"PLEASE, JARI

It was her use of his g.
With a hoarse strang n,
embracing her with a s?
Why are you marrying him?"

For a long moment, Tess didn't answer. Hunter waited, holding her close. He could feel the muscles of his chest pressing against her breasts, the scratchy stubble of his unshaved face rasping against her soft cheek, the hot insistent bulge of his desire straining against the front of her thin skirt. He wanted her so badly that he could hardly stand the tactile sensations of their bodies touching so intimately, but still he waited. Her answer was far more important than his desire.

When Tess finally spoke, her words came out in a fevered rush. "Don't do this to me," she begged. "Don't make me want you again. I know you don't want me so, please, just let me go."

"But, I *do* want you," he whispered, his voice rough with need.

"No!" she gasped, taking a lurching step away from him. "Not that again. Never that again."

Reaching out, he pulled her back to him. "That's not what I mean."

"What, then?" she sobbed. "What do you mean? I never know what you mean!"

"I mean . . ." *I mean that I love you.*

Pinnacle Books is proud to present this fourth book in a series of exciting romances where the hero takes center stage. Experience love through *his* eyes and rapture in *his* arms. Let the hero of your dreams lead you on an adventure to the frontiers of passion as you revel in . . .

HUNTER'S KISS

HUNTER'S KISS

Kate Charles

PINNACLE BOOKS
KENSINGTON PUBLISHING CORP.

PINNACLE BOOKS are published by

Kensington Publishing Corp.
850 Third Avenue
New York, NY 10022

First Printing: May, 1995

Printed in the United States of America

This book is dedicated to my editor, Tracy Bernstein, whose guidance, support and friendship have made many a dull scene brighter and many a tough day easier.

A special thank you for this one. Without your unfailing encouragement, none of us would have ever made it to Oregon!

Prologue

September, 1847

Death.

All around him, everywhere he looked, death.

He knew well its pungent odor. Indeed there had been a time when the sweet, sickening scent would awaken him at night.

But that was long ago. After two years of war, the sights and smells of death had long since ceased to interrupt his sleep. Now, the only smell that invaded his dreams was the acrid stench of spent gunpowder relentlessly burning his nostrils and searing his lungs.

Shaking his head to clear it of the nauseating smell, Colonel Jared Daulton Whitaker gazed dispassionately at the bodies strewn in the grass before him. Would it ever be over? The Mexican patriots were already reduced to marching out young boys and old men, but still they fought on, day after day, year after year.

And, tomorrow would be the same. Tomorrow he would again command his men to raise their guns against adolescent boys, and run their bayonets through wounded, half-starved peasants too weak to fight back.

Jared shifted wearily in his saddle. He had heard rumors among the men that General Winfield Scott, his commanding officer, was planning to reward him with a medal of commendation for leading the troops in today's slaughter. His shoulders shook with mirthless laughter. *A medal!*

Undoubtedly, the newspapers would write glowing reports of his heroism, young girls would send him perfumed letters, and well meaning matrons would pick up their needles and knit him hundreds of pairs of socks. When he returned to Washington, he would be wined, dined and fêted by society's finest hostesses. Propositioned, flirted with and fawned over by eager maidens and their ambitious mothers. Congratulated, toasted and glad handed by politicians eager to align themselves with one of the war's great heroes. And all because he'd led a charge that had killed a handful of school boys and their grandfathers.

Jared rolled his tense shoulders and, for the first time, seriously questioned his ability to go on. Maybe he should just leave. His commission had expired months ago but, still, he had stayed and fought on.

Why?

Deep down, Jared knew the answer to that question. His family was dead and Sophie . . . Sophie was married to another. Why should he leave? He had nowhere to go.

And yet, tonight, as he sat staring at the carnage his flawlessly executed military strategies had wrought, he knew he had to get away. Dear God, he had become "the brilliant killing machine" the newspapers touted him to be.

He wanted peace and, somewhere, there had to be a place where he would find it. An uncluttered, uncomplicated place where he could put behind him the horrors he'd witnessed, the slaughters he'd ordered, and the woman he'd loved and lost. A place where no one knew him, where he could make a new beginning and, hopefully, regain his humanity.

West. That was it. He would return to America and go west to the frontier where it was said that everything was clean and new and innocent. He would change his name, change his looks, change his history. He would find work—wholesome, honest work. He would stay uninvolved, unencumbered. Never again would he allow himself to truly care for another man or love another woman, for without care and love, there could be no pain. And, God knew, he had experienced enough pain in the past two years to last a man ten lifetimes.

With a grim nod, he reined his horse toward the spectacular sunset. He had made his decision. He would go west . . . and he would forget.

Chapter 1

April, 1849

"Hey, Hunter, there's a guy out here wants to talk to ya 'bout him and his folks joinin' your train."

The man named Hunter looked up from the stack of papers he was perusing, his irritation at being interrupted obvious on his handsome face. "What do you mean, 'folks'?" he asked, glancing out the door of his cramped office. "More merchants?"

"Naw, I don't think so. He's too young. They're probably homesteaders."

"You know I'm not taking homesteaders on this trip. Tell him they'll have to find another train." With a dismissive gesture, Hunter returned to his papers.

Jack Riley shifted his weight from one foot to the other, then spit an arcing stream of tobacco juice in the direction of a brass spittoon. "Aw, come on, boss. Why don't ya at least talk to him. He says they came all the way from St. Louis to see about joinin' up and he seems like a real nice sort."

Hunter threw down his pen impatiently. "Damn

it, Riley, I've got a million things to do before we leave next week and I don't have time to talk to a homesteader who I'm not gonna take on anyway. Tell him to go see Tom Johnson. His train might still have room and he's accepting families."

"I already done that," Riley argued. "But, this Chambers fella says that Johnson is leavin' day after tomorrow and there ain't time for them to provision."

At that moment, a young, blond man suddenly appeared behind Riley's shoulder. "Mr. Hunter?" he said hopefully, stepping around Riley and entering the office. "I'm Joe Chambers . . . "His words died in his throat as he got his first clear look at Hunter. "Why, you're . . . you're Colonel—"

"I'm not taking any homesteaders," Hunter cut in, stopping the man in mid-sentence. "You and your missus will have to find another train."

Joe Chambers didn't immediately respond to Hunter's rude interruption. Instead, he stood in stupefied silence, staring at him as if he were seeing a ghost. "Aren't you . . . What did you say your name was?"

"The name's Hunter . . . and, like I said, I'm not taking on any homesteaders. I'm afraid you're wasting your time here." Pointedly, he turned away.

Riley looked at the ashen faced Joe Chambers in bewilderment. "What's the matter with you, mister? Why are ya starin' at Hunter?"

Joe threw him an embarrassed look. "I'm sorry," he stammered. "I thought he was someone else. Again, his gaze flicked back to Hunter. "Mr. Hunter, did anyone ever tell you that you're a dead ringer for Colonel Jared Daulton Whitaker?"

"Jared Whitaker!" Riley guffawed. "You mean that missin' war hero that the papers keep writin' about? The one who disappeared after the battle of Chapultepec?"

Joe nodded, his gaze still riveted on Hunter. "Yeah,

that's the one. I served under him in Mexico and if I didn't know better, I'd swear Mr. Hunter was him. Of course, Mr. Hunter's hair is longer and the colonel had a mustache, but other than that . . ."

"Mr. Chambers," Hunter interrupted loudly, "I'm sorry to cut your reminiscing short, but I've got a lot of work to do here. Now, since I'm not taking on any more wagons, I'd appreciate . . ."

Hunter's dismissal seemed to finally sink in, and with an expression verging on panic, Joe Chambers leaned over the rough hewn table. "Please, mister, you can't turn me and Tess down. We've got to get to Oregon and yours is the last train goin'."

Hunter leaned back in his chair, trying to put as much distance as possible between himself and the frantic man. "Look, Chambers, I'd like to help you, but I'm just not taking any married couples on this trip. I'm taking lumberjacks to work in the Willamette Valley. It's an all male train. I don't want any women complicating things."

"But that's not true," Joe protested. "I talked to a couple today who told me they're on your train."

"An older couple?"

"Yeah. Middle-aged, I'd say."

Hunter nodded. "Probably George and Caroline Brooks. They're merchants. They're setting up a store near Fort Laramie."

"I don't see the difference. They're still a couple."

Hunter blew out a long, frustrated breath. "How old is your wife, Mr. Chambers?"

"Tess isn't exactly my wife," Joe admitted quietly.

"Oh?" Hunter asked. "Then who exactly is she?"

"She's my sister."

"Your sister!" Hunter exclaimed, throwing his arms wide. "That's worse yet. The last thing I need on a train filled with horny men is a young, single woman."

"Oh, but, she's not single," Joe quickly corrected, his words coming out in a rush. "She's a widow woman. And she's not that young, either. She's my older sister. Please, Mr. Hunter, we don't have anywhere else to turn. I've sold my place in St. Louis and we've got everything we own with us. You've just got to take us. We can't stay here in Independence for a whole year waitin' for next spring's trains."

Hunter emitted a long sigh and stared out the grimy window of his makeshift office. He'd rented a room in the back of one of Independence's many saloons to sign on passengers and organize his expedition. The little cubicle was hot, poorly ventilated and dirty, and the rent was exorbitant, but in the boomtown that Independence had become, he'd been lucky to find anywhere to set up business.

"Look, Chambers, the only way I'd consider taking a single woman, widowed or not, on this train is if she's willing to work her way 'cross country as a cook and a washerwoman."

"Tess will do that," Joe said promptly.

Hunter looked at him with a spark of interest. "Really? Do you know that for a fact?"

"Well, no, but after all, she's got to cook and wash for me. She might as well do it for you too."

Hunter studied the eager young man for a minute, then shrugged. "Okay. Bring your sister by and I'll talk to her."

Joe Chambers' eyes lit with hope. "Then you'll take us?"

"I didn't say that," Hunter retorted. "I said, I'll talk to your sister. That's all."

"Sure," Joe grinned, bobbing his head and backing toward the door. "I understand. Tess is right over at the hotel. I'll go get her."

Hunter held up a warning finger. "Don't count on anything, Chambers."

"No, sir, I won't." Nearly tripping over his feet in his haste to be off, Joe tore out the door.

Riley leaned against the wall and smiled at Hunter in wry amusement. "Thought you said you wasn't takin' on nobody else."

"I didn't say I was going to take them on. I just said I'd meet the sister."

"I don't get it. You told me yesterday you already hired a woman to cook for you."

"We didn't agree on anything firm. Anyway, you saw that girl who applied for the job. She's an ex-saloon girl and that kind of woman is bound to be trouble. If Chambers's sister really is a mature, respectable widow, then maybe I'll hire her instead. She'd probably be a lot less trouble."

Riley's mouth twisted in a knowing grin.

"What are you laughing about?"

"Nothin', really. It's just that you're not as tough as ya want everybody to believe. You feel sorry for that kid and you're tryin' to figure out some way to help him, ain'cha?"

Hunter's face hardened. "Quit giving me bouquets, Riley. I never feel sorry for anybody and I never do anything purely out of kindness. What I do, I do because it will benefit me, period. You'd be wise to remember that."

Riley shrugged, but the smile still lingered at the corners of his mouth. "Okay, boss, sure. I'll remember."

When Joe and Tess entered Hunter's office, he was absorbed in adding up a long column of figures and didn't immediately look up. When he finally did raise his head, he blinked several times in silent astonishment, barely able to conceal his surprise at the sight of the short, fat woman facing him. She was square.

That was the only word for her. Square. Actually, she was square and lumpy. Could something be square and also lumpy? Hunter wasn't sure, but if it could, this woman was it.

Her age was indiscernible, but based on her figure, Hunter pegged her to be at least forty. Briefly, his eyes flitted back to Joe. How could this boy have a sister as old as this woman obviously was? For a moment, he wondered if she was really Joe's mother and he, for some unimaginable reason, was trying to pass her off as his sister.

His eyes again settled on the widow. She was dressed in the drabbest clothes he'd ever seen—an unadorned brown dress, a brown shawl that completely concealed her hair and most of her face, and heavy brown shoes. All in all, Hunter thought her to be one of the most singularly unattractive women he'd ever encountered. So far, she was perfect.

Joe seemed to be entirely oblivious to Hunter's startled reaction to his sister and said simply, "Mr. Hunter, this here is my sister, Mrs. Tess Caldwell."

"How do you do?" Hunter nodded.

Tess murmured a reply and quickly lowered her eyes, not wanting the wagon master to see her startled reaction to his unbelievable good looks. He was, without a doubt, the most handsome man she had ever seen.

He was dark. Everything about him—his skin, his eyes, his hair. Contrary to the current style, he was clean shaven but, still, a dark shadow swept across his sculpted cheeks—hinting of a beard that no mere razor could conquer. Even his voice was deep and rich and dark, reminding her of thick, black molasses flowing over her when he spoke.

And his mouth. Tess found her eyes drawn again and again to the perfection of his full sculpted lips. There was a sensuality about his mouth that softened the chisled hardness of the rest of his face—a sensuality that despite her trepidation, she found disturbingly appealing.

She also noticed that despite his dark, forbidding appearance, there was nothing sinister about him. Rather, there was about him a sort of quiet, controlled sadness—as if he had borne much tragedy in his life and the unhappiness he'd endured had left a permanent sorrow within him.

Hunter gestured to Tess and Joe to sit down, then leaned back in his chair, eyeing Tess speculatively. "So, Mrs., ah, Caldwell, is it?"

Tess nodded, but didn't look up.

"Yes," Hunter continued, "well, Mrs. Caldwell, your brother here tells me that you want to join my wagon train and that you would be willing to hire yourself out to clean and wash for me."

Again Tess nodded.

Hunter frowned, finding her seeming unwillingness to look him in the eye irritating. "Tell me a little bit about your experience."

"I already told you she's a widow," Joe interjected quickly. "That's her experience. Takin' care of her man."

Hunter ignored Joe's interruption, keeping his attention trained on Tess's bowed head. "How long were you married, ma'am?"

"Over a year," Joe promptly supplied.

Hunter looked at Joe in annoyance. "Does your sister talk, Mr. Chambers?"

"Of course she talks."

"Then I'd appreciate it if you'd let her do so."

"Yes, sir."

"Don't call me 'sir'. I told you before, the name's Hunter."

Tess gazed surreptitiously at Hunter through the

veil of her eyelashes. Why would the man care that someone called him "sir"?

"Now, Mrs. Caldwell, will you please tell me about your experience with housekeeping chores."

"I was married for almost two years before my husband was stricken with a fatal case of influenza last winter."

Hunter's eyes widened. The last thing he'd expected was for this woman to speak in the soft, melodic voice he'd just heard. Somehow, he would have been less surprised if her voice had sounded like a foghorn.

"I see," he muttered. "Did your husband consider you a good cook?"

"I didn't cook."

"You didn't cook?"

"No. My husband and I had a household staff."

Joe groaned inwardly. Damn Tess, anyway, for always being such a stickler for the truth!

"I see," he repeated, his gaze again sliding over Tess's wide girth. "Well, how about cleaning or washing? Did you do any of those chores?"

Tess shook her head, her eyes fixed on her lap. "No, we had servants who did that also."

Hunter glared at Joe in exasperation. "I thought you told me that your sister could handle being a washerwoman and cook."

"I can," Tess answered, lifting her head for the first time. Although her face was almost completely concealed by her heavy shawl, her eyes met Hunter's unflinchingly. "I know how to do those things. I just did not do them while I was married."

For a moment, Hunter remained silent, his mouth slightly open, his eyes glued to the woman seated across from him. *Those eyes.* Who would have ever dreamt that this big brown brick of a woman would have eyes the color of a spring sky? And they weren't the lined, puffy eyes of a woman deep into middle age.

Rather, they were the fresh, sparkling eyes of a girl just entering the first full bloom of womanhood. He shook his head as if trying to clear it. Certainly, this woman was the most incongruous sight he had ever beheld.

Slapping his palms down on the desk, he said, "Okay, let me get this straight. You know how to cook and clean and wash, but you didn't do it while you were married because you had servants to do it for you. I take it, then, that you and Mr. Caldwell were quite comfortable."

Tess again lowered her head. "Yes, we were," she murmured.

"And are you aware of how *uncomfortable* you are going to be on this journey?"

"Yes, I am."

"And, yet, you still want to go."

"Yes."

"And you're willing to work for me in order to do so."

"Yes."

Hunter studied Tess closely. Something wasn't fitting together here. His long experience as a military man had given him an almost uncanny ability to gauge people after just a few moments' acquaintance and something about this woman did not ring true. But, for the life of him, he couldn't put his finger on it. She had obviously been truthful in answering his questions, championing her strengths and, unapologetically, owning up to her weaknesses. She was quiet and unassuming, unattractive enough not to cause any problems among the men and strong enough that she could probably pull their wagon over the Rockies herself if the mules faltered. She was exactly what he was looking for. But, for some reason that he couldn't quite pinpoint, those beautiful blue eyes of hers bothered the hell out of him.

Forget her damn eyes, he told himself firmly. She's just what you need, so quit worrying and hire her!

"All right," he said suddenly, "you can go."

Joe fumbled with his well worn hat. "I don't know exactly what you mean by that, Mr. Hunter. Do you mean "go" that we should leave, or do you mean "go" that you'll take us on your train?"

"I mean that I'll sign you on to the train."

Joe's eyes lit up with incredulous relief. "That's great!" he whooped. Turning to Tess, he added, "Isn't that great, sis?"

"Yes," she said quietly. "It's very kind of Mr. Hunter to accept us."

"There's nothing 'kind' about it, Mrs. Caldwell," Hunter snapped. "You're in for one rough trip and there's a few things you better understand before you start packing."

Again, Tess turned her unwavering blue gaze on him. "I believe you have been making that abundantly clear for the last several minutes."

Hunter nodded and returned her stare with one of his own. "Yeah, well, I'm gonna spend the next few minutes making it even clearer. The first thing I want you to understand is that as bad as you think this trip is going to be, it's probably going to be about ten times worse than that. Oregon isn't St. Louis and you better realize that right now. What's more, between here and there, we've got two thousand miles to cover. On foot, Mrs. Chambers, not in a well sprung carriage. There aren't going to be any warm, perfumed baths, any feather beds with silk sheets, and there sure aren't going to be any servants to scurry around cleaning up after you.

"You're gonna cook, wash, haul water, scrub pots,

sleep on the ground, and get dirtier than you've ever been in your life. You're gonna cross rivers full of snakes and mud and quicksand, walk across desert land so dry and dusty that it will turn your saliva into mud, and haul yourself over mountains that would be a challenge for a goat. You'll be up before dawn and you'll work till sunset, then you'll sleep for a few hours and get up and do it all over again. Your skin is gonna get burned and cracked from the wind and sun, and welted from mosquitos and gnats. You'll probably see people die from cholera and smallpox, and if luck runs against us, you'll see a few more die from Indian attacks. Right now, the government is saying that there are seventeen graves along each and every mile of the Oregon Trail. Seventeen, Mrs. Chambers. It's not a pretty sight, so you better think about it real hard before you decide if you really want to go a'journeying."

Tess had sat silently through Hunter's long tirade, but now she said, "You don't hold women in much regard, do you, Mr. Hunter?"

Hunter was nonplussed by her softly voiced question. "On the contrary. I enjoy the company of women very much." He paused. "My concern is that so do all the other men who'll be on this train. As I told you, there will be almost no women. Only men. Lonely, love starved men who are going to be out on the trail for months without the, ah, comfort of women. Do you understand what I'm saying?"

Tess nodded. "I will stay out of sight as much as possible."

Hunter stared at her for a long moment. "Then, despite everything I've just told you, you still want to go?"

Tess's nod was echoed by her brother's.

"All right, then. The fee to join is two hundred fifty dollars."

"But that's going to be waived since Tess is working for you, right?" Joe asked.

Hunter shook his head. "No. The fee is two hundred fifty *apiece*. Mrs. Caldwell's fee will be waived, but you will still have to pay yours." He paused, waiting to see what the couple's reaction would be to this announcement.

To his surprise, Joe merely nodded and looked expectantly over at Tess.

"Would you like that in cash?" Tess asked, pulling open the strings of her reticule.

"You mean to tell me that you're carrying around two hundred fifty dollars in cash in your bag?" Hunter gasped. "Are you nuts, lady? With all the pickpockets and chiselers roaming the streets of Independence just waiting to prey on innocent women like yourself?"

Angrily, he swung his gaze over to Joe. "Why would you allow your sister to carry that kind of money on her person?"

Joe shrugged guiltily. "I guess I didn't think . . ."

"No," Hunter barked, "I guess you didn't."

"I can assure you, Mr. Hunter," Tess said firmly, "that I am quite used to taking care of myself. And, I don't see that where I carry my money is any of your business anyway."

"Well, it is, Mrs. Caldwell. Everything about you is my business if you're going to be on my train."

"Surely you're not planning on being my keeper all the way to Oregon."

"You're damn right I'm not!" As soon as the profanity left his lips, Hunter noticed the subtly insulted lift of Tess's eyebrow.

"I'm sorry," he said quickly. "You're *absolutely* right, I'm not. I have far more important things to do than watch over one woman, who's too foolish to know that she should hide her money. I'm letting you join this train to help *me*, Mrs. Caldwell, not the other way around."

"And she will," Joe assured him quickly.

Hunter looked at the slight young man dubiously, but reluctantly nodded. "Good. Then we understand each other."

Tess again reached into her reticule and pulled out a large roll of bills.

Hunter gaped at the money for a moment, astonished by the size of the wad, then quickly turned his attention back to Joe. "Do you have a wagon?"

"Bought one yesterday," Joe said proudly. "A good one too—all hickory."

Hunter nodded his approval. "How about mules and provisions?"

"I have two teams of four, but we haven't bought provisions yet. I was hoping maybe you could tell us which vendors are honest. There are so many lined up along the riverfront that I'm not sure who to deal with."

Hunter pulled a scrap of paper out of his pocket and picked up a pen. "I'll give you the names of several to deal with . . . and several to stay away from. I expect the trip is going to take about four and a half months and . . ."

The rest of his sentence died in his throat as he heard Tess's sharply indrawn breath. "Is something wrong, Mrs. Caldwell?"

"No!" she answered quickly, shaking her head. "Nothing's wrong. Four and a half months, you say?"

Hunter nodded. "And that's if everything stays on schedule. I'll be happy if we make it in five."

"Five months," Tess muttered. "That means we won't get to Oregon until sometime in October."

"Right. My goal is to get there before the first snow flies. If we can make it sooner, all the better. I don't think it will be a problem since we're such a small outfit."

"How many wagons will there be?" Joe asked.

"Counting yours, thirty-three."

"And when do we leave?"

"A week from today. And that's firm. If you're not ready by then, we'll leave you behind."

"We'll be ready, Mr. Hunter," Tess said firmly. "You have Joe's two hundred and fifty dollars and, somehow, you don't seem like a man who would give a refund if someone dropped out at the last minute. Believe me, we'll be ready."

"Well, I'm glad to hear that Mrs Caldwell, because you're right in your assumption. I don't give refunds."

Tess stood up. "Then I'd say we better get going. We have a lot to do before next Monday."

Joe rose also and took Tess's arm. With as much grace as she could manage beneath her many layers of clothing, Tess swayed toward the door.

"See you next week, Mr. Hunter," Joe said jauntily.

"Yeah," Hunter grunted. "Mind you're not late. We're pulling out at dawn."

"I don't think the widow liked you much," Riley grinned, stepping back into Hunter's office.

Hunter shrugged. "I don't care if she likes me or not. The only thing I care about is whether she can handle the work."

"Oh, I don't think you need to worry 'bout that," Riley chortled. "By the looks of her, she could prob'ly take care of ev'ry man on the train."

A rare smile crooked the corner of Hunter's mouth. "Yeah, she's a hefty one."

"That's putting it nice enough. Let's just say that I don't think you're gonna hafta worry much about her turnin' the men's heads. Except for them eyes. Did you notice 'em, Hunter? Why, they're blue as the sea. Funny for a woman that plain to have such amazin' eyes."

Hunter threw Jack a jaundiced look. "You're a crazy old coot, you know that? Now, quit wasting time babbling on about women's eyes. I've got work to do and so do you, so let's get at it."

Jack threw his boss an offended look, but dutifully put on his old hat and ambled out the door.

After he was gone, Hunter stared thoughtfully through the dingy little window. Although he'd never admit it to Jack, he *had* noticed Mrs. Caldwell's eyes, and his reaction to their azure brilliance and crystalline clarity had been identical to his friend's. They *were* amazing. And for some reason he couldn't quite put his finger on, that fact bothered him. It bothered him a lot.

Chapter 2

"I see you made it."

Joe looked down at Hunter from the high seat of his covered wagon and grinned. "We sure did, Mr. Hunter. And we're just itchin' to be on our way."

Hunter looked over at Tess who was staring at something off in the distance. "And are you 'itchin' too, Mrs. Caldwell?"

Tess shot him a quick glance, nodded, and went back to perusing the horizon.

"Gonna be pretty hot out there once the sun's up, ma'am," Hunter noted. "You're gonna swelter under that shawl. Maybe you should find something cooler to cover your head with before we get going."

Tess nodded again, still not making eye contact. "Thank you for your concern, but I'm fine."

Hunter's heavy, black eyebrows rose at her curt response. "Up to you," he muttered. If the woman wanted to suffocate beneath that stupid shawl, it was her business. Pulling his eyes away from Tess's shrouded face, he looked back at Joe. "How much gear do you have?"

"Plenty," Joe said happily. "We're packed tight back there."

This was not the answer Hunter wanted to hear and with a dubious frown, he reined his horse around and headed for the back of the wagon.

"You've got way too much stuff here," he called irritably after peering into the wagon's interior through the oval hole in the canvas cover. "You've got to get rid of some of it."

"Get rid of it!" Tess cried, craning her head around to glare at him. "I think not. We need everything we have back there."

Hunter shook his head. "I'm telling you, you've got to lighten up. You'll never make the pull over the Rockies with all this junk weighing you down. It'll break down your team for sure."

"I beg your pardon," Tess snorted, "but there's nothing back there that is 'junk'."

Hunter stared at the stacks of furniture, the trunks of clothing and the piles of carefully wrapped trinkets and nicknacks wedged tightly against the wagon's canvas sides. "Suit yourself," he shrugged, riding back to the front of the wagon, "but, I'm warning you. If it isn't food, ammunition or housekeeping necessities, it's bound to end up at the side of the trail somewhere between here and Oregon. You might as well unload the excess now and save your mules the strain of hauling it across the prairie."

"No," Tess said stubbornly. "I'm not throwing anything away, and that's that."

Hunter studied the mutinous set of her mouth for a long moment, then said simply, "Okay. Just don't say I didn't warn you." Without giving her a chance to argue further, he flicked his gaze back to Joe. "We're gonna get started now, so get your mules lined up."

Joe nodded and gathered the reins more tightly in his hands. "We're ready whenever you are."

Hunter shot one more disparaging glance at Tess, then nudged his horse into a trot and headed for the front of the train. "Stretch out!" he bellowed as he rode along. "Come on, mules! Gee up! Come on there!"

Suddenly, the quiet prairie dawn came alive with the sound of men yelling, wheels creaking and recalcitrant mules braying as they were prodded into action. Slowly, very slowly, the wagon train started forward, snaking away from Independence as it began its great trek.

Joe and Tess's wagon was the last one in line and it was a full ten minutes before it was their turn to roll. "Here we go!" Joe cried excitedly when he finally slapped the heavy reins over the mules' backs. "My God, Tess, we're actually on our way! Can you believe it?"

"Hardly," she gasped, grabbing on to the wagon's seat as they lurched forward. "If anyone had told me a year ago I'd be on my way to Oregon in a covered wagon . . ."

"Everything's gonna work out fine," Joe assured her, looking over and smiling encouragingly. "The worst is behind you now."

Tess looked down the long line of wagons to where Hunter was waving his hat and impatiently shouting instructions at someone. "I hope you're right, Joe," she muttered, "but, I can tell you right now, I don't like Mr. Hunter. Imagine him demanding that I throw my possessions away! Just who does he think he is?"

Joe looked at his sister beseechingly. "Try to make peace with the man, Tess. Our entire fate rests in his hands."

"I know," Tess sighed, "and that's not something I'm pleased about."

"I know, but please try to get along with him anyway."

"I will," Tess promised. "As long as he tries to get along with me too . . ."

By mid-afternoon, the heat was nearly intolerable. The sun blazed down unmercifully from the cloudless blue sky, causing sweat to run down Tess's back and pool uncomfortably between her breasts. But, despite her discomfort, she stubbornly kept her shawl pulled over her hair and her heavy, dark dress buttoned all the way up to her neck.

Several times Hunter had ridden by their wagon, looking at Tess quizzically, but saying nothing about her stubborn refusal to discard the hot shawl. Finally, about three in the afternoon, he rode ahead of the train, catching up with his scout, Dash McLaughlin.

"Hi, Jared," Dash greeted as Hunter trotted up to him. Dash was a big, handsome blond man who had once been a Texas Ranger and now enjoyed the reputation of being one of the finest western scouts in the country. His years spent with the famous troupe of lawmen had given him almost an uncanny sense for danger and it was said that he could sense an Indian two miles away.

Every wagon master in Independence vied for McLaughlin's services and it had long been a topic of speculation as to why the much sought after scout would sign on with Hunter again and again, especially when it was common knowledge that his usual fee was far greater than what Hunter's modest trains could support.

What the other adventurers didn't know, however, was that the men shared a friendship that went all the way back to when they had attended West Point together. Dash McLaughlin was one of the few men on earth whom Hunter trusted and the only one of his current acquaintance who knew who he actually was.

Dash had never asked his friend why he had made the transition from Jared Whitaker, the celebrated army colonel, to Hunter, the enigmatic wagon master. In his mind, the reasons for his friend's decision were his own and he did not deem it his business to question them.

"So, how are they all holdin' up so far?"

"Well enough," Hunter nodded, "except for one stupid woman who's wearing enough clothes to weather the arctic and refuses to shed any of them. I swear she'd gonna pass out from the heat before the day is over."

Dash chuckled and shook his head. "There's always one, isn't there? I've never understood why some women would rather collapse from heat prostration than unbutton their bodice an inch."

"Bodice!" Hunter scoffed. "This one won't even take off her shawl, much less unbutton her bodice."

"She's wearing a shawl? You're joking! In this heat?"

"Yes. And not only that, but she has it pulled around her head and face so tight that you can hardly see her. Why, I've seen more exposed flesh on a nun!"

Dash smiled at his friend's quip. "You know, Jared, maybe it's all for the best. If a woman is going to that much trouble to hide her face, we're probably all better off for it."

Hunter's lips twitched with amusement. "And, you don't know the half of it. The rest of her looks like a big, brown brick."

"You mean she's fat too?"

Hunter rolled his eyes.

"Oh, no!" Dash guffawed. "I definitely have to see this one."

"Why don't you come around tonight after we get settled in?" Hunter suggested. "I want to introduce you, anyway, so that none of these crazy lumberjacks sees you skulking around and shoots you for a outlaw."

"Good idea," Dash nodded. "We can review tomorrow's route at the same time. Just be sure, though, that you point out your girlfriend. I wouldn't want to miss her."

Hunter slanted Dash a look. "It would have to be a mighty long dry spell for me to need a woman that bad!"

"Never say never," Dash warned. "We've got a lot of territory to cover before we get to Oregon and you know how cold it can get up in those mountains. By September, you might be real happy to share that shawl of hers."

Jared reached out and gave his friend a good natured shove. "Go find a stream somewhere, would ya, McLaughlin?"

"A stream?"

"Yeah, a good cold one."

"What for?"

"For you to soak your head in!"

"Hey, Mrs. Krenzke?"

"Yes, Mr. Hunter?" Mary Krenzke, one of the three merchant's wives on the train peered out of the back of her wagon. "What can I do for you?"

"Do you have any sunbonnets in your wagon that aren't packed in boxes?"

"Bonnets of my own, or ones for sale?" Mary asked, surprise apparent on her pleasant, round face.

"For sale."

"Well, I imagine I could find one in here someplace. Any particular color you're looking for?"

Jared shook his head. "Naw, anything will do. Just as long as it keeps the sun off."

"Just a minute," Mary smiled. "Let me check."

The friendly woman disappeared inside her wagon, emerging again a moment later with a bright red sunbonnet dangling from one finger. "Will this one be all right?"

Jared nodded. "Just fine." Riding closer, he plucked the hat out of Mary's outstretched hand. "How much do I owe you?"

"Fifty cents," Mary answered, "but don't worry about it now. I know where to find you."

As Hunter wheeled his horse around and headed for the back of the train, Mary crawled through the lurching wagon and resumed her seat next to her husband.

"What was that all about?" Gerald Krenzke asked, looking over at his wife curiously.

"I think we already have the makings of a romance on the train," she said excitedly.

"What? What are you talking about?"

"Mr. Hunter just bought a sunbonnet from me."

"A sunbonnet? Now, what in tarnation would he want a sunbonnet for?"

"I don't think 'for what' is the question, Gerald. I think 'for *who*' is more to the point."

"You think he's buying a sunbonnet for some woman on the train?"

"Well, I don't think he's going to wear it himself!"

"But, who would he be buying it for? All the women on the train are married."

"Not all," Mary corrected. "There's that widow travelling with her brother. The one who's going to be cooking and washing for Mr. Hunter. Maybe he's sweet on her and he's buying her a gift. That could be why he hired her in the first place."

"Widow . . ." Gerald mused. "Do you mean that fat, old lady in the last wagon?"

"Gerald, that's not nice!"

Gerald forced a look of contrition. "Sorry," he muttered. "But, is that the one you mean?"

"Yes," Mary admitted. "That's the one."

Gerald shook his head. "You're dreamin', Mary. There's not a chance in the world that that handsome young buck would be interested in her."

"We'll see," Mary said smugly. "But, you mark my words. Tomorrow morning, you're going to see Mrs. Caldwell wearing a red sunbonnet."

"You're plum crazy, woman. Why, she could be his mother."

"I don't think so. I saw her up close this morning while we were loading. She's not nearly as old as you think she is and from what I could see beneath that shawl she was wearing, she's very pretty."

"Pretty! What's pretty about her?"

"Her eyes," Mary answered promptly. "She has, without a doubt, the most beautiful blue eyes I've ever seen . . ."

Hunter cantered along the length of the train, stopping now and again to offer a word of advice to the neophyte travellers.

Noticing a loose harness strap on the Bennington brothers' wagon, he paused to tell them about it. He hadn't even opened his mouth, however, when he noticed the three men staring in amusement at the bright red sunbonnet he was carrying. Quickly, he stuffed the garment inside his shirt, cursing himself for not thinking to hide it earlier. Tersely, he informed the grinning brothers of their broken harness, then rode away before they had time to make a comment about his choice of apparel.

By the time he reached Tess's wagon, his good mood of a few minutes before had changed into infuriated embarrassment. There was no doubt in his mind that the story of his riding around clutching a red sunbonnet would be the main topic of conversation around every campfire tonight. When he spied Tess still suffering beneath the confines of her heavy shawl, he was so annoyed that he whipped out the sunbonnet and threw it at her. "Put this on before you pass out!" he barked.

"I beg your pardon!" she retorted, plucking the bonnet off her lap where it had landed and holding it up as if it smelled. "I'm perfectly fine."

"You're not fine," Hunter yelled. "You're red as a beet. You get heat prostration and you won't be worth a damn to me. Now, take off that idotic shawl and put on that bonnet!"

Tess's eyes widened in outraged offense, but before she could think of a suitable set down, Hunter had kicked his horse and taken off toward the front of the train.

"Can you believe that man's nerve?" she gasped, turning to Joe with flashing eyes.

Joe, who had found the whole exchange extremely amusing, now struggled mightily to control his mirth. "Your face *is* red, Tess. Maybe you should put the bonnet on. It would certainly be cooler than that shawl."

"I know that!" Tess snapped. "But I thought you said I had to keep my face hidden until we were far enough out of Independence that he couldn't send us back."

"I know what I said, but the bonnet should cover you just fine. Go ahead and put it on."

"Oh, all right!" With an irritated jerk of her head, Tess threw off the heavy shawl, breathing a sigh of relief as the late afternoon breeze wafted across her damp face.

Joe looked at her sympathetically. "Feels good, doesn't it?"

"Oh, yes," she sighed, turning her face into the wind and letting the cool air riffle the loose tendrils of hair near her temples. "It feels wonderful." She closed her eyes, thoroughly enjoying her release from the suffocating shawl. Her brief respite was soon interrupted, however, when Joe whispered urgently, "Put that bonnet on, quick. Here he comes again."

With a start, Tess pulled the sunbonnet over her blond curls, tying it tightly under her chin and pulling the long, floppy bill as far down over her face as she could.

"Feel better now?" Hunter asked as he rode up.

"Yes," she murmured, "thank you. The bonnet *is* a lot cooler than my shawl."

"Good. I thought it would be."

Glancing down, Hunter's eyes lit upon Joe's old rifle leaning up against the seat. "Move that rifle down to the floor," he said curtly, throwing Joe a look that brooked no argument. "Never, ever lean your rifle up against the seat like that. It's dangerous."

His face suffusing with embarrassed color at his naivete, Joe hurriedly laid the rifle on the floor.

"Barrel point out," Hunter added. "That way, if it goes off, it won't shoot your sister's foot off." Silently, he watched Joe again adjust the rifle's position, then turned his attention back to Tess and said, "I just came back to tell you that we've spotted a stream about half a mile ahead, so we're going to stop for the night. I'm starving and I'll be wanting supper as soon as you can make it, so get a fire going right away."

From within the deep recesses of the bonnet, Tess's placid expression changed to a furious glower. "Have you ever heard of the word, 'please', Mr. Hunter?"

Hunter's eyes narrowed at her unexpected rebuke, but with exaggerated politeness, he whipped off his hat and said, "*Please*, Mrs. Caldwell. I would very much appreciate it if you would prepare my supper at your earliest possible convenience."

"That's much better," Tess nodded. "And is there anything in particular you'd like to eat? Some hard-tack and jerky, maybe?"

Hunter grimaced. "Lord, no! I want something hot. Bacon and biscuits would be good."

"Bacon and biscuits," Tess muttered. "Certainly, Mr. Hunter." She watched Hunter ride off, then turned back to Joe. "Did you hear what he said? He wants bacon and biscuits!"

Joe tried hard to muster an encouraging smile. "Don't worry, I'll get the fire started for you."

"The fire isn't the problem," Tess moaned. "I don't have the slightest idea how to make biscuits."

"There's not much to them," Joe shrugged. "I think they're pretty much just flour and milk. There might be something else in them, but I don't know what it is."

"Milk!" Tess gasped. "Where am I supposed to get milk out here in the middle of nowhere?"

Joe looked over at the two milk cows plodding along next to the wagon. "I suppose from one of them."

"What? Oh, Joe, you can't be serious."

"You're not in Boston anymore, Tess. No one is going to bring milk to your door in shiny little cans."

"But, I don't know how to milk a cow!"

"Then, I guess I'll have to do it."

"You don't know how either. You're a clock maker, for heaven's sake. Don't you think I could just use water to make the biscuits?"

Joe's expression was dubious. "I don't know. I think you're supposed to use milk."

"I'm sure they'll be fine made with water," Tess said stoutly. "They might not be quite as tasty, but if Mr. Hunter is as hungry as he says he is, he probably won't even notice."

Joe shrugged. "Maybe you're right. If he's hungry enough, he probably won't even notice."

Chapter 3

Hunter walked up to Tess's small campfire and sniffed appreciatively. "Bacon smells good."

Tess acknowledged his compliment with a nod, but kept her eyes on the fire, poking gingerly at the sizzling strips of smoked pork.

"Looks like it's about done."

"It is."

Hunter stepped closer, looking curiously down at a covered pot. "Are those the biscuits?"

"Yes."

"Are they done too?"

"I think so."

Hunter brows furrowed in bewilderment at her strange answer. *I think so*? Didn't she know?

"Well," he said, rubbing his hands together in anticipation. "I'm ready." Walking over to the wagon, he picked up a tin plate and cup, then returned to the fire and held them out. "I hope you made a lot because I sure am hungry."

Without turning around, Tess reached out for his plate. He handed it to her, along with the cup. "You did make coffee, didn't you?" he asked, looking around for the coffee pot.

Tess sucked in a startled breath. "You wanted coffee? You didn't say you wanted coffee."

Hunter let out a snort of annoyance. "Of course, I want coffee. I want coffee with every meal."

"Yes, sir."

"Don't call me 'sir'."

"Yes, Mr. Hunter. Do you want me to make some now?" Tess cringed, hoping desperately that he'd say no since she didn't have the slightest idea how to make coffee.

"No, don't bother. I'll get a cup from somebody else. But don't forget tomorrow."

Tess silently speared some bacon and slapped it on the tin plate, then lifted the cover off the dutch oven and plucked out two biscuits.

"By the way," Hunter said, peeking under the brim of the sunbonnet she was still wearing, "it's probably safe to take off your hat now since the sun went down an hour ago."

Tess ignored his comment and handed him his plate.

Hunter looked down at his supper. "What are these?"

"What are what?" Tess asked, looking up for the first time.

"These little brown things."

"They're biscuits, of course."

Hunter shook his head. "No, they're not."

"Well, I'm sorry, Mr. Hunter, but, yes, they are."

Carefully, Hunter picked up one of the flat little disks and studied it. "These aren't biscuits, Mrs. Caldwell. These are weapons." He paused, hefting the heavy little lump in his hand. "I could put one of these in a slingshot and kill small game with it." As if to demonstrate, he threw the biscuit at a nearby sapling, neatly shearing off a small branch. "See? They're lethal. In fact, I bet these biscuits are what David used to slay Goliath."

Tess's mouth pursed in offense. "I'm sorry if my biscuits don't meet with your approval," she huffed.

Hunter dropped the tin plate on the tailgate of the wagon, then planted his hands on his hips. "These biscuits wouldn't meet with anybody's approval. I thought you told me you could cook, Mrs. Caldwell."

"I can!" Tess lied. "It's just that . . . I'm not used to having to do it outside over a campfire. I'm used to a kitchen . . . with a stove!"

Hunter stared down at the rocklike little biscuits in the dutch oven, not believing that excuse for a minute. There was far more wrong with these biscuits than just the way they were baked. From their consistency, they looked like she had forgotten the leavening altogether.

Silently he cursed himself for hiring a woman he knew so little about. If he'd used his head, he would have made her cook a meal for him before they'd left Independence. That way he would have found out the truth about her culinary skills—or lack of them—before it was too late to do anything about it. As it was, it looked like he'd been hoodwinked—and he didn't like it one bit.

"Well, since your biscuits are inedible, what do you expect me to eat tonight?"

"The bacon is fine. You can have that."

"And what else? I can't make a meal out of just bacon."

"We have hardtack," Tess suggested hopefully. "And, I brought along some strawberry preserves. You could put some on the hardtack. I'm sure it would be quite delicious."

"Quite delicious?" Hunter asked sarcastically.

"Well, passable, anyway."

Hunter's eyes narrowed angrily. "Now you listen to me, lady. Passable doesn't cut it with me. You hired yourself out as a cook and I expect a whole lot better than 'passable' food from you. You say the problem tonight is that you're not used to cooking outdoors. Since I consider myself a fair minded man, I'll buy that once. But, I suggest you get used to it, and fast, because I expect edible meals tomorrow. I want biscuits I can bite into without breaking my teeth and I want coffee—lots of strong, black, hot coffee. Am I making myself clear?"

"Perfectly."

"Good, because unless tomorrow's food is a *whole* lot better than today's, you and your brother are both going to be on your way back to Independence."

"You don't need to threaten me, Mr. Hunter. I said I understand."

"I hope so. Now, you better get this mess cleaned up and get bedded down for the night. We're starting early tomorrow."

Tess nodded, the wide brim of her sunbonnet bobbing up and down.

"And take off that hat, for God's sake," Hunter growled. "You look ridiculous wearing a sunbonnet when it's pitch dark." With a last frown of annoyance, he strode off into the darkness, pausing long enough to pick a piece of bacon off the tin plate and take a frustrated bite out of it.

Tess watched his departure, then turned and angrily kicked the dutch oven over.

"Guess he didn't like your biscuits, huh?" Joe muttered, emerging from behind a clump of bushes.

"No, he didn't," Tess snapped. "And thanks so much for all your support while he was dressing me down."

Joe shrugged. "There wouldn't have been anything I could have said to change things, so I just decided to stay out of it. No sense havin' him mad at both of us."

Tess stared at her brother accusingly. "You act like you're scared of him."

"I'm not scared of him," Joe protested hotly, "but there's something about the man that commands respect. You know, I still can't get over how much he reminds me of Colonel Whitaker. The way he talks, his gestures, even the way he walks. He's so much like the colonel, it's eerie. I just can't help thinkin' that he *is* him."

"Well, he's not him," Tess snapped, "so I wish you'd quit acting like he is. All the newspapers say that Colonel Whitaker must be dead or he would have shown up in Washington to accept that medal they wanted to give him. Besides, if he's not dead, then where did he disappear to after the battle of Chapultepec?"

Joe shrugged. "Nobody knows, Tess. But, you know, they never found his body and General Scott told the papers that he spoke to him after the battle and he wasn't even wounded. I just keep thinkin' that maybe the colonel got hurt somehow and got that disease where you lose your memory."

"Amnesia?"

"Yeah, that's it. Who knows? Maybe the colonel thinks he's this Hunter because he's forgotten who he really is."

"Oh, you're talking nonsense," Tess scoffed. "Mr. Hunter is exactly who he says he is. You're just letting your imagination run away with you because you idolized Colonel Whitaker and you want Hunter to be him. Besides, who he is or isn't is the least of my worries, and it should be the least of yours. If I don't figure out some way to make decent meals for him by tomorrow, he's going to send both of us back to Independence!"

"Yeah, I heard him say that."

"Then quit fussing about whether or not he's your Colonel Whitaker and try coming up with some suggestions about what we're going to do to get out of this mess."

Joe looked at her thoughtfully for a moment, then said, "Why don't you go talk to the other women on the train? Maybe one of them could tell you how to make proper biscuits."

Tess's pondered this for a moment, then her eyes widened and her face lit with a dazzling smile. "I have a better idea."

Hurrying over to the wagon, Tess pulled off her sunbonnet and threw her heavy shawl over her head. "Clean up this mess, will you, Joe? I'm going to go see Mary Krenzke."

"But, Tess . . ."

"Don't worry!" she smiled. "Everything is going to work out fine. You just wait and see."

Mary Krenzke stared at Tess in astonishment. "But, I thought Mr. Hunter hired you to cook for him. Now you want to pay me to do it for you?"

"Yes."

"I'm sorry, but I don't understand, Mrs. Caldwell."

Tess sighed, annoyed that the woman was asking so many questions. Why didn't she just agree or refuse? Why did she need reasons? "It's like I told you before, Mrs. Krenzke," she said patiently, "Mr. Hunter doesn't like my cooking."

"How could he have decided that already? After all, you've only cooked him one supper."

"I'm afraid one supper was enough," Tess sighed. "Look, ma'am, I am willing to pay you a dollar a day in addition to supplying all the food if you will just cook it for me."

Mary Krenzke's eyebrows shot up in astonishment. "A dollar a day?" she gasped.

"Yes."

"Every day? Seven days a week?"

"Yes, every day."

"I'll do it!"

Tess breathed a long sigh of relief. "Thank you. Now, just remember, not a word to Mr. Hunter. He has to believe that I'm doing the cooking. I'm afraid he might be put out with me if he thought I wasn't."

"I won't tell a soul," Mary promised, her eyes gleaming at the thought of how much money she was going to make over the next five months. "What do you want me to make for breakfast?"

"Biscuits," Tess answered promptly. "You do know how to make biscuits, don't you? Big, flaky ones?"

"Of course," Mary nodded. "What woman doesn't know how to make biscuits?"

Tess smiled and pulled a five dollar gold piece out of her pocket.

"Much better," Hunter complimented, sinking his teeth into his third, honey drenched biscuit. "I don't know what you did between last night and this morning, Mrs. Caldwell, but these are delicious."

"I told you that I just needed to get used to cooking over an open fire," Tess said. "Once I figured that out, the rest was easy."

Hunter licked a drop of honey off his thumb and looked at her speculatively. Easy? Somehow, he doubted that. In his estimation, the difference between last night's biscuits and these was little short of a miracle, but he kept that thought to himself. Out loud, he simply said, "Well, whatever you did, it worked."

"Thank you," she answered, careful to avert her

face so he wouldn't see her smug smile beneath the brim of her bonnet. "What would you like for supper?"

Hunter thought a minute, then said, "Tell you what. I'll see if I can shoot a rabbit or a prairie chicken sometime today and we can have that." Standing up, he brushed a crumb off his shirt, then looked at Tess warily. "You do know how to skin and spit a hare, don't you?"

"I'm sure that . . . I mean, yes, of course I do. What woman doesn't know how to skin a hare?"

The corner of Hunter's mouth crooked doubtfully, but he decided to give her the benefit of the doubt. "None that I can think of—if they're worth their salt, anyway." Picking up his hat, he began to walk away. "If I shoot anything, I'll bring it on back."

"The sooner, the better," Tess called after him.

Hunter held up an acknowledging hand, then strode off down the line of wagons. "Come on, everybody, time to mount up," he called. "Wagons ho! Let's move 'em out!"

Tess turned back to Joe who was happily finishing up the last of the biscuits. "See?" she whispered excitedly. "I told you this plan would work!"

"Well, it worked this morning, anyway," Joe responded. "But, you just better hope that Mrs. Krenzke knows how to skin a hare."

"She will," Tess said confidently. "After all, you heard Mr. Hunter. Every woman worth her salt knows how to skin a hare, and after seeing his reaction to her biscuits this morning, I'd say that Mrs. Krenzke is definitely worth her salt!"

Chapter 4

"You've got to get out of that wagon and start walking, Mrs. Caldwell."

Tess shifted nervously on the wagon seat and sneaked a peek at Hunter from under the brim of her red sunbonnet.

"Mrs. Caldwell, did you hear me?"

"Yes, Mr. Hunter, I did."

"Well then, get down and start walking."

"I can't walk. I have a bad . . . hip."

Hunter's eyes narrowed ominously as he stared at the obese woman. Her hip had probably gone bad from trying to hold up that fat body.

"Are you telling me that you expect to ride all the way to Oregon? That you can't walk at all?"

"It's difficult," Tess muttered.

"Tell you what," Joe chimed in. "I'll walk."

Hunter's speculative gaze swung over to the young man. "Can she drive?"

"No!" Tess blurted. "Joe, please, I don't think I can handle these mules."

"Sure you can," Joe smiled encouragingly, holding

out the heavy leather reins. "It just takes a little practice."

Tess immediately thrust the reins back at him. "No. I'll . . . I'll walk."

Hunter frowned and shook his head. "Look, I don't care who does what, but one of you has to walk. These mules have a heavy enough load without pulling an extra two hundred pounds. Somebody has got to get down, now." With a look that invited no further discussion, he rode off.

Tess's eyes widened in outraged offense. *Two hundred pounds*! Did the man seriously think she weighed two hundred pounds? She glanced down at her many layers of clothes, then grimaced. In actuality, she probably *did* look like she weighed that much. Her vanity thoroughly piqued, she scrambled into the back of the wagon and furiously pulled off two of her heavy petticoats. There's about twenty pounds right there, she thought with satisfaction, looking down at her instantly slimmer figure.

"Tess, what are you doin' back there?" Joe called.

"Taking off a couple of these petticoats."

"But, Tess," he protested, craning his neck around to look at her, "he's gonna notice."

"I don't care! I'm not going to walk lugging all these clothes around. They're hot, they're heavy, and I'm sick of them."

"Okay. Whatever you think."

Crawling back up to the front of the wagon, Tess re-settled herself on the hard seat. "Whenever you get a chance, pull over and I'll get down."

"Do you really think you should?"

Tess shrugged. "I don't see that I have much choice. You heard Mr. Hunter. One of us has to walk. I think it would be harder on me to try to control those cantankerous mules, so I guess I'm it."

"Maybe we should just tell Mr. Hunter the truth."

"No!" Tess shook her head vehemently. "We can't do that. You know we can't. I'll be fine. I'm much cooler now that I've taken off some petticoats."

Joe looked worriedly at her flushed face. "Tess, I'm real concerned about you . . ."

Tess's angry expression softened. "Don't be, Joe, I'm fine. A little walking never hurt anyone."

Just then, Joe saw Hunter riding toward them again and quickly pulled their wagon out of line, stopping by the side of the rutted trail. As Hunter approached, Tess stepped awkwardly down on to the wagon wheel, then jumped to the ground. "You don't need to check up on me, Mr. Hunter," she snapped, "I'm walking."

Hunter opened his mouth to retort, but as he took a closer look at her, his words died in his throat.

"What's the matter?" Tess questioned.

"Nothing. It's just that you look like you've lost about forty pounds since breakfast."

Tess could barely conceal her smile of pleasure. Forty pounds! Forcing herself to remain sober, she tossed him a reproving look. "Really, sir, I do not think my weight should be a subject for discussion."

Hunter threw her an annoyed glare. God, she was testy! What was wrong with the woman that she wouldn't even allow him to give her a little compliment? "You're absolutely right, Mrs. Caldwell, so I'll just tell you what I came back here to say."

Tess reached up to wipe her perspiring brow. "And, what was that?"

"Just this," Hunter answered, reaching behind him and untying a dead rabbit from the back of his saddle. "I caught us some supper."

Tess looked at the luckless animal, her stomach churning. "I see," she croaked, averting her face.

Hunter frowned and held the rabbit out toward her. "Take it. We're gonna be stopping in a few hours. You can skin it and spit it then."

Gingerly, Tess reached out and took the dead rabbit. "What should I do with it until then?"

"I don't care. Carry it if you want to."

At her horrified look, he started to laugh. "I'm teasing you, Mrs. Caldwell. Why don't you tie it on to the side of the wagon?"

Tess nodded weakly and turned away to do as he bade. Carefully, she tied the rabbit to the wagon, then stood with her back to him, hoping he'd leave before he saw how nauseated this whole episode was making her. But, he didn't move and, finally, she was forced to turn around and face him again.

"You sure you know how to skin that thing?" he asked, peering at her ashen face closely.

"Of course, I do. Why do you always presume that I don't know how to do things?"

"Because I don't know too many ladies who had household staffs, like you say you did, who would know how to skin a hare."

Tess lifted her chin a notch and glared at him. "Well, I do."

"Okay," he shrugged. "Just keep your eye out for a good, strong willow sapling as you walk. When you see one, cut a branch you can use for a spit. That way you won't have to waste any time looking for one after we've camped."

"I know, I know," Tess sighed, "after we camp, you want to eat as soon as possible, right?"

"Right." A quick smile flashed across his face, treating Tess to a rare glimpse of his even white teeth. His dark good looks sent an unexpected little shiver through her and she was disappointed when his smile faded.

Noticing that Tess was scrutinizing him from beneath her concealing bonnet, Hunter cleared his throat uncomfortably and said, "Well, I'd like to stand here and socialize, but you're already falling behind. Better move back into line now or else you'll have to run to catch up."

Again his mouth quirked at the corners, but this time his smile had a far different effect on Tess. She guessed his amusement stemmed from the thought of her running and his silent statement about her girth infuriated her. And to think that only a moment before, she had been musing over how handsome he was! With a haughty toss of her head, she gathered up her heavy skirts and hurried off to catch up with her wagon.

Hunter watched her for a moment, surprised by her quick, lithe movements, then thoughtfully rode back to the front of the train.

Dash McLaughlin, who was just returning from his day's scouting fell in next to him. "I saw you back there talking to your lady friend."

Hunter threw him a jaundiced look. "For God's sake, Dash, will you knock it off?"

Dash's grin widened. "You know, she looks different today than she did last night. I don't know what it is, but there's a definite change."

Hunter nodded. "I can tell you what it is. She peeled off about ten of those petticoats she was wearing and she looks forty pounds thinner."

"You're right! Hey, Hunter, maybe there's hope yet. If she keeps takin' off a couple layers every day, maybe by the time we reach Fort Laramie, she'll have a figure worth gapin' at."

"Don't count on it," Hunter muttered.

Dash looked back to where Tess was plodding slowly along next to her wagon. "I still don't understand why a woman would wear every stitch of clothing she owns at the same time."

"Who knows? Maybe she's got all her valuables

sewed into her petticoats and she doesn't want to let them out of her sight."

Dash craned his head around again, then grinned. "You know, Hunter, that's probably a good idea, her carrying her valuables in her petticoats."

"Oh, yeah? Why?"

"Well, from what you've said about her, I doubt there's a man on the train who'd risk ripping them off to find out. So if she's actually hidin' something valuable under those skirts, it's probably safer than in a bank."

The men shared a hearty laugh and then spent the next several minutes in outrageous conjecture about what Mrs. Caldwell could be stashing under her voluminous skirts. Although they ran the gamut from gold to guns to biscuits, neither of them came close to guessing what she was really hiding, a fact for which Tess, had she been aware of their conversation, would have been exceedingly grateful . . .

By the time supper was over, Tess was exhausted. It had been no small feat to get the disgusting little rabbit over to Mrs. Krenzke's for cooking without Hunter seeing her. And, even though she was careful to stay out of sight by ducking between wagons, he'd still caught her as she'd carried the cooked hare and a pot of baked beans back to her wagon.

"What in the hell are you doing?" he demanded, coming up behind her so silently that she nearly dropped the beans.

"Oh, Mr. Hunter!" she gasped. "You scared me to death!"

"Sorry. Now, what are you doing?"

Tess swallowed hard, trying desperately to think of a plausible excuse for why she was carrying a cooked hare on a spit. "Well, I . . . um . . . Mrs. Krenzke and

I decided to cook together tonight. We're sort of . . . sharing."

At Hunter's quizzical look, she held up the bean pot. "See? She baked beans and gave me some."

Hunter nodded approvingly, then reached out and took the bean pot. Together, they continued walking toward the wagon. "So, what did you give her?"

Tess looked over at Hunter blankly. "What do you mean?"

"You said Mrs. Krenzke made beans to share with you. What did you give her in return? It's obvious that you still have the whole rabbit."

"Ye . . . yes," Tess stammered, "I do." Suddenly she smiled, and added, "Mrs. Krenzke doesn't like rabbit. After I cooked this, I took it down to give her some and she said she didn't want any."

"I can't imagine anyone not liking roasted rabbit," Hunter muttered. "God knows, there were times when I would have sold my soul for a piece of roasted anything."

"Really?" Tess questioned. "When was that?"

Hunter's pleasant expression suddenly became shuttered. "Never mind. I'm just talking to myself."

But Tess's curiosity was piqued and instead of taking his hint and letting the subject drop, she plunged heedlessly on. "You sound like a man who's known what it is to be hungry, Mr. Hunter. Did you serve in the war with Mexico?"

Hunter's head snapped around. "Why would you ask that?"

Tess shrugged. "I don't know. It seems that most of the men who were involved in that war were hungry at least some of the time. I just thought maybe you were one of them."

Hunter said nothing, but his silence was more telling than any answer could have been. Getting a response from him now had turned into a challenge for Tess and even though she knew he was trying hard to avoid her question, she couldn't seem to let it go. "You didn't answer me, Mr. Hunter. Did you fight in the war?"

"Yeah, I fought in the war," he answered, his voice cold. "For awhile, anyway."

Tess threw her head back, trying to glimpse his expression, but he was staring straight ahead and all she could see was his darkly chiseled profile. "It know it was terrible," she murmured. "Joe told me about some of the hardships he was forced to endure. I'm sure you suffered the same and, for what it's worth, I'm sorry."

Hunter was so astonished by the genuine note of caring in her voice that for a moment he was speechless. Finally, he muttered, "It doesn't matter. It's over now and I don't want to talk about it."

Tess's heart wrenched at the fleeting look of pain that crossed his eyes. "At least, you have the satisfaction of knowing that we won," she said softly. "Certainly, it helps to make the hardships worthwhile when the ultimate victory was ours."

To her surprise, Hunter stopped in his tracks, rounding on her with a black look. "We didn't 'win', Mrs. Caldwell. We invaded the Mexicans' homeland and slaughtered them on their own soil. We had them outnumbered, out-equipped and out-gunned. We starved them, then we killed them without mercy. There's no victory in that." With a disgusted shake of his head, Hunter set down the pot of beans and walked away.

For a long moment, Tess just stood and stared after his retreating figure, trying to figure out what she had said to set him off. When, after several seconds, she still hadn't come up with an answer, she gave up pondering the enigmatic man's quicksilver turn of moods and returned to the wagon.

Later, when Joe asked her where Hunter was, she merely shrugged and set the wagon master's plate of rabbit and beans on a rock by his saddle.

It was still there the following morning.

Chapter 5

"Did you fight in the war, Mr. Hunter?"

Hunter sat on a cliff overlooking the bank of the Blue River, gazing sightlessly into the sluggish water beneath him as he tried to banish Tess's haunting question from his mind. Two weeks had passed since their conversation, but still, her words rang through his brain like a litany.

The war. It had been over a year since he had allowed himself to think about anything connected with those terrible months spent in Mexico fighting a war propelled mainly by greed and arrogance. Even now, as memories again assailed him, he was haunted by visions of the innocent citizens he had unwittingly killed, the friends he had buried, and the woman he had lost.

Even during the dark, lonely hours just before dawn when torturous visions would rise before his weary eyes, he always managed, somehow, to overcome them. To vanquish the pain, the despair, and the paralyzing sense of failure he suffered when memories of Colonel Jared Daulton Whitaker, the man he had left behind, insinuated themselves into his tired brain. For awhile, he'd actually thought he'd put it behind him. As the months had passed, the nightmares came less frequently and even the stabs of remorse he endured, knowing that he had given up his name and his birthright, didn't knife at him as often.

Slowly, he had settled himself into his new, untethered life, and the pain had almost stopped. Or at least, he thought it had until Tess Caldwell had asked her simple question.

Since that moment, he had thought of little else and the memories were as excruciating as ever.

"Damn her," he muttered, breaking off a brittle piece of grass and crushing it in his hand. "Damn her for a meddling old busybody."

He closed his eyes. A vision of Tess's earnest, upturned face as she stood holding her cooked hare and her bean pot floated before him. There had been something in her voice that day that he couldn't seem to get out of his mind—a note of caring that he had almost forgotten existed.

Was that what it was about Mrs. Tess Caldwell that seemed to draw him to her? What else could it be? It certainly wasn't that he was romantically interested in her. Not only was she significantly older than he, but she was far too quiet and lackluster for his liking. She rarely spoke to him except in monosyllables, and the only time she had ever tried to strike up a conversation, she had asked him the one question he didn't want to answer.

And yet, there was something about her that was keeping him awake nights, something elusive and intriguing that, try as he might, he couldn't quite define. Maybe it was the fleeting glimpse he sometimes got of her beautiful blue eyes before she hurriedly looked away. Maybe it was that warm, melodic voice that seemed to ripple over him like a merry little brook on the rare occasion when she spoke to him. Or, maybe it was that little bit of alabaster skin he could see beneath her concealing bonnet—skin that looked as soft and smooth as a young girl's.

"But she's not a young girl," he berated himself. "She's a middle aged matron—a widow, for God's sake."

So, why did he continually seek her out? A dozen times a day, he found himself riding back to her wagon, dawdling next to her as she trudged along, silently assuring himself that she was all right.

Over and over, he told himself that his concern stemmed only from his fear that she would overtax herself and be unable to cook his meals. But, that was a lie and he knew it.

With a heavy sigh, Hunter flopped onto his back, staring up at the cloudless sky. "It's because she's so damned mysterious about everything," he told himself. "She never shows her face. If you saw her close up, you'd find that she's exactly what she appears to be."

Suddenly, he sat up. That was it! Somehow, he had to find a way to see her—*really* see her. Her hair, her eyes, her lips. Just one quick look and then he would quit thinking about her, would quit hearing her soft voice flowing over him late at night as he lay on the hard ground.

Just one quick look—and then he would forget her.

"Okay, folks, we're going to take a day's rest before we cross the Platte."

A boisterous cheer arose from the seventy three people gathered around Hunter.

Florette Kubes, the youngest of the three merchants' wives on the train let out an excited little squeal and turned to Mary Krenzke. "Isn't this wonderful? A whole day without having to move. We can wash clothes."

"Wash clothes, hell," muttered a lumberjack standing nearby. "We can sleep as late as we want and then spend the rest of the day gettin' drunk!"

Florette sent the burly man a shaming look, then addressed Mary again. "Perhaps we ladies should get together to do chores tomorrow. With a whole day to spend, we can wash, mend, maybe even bake some bread."

"Yes," Mary nodded excitedly, "and we'll probably still have time left over to air out the linens in our wagons and," her voice dropped to a conspiratorial whisper, "sneak down to the river and take a real bath."

"Oh," Florette groaned ecstatically, "what a heavenly thought!"

"All right," Mary smiled, "then it's all settled. You go talk to Caroline Brooks and I'll tell Tess Caldwell. We'll make a day of it."

Florette nodded, then threw Mary a mischievous look. "Do you suppose we can get Tess to take off that red sunbonnet long enough to wash it? I swear, she wears that hat even after it gets dark at night. It's almost as if she's trying to hide something. What do you want to bet her hair is gray and she's embarrassed about it."

"Nonsense," Mary snorted. "I know the reason Tess wears that hat so much and it has nothing to do with the color of her hair."

Florette's eyebrows rose with sudden interest. "Really? What *is* the reason, then?"

Mary cast a furtive look around her, then whispered loudly, "It's because Mr. Hunter gave it to her as a gift."

"No!" Florette gasped. "Are you sure?"

"Well, I should be. I sold the bonnet to him."

Florette's eyes lit up with glee at this titillating bit of gossip. "Do you mean that Mr. Hunter and Tess Caldwell are . . ."

"I'm not saying a thing," Mary interrupted primly. "But, when a man buys a lady a bonnet and she refuses to take it off, well . . ."

"You're right," Florette nodded. "There *must* be something going on between them. I guess I'm just going to have to keep my eye on those two. Oh, Mary, I just can't wait for tomorrow!"

As Hunter lay with his head braced on his saddle and looked up at the stars, he, too, was contemplating the following day's respite.

So, the ladies are going to wash clothes, he thought smugly. That'll be my chance. She has to take that bonnet off if she's going to wash it. He smiled with satisfaction. Finally, he was going to solve the mystery of Tess Caldwell.

Rising early the following morning, Hunter gathered his soiled clothes into a tight bundle and headed for Tess's wagon. Even from a distance, he could see steam rising from a large pot of hot water and knew that wash day was already underway.

With a feeling of high anticipation, he rounded the back of the Bennington brothers' wagon, looking eagerly over at the wash pot. What he saw, however, made him stop in his tracks and let out a long, disappointed sigh.

Tess was standing over the pot of water, stirring the soapy contents with a large paddle—and over her head, completely concealing her hair and most of her face, was her heavy brown shawl.

"Damn it," Hunter muttered. "Damn it, damn it, damn it!"

His face tight and angry with frustration, he stalked up to Tess and thrust the large bundle at her. "Here are my dirty clothes. Just throw them in the soapy water and let them soak. Don't scrub them on a washboard. It wears them out too fast and I don't really care how white my longjohns are as long as they're clean."

Tess's eyes widened with horror. His longjohns! She didn't want to wash his longjohns. Of course, she was washing her brother's underclothing, but that was different. Somehow, there was something terribly intimate about handling Hunter's underwear. Why, just the thought of it made strange little goose bumps skitter up her spine.

Silently, she nodded her understanding of his instructions, then quickly turned away before he could see the embarrassed flush heating her cheeks.

"Oh, by the way, Mrs. Caldwell . . ."

Tess reluctantly turned back toward him. "Yes?"

"You better take that hot shawl off your head. You're red as a beet again."

"As always, Mr. Hunter, I appreciate your concern, but I'm washing my sunbonnet."

"So? Just leave your head uncovered, why don't you?"

Tess compressed her lips tightly. Why was Hunter always so concerned about what she wore on her head? "Mr. Hunter," she said, trying hard to keep her voice from betraying her discomfiture, "I prefer to keep my head covered. I have very fair skin and I don't want to get a sunburn."

"A sunburn isn't as much of a threat as passing out from wearing that blanket over your head."

"It's not a blanket, sir, and I don't see why you—"

"Forget it!" he snapped, interrupting her. "Wear whatever you want. Just make sure you get my clothes washed before you have to take to your bed from heat prostration!"

Wheeling around, he stomped away, leaving Tess to stare down with distaste at the dirty bundle of clothes she still held. "I can't *believe* he expects me to wash his longjohns," she muttered crossly, hurling the bundle to the ground.

For a long moment, she stared at the smelly clothes, then, with a grimace of distaste, she leaned down and gingerly scooped up the bundle. Shaking it out, she began adding the offensive items to the clothes already boiling in the pot.

"WHAT IN THE HELL DID YOU DO TO MY CLOTHES?"

Tess looked up from the petticoat she was mending. "I beg your pardon?" she asked blandly.

"You heard me!" Hunter raged. "What in the hell have you done to my clothes? They're pink! My white shirts, my longjohns, my socks. Everything is PINK!" His voice crackling with fury, he thrust a neatly folded pile of pastel underwear at her.

Tess threw a cursory look at the clothes and bit off a length of thread. "You told me just to throw them in the water and not to scrub them."

"Scrub them!" Hunter fumed. "What the hell has scrubbing got to do with anything? I give you white clothes to wash and you give them back to me pink! Now, you've got some explaining to do, lady, and I want to hear it."

Tess blew out a tremulous breath, careful to keep her eyes averted from the furious man. "Well, I had sort of an accident."

Hunter waited for her to continue, but when she

merely threaded her needle and began sewing again, he took an impatient step forward. "And?"

"And, your clothes ended up in the same wash pot as my sunbonnet.

"Your sunbonnet!"

"Yes. You know, the red one you gave me?"

"I know about your damn sunbonnet," Hunter gritted. "You never take the thing off your fool head, even in the dead of night. How could I help but know about it?"

"Well, I took it off today," Tess tittered nervously, "and that's why it ended up in the wash pot with your clothes."

Hunter misread her nervous little laugh, interpreting it as a total lack of remorse for the destruction of his clothes. If possible, his expression became even blacker.

"Lady, I have had it with you!" he bellowed. Leaning forward, he grabbed the offending sunbonnet off Tess's head. "Can't you do anything right?"

Taking a step backward, he drew a breath to let loose another epithet, but the curse died in his throat as he saw the honeyed mass of Tess's long, luxuriant hair tumble down her back.

An endless moment passed as Hunter's eyes widened with astonishment at the sight of the gorgeous woman before him.

"My God," he breathed, "you're . . . you're . . ."

"Give me my bonnet back!" Tess cried, lunging for the hat which still dangled from his fingers.

Despite his awestruck astonishment, Hunter's reactions were still lightning fast and before Tess could grab the concealing bonnet from him, he whipped it behind his back. "Now I understand," he whispered.

"Give me my bonnet!"

"No."

"Mr. Hunter, I'm warning you . . ."

"How old are you, Tess?"

Tess didn't know if she was more astounded by his unexpected question or by his unprecedented use of her first name. Too stunned to prevaricate, she said simply, "Twenty-three."

Hunter stared at her for a moment longer, then his eyes narrowed ominously. "Your brother lied to me."

"No, he didn't! He just said that I'm older than he is, and I am."

"By what? A year?"

"No, three. Joe is twenty. Now, please, give me back my bonnet."

"Why?" he asked, his ebony eyes riveted on the beauty of her exquisite face. "It doesn't make any difference if I see you now. Your secret is out."

Tess sighed wearily and covered her face with her hands. "We were afraid you wouldn't let us on the train if Joe told you my real age."

Hunter's voice was frighteningly quiet when he answered. "I wouldn't have. I told him I wasn't accepting any young women."

Slowly, Tess raised her eyes to his. "Are you going to throw us off now?"

Hunter tipped his head back and stared at the dark sky, contemplating her question. "I don't know," he answered honestly. "I don't know what I'm going to do." His gaze shifted back to her and, again, his eyes roamed over her pale hair. "Here's your bonnet," he said, tossing it into her lap. "Maybe you better keep it on after all."

Tess picked up the bonnet and quickly pushed her curls up under it. "Mr. Hunter . . ."

"No," Hunter interrupted, holding up a hand. "Don't say anything else, Mrs. Caldwell. It *is* Mrs. Caldwell, isn't it?"

Tess nodded mutely.

"I'll tell you in the morning what I've decided to do about you."

"Mr. Hunter, please . . ."

"Good night, Mrs. Caldwell."

"But, Mr. Hunter!"

Holding up a warning finger, Hunter said stonily, "This conversation is over, Mrs. Caldwell. Now, good night."

And before Tess could say anything more, he turned and disappeared into the night.

Chapter 6

Now he understood.

Tess Caldwell was twenty-three . . . and beautiful. It explained a lot. The melodic voice, the soft skin, the crystalline blue eyes. His unreasonable attraction for her suddenly all made sense. She was young and gorgeous. A bit plump for his taste, he admitted silently, but gorgeous nonetheless. And, so alluring that it was frightening.

Frightening because a beautiful, young woman had no business being on a rough and tumble men's wagon train. Frightening because he didn't know how he would control the men on the train if they discovered what he had tonight. But, most of all, frightening because the moment he had looked down at her exquisite face, feelings he had thought long buried had surfaced with staggering intensity.

Turning over on to his side, Hunter gazed thoughtfully into the dying embers of the evening's campfire.

"So you felt lust," he muttered aloud. "So what? You've been alone for months and you reacted to the sight of a beautiful woman. Quit worrying about it and go to sleep."

But sleep wouldn't come, and as the moon arced its way across the velvety night sky, Hunter's tired brain continued to spin.

Actually, he should be happy, he told himself. It had been so long since a woman had affected him sexually that he had almost forgotten how it felt. He should be pleased by the fact that, obviously, he wasn't quite as dead inside as he'd thought he was. But "happy" and "pleased" were definitely not words he would use to describe his feelings concerning Tess Caldwell.

Rather, his immediate physical reaction had left him conflicted, confused, and madder than hell. Tess Caldwell had duped him, and the fact that he had been taken in so easily was infuriating.

He should throw her off the train—her and that lying brother of hers. Send them back to Independence and let them cool their heels in the bawdy, expensive, dangerous town over the winter. He could think of no more appropriate punishment for their duplicity than six months of being trapped in Independence.

But, could he actually do that?

With an irritated grunt that he was still vascillating as to their fate, Hunter rolled over on his back and glared at the fading stars. Of course, he could do it. It was the only logical thing to do. He'd have to send Jack Riley along with them to show them the way back, but he could certainly make one trip without his trusted assistant. And Jack, with his Irishman's love of whiskey and women, would probably delight in being stranded in Independence for the winter.

Unbidden, a vision of Tess holed up in a seedy hotel room as she waited for the spring thaw, rose in his mind. There was no telling what would happen to her in the unholy environment that Independence had become in the last few years. It was certainly no place for a young, naive woman, especially when her only security would be the dubious protection of her even younger and more naive brother.

Hunter's mind twisted in another direction. Could he really spare Jack to escort the couple back to Missouri? Now that he thought about it, probably not. He needed the gritty little man. Needed him for a thousand reasons—none of which he could think of right at this moment—but a thousand reasons, nevertheless.

Pressing his lips together in a thin line, Hunter shook his head. No, he definitely could not get along without Jack. And if he couldn't spare Jack, then he couldn't send Tess Caldwell back to Independence.

So, that was the end of it. His decision was made. Tess and her brother would have to stay—not because he wanted them to, of course—but because he couldn't possibly spare Jack Riley.

Slamming his eyelids shut, Hunter let out a long, weary sigh and willed himself to relax. "Go to sleep," he mumbled. "Quit thinking and go to sleep."

And he finally did go to sleep, but not before a niggling little voice in the back of his mind whispered, "You made your first two crossings without Jack Riley . . . and you got along just fine. What makes you think you can't make it without him now?"

"I've decided you can stay."

Despite the iciness of Hunter's curt statement, Tess felt almost lightheaded with relief. For a crazy moment, she wanted to rush forward and hug him, but the forbidding expression in his dark eyes stopped her before she took a step.

"Thank you," she said simply, handing him a plate of eggs and bacon.

Hunter set the plate down on the tailgate of the wagon and turned toward her. "Let's get something straight, Mrs. Caldwell. The only reason I'm letting you and your brother remain with the outfit is because I can't spare a man to take you back to Independence."

Tess blanched at the hostility in his voice. "I understand."

"Then understand this too. You've already lied to me more than once—"

"No, I haven't!"

"Don't interrupt me. You and your brother tried to pull the wool over my eyes about your age, after I had told him I wouldn't accept young women on this train. Then, you lied about your housekeeping skills. Obviously, you don't know how to wash clothes even though you assured me you did. Tell me, Mrs. Caldwell, do you lie about everything?"

"No!"

Hunter's eyes narrowed. "What about your cooking?"

Tess's breath caught in her throat. Did he know about Mary Krenzke doing the cooking for her? And, if he did, how had he found out? Swallowing nervously, Tess decided to brazen it out. "What about my cooking?"

"It just seems kind of strange to me that the first night out you made a meal that was so bad I couldn't eat it, yet the next morning and ever since, your cooking has been fine. I also think it's strange that I never see you fixing anything. The food just seems to appear, almost like someone else was cooking it and bringing it to you."

Tess's shoulders sagged in defeat. He *did* know.

Somehow, he had found out she was paying Mary to do her chores. "All right," she sighed. "I admit it. I haven't been doing the cooking."

An unexpected jolt of disappointment ripped through Hunter. Tess's perfidy in this matter had been a wild guess on his part and he hadn't realized how much he'd wanted to be wrong.

"You haven't?"

She shook her head.

"Then, who has?"

"Mrs. Krenzke," Tess murmured, her gaze fixed on her clenched hands.

Hunter nodded slowly. "Of course. That's why I saw you coming from her wagon that night with the hare and the beans. You two weren't cooking together, you were just picking up food from her, weren't you?"

"Yes." Tess's admission was barely more than a whisper.

Hunter sucked in a deep breath, trying hard to clamp down on his rapidly igniting temper. He clenched his fists, then willed himself to unclench them again. He was so angry that he wanted to hit something, kick something, bellow at Tess for betraying him. And what made him angriest was the fact that this woman, who should mean nothing to him, could make him feel this way. When he finally spoke again, his voice was so low, so controlled, that Tess had to lean toward him to hear.

"Mrs. Caldwell, you are, without a doubt, the most deceitful woman I've ever met."

Tess squeezed her eyes shut, hating him for his cruel words, even though she knew they were true. Even more, she hated the circumstances of her life that had forced her to become the woman he accused her of being.

"I'm sorry, Mr. Hunter. I know what you must

think of me and you have good reason." She paused, waiting for him to say more. Several seconds passed in silence.

Finally, she gathered up her courage and voiced the question that hung between them. "Now that you know about the cooking, do you still want me to work for you?"

Hunter's expression was incredulous. "Work for me? Is that what you think you've been doing? You haven't *worked* for me, Mrs. Caldwell, except to make me one inedible meal and ruin most of the clothing I own. What you have done though, and very successfully, is *lie* to me."

Tess tipped her head back and peered out at him from under the brim of her red sunbonnet. "I know that. You don't have to keep reminding me. I also know that what I did was wrong, but I thought if I told you the truth, you would send Joe and me back."

"And, that's exactly what I should do," Hunter growled, and at that moment he meant it. How could he spend the next three months in close company with this dishonest, deceitful woman when he knew that despite all of her lies, he was still so attracted to her that even now, in the midst of his anger, he longed to rip that stupid bonnet off her head and bury his lips in the long blond tresses he knew it concealed. Tess Caldwell personified everything he disliked in women and yet, all he could think of as he looked at her was what her lips might feel like beneath his.

Hunter frowned, annoyed by his own traitorous thoughts. "But, I've told you that you and your brother can stay on with the train and, unlike you, I am a person of my word."

Tess winced at this latest insult, but remained silent.

"However," Hunter continued, his voice icy, "if you're going to stay, there are several conditions that you will meet."

"What are they?" Tess gulped.

"First of all, you will start doing the chores you were hired to do. All of them. *You* will cook, *you* will clean, *you* will wash."

"But, I promised Mrs. Krenzke that I would pay her a dollar a day till we reached Oregon for doing the cooking for me."

Hunter shrugged. "That's between you and her. If she holds you to your agreement, that's your problem, but, you will do the cooking yourself."

"That doesn't seem quite fair," Tess huffed.

"Fair?" Hunter gasped. "You have the audacity to stand here, look me in the eye, and tell me what's fair? My God, woman, I have to give you credit. You do have cheek."

Tess threw her head back haughtily. "I beg your pardon, sir, but, regardless of what you think about me, you have no right to stand here and insult me." Whirling around, she started to walk away.

It took Hunter less than a second to catch up with her. "Lady," he growled, catching her by the arm and turning her back to face him, "I think you would be wise—very, *very* wise—to try your damnedest not to upset me right now. Otherwise, you and that brother of yours might just find yourself headed back across three hundred miles of prairie all by yourself."

"Quit threatening me!"

"Then, quit lying to me!"

His thundering command brought immediate silence. Tess blinked several times as his obsidian eyes bored into hers. Finally, she lowered her gaze. "Are you through, Mr. Hunter?"

"No. I have a couple more things to say first. Number one, I expect the meals you cook me to be edible and the next time you wash, I expect my clothes to come out of the water the same color as they were when they went in. Therefore, I think it would be an excellent idea if you spent the next few days at Mrs. Krenzke's side learning the trade for which I am paying you."

Tess nodded a grudging agreement. As much as she hated to admit it, his idea was sound. In fact, if she'd listened to Joe when he'd first suggested that very thing, it might have saved her the embarrassment she was suffering this morning. "All right, I'll speak to her right away. What else?"

"Come around here to the back of the wagon where we can talk without being overheard."

Tess glanced around, surprised by Hunter's sudden demand for privacy. There was no one within earshot that she could see and she found it strange that after the tongue lashing he'd just given her, he'd be worried about it now. What in the world could he want to discuss? Biting her lip, she looked at him apprehensively, wondering if she dare refuse his command, but before she could make a decision, he grabbed her by the wrist and pulled her over to the back of the wagon.

"Take off that bonnet," he ordered when he was sure no one could see them.

"Why?"

"Because I'm going to ask you a question and I want to see your face when you answer."

Slowly, Tess untied the strings of the red sunbonnet and lifted it off her head.

Hunter's eyes feasted hungrily on her for a moment, then he quickly looked away, balling his hands into fists and jamming them in his pockets. "Now," he gritted, "I'm going to ask you a question and I want you to look me straight in the eye when you answer."

Tess felt like a trapped animal, but she was determined not to let the autocratic man see how apprehensive she was. Resolutely she raised her eyes until she was staring into the black depths of his. "All right," she whispered. "Ask."

"Have you lied to me about anything else besides your age and your housekeeping experience?"

Tess's breath caught in her throat and for a moment, she didn't think she was going to be able to answer. Several long seconds passed as she tried to compose herself.

"Well?" Hunter prodded. "Yes or no?"

Begging heaven's forgiveness for the lie she was about to tell, she drew a deep breath and said, "No."

Hunter riveted her with a look that seemed to pierce right to her soul. "You're sure?"

"Yes."

Another endless moment passed as his dark gaze searched her face, then, finally, he nodded. "All right. Now, you better put your bonnet on and get back to your wagon. We're heading out in less than an hour."

Gratefully, Tess replaced the bonnet and picked up her heavy skirts, hurrying back to the relative security of her wagon. She barely looked up when Hunter joined her, picking up his plate and shoveling the now cold eggs into his mouth. Silently, he finished his hurried meal, then handed the plate back to her. "One more thing," he said, wiping his mouth on the back of his sleeve.

"Yes?"

"You better take off a couple more of those petticoats you love so much. You fall into the river today wearing all those clothes and you'll drown for sure."

Chapter 7

Tess stared down from the high seat of her wagon into the shallow, muddy river, then lifted her gaze to Hunter, throwing him a jaundiced look. The South Platte, at the point where they were crossing, looked to be no more than three or four feet deep. Drown, indeed!

Hunter saw Tess's doubting glance and separated himself from the lead wagons, riding over to her and holding up a warning finger. "Don't look at me like that, Mrs. Caldwell. More than one traveller has died in this river because they didn't take it seriously."

Wheeling his horse around, he took off his hat, waving it over his head to get everyone's attention. "Listen to me, folks," he called. "I know that most of you think this river doesn't look like much and that we've got an easy crossing here, but I want you all to keep your heads up. The Platte may be shallow, but there are eddies that can spin you around like a twig and patches of quicksand that can pull you under faster than you can blink an eye. If anybody feels their wheels sinking, you're to yell for help and yell loud.

I don't want anybody trying to play the hero here. I just want us all to get to the other side in one piece. Understood?"

Seventy-three heads nodded soberly.

"Good. Then let's move the first wagon out." Turning back briefly to Tess, he added, "When your turn comes, you get in the back. I want Joe up front alone."

He could see Tess opening her mouth to protest, but before she could utter a word, he snapped, "Don't argue. Just do it." Then he rode back to the head of the long column, stopping frequently to offer words of encouragement and advice.

The wagon train had taken on a rather bizarre appearance since, in preparation for the river crossing, green buffalo hides smeared with tallow and ashes had been tied to the bottom of the wagons to waterproof them. As Tess stared down the long line, she couldn't help but smile at how much the wagons resembled white haired old men with dark, furry beards growing from their chins.

Double and triple teams of mules were chained together to haul the wagons across the rapidly flowing river. As the first team stepped into the water, a tense silence descended over the travellers. It was the train's first major river crossing and everyone was nervous, although the brash and rowdy lumberjacks would have sooner died than admit it.

The first wagons crossed safely except for a luckless cow, who got caught up in one of the swirling undercurrents Hunter had described and was carried downstream, bawling and struggling. Tess felt a moment of panic as she watched the terrified animal being hurtled down the river, but she fought back her trepidation. As much as she feared her turn in the muddy river, she knew she had no choice. It was either cross or be left behind.

When the moment finally came, she held her breath as she felt the wheels sink into the soft river bottom. She had heard the South Platte described as being so muddy that it looked like it flowed upside down and the sound of the wheels squishing through the muck as they inched torturously along certainly gave credence to the description.

At one point, halfway across, the wagon suddenly gave a sickening sideways lurch, throwing Tess painfully against the wooden side and causing her to grab desperately for the edge of her cot. She heard Hunter yell something at Joe. His command was followed immediately by the sharp cracking sound of a whip hitting the water. One of the mules let out an ear-splitting bray of protest, but the wagon righted itself.

For a long moment, Tess sat on the edge of her cot, her lips white with fear and her eyes squeezed shut so tightly that they stung. Finally, she let out the breath she didn't even realize she was holding and hazarded a glance over Joe's shoulder. To her extreme relief, the opposite edge of the river was much closer than it had been the last time she'd looked and as she continued to watch, she saw Hunter's big roan horse scramble up onto the grassy bank. Then, after one last crack of the whip, the mules clambered onto dry ground, hauling the heavy wagon, bucking and lurching, up the bank behind them.

Tess closed her eyes and uttered a heartfelt prayer of thanks, then crawled forward and threw her arms around Joe, hugging him fiercely.

"Praise God, sis, we made it!" Joe crowed, reaching up to touch her face with shaking fingers.

"You did a wonderful job, Joe. Didn't he, Mr. Hunter?"

Hunter, who had ridden over to where their wagon

stood dripping in the morning sunlight, looked up at Joe and smiled. "Yes, that he did, especially when the lead brace almost went down."

"What?" Tess gasped.

Hunter threw her a perplexed look. "You didn't feel it when the mules floundered?"

"You mean when the wagon lurched sideways in the middle of the river?"

Hunter nodded. "That was it, and your brother got them back on their feet before they could drag the brace behind them down too. It probably saved the wagon from tipping over." Turning toward Joe, Hunter graced him with one of his rare smiles. "A capital job, young man."

As he rode away, Tess beamed at Joe, but her smile faded to bewilderment as she noticed the pensive expression on his face. "What are you thinking about?"

Joe shook his head. "I tell you, Tess, that man is Colonel Whitaker."

Tess frowned impatiently. "Oh, come on, are you going to start that nonsense again?"

Joe hitched around on the seat and looked at her earnestly. "It's not nonsense. Did you hear him when he was praising me?"

Tess nodded. "What about it?"

"He used the expression, 'a capital job'."

"So?"

"That's the expression Colonel Whitaker used when he praised one of the men in the company. It was always the same. 'A capital job, young man.' Those were his exact words - every time."

Tess sighed, tired to death of her brother's unrelenting fascination with Hunter's "secret" identity. "Maybe you're right, after all, Joe. Maybe he *is* Colonel Whitaker." There. She had finally said what he wanted to hear. Now, maybe, he'd quit talking about it.

"But, don't you find that fascinating?"

Tess pursed her lips together in annoyance. "No, Joe, like I've told you before, I really don't care if he is or isn't. I have absolutely no interest in Mr. Hunter other than his competence as our trail guide. I couldn't care less about his past."

Joe started to say something else, but seeing her annoyed expression, thought better of it. Instead he asked, "Are you going to have your first cooking lesson with Mrs. Krenzke today?"

Tess nodded, relieved that they were finally off the subject of Hunter. "I'm supposed to, although after all the excitement of the crossing, I don't think anyone will be doing much cooking tonight."

"It *was* exciting, wasn't it?" Joe chuckled. "I've got to tell you though, when I saw those mules go down, I thought we were goners."

Tess looked over at Hunter who was riding just a few wagons ahead of them. "I guess it's like Mr. Hunter says," she smiled. "You did a capital job, young man. A capital job."

They travelled another three miles that afternoon before setting up camp for the night. When the wagons were finally squared off, Tess hurried down to Mary Krenzke's for her first cooking lesson. Her suspicion that supper might be a light repast proved to be true, however, and all she ended up doing was slicing a loaf of the bread Mary had made the previous day. Mary gave her a large chunk of antelope that had been caught and roasted two days before and Tess headed back for her wagon with the simple meal.

"There's no hot food tonight," she warned as Hunter walked up to their wagon.

To her surprise, he smiled. "Didn't figure there

would be. Anytime there's a river crossing, I can pretty much count on a cold supper."

Tess neatly sheared a thick slice of meat off the piece Mary had given her, slathered mustard on the soft bread and handed Hunter a sandwich. With a nod of thanks, he walked over to the campfire and sat down, biting into his food hungrily.

After making another sandwich for Joe as well as one for herself, she joined him by the fire. "So, now that we're across the Platte, what comes next?"

A moment of silence passed as Hunter swallowed his food and took a swig of coffee. "We've got some pretty country coming up. There's a long line of bluffs that follow the North Platte. They're called the Coasts of Nebraska. We're going to pass along those, then we'll come to Court House Rock, Chimney Rock and Scotts Bluff. After that we'll continue on to Fort Laramie."

"Fort Laramie," Tess sighed. "I can't wait."

"Most women I've guided across feel that way. We'll stay there for three or four days so everyone can re-provision and rest up for the pull across the Rockies."

"I don't even want to think about the Rockies," Tess said. "I'm just concentrating on four heavenly days of being back in civilization."

"Well, I don't know if I'd call Fort Laramie 'heavenly'," Hunter chuckled, "but I guess it's as close to civilization as you're gonna find out here."

"I've heard it's a wonderful place," Tess stated positively.

"Really? Who told you that?"

"The other ladies on the train."

"I suppose they would think that since that's where they're all settling."

Tess turned incredulous eyes on him. "All of them?" she gasped. "I thought it was just the Brookses who were settling in Fort Laramie."

"No. All three couples are. They've decided to pool

their resources and start one big store. Three times the inventory, three times the profit."

Tess was visibly upset by this piece of news.

"What's the matter?" Hunter asked.

She shrugged, trying desperately to act nonchalant. "Oh, it's nothing, really. I'm just going to miss having the other ladies for company. Once they leave, I'll be the only woman on the whole train."

"That's right," Hunter nodded. "That's why I told you to keep that sunbonnet on. I don't want any of the men knowing what you really look like."

Tess wasn't sure whether to be frightened or flattered by his words. She didn't give them much thought, though, since she was far too distraught by the realization that she was soon going to be completely without female companionship—or assistance—to worry about the meaning behind his ambiguous statement. "Don't worry," she said absently. "I'll keep to myself."

Hunter's eyes ran over her shapeless form, knowing he should probably be relieved that she was not more curvaceous. Now that he knew how young and pretty she really was, he couldn't understand why she didn't take more heed of her figure. If her body were as gorgeous as her face, she'd be truly spectacular.

They sat in silence for a moment, each lost in their own thoughts. Their reverie was finally interrupted by Joe who suddenly appeared out of the darkness, his hair and shoulders wet from a recent dousing in the river.

"Got the animals hobbled for the night," he announced, picking up his plate and settling a hip against the wagon's tailgate.

"Did you find them a good grazing spot?" Hunter asked.

Joe nodded. "Sure did. They've got plenty of grass, so they should be happy."

"That's not hard to find around here," Tess sighed, her eyes sweeping across the endless panarama of tall, waving grass. "Grass is all you see as far as you look. It's so boring. I wish we'd see some trees or at least some hills. Anything but these never ending fields of grass."

"Enjoy it while you have it," Hunter warned. "Once we get to Wyoming and you're walking over rocks every day with nothing more than an occasional clump of sagebrush to cushion your steps, you'll be wishing for some of that soft, boring grass."

Silence again fell as the threesome thoughtfully ate their sandwiches. Then Joe said, "Tess tells me that you were in the war with Mexico, Mr. Hunter."

Hunter's shoulders stiffened. "Yeah, I was."

"What outfit were you with?"

For a moment, Tess didn't think Hunter was going to answer, but finally he muttered, "General Scott's."

Joe's eyes widened. "Then you must have been with Colonel Whitaker. Why, that was my outfit too. Funny we never met."

Hunter shrugged. "It was a big company."

"Yeah," Joe mumbled, "but still . . ." He paused a moment, wondering if he dared say more, then recklessly plunged on. "Didn't anybody in the outfit ever mention to you how much you look like the colonel?"

Hunter tossed his plate aside and got to his feet. "No," he said shortly. "Nobody ever did. Better bed down now. We've got a lot of ground to cover in the next few days if we're gonna make Fort Laramie by the fifteenth."

He started to walk away, but was halted by Joe's insistent voice. "Hey, Mr. Hunter, tell me something. Were you at Chapultepec?"

Hunter didn't turn around. "No. I was mustered

out before that." Without waiting for Joe to respond, he disappeared into the darkness.

Joe whirled around to look at Tess who was gathering up the dirty dishes. "He's lying. You could tell just by the way he said it that he's lying."

For the first time, Tess was actually beginning to believe Joe's wild speculations concerning Hunter's true identity. "I think you're right," she agreed. "I also think that if you know what's good for you, you won't ask him any more about the war."

"Ah, come on, Tess, don't be such a spoilsport. I just have to know if he's really Colonel Whitaker and I bet if I just keep workin' on him a little bit here and there, eventually he'll tell me."

Tess glared angrily at her brother. "Joe, I want you to drop this whole thing right now. You're not to "work" on Mr. Hunter, do you understand me? Even if he is Colonel Whitaker, he obviously doesn't want anybody to know it and if you persist in questioning him, he may get so fed up that he'll toss us off the train. With everything that's already gone wrong, I don't want you antagonizing him any further. Promise me you'll let it drop."

Joe threw her a mutinous look.

"Promise me, Joe."

"Oh, all right," he snapped. "If you're gonna get into such a state about it, I won't ask him anything else."

"Good," Tess nodded. "Now, we better take Mr. Hunter's advice and go to bed. I'm so tired I could sleep for a week."

Joe's expression softened. "Poor Tess," he said sympathetically. "I know how hard this is on you. Why don't you just go on to bed. I'll finish up out here."

Tess looked at him gratefully. "Are you sure?"

"Absolutely."

With a smile and a last little wave, Tess climbed into the back of the wagon.

Long after she'd fallen into an exhausted sleep, Joe sat outside in the cool night air, trying to figure out some way to subtly coerce Hunter into admitting who he really was. He'd never broken his word to Tess and he wouldn't do it now, but somehow, there had to be a way to get Hunter to confess. And, if there was, he was going to find it.

Chapter 8

Hunter squatted down near Dash McLaughlin's small campfire and accepted the glass of whiskey his friend offered.

"Mrs. Caldwell's brother knows I'm Jared Whitaker," he said without preamble.

Dash looked at him in surprise. "Are you sure?"

Hunter nodded. "I've suspected he knew ever since the first day I met him. He mentioned at that time that he thought I looked like Colonel Whitaker. Now, tonight, he brought it up again."

"But, how would he know what you looked like?"

"He told me tonight that he served under me . . . under Whitaker, that is."

Dash took a long swallow of his whiskey, thinking how strange it must be to refer to oneself in the third person. "Do you remember him?"

"No. There were hundreds of kids just like him, especially toward the end. They all became faceless. Faceless and meaningless . . ." Hunter's voice trailed off and an expression of pain filled his eyes.

"So," Dash said thoughtfully, "what are you going to do about it?"

"Do? What can I do, except keep denying it?"

"But, what if Chambers starts tellin' his suspicions to the other men?"

Hunter shrugged and upended his glass, draining the contents. "If that happens, I'll just have to deal with it. I don't really think anyone will much care, even if he does talk. After all, it's been over a year."

Dash threw him a dubious look. "You're kidding yourself, Jared, if you think people aren't still interested in your 'disappearance'." He paused for a moment, then added, "You know, maybe you should just go ahead and admit who you are. Go back to Washington, pick up your damn medal and put an end to this sham."

Hunter's answer was quick and final. "No."

Picking up the whiskey bottle, he poured himself another liberal shot. "For all intents and purposes, Jared Whitaker is dead . . . and that's exactly how I intend to keep him."

Dash refilled his glass too, debating whether to pursue the touchy subject. In the past, he had made it a point not to ask his friend about his surprising decision to forsake his birthright but, somehow, tonight, as they drank together hunkered down by the fire beneath the vast Nebraska sky, it seemed natural to voice the questions he had so long suppressed. Finally, throwing caution to the wind, he said quietly, "Why did you do it, Jared?"

Hunter looked at him in surprise. "Why did I do what?"

"Everything. Walk away without a word, change your name, take up this aimless life you're leading?"

A shadow of a smile touched Hunter's lips. "Is this something you've been wondering for a long time, McLaughlin?"

"As a matter of fact, yes."

"Why didn't you ever say anything before?"

"The time just never seemed right."

Hunter leaned back on his elbows, staring at the inky sky. "And, yet, out here in the middle of this God forsaken prairie, it does?"

"Yeah."

Hunter sighed, a sound so mournful that Dash almost wished he hadn't pried.

"Okay, I'll tell you, but I'm afraid you're going to be disappointed by my answer."

"Try me," Dash said softly.

Hunter swallowed hard, clenching his teeth together so his words came out in a long, hissing breath. "I left because I couldn't stand any more praise."

For a long moment, Dash just stared at him, blinking several times as he tried to make sense of Hunter's strange statement. He took another swallow of his drink, then stared at him some more. "What the hell does that mean?"

Hunter's face took on a haunted look as visions of that last terrible battle rose before his eyes. *The bodies . . . So many bodies, and most of them so young. It was such a waste. All of those proud, misguided boys dead before they even had a chance to really live.*

When he finally spoke again, Hunter's voice was so thick with pain that Dash had to lean forward to hear. "The night after the Battle of Chapultepec, I was sitting up on the hill, looking down at the field. There were bodies everywhere—mostly Mexicans. But, they weren't soldiers, they were young kids and old men. It made me sick to my stomach to know that I had ordered the slaughter. It was then I knew I had to go."

"My men told me that General Scott was saying that he was going to see that I got a medal." Suddenly,

Hunter turned to Dash, his look tortured and his voice rasping. "Don't you see, Dash? I didn't want his praise and I sure as hell didn't want a medal. So I left. I just turned around and rode away."

"That's it?" Dash cried, disbelief evident in his tone. "You didn't say anything to anybody? You just rode away?"

Hunter let out a long, shuddering breath and drained his glass again. "Yes. I just rode away."

Dash studied his old friend for a moment, relieved to see that the haunted look was fading from his eyes. "But, why this, Jared?" he asked quietly. "Why a wagon train, for God's sake? You were never a scout. You were a high ranking officer. It just doesn't fit."

"You're wrong. It fits perfectly. No ties, no involvements, no permanence . . ."

"No loss, no grief, no emotions," Dash finished.

"That too. At any rate, it suits me fine, and the money's good."

"What difference does the money make? You never spend any of it."

"I'm putting it away. One of these days I'll get too old or too bored for this. By then, I'll have enough set aside to buy a little place somewhere."

"And do what?"

"I don't know. Ranch a little, maybe. I like Colorado a lot. Maybe I'll eventually buy myself a little spread there and raise some cattle. Or, maybe I'll just sit out on a front porch somewhere and watch the sun come up in the morning and go down at night."

"Sounds fascinating," Dash chuckled wryly.

"There are worse things. Anyway, it's not something I think about much. This life is fine for now."

Dash took the hint Hunter was so obviously dropping and tactfully changed the subject. "So, how's your widow doing with her cooking lessons?"

Hunter relaxed as the conversation moved to less

sensitive ground. "She was supposed to have her first one today, but with crossing the river, there wasn't any time to cook, so I guess she'll have to start tomorrow instead."

Dash pulled a piece of beef jerky out of his saddle bag and broke it in two, tossing Hunter half. "You know," he said, gesturing with the piece he still held, "I still cannot understand a woman her age not knowing how to cook and wash clothes."

"She had a rich husband," Hunter said evasively.

"Nobody's that rich!" Dash scoffed. "Anyway, being married as long as she must have been, you'd think she would've picked up some knowledge just by association with her servants, if nothing else."

"She told me she was only married for a couple of years."

"Really! Well, with her looks, I'm not surprised that it took her till she was forty-five to catch herself a man. Probably some old geezer with lots of money, but not much of anything else, if you get my drift."

Hunter didn't laugh at Dash's quip. Rather, he looked at him closely for a moment, then said, "She's not forty-five."

Dash shrugged. "Okay, so forty, then. When a woman gets that old, who can tell?"

"She's not forty, either. She's twenty-three."

Dash, who was just taking another bite off his jerky, gaped at Hunter in disbelief, the tough piece of meat still clamped in his teeth. "Sure she is."

"She's twenty-three," Hunter repeated.

"Oh, come on, you're joshin' me, right?"

Hunter shook his head.

Dash tore a piece off the meat, then laid back, chewing it thoughtfully. "Who told you she's twenty-three?"

"She did."

"And you believed her?"

"I didn't have to take her word for it. I've seen her."

"I've seen her too. That's why I think she's pullin' your leg. If that woman is twenty-three, then I'm sixteen."

Hunter shook his head. "You don't get what I'm telling you, Dash. I've *seen* her . . . up close . . . with her sunbonnet off. She's young, blond, and pretty enough to make a man need a dip in a cold stream just from looking at her."

Dash chewed a few times, then swallowed and chased down the dry meat with a drink of whiskey. "You know I'd never call you a liar, Jared, but I'm just havin' a hell of a time tryin' to picture the Widow Caldwell makin' my flag fly."

This comment did bring a rumble of laughter from Hunter. "Like I'm telling you, you haven't seen her with that bonnet off. And, knowing your penchant for pretty women, I'd lay odds that if you did, your flag would not only be flying, it would be singing Dixie too."

"Well," Dash chuckled, "guess I'm gonna have to make a point of gettin' a peek at the widow minus her bonnet. Regardless of what her face looks like, though, she's still built like a brick shithouse."

"I told you before that I think a lot of that is all those petticoats she wears. Sometimes, when it gets so hot that she has to take a few of them off, she looks a lot thinner. Even you noticed it that one day."

"Yeah, I did," Dash agreed, "but she was still pretty square. In my opinion, potatoes and gravy are responsible for her looks, not petticoats."

"Maybe you're right," Hunter conceded, "but I still think there's a whole lot about Tess Caldwell that neither one of us knows. She's full of surprises."

Dash chewed his jerky for a moment, considering

all that Hunter had just told him. "You really think there's a gorgeous little woman under those clothes?"

"I didn't say that. What I said is that I don't think she's as fat as she wants us to believe she is. But, I wouldn't go so far as to say that she's a 'gorgeous little woman'. I think she's . . . well . . . plump. But, for some reason, she wants us to think she's obese."

"Plump, huh? Well, plump isn't all bad, I guess, although, personally, I prefer 'voluptuous'."

"Yeah, well, who doesn't? Hell, Dash, I don't know why we're discussing this anyway. It's not like either one of us is going to court her."

"I know, I know, but it's more fun to speculate about the widow than to talk about those ugly lumberjacks we're haulin'. Hellfire, Jared, I've never met a rougher group of men than this bunch. Whatever made you decide to take them on?"

"Figured they wouldn't be any trouble. And I was right. So far, they haven't been."

"Except for the damn fights that break out every other night when they get liquored up."

"I'll take a couple of drunken brawls any day over a bunch of homesteaders and their wives. Have you forgotten the last crossing? I swear, we had to stop every two days while some woman had a baby. God save me from ever making another trip like that one."

"Well, yeah," Dash admitted, "now that you mention it, there were a lot of delays. But, there were compensations too. At least with women on the train, I could always count on gettin' an invitation to supper if I wandered around to enough wagons."

"Supper, hell. What you were counting on when you wandered around was finding a pretty young girl with no particular plans for an evening."

Dash's grin was unrepentant. "That too . . . Anyway, I say, next time, let's just start a week earlier to make up for the delays and go back to takin' women . . . lots and lots of 'em."

Hunter swallowed the last of his whiskey and got to his feet, brushing off the back of his pants. "I'll keep that in mind. I can see the advertising posters in Independence now. WANTED FOR EXPEDITION TO OREGON: LOTS AND LOTS OF SINGLE, AVAILABLE WOMEN."

"Oh, don't do that!" Dash protested. "All an advertisement like that would get us is lots and lots of single, horny men!"

Chapter 9

"The worst thing about this whole trip is the lack of privacy," Tess grumbled to herself. Jumping awkwardly down from the back of her wagon, she tightened the sash of her heavy wrapper, then crept stealthily off toward a nearby clump of bushes, careful not to awaken Joe or Hunter as they lay sleeping beneath the dark, starless sky.

Hitching up the loose skirts of her voluminous nightclothes, Tess squatted down behind a bush. *What I wouldn't give for a real privy with a door—and a lock.*

Her wistful thoughts were suddenly interrupted by a low, moaning sound coming from a nearby bush. With a gasp of fear, she leapt to her feet, whirling around and peering in the direction from which the sound had come. Almost immediately she heard it again.

Clapping her hand against her chest to still her pounding heart, she took a cautious step forward. "Is anybody there?" she whispered.

The moan became louder, accompanied by a rustle

of leaves, like someone was moving through the heavy undergrowth.

"Hunter, is that you?" she called softly. "Come out where I can see you." She listened intently, but the only sound she heard was the creaking of wagons and an occasional snore from an exhausted traveller.

After several silent moments, Tess began to think that maybe she had imagined the eerie sound and turned back toward her wagon.

Then she heard it again. This time the sound was loud enough that she could discern that it was coming from a bush directly to her right. Spinning on her heel, she squinted her eyes, trying to see more clearly in the consuming blackness of the cloudy night.

She took another cautious step forward, stifling a scream when her bare toe butted up against something solid and warm. She jumped back, fearful that she'd inadvertently unearthed some dangerous, wild animal in his lair. Picking up her skirts, she began to run. Whatever was under that bush was alive and there was every possibility that if she stayed where she was, she could come to serious harm. She was halfway back to her wagon when her flight was again halted by a soft, guttural call.

Tess suddenly realized it wasn't an animal under that bush. It was a man and he was obviously in some kind of pain.

For a long moment, she stood still, riddled with indecision as she stared into the darkness. Then, she heard the strange call again. Turning, she retraced her steps. When she reached the spot from where she'd heard the sound, she squatted down, her eyes roving the area carefully. Suddenly, her heart leaped into her throat and she clapped a hand over her mouth, muffling the scream of terror that erupted. There was indeed a man lying stretched out beneath the bush. But, not just any man—an Indian.

Tess jumped to her feet, quickly sidestepping the man's outstretched arm. Something warm and wet squished between her toes, making her stomach roll sickeningly. Hobbling away as fast as her girth would allow, she grabbed on to a branch and held her foot up to examine it. Even in the dark, she could tell that it was covered with blood.

For a long moment, she stood as if paralyzed, staring down at her bloody foot, then looking over at the wounded man. "Are you badly hurt?" she whispered into the darkness.

Another faint moan was her only answer.

"Have you been shot?"

Silence.

Every protective instinct Tess possessed warned her to turn around and run for help. But she didn't. Instead she crept slowly forward, drawn by some instinctive force that demanded she answer the man's plaintive calls.

When she again reached the bush, she knelt down next to the Indian and cautiously pressed two fingers against his neck. Thank God, he was still alive. "Where are you hurt?" she asked quietly.

He didn't answer, but slowly lifted a bloody hand and pointed at his left side.

Tess leaned forward, cursing the lack of starlight which made close examination impossible. She needed a lantern.

"Have you been shot?" she asked again.

Weakly, he nodded, his hand falling back on the ground beside him.

With trembling fingers, Tess pushed back his long, black hair and placed her palm on his forehead. His skin was dry and hot, indicating that a fever was setting in.

"Stay here," she whispered, brushing her hand down his cheek. "I'm going to get help."

As she scrambled to her feet, the Indian grabbed for the hem of her robe, startling her with his unexpected strength. "No," he whispered, his voice barely audible. "Stay."

"You need help," Tess protested. "I'll be right back, I promise." Jerking her wrapper out of his clutching hand, she sped back toward the camp, heading straight for Hunter's bedroll.

"Mr. Hunter," she whispered, kneeling down next to his sleeping form and shaking him. "Mr. Hunter, wake up!"

Hunter came awake instantly, shooting up into a sitting position and reflexively reaching for his gun.

"No!" Tess gasped, grabbing his forearm as he started to pull the weapon from its holster. "There's no need for that."

Hunter squinted at her groggily. "What's wrong? Is someone hurt? Are you sick?"

"I'm fine," Tess assured him. "But, yes, someone *is* hurt and I need for you to come with me. Now."

Hunter immediately got to his feet, running a lean hand over his face to rub away the last vestiges of sleep. "Who's hurt?"

"He's right over here," Tess answered evasively. Reaching out, she grabbed Hunter's hand, leading him back to the bush where she had found the wounded Indian. The man made no sound as they approached him and Tess felt a rush of fear that he might have died while she was gone. Hurrying her steps, she peered closely down at him. To her extreme relief, she saw the labored rise and fall of his chest and realized that he had only lost consciousness. "Here he is," she whispered loudly, gesturing to Hunter to join her.

Hunkering down next to her, Hunter pushed some brush out of the way to get a better look. Then, with a startled grunt, he stood up again. "It's an Indian."

"I know that," Tess said impatiently, rising also. "But he's hurt and we have to help him."

To her surprise, Hunter grasped her upper arm and began propelling her back to her wagon.

"What are you doing?" she cried. "Why are we going back to camp?"

"We're going back to bed," Hunter answered curtly.

"What? We can't do that!" Wrenching her arm out of his grasp, Tess wheeled around, intending to return to the wounded man.

"Don't go back there," Hunter ordered, again reaching for her arm.

"But he's hurt! He might die if we don't help him."

"I know. And that's exactly what we're going to let him do."

Tess gasped in outrage at Hunter's callous statement. We are not!" she spat. "At least *I'm* not." Picking up the hem of her robe, she evaporated into the darkness like a wraith.

With a muttered curse, Hunter followed her. "Tess," he hissed when he finally caught up, "you don't understand. You don't know what caused this man's injury."

"A bullet caused it," she snapped. "What do you think it was?"

"I know it was a bullet, but you don't know who shot it."

"What difference does it make?"

"A hell of a lot! His own tribe might have done this to him and we would be doing him a disservice if we interfered by trying to save him."

"That's nonsense! Why would his tribe shoot one of their own people?"

"Lots of reasons. He may have disgraced them some way, brought shame to the chief, shown himself to be a coward. There are any number of things an

Indian warrior can do that will cause the other members of the tribe to kill him."

"But he's not dead. He's only wounded, so that proves your theory is wrong."

Hunter gritted his teeth in frustration. "Whoever shot him, it's none of our business. The smartest thing for us is to just leave him. What is meant to happen will happen. It's the Indian way."

Even in the darkness, he could see Tess's eyes blaze with fury. "Fine," she snarled. "If that's the way you feel, then go back to the camp, crawl into your warm blankets and go back to sleep. I'm sorry I disturbed your rest. I thought you were a human being who would be concerned about the plight of another human being, but I see now that I was wrong. You, obviously, don't care about anyone or anything—except yourself. As far as you're concerned, as long as your belly is full and your clothes are clean, everyone else can go to hell."

Hunter said nothing to interrupt Tess's tirade so, recklessly, she plunged on. "Well, Mr. Hunter, some of us don't feel that way. Some of us care about the suffering of other human beings and some of us feel that if there is anything we can do to help alleviate suffering when we see it, we should try to do so."

At that moment, the warrior regained consciousness and let out another pain filled moan. Tess abruptly ended her speech and tore off in the direction of the bush. Kneeling down, she murmured, "Just lie still and relax. You're going to be all right. I'm going to help you."

The man growled something in response, his guttural tones causing the hair to stand up on the back of Tess's neck. Forcing back her instinctive terror, she got clumsily to her feet. "I'll be right back," she promised softly. Turning, she again headed back toward the camp.

Although Hunter heard her talking to the wounded man, he wasn't really listening to her soothing murmurs. Rather, his mind was still digesting her hard words of a few minutes before. *I thought you were a human being who would be concerned about the plight of another human being, but I see now that I was wrong.*

Hunter squeezed his eyes shut, trying to deny the truth in Tess's cruel statement. But he couldn't—because she was right. He didn't care, not anymore. After all the hundreds of men he had killed during the war, after the thousands of bodies that he'd witnessed strewn haphazardly in the bloody grass of countless battlefields, what was one more death?

Death. So much of his adult life had been spent doling out or dealing with death that he could barely tolerate the thought of it. Unbidden, visions of that final slaughter at Chapultepec rose in his mind. Bile clogged his throat as he remembered the pungent, nauseating stench of blood, the horrifying screams of the dying, the equally horrifying silence of the thousands of corpses as they stared up into the merciless Mexican sun with sightless eyes.

A cry of despair erupted from him and he clapped his hands on either side of his head, shaking it miserably. He had to forget, had to put it behind him. He *had* to.

With the crystal clarity of tortured self-realization, he suddenly knew that Tess was right. It was inhuman to let the wounded Indian die under that bush, unattended.

With a strangled cry of denial, Hunter started to run, not slowing his pace until he reached Tess's side.

"The first thing we have to do is get him good and drunk."

Tess looked up from where she knelt, gazing at

Hunter as if he'd lost his mind. "Are you crazy?" she whispered.

"No, I'm not crazy, and if you really want to help him, you'll quit arguing and do as I say. Now, lift his head so I can pour some of this whiskey down his throat."

In the dim light of the single lantern they'd brought with them, Hunter saw Tess throw him a withering look, but she lifted the man's head and propped it against her lap, allowing Hunter to tip the whiskey bottle into his mouth.

The brave coughed and choked on the fiery liquid, but Tess saw him swallow and knew that he had gotten some of it, anyway. After several minutes of forcing the liquid down the man's throat, Hunter watched with satisfaction as his head lolled to the side.

"Okay, now move the lantern over here and hand me that damp cloth."

Tess did as Hunter bade, watching, despite her suddenly churning stomach, as he gently washed away blood and gore from the man's side, revealing a ragged hole the size of a quarter just below his ribs. "Ah, here it is," Hunter muttered.

Looking over at Tess, he was surprised to see that her eyes were closed. "What's the matter? Are you gonna be sick?"

"No," she answered, her voice sounding strained and slightly breathless, "I'm fine."

"Don't you faint on me. Remember, this was your idea."

"I'm fine."

Hunter studied her closely for a moment, then said, "Hand me my knife."

With shaking hands, Tess picked up a long bladed knife and handed it to him, turning her head away as he leaned over the comatose warrior and cut an

X across the hole the bullet had made. "Now give me those tweezers you brought."

Again, Tess did as he asked, closing her eyes as soon as the small implement was safely in his hand.

Hunter probed around for several silent moments, then sat back on his heels. "Got it."

Warily, Tess opened her eyes, astonished to see him grinning at her.

"Look!" There was such a tone of satisfaction in his single word that Tess couldn't help but look at the bloody lump of metal he thrust toward her.

"I see," she choked.

"Hand me that needle and thread."

After she gave him the requested item, he again bent over his patient, taking several careful stitches before straightening and snipping the thread with the bloody knife. "There," he said proudly. "Done. Pass me the whiskey again."

"But, he's out cold!"

"I'm not gonna try to make him drink it. I'm just going to pour some over the wound to seal and clean it."

"Oh," Tess mumbled contritely, handing him the bottle.

Hunter poured a generous amount of liquor over the wound, then tipped the bottle back and took an equally generous swallow. "Want somc?" he asked, holding the bottle out toward her.

"No. Thank you, anyway."

Wiping his forehead on the back of his sleeve, Hunter rose to his feet, extending a hand to help Tess up too. "That's all we can do for him. The rest is up to providence."

Tess nodded and rose on shaking legs. Gathering up their meager supplies, they began walking back to the wagons.

"Remember," Hunter warned as they walked along, "you're not to say a word to anyone about this. There are plenty of men on the train who would love to kill themselves an Injun, if for no other reason than to be able to brag to their friends about it. You start talking about this and any hope that warrior has of making it is gone—I guarantee it."

"I won't say a word," Tess promised.

They walked in silence for another few steps, then Tess suddenly reached out and clasped her slender fingers around Hunter's forearm. He stopped and looked at her expectantly. "What?"

"Thank you for what you did tonight," she whispered. "I know you did it for me since you didn't care whether that man lived or died and I just want you to know that I . . . appreciate it."

"I did it because I wanted to, nothing more," Hunter said abruptly. "It wasn't for you."

Tess tilted her head, studying him closely. Finally she shrugged, but a small smile played around her mouth. "Whatever your reasons, thank you."

Hunter gazed into her clear, azure eyes. She was still holding on to his arm and the touch of her hand on his skin sent rivers of sensation throbbing all the way up to his shoulder. "You're welcome."

To his dying day, he never knew why he made the next move. One minute, he was just looking at her, responding to her thanks, and the next, he was kissing her, his mouth covering hers in a gentle caress. Instinctively, he reached his hand back, pulling off her concealing nightcap and burying his fingers in her thick, soft hair.

To Hunter's astonishment, he felt her lips part beneath his. Holding her face in both his hands, he deepened the kiss, his mouth moving over hers provocatively as their tongues tangled.

A surge of passion coursed through him, its primitive demand making his knees nearly buckle. His breathing became harsh and ragged as his man's body quickened in response to the soft little moan that escaped Tess.

He stepped closer, intending to circle Tess's waist with his arm and pull her up against him but, suddenly she backed out of his arms.

"Mr. Hunter!" she gasped, taking a staggering step backward. "I . . . we . . . can't . . . this is wrong."

Hunter clenched his fists at his sides, tamping down hard on his rampaging desire. "You're right," he rasped. "We can't. Go to bed—NOW!"

Tess bristled at his high handed command, but seeing the passion flaming in his eyes, she prudently remained silent. "You'll check on him before morning?" she asked shakily.

Hunter nodded. "Yes. Just go to bed. Please."

Instinctively understanding his need to have her out of his sight, Tess turned away. It wasn't until she was nearly back to her wagon that she finally allowed herself to look back at the dark, handsome man. She shivered as she realized that his ebony hair and massive shoulders reflected in the lantern's dim light were, perhaps, the most arousing sight she had ever beheld.

"Oh, Mr. Hunter," she sighed into the darkness, "you *do* have a way about you."

Chapter 10

Tess didn't go to sleep the rest of the night. Instead, she lay on her hard, narrow cot thinking about all that had transpired in the last few hours. The wounded Indian, the time spent with Hunter trying to save him—and the kiss.

Most of all, she thought about Hunter's kiss. Never, ever had a kiss had such an effect on her. Even the most intimate moments with William had not raised the fever of passion that had shot through her when Hunter's mouth had covered hers.

But as the initial thrill of the kiss dimmed, so did Tess's feelings of contentment. She should feel guilty, not content. It was sinful. The feelings she'd experienced as Hunter's mouth had sensuously caressed hers, hoping the kiss would never end, craving the feel of his hands on her breasts and wondering what it would be like to lie in his arms for a whole, long, passionate night.

"Maybe you *are* a wanton," she berated herself. "Just like Margaret said you were. A greedy, no good wanton who thinks of nothing but her own pleasure."

Turning her face to the flimsy canvas wall of her wagon, Tess gave vent to long held tears. Maybe Margaret *was* right. Maybe she was everything the cruel woman had accused her of being.

"Maybe you're just lonely," a small voice deep in her mind comforted. "And maybe it will never happen again."

"It *will* never happen again," Tess vowed to the silent voice, "because I won't let it. Ever."

Hunter lay with his hands behind his head, staring up at the inky black sky.

He felt good—better, in fact, than he'd felt in a long, long time. Tonight had been a catharsis. He'd helped a wounded man and kissed a beautiful woman—two things that he had thought never to do again. And it had felt good. Damn good.

Maybe he had gotten a little carried away with Tess, but he had stopped himself long before anything regrettable had happened, and she had not seemed overly upset at his boldness. In fact, she had answered the passion in his kiss with an equal portion of her own—a fact which astonished and secretly pleased him.

Hunter stared down the length of his body, surprised to see that just thinking about those moments when he'd held Tess in his arms was causing an erection to stir within the tight confines of his pants. "Guess you're not completely dead, after all," he chuckled.

He lay back, smiling into the darkness until an irritating little voice deep in his mind pricked him. *Better figure out where you go from here. It's still a hell of a long way to Oregon.*

Hunter sighed. The damned voice of reason. Never, at any time in his life, had he ever been able to escape it.

"It goes nowhere," he whispered. "It's just something that happened. The night was crazy, I was lonely, she was there. It just happened. Tomorrow, everything will be like it always is. She'll burn my breakfast, turn my clothes pink and infuriate me in a dozen different ways. Nothing will have changed. And, what happened tonight will never happen again, because I won't let it. Ever."

Dawn was just tinging the dark sky with violet when Tess climbed down from her wagon, slinging a small cloth sack over her shoulder, and heading off for the copse of bushes where she knew the Indian warrior lay.

The man was just where she and Hunter had left him. Tess paused, studying him intently. His eyes were closed, but even from this distance, she could see the slow rise and fall of his chest. Thank God, she thought gratefully, he's still alive. Approaching him quietly, she knelt down, placing her hand on his forehead as she had done the night before.

She smiled. His skin was cooler and not so dry. Obviously, removing the bullet from his side had done much to aid his recovery. Sitting back on her heels, she stared at him, noting how much more fearsome he appeared in the daylight. His facial features were lean and chiseled, set off by a long, straight nose and a hard, unforgiving mouth. Black hair streamed over his shoulders—shoulders that were as wide and muscular as Hunter's.

Good Lord, she thought, shivering delicately, if I had seen him this clearly last night, I would have run for sure.

Just then the Indian opened his eyes, pinning her with a look that seemed to pierce right through to her soul.

"Are you feeling better?" Tess asked, mortified at how her voice was shaking.

The brave didn't answer, but continued to look at her with a hooded, distrustful gaze.

"I brought you some food," she continued, trying hard to summon a smile. "And some water. I have to move on this morning—I'm part of a wagon train—but I thought these provisions would keep you for a day or two until you are strong enough to go back . . . wherever you came from."

I'm babbling, she thought desperately. Babbling like an idiot . . . and in front of a man who probably can't understand a word I'm saying anyway.

The Indian remained silent, but Tess thought she saw some of the distrust fade from his eyes. Slowly, he shifted his position, wincing slightly as the movement pulled at his wound.

"Are you in a great deal of pain?" Tess whispered, her brows knitting together with concern. "Perhaps if I got you some whiskey . . ."

To her surprise, the man seemed to understand this last sentence and he emitted what Tess took to be an assenting grunt.

"Whiskey?" she asked eagerly, nodding her head. "You'd like some whiskey for the pain?"

Almost imperceptively, the brave nodded.

"All right, I'll go talk to Hunter and see what I can do." Whirling away, Tess tore back through the early morning haze to the wagons.

By now, many of the men were up and moving around, relighting the previous evening's campfires and sleepily spooning coffee into huge, black pots.

"Hunter?" Tess called, craning her head around in an attempt to spot him. "Hunter? Are you here?"

"What do you want?" he asked, appearing out of nowhere with his shaving cup in one hand and a razor in the other.

"I need to talk to you."

Hunter looked down at his shaving supplies, then set them on the tailgate of Tess's wagon and wiped the lather off his face. Throwing Tess a jaundiced look, he realized he'd been right last night. It wasn't even six o'clock yet and, already, she was annoying him.

"Over here," she whispered, gesturing for him to join her behind the wagon.

"What is it?"

"Our *friend* wants some whiskey—for the pain. I told him I'd get your bottle and bring it to him."

"What?" Hunter barked, causing several men to turn and look at them curiously.

"Lower your voice, for heaven's sake," Tess ordered. "You're the one who said that no one can know about him."

Hunter glanced around uneasily. "Are you telling me that you've been out to see him already this morning?"

"Well, yes! I took him some food and water. He's much better, too, so you see, we did do the right thing last night."

"You mean he was conscious?"

"Yes, he's conscious."

"Well, that was a damned stupid thing for you to do."

Tess's eyebrows shot up in surprised offense. "I beg your pardon . . ."

"You don't know anything about this man. He's an Indian, for God's sake. Why, he might just as well have scalped you as looked at you."

"Don't be ridiculous! He was lying under that bush, right where we left him. I just asked him how he was feeling and gave him some food and water. Then, he told me he wanted some whiskey for the pain. That was all there was to it. I was never in any danger."

Hunter rolled his eyes heavenward. "He *told* you he wanted whiskey?"

"Well, he didn't *tell* me, exactly. I don't think he speaks much English."

"No, I imagine he doesn't . . ."

"But, when I mentioned whiskey, he seemed to know what I was talking about and he let me know that he'd like some."

"I'm sure he did. He probably would have also let you know he'd like some guns if you'd mentioned them."

"Oh, I think you're being horrible," Tess sniffed, turning away in a huff. "How could you have been so nice last night and such a beast this morning?"

Gently, Hunter reached out and turned her back to face him. "Actually, I thought you might be thinking just the opposite."

"What?"

"I thought you'd think that I'd been a beast last night."

His low intimate tone made a shiver run all the way up Tess's spine. "No," she murmured, looking away shyly, "I didn't think that. But . . ."

"But, what?" Hunter asked, tipping her chin up so he could see her face.

"But, I think it's better if we just forget about what happened between us."

Despite Hunter's vow to do just that, a ripple of disappointment shuddered through him. "It's already forgotten," he muttered. Quickly, he released her shoulders and stepped back. "Now, as far as our 'patient' is concerned, I want it clearly understood that you are not to go back there. We're going to be pulling out soon, anyway, and you need to get ready for the day's trek."

Tess looked up at him with stricken eyes. "Are we just going to leave him?"

"Of course, we're just going to leave him. Did you think we were going to take him with us?"

"Well, no . . ."

"Look, you said you've taken him food and water. That's all we can do."

"But, you will take him the whiskey he asked for, won't you? I promised him I'd bring it."

"I know what you promised."

"Then you'll take it to him?"

Hunter hesitated for a moment, trying to decide whether he should tell her the truth or lie to appease her. Looking down at her earnest, upturned face, he knew he couldn't lie to her. Funny that he felt that way, he thought wryly, since she had no compunction about lying to him.

"I'm not taking him any whiskey, Tess."

Tess's chin rose defiantly. "Why not? You said yourself that it numbs the pain."

"Yes, and it also numbs the senses. How would you feel if something happened to him because he was met with some danger and was too drunk to defend himself?"

Tess paused for a moment, thinking about this. "I guess you're right," she admitted, "but I still think it wouldn't hurt to take him a little. Not enough to make him drunk, of course, but just enough to dull his pain."

"No. Now that's the end of this conversation. I have things to do and so do you. We can't spend the day standing here arguing about whiskey."

"I hate it when you say that," Tess blurted.

Hunter looked at her quizzically. "Say what?"

" 'That's the end of this conversation.' I just hate it when you say that to me. It makes me feel like a child."

Hunter's gaze swept across Tess's beautiful face, feasting briefly on her crystalline bluc eyes before settling on her full, pouting lips. The slightest hint of a smile quirked the corners of his mouth. "Oh, you're anything but a child, Mrs. Caldwell."

With a parting nod, he turned on his heel and walked away.

They'd been on the trail about two hours when Hunter sought out Jack Riley. "Watch over things here for awhile, would you?" he asked. "I've got something I have to do."

Jack looked at his boss curiously, but didn't question him. After three trips with the enigmatic wagon master, the little Irishman had come to realize that if Hunter wanted him to know something, he'd tell him. It did no good to ask.

"Sure, boss. How long ya gonna be gone?"

"Just a couple of hours."

Jack nodded and reined his horse toward the front of the train, his unappeased curiosity rampant. What could Hunter have to do that would take him away from the train for a couple of hours?

The obvious answer made Jack chuckle lecherously. But, it couldn't be *that.* There wasn't a town with a whorehouse or even a saloon for a hundred miles in any direction. "Unless, of course, he's found himself some Injun gal somewhere," Jack mused, muttering to himself. But, no, it couldn't be that either. In all the time he'd been with Hunter, he'd never heard him mention *wanting* a woman, much less go looking for one.

Jack bit his lower lip, trying to unravel the puzzle of Hunter's unprecedented request. Try as he might, though, he couldn't come up with a single reason why the boss would leave the train for two hours right in the middle of the morning.

"Well, boyo, you're probably never gonna know

unless he decides to tell ya later on." Jack sighed, shaking his head with disappointment. "Guess you'll just have to chalk it up to another one of his strange twists of mood."

In Jack's estimation, Hunter had a lot of those but, despite the man's peculiarities, Jack admired him. And that, in itself was peculiar. If there was one thing Jack Riley had learned during his long, hard life, it was that there weren't many men on God's green earth who were worth his admiration.

It was nearly noon by the time Hunter reached the previous night's camp. Dismounting, he walked over to where the Indian warrior lay sleeping beneath the shelter of the scraggly bush.

Squatting down, he peered closely at the makeshift bandage he'd fashioned, nodding with satisfaction when he saw that the man had not bled through it.

He stood up, continuing to gaze down at the brave as he tried to gauge how long it might be before the man would be fit to travel. Just then, the Indian opened his eyes, jumping reflexively at the sight of the huge, heavily armed white man looming above him.

"It's all right," Hunter said quickly, holding up an open palmed hand in a universal gesture of friendship. "I brought you a horse so you can return to your people."

Seeing the Indian's uncomprehending stare, Hunter turned and pointed at the unsaddled horse standing quietly next to his own mount. "Horse." Swinging around, he then pointed at the warrior. "For you."

The brave looked at him unblinkingly, one set of ebony eyes boring into the other.

Hunter walked over to his horse and unwound a

small sack from around the saddle horn. Returning to the Indian, he tossed the bag to the ground. "Whiskey."

The wary tension faded from the brave's eyes. Hunter stood over him for another moment, then nodded and started to move away. His departure was almost immediately halted, however, as the warrior's arm snaked out and grabbed him around the calf of his right leg.

Startled, Hunter pivoted around. The Indian was braced on one elbow, looking up at him gratefully. As their eyes met again, he grunted something in a guttural language that Hunter didn't understand, but his meaning was clear.

Hunter looked down at the hand clamped around his leg, then lifted his eyes back to the Indian's and said simply, "You're welcome."

He was still nearly a mile away from the wagon train when he noticed that it wasn't moving. "Damn," he cursed, whipping his horse into a gallop. "Now what?"

Thundering down a hill, he raced across the deeply rutted prairie, arriving at the tail end of the train no more than five minutes later.

Spotting Jack Riley, he yelled, "What the hell is going on?"

Riley spun around in his saddle, his homely face reflecting his relief that Hunter was back. Kicking his horse hard, he cantered up to his boss. "Next time you decide to take a bunch of wild ass lumberjacks west, I'm stayin' in Independence."

Hunter frowned at him. "What the hell is going on?" he repeated.

"They all decided they wanted to stop and write their names on Courthouse Rock. I couldn't stop 'em,

Hunter, even when I told 'em you wouldn't like it. It's damn stupid too, since most of 'em can't even write."

"Oh, for God's sake!" Hunter swore, wheeling his horse away from Riley and galloping toward the many-tiered, four hundred foot high heap of clay and volcanic ash.

Sure enough, when he reached the base of the famous rock, he found every single member of his little troupe—both male and female—crawling over the giant edifice like a bunch of frenzied ants.

"What in hell are you all doing?" he bellowed.

Instantly, the activity came to a halt as seventy-three faces turned toward him, their expressions as guilty as a bunch of children caught with their hands in a cookie jar.

Hunter's eyes scanned the crowd, finally coming to rest on Tess who was standing with a large group of lumberjacks clustered around her. "What's the meaning of this, Mrs. Caldwell?"

Tess looked around in surprise, embarrassed that she was being singled out to justify the actions of the entire group. Hitching up her skirts, she marched over to where Hunter waited, glaring up at him mutinously. She was quickly joined by Mary Krenzke, Florette Kubes and Caroline Brooks.

"The men wanted to write their names on the rock," Tess explained. "Jack Riley told us the other night that it's become a tradition of sorts for travellers passing by to do so."

Hunter wheeled around in his saddle, throwing a ferocious, accusing glare at the hapless Jack. "He did, huh?"

"Yes," Tess nodded. "He did."

"Well, we don't have time for this nonsense," Hunter growled. "And I would think that you ladies, at least, would have more sense than to participate in it."

"Actually, we were attempting to help speed things up," Caroline Brooks said defensively. "Many of these men don't know how to write, so we ladies were doing it for them. We were just trying to get everyone's name written as quickly as possible so we could get underway again."

For a long moment, Hunter stared down at the three women, a tight, angry expression mottling his face. Finally, he shook his head and sighed with resignation. Dismounting, he shouted, "You've got a half hour. I don't care if you spend the time eating, writing your names, or drawing pictures in the dirt, but in thirty minutes, we're pulling out."

As he turned to lead his horse away, Tess trotted after him. "Mr. Hunter," she called, smiling broadly as he pivoted around to look at her, "as long as we're going to be here another half hour, wouldn't you like to write your name on the rock too?"

"No," he said shortly.

"But, why not? Have you done it already on a previous trip?"

"No."

Planting her hands on her hips, she frowned at him. "Oh, come on, it'll be fun."

Hunter snorted his opinion of that statement, then continued leading his horse toward a water bucket.

Tess watched him for a moment, her eyes widening as a sudden realization gripped her. Hurrying to catch up with him again, she wrapped her fingers around his forearm. "I understand," she said softly. "You can't write, can you?"

"Of course I can write! I'm just not going to waste my time chiseling my name into a stupid rock."

Tess looked so dejected that Hunter felt an unexpected surge of guilt. "Why is it so important to you that I do this?"

Tess shrugged. "I just think you should. Someday, a hundred years from now, people may come to this rock just to see our names. I think yours should be there—along with a list of all the years that you've made crossings."

Hunter shook his head, still not understanding why Tess cared whether his name was on the rock or not. For a long moment, he just stared at the huge boulder. "Well, what the hell," he muttered. "Come on. You can help me find a place."

With a smile that could have lit up the whole state of Nebraska, Tess scurried toward the rock, pulling Hunter along by his arm. "Hurry!" she commanded. "We don't have much time if we're going to pull out in a half hour."

With an agility that belied her girth, she climbed up the towering rock, peering intently at its surface until she found a place smooth enough to suit her. "Here," she pointed.

Hunter nodded and pulled out his knife. Kneeling down, he brushed loose sand away from the stone, then paused, as if trying to determine what to write. Finally, he leaned forward and began diligently carving lines and circles into the stone. Several minutes passed with the only sound being the scraping of the knife. Finally he sat back. "There. I left room to add another date in case I come back next year or the year after."

Tess smiled, stepping forward to look at what he had written. "Hunter—'48, '49".

"No first name?" she asked, her voice betraying her disappointment.

"No first name," he echoed. "'Hunter' is enough."

"But, you must have a first name. Everyone does."

"I don't," he said flatly. "Not anymore."

Folding his knife, he jammed it back into his pocket. "Come on. We have to get back."

Tess nodded and followed him down the hill. At least, he signed it, she thought wistfully. He may not have divulged his first name, but at least he signed it.

Despite the exhaustion weighing down his body, Hunter lay awake far into the night. It had been a hell of a twenty-four hours. The Indian, the kiss, signing his name on the rock . . . A great many things had happened. A great many things that had caused the tiniest seed of re-discovered humanity to take root deep inside him.

Most importantly, he had once again experienced the ebb and flow of human emotions—pity, desire, satisfaction, and even the faintest sense of belonging. And as much as he hated to admit it, Tess Caldwell was responsible for all of it.

Hunter sighed deeply. Right at this moment, he wasn't sure whether he loved or hated her for it.

Chapter 11

Hunter stepped up on to the tongue of a parked wagon and looked down on the assembled crowd. "Okay, listen up, everybody, because we've got several important things to talk about today."

It was seven o'clock Monday morning, the hour designated each week for the entire population of the wagon train to gather for a formal progress meeting. Hunter's eyes swept over the people standing in front of him, then he nodded, satisfied that everyone was present.

Hunter knew that a wagon train was very much like a small town, with the same power struggles, moments of dissension and petty jealousies inherent in any community. He had discovered that many of the political disasters that plagued other trains, often splitting them apart and even resulting in bloodshed among the travellers, could be averted by holding meetings and letting people publicly air their problems, disagreements and concerns. The meetings also served as an opportunity for him to share with the members of his expedition information they might need for the next few days of travel, warn them of potential dangers, and render advice on how best to cope with new situations they were likely to meet.

"I thought you'd all like to know that when we passed Chimney Rock yesterday, we also passed the one-third point of the trip."

A cheer rose from some members of the party while others groaned with dismay. Hunter smiled at the groaners, surmising that they had obviously lost track of time and distance and thought the expedition farther along than just six hundred miles.

"I figure to be at Fort Laramie by the fifteenth, but in order to achieve that, we're going to have to pick up the pace a little. Now, I don't want any of you to get nervous. We're not far behind schedule and there's no worry at this point that we won't make Oregon before the snow, but the rain that we had last week, coupled with how long it took us to cross the Platte has put us back a couple of days. So, at least until we reach the fort, I want to get started a half hour earlier and travel a half hour later. We're also going to cut rest and water periods to fifteen minutes. That way, we can add about two hours a day in travel time and, barring anything unforeseen like weather or Indians, we'll make it to the fort as planned."

There was a distinctly uncomfortable rumble at the word "Indians" and as Hunter paused to take a breath, a brawny, bearded lumberjack yelled, "Think we're gonna run into savages?"

"No," Hunter said quickly, purposely not looking in Tess's direction. "We're staying on the main trail, not taking any shortcuts and I haven't had any trouble in past trips. But, you still all need to be aware that this is Indian country we're crossing and there is always the *possibility* of trouble. Just keep your heads up and your guns at the ready and we should be fine."

"But, remember," Jack Riley chimed in, "no rifles leanin' against wagon seats barrel up. Keep 'em handy, but keep 'em layin' flat on the floor with the barrel pointed out."

"Right," Hunter agreed. "Leaning your rifle against the seat is a good way to blow your own head off. All it takes is one good bump in the road."

Another wave of conversation rippled throughout the men. The subject had been discussed before and there was widespread disagreement as to whether the threat was greater having the rifle close at hand but vulnerable to misfire, or in the safer but less easily accessible horizontal position on the wagon floor.

"I don't want any arguments about this, men," Hunter warned. "Guns are to be kept on the floor, period."

The buzz of conversation trailed off.

"Now, is there anything else anybody wants to discuss? The next week should be relatively easy going. Good water, flat land and a well marked trail. I'm sure we won't have any trouble making up the time we've lost."

Several issues were presented by various members of the group. A stolen bottle of whiskey, a mule that had been injured due to a drunken man's negligence while on watch, and a slightly embarrassed plea from Florette Kubes for more privacy for the ladies when seeing to their personal needs.

The problems and complaints were quickly and satisfactorily dispatched and the group dispersed to harness up the mules and get started.

Tess, who after two weeks under Mary's careful tutelage, was becoming quite adept at setting up and breaking camp, efficiently stowed the remains of their breakfast and prepared the interior of the wagon for the day's journey.

"Any chance of some fresh meat tonight?" she

asked shyly as Hunter brought her three freshly filled water canteens. "A prairie chicken, perhaps, or maybe a squirrel?"

"Could be a whole lot better than that," Hunter grinned.

Tess's eyebrows rose at his uncustomary effusiveness. "Oh? And what could be better than chicken?"

"How about buffalo?"

Tess gasped, her eyes widening with astonishment. "Are you serious? Buffalo?"

Hunter nodded. "We've been deep into buffalo territory for several days now. Dash hasn't seen any herds yet since they've been pushed west by other trains passing through but, even so, we're bound to come upon one soon. If Dash or I can bring one down, there would be enough meat to feed the whole train."

Tess closed her eyes in wistful anticipation. "That sounds wonderful." Opening her eyes again, she scanned their barren surroundings, a small sigh escaping her. "Except for the fact that we don't have enough wood to build a big enough fire to roast a real piece of meat."

"You don't need wood. There are other kinds of fuel that will work just as well."

"Like what, for instance?"

With a mischievous smile, Hunter bent down and picked up a chunk of dark, dry material that resembled rotting wood. "Like this, for instance."

"What is it?"

His smile widened. "Do you really want to know?"

Tess nodded.

"Okay, but remember, you asked. It's a buffalo chip."

Tess's brows knit together in bewilderment. "A buffalo chip? What's a buffalo . . ." Suddenly her eyes widened and a look of revulsion crossed her face. "Oh, no! You're not telling me that that's a . . ."

"That's exactly what it is," Hunter laughed.

"That's disgusting."

He shrugged. "You may think so, but it burns like crazy and makes a damn fine fire to cook over."

"Oh, my Lord," Tess groaned, turning her head away from the offensive piece of dung. "Do you really expect us to cook with that?"

Hunter made a great show of looking over the flat, treeless expanse of prairie. "Well, I'll tell you, Mrs. Caldwell, I don't think there's much choice. Unless you want to eat your meat raw for the next couple of weeks, this is about all we've got."

Tess closed her eyes and shook her head, trying hard to conquer the queasiness she felt at the thought of cooking with animal droppings. "But, doesn't it make the food taste like . . ."

"No, it doesn't."

She sighed, vastly relieved to hear that. "Well, all right. If we have to, we have to, I guess."

Hunter considered her for a moment, a small, impressed smile playing around the corners of his mouth. "So, do you think you and the other ladies can handle cooking buffalo steaks over a chip fire if I can bring one down?"

Tess nodded. "You bring it to us and we'll cook it."

Hunter laughed, the deep, rich sound of his amusement making Tess's heart rate quicken. "Mighty bold words from a lady who couldn't make a pot of coffee a couple of weeks ago—over any kind of fire."

Tess smiled saucily. "I'm very adaptable, Mr. Hunter. And a quick learner too."

"Yes, you are," he agreed. "Those biscuits this morning were the best yet."

"And I made them all by myself."

"I know. I saw you."

Tess looked at him quizzically. "You did? When? I didn't see you anywhere around when I was making breakfast." To her complete astonishment, Hunter appeared to blush beneath his dark tan. "Mr. Hunter?" she asked incredulously "Are you all right?"

"Yeah, I'm fine."

"So, where were you when you saw me making the biscuits?"

"Behind those bushes over there," he muttered, wishing he hadn't brought up the subject.

Tess glanced over to where he pointed. "What in the world were you doing over there?"

He hesitated for a moment, then blurted, "Getting dressed."

Tess's confusion deepened. "Behind the bushes? But, I thought . . ."

"Thought what?"

Averting her face, she murmured, "It's not seemly for us to be having this conversation."

I don't see anything unseemly about it," Hunter protested. "Now, what was it you thought?"

"Well, I thought . . . that is, Joe told me that you and the other men all wash and dress together down by the stream every morning. He said that's why we ladies can't go down there before breakfast."

"That's right."

"But, you just said that you were dressing behind those bushes."

"That's right too."

"Do you prefer more privacy?"

"Didn't used to, but I do now."

Tess threw him another bewildered look.

Hunter took a step closer and cast a furtive look around to make sure they couldn't be overheard. "You see, Mrs. Caldwell," he drawled, "since a certain lady threw her sunbonnet in with my unmentionables, I now have three sets of pink longjohns. I just don't want the other men to . . ."

"Tease you?" Tess whispered.

"Yeah, something like that."

Now it was Tess's turn to blush. "I'm so sorry about that, Mr. Hunter. I wish there was some way that I could make up for what I did to your clothes."

Hunter's face, as always, remained void of expression, giving Tess no clue as to whether he was truly put out with her or just teasing. Thankfully, his next words put her doubts to rest.

"Don't worry about it. I should be able to buy some new longjohns when we get to Fort Laramie."

Tess's face immediately lit up with a smile, reflecting her relief that the situation did, indeed, have a remedy. "They'll have them available there?"

"Always have in the past."

"Then I insist on buying them for you."

Hunter shook his head vehemently. "I don't think that would be a good idea."

"But, Mr. Hunter, it's my obligation."

"Mrs. Caldwell," he said patiently, "what do you think the men on this train would think if they found out that you were buying me underwear? And they *would* find out. Things like that always have a way of getting around."

Tess's becoming blush deepened to crimson. "I see. Well, perhaps, you could purchase them and just tell me the cost. I'll be happy to pay you for them."

Hunter gazed at her for a moment, surprised at how much her innate sense of honor pleased him. "We'll talk about it later. I do appreciate the offer, though. Now, I better get up to the front of the train. We've got to get rolling or we'll never make twelve miles today."

Tess nodded and turned back toward her wagon.

"Would it be all right if I rode in the wagon for a little while? I'm . . . rather tired this morning."

Hunter looked at her with concern. "Are you sick?"

"No," she said quickly, "I just . . . didn't sleep well last night. Please, could I ride a bit? Just this once?"

At Hunter's assenting nod, Tess smiled and awkwardly began climbing up into the wagon. Before she had even one foot up on the wheel spoke, however, she suddenly found him at her side, his hand at her elbow as he assisted her up on to the high seat.

"You should have an extra step here," Hunter noted, pointing to the bottom of the wagon bed. "Tell Joe to nail a horseshoe right there and it will make getting into the wagon much easier for you."

"Thank you," Tess murmured, embarrassed by her obvious clumsiness. "I'll tell him."

Hunter nodded and tipped his hat. "Have a good day, and if the afternoon sun gets too hot, lie down for awhile in the back."

With that, he rode away, leaving Tess to stare after him in wonder. Could this be the same man who, just a few weeks before, had ordered her to walk? What in the world had changed his attitude so much?

Tess pondered the question for a moment, then shrugged it off. Far be it from her to tempt Hunter's unusual good humor by asking questions. It was enough that she was going to be able to rest a bit today. God knew, the way she felt this morning, she needed it. With a weary sigh, she crawled into the back of the wagon and lay down on the hard little cot, promising herself that she'd rest only until they were underway.

When she again opened her eyes, she was surprised to see the sun high in the sky. Feeling a stab of guilt that she had obviously been sleeping for hours, she got up and moved to the front of the wagon, crawling over the seat and sitting down next to her brother.

"Did you have a good rest?" Joe asked, smiling over at her.

Tess nodded. "I can't believe I slept the whole morning away, especially with the wagon moving. You would think that the bumps alone would have woke me up."

"You must have been really tired," he agreed. "This section of trail has been driven over so many times that it's like a washboard."

"Yes it is," Tess chuckled. "I heard that Mrs. Brooks set a churn full of cream on the tailgate of her wagon yesterday morning and by dinnertime, she had butter!"

As if to give credence to their conversation, the wagon suddenly hit a deep rut, nearly throwing Tess off the seat. As she grabbed for a hickory bow to steady herself, her eyes lit on Joe's rifle leaning against the seat near his knees. "Joe! Mr. Hunter specifically said that you're not to have your gun propped up like that."

Joe's mouth tightened mutinously. "I know what he said."

"Then you should listen to him. You know very well that it's dangerous, particularly on a rutted road."

"I don't care. We're in Indian country now and I'm not gonna have my gun somewhere where I can't get to it fast."

Tess glared at her brother angrily. "You should keep it on the floor like Hunter said."

"No."

Tess's frustration with her brother's obstinacy was increasing by the moment, but seeing that making demands was having no effect on him, she decided to change her tack. "Please, Joe, for my sake, put the gun on the floor. What would I do if something happened to you?"

"Nothing is gonna happen to me. Now, just drop it, Tess. The gun's stayin' where it is."

Tess blinked with surprise at his uncustomary rudeness, but she said no more. They rode along silently for another hour, but with each bump they hit, Tess found herself gazing nervously at the rifle.

Then it happened.

The rut was huge, at least two feet across and six inches deep and, yet, Joe made no attempt to skirt it. Tensely, Tess watched the mules step over it, then the front wheels dropped into the hole. At the same instant as she felt her teeth jar together, she heard the rifle go off.

With a cry of terror, she grabbed the wagon's side, then snapped her head around to look at her brother. To her surprise his expression was bland, his eyes staring straight ahead, his hands slack on the reins.

"My God, Joe," she gasped, grabbing for the gun before the wagon's back wheels hit the rut, "don't let the . . ."

She never finished her sentence because, at that moment, the back wheels plunged into the pothole and Joe slowly toppled forward, falling off the seat into a heap on the wagon's floor.

Hunter heard the gun's sharp report followed by Tess's scream all the way at the front of the train. "What the hell . . ." he barked, jerking his horse's reins around and taking off toward her wagon.

"What's the matter?" he shouted as he thundered up upon her. "Where's Joe?" Glancing over at the nervously prancing mules, he instinctively grabbed their harnesses. "Whoa, there, mules!" Immediately, the team quieted. "What the hell is wrong?" he bellowed again, turning his attention back to the screaming Tess as he tried to make his voice pierce her hysteria.

But Tess just kept screaming, her shaking hands covering her mouth as she stared down at something on the floor beneath her.

Spurring his horse forward a few steps, Hunter looked over the front lip of the wagon. "Oh, my God!" he gasped, seeing the prostrate man lying on the wagon's floor.

To his horror, Hunter saw again the crumpled, bloody figures of hundreds of men, grotesquely sprawled out in front of him. He drew in a strangled breath, fighting the hot, sour taste of revulsion that rose in his throat. Raising his eyes, he stared for a long moment at the strange, hysterical woman before him, wondering, briefly, where he was. Then, as quickly as the vision had arisen, it faded. Shaking his head as if to clear it, he turned in his saddle and yelled, "Man hurt! Help! Now!" He leaped off his horse and scrambled into the wagon, kneeling down next to Joe and carefully turning him over.

Men came running from every direction until a large cluster of them circled the wagon. "What happened? How bad hurt is he?"

Hunter gazed for a brief moment at the rapidly spreading red stain on the front of Joe's shirt, then placed his fingers against the man's neck. He held them there for several seconds before looking up at the men hurling questions at him and giving his head a slight shake.

Rising to his feet, he turned to Tess. She had stopped screaming and was now standing rigidly erect, her hands still clamped over her mouth, her eyes glazed with fear and disbelief.

"I'm sorry, Mrs. Caldwell," Hunter said quietly, placing a supporting arm around her shoulders. "He's dead."

"No," Tess moaned, shaking her head violently back and forth in denial. "NO! My God, Joe, wake up!" Wrenching herself away from Hunter, she lunged toward her brother's inert form.

"Go get Mary Krenzke," Hunter ordered a man near the wagon. "NOW!" With a quick nod, the man sprinted off in the direction of Mary's wagon.

Hunter looked down at where Tess now lay sprawled across Joe's body. "Come on, Tess," he coaxed, taking her by the shoulders and pulling her to her feet. "Let's get out of the wagon now."

"No!" she shrieked, again trying to wrest out of his grasp. "I have to see to my brother. Can't you see he's hurt?"

Hunter flicked a look of concern at Jack Riley who immediately stepped up to the wagon and held out his arms to Tess. "Come on now, little lady. Lemme help you. We need to get your brother out of the wagon and we can't do that till you get down."

Tess looked at Jack as if she'd never seen him before, but something about his grizzled face and gravelly voice seemed to finally penetrate her shock. Obediently, she allowed him to assist her down. "Please hurry!" she whispered hoarsely. "We have to get Joe out of there so I can tend to him."

Jack looked helplessly back at Hunter who again stepped forward, placing a finger under Tess's chin and tipping her head back until she was forced to look directly into his eyes. "Tess, look at me and listen to what I'm saying."

When he was satisfied that she was at last focused on him, he said, "Joe is dead, Tess. He's dead. There's nothing we can do for him now. He's gone."

Tess stared at Hunter for a long moment, her face devoid of expression. "He is, isn't he?" she responded dully, gazing over at the men lifting Joe's body out of the wagon.

"Yes. He is."

Looking back at Hunter, she nodded absently. "I

knew he was. I knew it as soon as I heard the shot and saw him fall. I told him not to put the gun there. I told him and told him all day long. Just like you said this morning. It's dangerous to prop a gun against the wagon seat. I told him that, but he wouldn't listen." She babbled on for a few moments longer until her attention was diverted by the sight of Joe's body being laid carefully on the ground.

Suddenly, with a strength borne of shock and grief, she again wrestled away from Hunter and raced back over to where her brother lay. Dropping to her knees, she leaned over and shook him furiously. "I told you!" she shouted. "I said it was dangerous, but you wouldn't listen, would you? You never listen to me and now look what's happened? You've gone and killed yourself." Her breath caught in her throat in an anguished choking sound and, again, she pressed her fist to her mouth. "Now, you're dead and all because you wouldn't listen to me!"

Suddenly the dam of tears broke and with a wrenching sob, Tess again threw herself across the body. Hunter immediately stepped forward and pulled her to her feet, holding her shaking form in his strong embrace and running his hands lightly up and down her back in an age old gesture of comfort. Without thinking, he pushed her sunbonnet back off her head and pressed his lips to her thick, blond hair. "There, now," he murmured, gently kissing her temple, "it's all right, sweetheart. Just go ahead and cry."

So absorbed in Tess's grief was he that he didn't even notice the gasp of shock that rippled through the crowd of men as they viewed, for the first time, Tess's magnificent golden hair and beautiful face. Seemingly unconscious of everyone around them, Hunter merely stood, holding Tess against the solid security of his chest and crooning words of sympathy as they slowly rocked back and forth beneath the bright, July sun.

It was Mary Krenzke who finally interrupted them. Running up to the wagon as fast as her aging and arthritic legs would allow, she took one look at the body on the ground and the girl in Hunter's arms and immediately took over. "Give her to me," she ordered softly. "She needs a woman now."

Slowly, Hunter dropped his arms from around Tess and stepped back, allowing Mary to guide the sobbing girl to the wagon.

"Come on now, love, let's get up in here. You're going to lie down for a few minutes and I'm going to get a cool cloth for your head."

She coaxed Tess into the interior of the wagon and helped her lie down on the cot. Then she leaned out through the oval slit in the canvas and whispered to Hunter, "Get one of the other women to clean the body up. She shouldn't see him all bloody like that. And tell one of the men to build a coffin. We'll have to bury him as soon as possible."

Hunter, the man so accustomed to giving orders, was just as adept at taking them and with a nod of understanding, moved off to do Mary's bidding.

With a mournful shake of her head, Mary returned to the little cot and sat down next to the sobbing Tess. It was going to be a very long night.

Chapter 12

"Rock of ages, cleft for me . . ."

Hunter stood, hat in hand, next to the deep hole carved into the Nebraska prairie and gazed around at the seventy-two singing people.

Death. Wherever he went, whatever he did, there was always death.

He closed his eyes, trying to block out the sight of Tess's ashen face. "People die on wagon trains," he told himself silently. "Every trip, every train, people die."

But, his mind screamed, why, oh, why had the first death to befall this particular expedition have to have been this woman's brother?

Hunter looked over at the crude coffin sitting next to the gaping hole. Tess had been right as she'd screamed out her anguish over her brother's dead body. Joe Chambers's death had been his own fault. He hadn't listened to Hunter's warnings, hadn't listened to his sister's pleas that he move his rifle to a safer position. And, because of his stubbornness, he had paid the ultimate price.

Hunter's gaze again swung over to Tess. So, now what? Joe was gone and this helpless, pampered woman who could barely cook a meal or wash a load of clothes was suddenly alone. Alone and vulnerable - in the midst of his wagon train.

There was no doubt in Hunter's mind that Tess could not complete the trip to Oregon. But, that was not his main concern. Right now, he was more worried about how she would manage as far as Fort Laramie. Once they arrived there, his problems were over since he had every intention of leaving her at the fort. She could winter there with one of the merchants' families and if, by spring, she still insisted on going to her sister in Oregon, she could join another larger, better equipped train. A settlers' train full of good, Christian families. Certainly, in a group like that, at least one of them would allow her to join them for the remainder of the journey.

Leaving her at Fort Laramie was the only sensible course of action to take. Even she would have to agree with that. But, even as he told himself this, Hunter knew he was probably in for a fight. Tess Caldwell was nothing if not determined. The act she had put on in Independence, hoodwinking him into believing she was a middle-aged matron well attuned to the rigors of housekeeping was proof of that. She was obviously set on getting to Oregon this season and he knew it was not going to be easy to talk her out of it.

But, he reminded himself, he was determined also, and very accustomed to giving orders and having them followed without resistance. If he could marshal a platoon of men to attack a foe under the most adverse of conditions, surely he could convince one lone girl to give up the perils of travelling unescorted and remain behind in the safety and security of a well guarded and provisioned fort.

But, in the days until they reached the safety and security of that fort, what was he going to do with her?

As the mournful, funereal hymn droned on, Hunter's gaze drifted over the rough group of men clustered around the makeshift grave. Perhaps there was one of them who could be trusted to drive her wagon and look out for her. But, who? His eyes roamed over the possibilities. Rowdy, Blackie, Goldtooth, Skunk. Their nicknames alone were enough to give him pause in choosing any one of them as Tess's protector.

As if reading his thoughts, Dash McAllister leaned over and murmured, "You know there's not one of them you can trust. You're gonna have to see to her yourself."

Hunter started with surprise. How could Dash have guessed what he was thinking about? Was his expression that transparent? Darting a quick glance over at his friend, he frowned, annoyed by Dash's knowing little smile.

But, even as he frowned at Dash, Hunter realized it wasn't his expression that had given his thoughts away. It was just another example of the unbreakable bond between the two men—a bond that had been forged while they were cadets at West Point and that had grown so strong over the years that they could often read each other's thoughts.

"I don't have time to take care of a woman," Hunter muttered. "You know that."

"You'll find time," Dash whispered positively.

"I don't *want* to take care of her."

"I know. But, you will, anyway."

The last strains of the hymn faded away and the travellers looked at Hunter expectantly. Clearing his throat, he stepped forward, placing his arm gently around Tess's drooping shoulders and leading her over to the coffin. He murmured a few words—words he had repeated over the bodies of dead soldiers so many times that he could say them by rote—then reached down and scooped up a handful of dirt, placing it in Tess's palm.

With a slight inclination of his head, he gestured to several nearby lumberjacks to lower the coffin into the ground, intoning,

> "We commend the soul of our brother departed, and we commit his body to the ground, earth to earth, ashes to ashes, dust to dust . . ."

Mechanically, Tess stepped forward and sprinkled the rich, black Nebraska dirt over the coffin, the tiny clumps pelting the wooden box as it disappeared into the ground. When her hand was again empty, she looked at it forlornly, a strangled cry escaping from deep within. For a moment, she swayed on her feet, looking like she might fall. With lightning speed, Dash stepped forward, curling a strong arm around her waist to support her. Tess leaned against him gratefully, so distraught that she didn't notice the look of shocked surprise that crossed his face as he held her close to his side.

Hunter led the mourners in the Lord's Prayer, then raised his head and said quietly, "We'll stay here for the rest of the day and move on in the morning."

The raucous lumberjacks nodded silently and began to disperse, their usual high spirits greatly subdued by the tragedy that had befallen their ranks. Although Joe Chambers had not been one of their immediate party, he had been a member of the wagon train and his loss was felt by all the members of the small, rolling community. In addition, every man who had ignored Hunter's warnings and propped his rifle against the seat of his wagon realized that it could very well have been him who was being buried that day. It was a sobering thought.

Mary Krenzke walked up to where Dash still stood with his arm around Tess. "Come with me, dearie," she said softly, "and I'll make you a cup of tea."

Tess looked at her as if she didn't know what tea was, but obediently detached herself from Dash's embrace and followed Mary back toward the wagons.

For a long moment, Hunter watched them go, then he placed his hat back on his head and turned to Dash. "What a damn waste," he muttered.

Dash slowly nodded his agreement. As they started back toward the camp, he threw several sideward glances at Hunter, silently debating whether to tell his friend what he'd discovered. He hated to do it since the last thing Hunter needed was another problem with Tess Caldwell, but, there was no help for it. He had to tell him what he knew and now was as good a time as any. "I need to talk to you, Jared."

Hunter looked at Dash quizzically, concerned by the unaccustomed seriousness in his voice. "What's up?"

"Not here," Dash answered, looking over at the small group of lumberjacks who were shoveling dirt into the grave. "Privately."

"Okay. Let's go down by the river."

Dash nodded. "I think we should stop by my camp first and get my bottle. You're going to need it."

"What's wrong?" Hunter asked, his voice wary. "Have you seen Indians?"

"No," Dash said. "It's not Indians. It's Mrs. Caldwell."

Hunter's expression registered relief. "What about her? I already know she's going to be a problem."

"You've got more problems than you know," Dash said tiredly. "Come on."

* * *

The two men lay stretched out in the tall grass near the bank of the North Platte, idly passing Dash's bottle back and forth.

"Okay," Hunter said, "we've got all the privacy you could ever want, we've had a drink, so tell me what's going on."

"What's going on is that Tess Caldwell is pregnant."

Hunter's glass froze in mid-air, halfway to his mouth. "What?"

"I said, Tess Caldwell is pregnant. Very, very pregnant."

Hunter completed his glass's trip to his lips, draining the contents with one swallow. "You're crazy. We just talked about her weight the other day. She's plump, that's all."

Dash shook his head. "Wrong, buddy. She's not plump, she's pregnant."

Hunter's mouth tightened ominously. "What makes you think so?"

"It's simple. I had my arm around her waist for most of the burial service. It's pretty hard to miss. The woman is huge with child."

Hunter closed his eyes and slowly shook his head, trying desperately to think of a plausible denial to Dash's suspicions. "You must be wrong. I've helped her in and out of her wagon any number of times. I didn't notice anything."

Dash shrugged. "She's done a damn good job of hiding her condition under all those petticoats. I don't think I'd have noticed it helping her into a wagon, either. But, when we were standing by the grave site and I had my arm around her waist, I could feel it. Fat is soft, Jared. Her stomach is hard as a rock. There's a baby in there, all right, and my guess is that from the size of her belly, it's gonna make its appearance real soon."

Hunter expelled a long breath and flopped back into the tall, coarse grass. "Damn her!" he cursed, feeling a devastating sense of betrayal.

Dash remained silent for several minutes, letting his news sink in. Finally he said, "So, what are you going to do, now that you know?"

Hunter's pain quickly turned to fury and he now turned that roiling anger on Dash. "How the hell do I know what I'm gonna do?" he barked.

"Well, if I were you, I'd be doin' a whole lot of praying that she doesn't deliver that baby before we reach Fort Laramie. If she does, you're really gonna have your hands full."

"Me? Why, me? If she has the baby before we reach the fort, the women will take care of her. It's really not that big a thing. We've had babies born on trains before."

"Yeah, we've had babies born before, but never without the father around. And, speaking of that, where do you suppose the father is?"

"Who the hell knows? Her story is that her husband died last winter."

Dash poured another liberal portion of whiskey into both glasses. "I suppose that's possible. If she's ready to have the baby now, she would have conceived it last fall. He probably died early in her pregnancy. That much of her story, at least, is most likely true."

"Well, if it is, it would be the first true thing she's told me since the day I met her," Hunter growled.

The men drank in silence for a few moments, then Dash set down his glass and looked at Hunter thoughtfully. "You know, the fact that Mrs. Caldwell is going to have a baby might actually work in your favor."

"What do you mean?"

"Well, I'm sure you were planning to leave her at Fort Laramie even before you knew she was pregnant."

"Right . . ."

". . . and I know as well as I know my own name that she would have fought you on it."

"Right, again."

"Well, now that you know she's about to give birth, you have the perfect excuse for insisting that she stay at the fort. Even *she* can't expect you to let her continue with the train, now that you know her secret."

Hunter pondered Dash's statement for a moment, then nodded. "I think you're right. This actually might solve a whole lot of problems. Except . . ."

"Except what?"

"Except, how do I let her know that I know?"

"Simple. You just tell her that you're on to her."

"Oh, right," Hunter snorted, "I just walk up to her and say, 'I've finally figured out that you're pregnant, not fat, so I'm leaving you behind at Fort Laramie.' "

"Well, you might want to use a little more tact than that," Dash chuckled, "but you've got the general idea."

"It's not going to be that easy. She's . . . she's hard to talk to."

"What had you planned to say to her to convince her to stay behind before you knew this?"

"I was just going to tell her that there weren't any men who could drive for her, and that no woman could make the trip alone."

"And she would have told you that any number of the lumberjacks had already offered to drive for her - and you know they will, if they haven't already. I saw at least six of them head back to Gerald Krenzke's wagon right after the burial. I'll bet every one of them was going there to make that very offer. None of them know she's pregnant and even though she's done her best to hide the fact that she's young and pretty, you did a damn good job of blowing her cover when you took her bonnet off in front of all of them yesterday. Hellfire, Jared, there isn't a man jack among them who wouldn't leap at the chance to spend the rest of the trip playing Romeo to a gorgeous little piece of fluff like that."

Hunter's eyes flared angrily. "I won't allow that, no matter which of them offers! They all have their brains in their pants. There's no way I'm going to let any one of them—"

Dash burst out laughing, effectively cutting off Hunter's tirade. "You don't have to lecture me, Jared. I've known you for fifteen years and I know exactly what you will and will not allow. But, now you won't have to argue with her about it. You can just tell her that you know she's pregnant and that she can't continue on after Fort Laramie. Enlist the other women if you have to. You know if any of them knew of her condition, they'd encourage her to stay with them at the fort, if for no other reason than there's not a middle aged matron in the world who can resist having a baby around. Why, once they know she's about to give birth, they'll probably be fighting over who gets to care for her."

Hunter shook his head. "I can't tell the other women."

"Why not? Seems to me you're gonna need all the help you can get if she's as stubborn as you keep saying she is."

"She *is* stubborn, but it's her secret to tell, not mine." *God knew, he was aware of how painful it was to harbor a dark secret, and regardless of how much he might want to enlist the other women's aid to convince Tess of her folly, he wouldn't betray her.* "Besides, I don't want her to feel like the whole world is ganging up on her. She's been through enough as it is. I'll just have to handle it myself."

"Suit yourself," Dash yawned, upending his glass to get the last drops of whiskey from it. "But, if I were you, I'd use any means at my disposal to convince her that she has to stay at the fort."

"I'll handle it."

Together, the men rose and sauntered back toward the camp. "You know, Dash," Hunter said hopefully, "we might be worrying for nothing. Maybe, now that Mrs. Caldwell's brother is dead, she won't want to continue on all the way to Oregon alone. She has to realize that staying at the fort would be the best thing for her. Hell, there's probably even a doctor there who can help her when her time comes. I'd think that fact alone should be appealing enough to make her want to stay."

"Yeah," Dash nodded, "I'd think so too. And, besides that, there are hundreds of love-starved trappers and soldiers who would probably be more than happy to marry her. She's bound to find a new daddy for that baby before long."

Hunter stopped walking and angrily planted his hands on his hips. "What makes you think she's looking for a new husband?"

Dash shrugged innocently. "Seems logical to me that she would be, now that her brother's gone. After all, the woman is a widow, soon to have a child to raise. Doesn't it make sense to you that she'd want to find a new husband as soon as possible?"

"Not necessarily."

Hunter's belligerent tone brought a rumble of laughter from Dash. "Jared, old man," he quipped, slapping his friend on the back, "if I didn't know you so well, I'd swear those were the words of a smitten man."

"Don't be ridiculous. Tess Caldwell doesn't mean anything to me. No woman does."

"I don't know," Dash teased. "It's like I've told you before, you were in love once and if it happens once to a man, it can happen again."

"For God's sake, Dash, you just got done telling me the woman is great with child! What kind of man would I be if I had designs on a lady who's in that condition?"

"How about a man who began having designs before he knew the lady was great with child?"

"Well, you're wrong. Dead wrong. I can't think of anything in this world I want more than to reach Fort Laramie and get Tess Caldwell off my hands. And that's the end of this conversation."

"Okay, Whitaker, okay," Dash chuckled. "Have it your way."

"Smitten with Tess Caldwell," Hunter muttered. "You must be out of your mind."

The men reached the edge of the camp and, after a quick farewell, Dash headed off toward the leading edge of the wagons. He'd only walked a few steps, however, when he turned around and called, "Hey, Hunter, you know what?"

"What?"

"Methinks thou dost protest too much!"

Dash barely had time to dodge the clod of dirt that came hurtling his way.

Chapter 13

"What are you doing, Mr. Hunter?"

Hunter looked up at Tess from where he squatted next to her wagon. "I'm nailing a horseshoe to the wagon bed so you'll have a step up to the seat. It'll make it easier for you to get in and out."

A wan smile crossed Tess's face. "I remember, you suggested that I ask Joe to do that." Her voice trailed off forlornly.

Hunter straightened, his heart wrenching despite his anger as he saw tears fill Tess's eyes. "I remember too," he said softly, "but since Joe didn't get around to it, I thought I'd do it."

"That's very kind of you," Tess murmured. "Everyone has been very kind."

"How is Matthew working out?" Hunter asked.

"Fine. He couldn't be nicer or more polite."

Hunter nodded in satisfaction. Matthew Bennington was one of the youngest of the men travelling with the train. For several days after Joe's death, Hunter had kept a close eye on the lumberjacks, trying to determine who would be the best candidate to serve as Tess's driver till they got to the fort. Young Matthew had been his choice. He and his older brothers were among the quietest and most well behaved of all of his travellers. There were no sounds of drunken revelry, swearing, or brawling coming from their wagon late at night, only soft male voices engaged in good-natured conversation. The Bennington brothers' lamp was always one of the first extinguished, giving Hunter the impression of a seriousness of purpose. Where many of the lumberjacks drank and gambled so late into the night that they could hardly open their eyes the next morning to harness their teams, the Bennington camp was always packed up and the team ready and waiting long before the cry of "Wagons Ho" began the day's trek.

Hunter's favorable impression had been borne out by Caroline Brooks who had informed him that Matthew and his brothers were among the few men who joined the merchants' families at their Sunday night prayer meetings. This knowledge, along with Matthew's solemn promise that he would say or do nothing untoward to upset the grieving woman had convinced Hunter that he was the right choice. And, as the days passed without incident, Hunter felt more and more confident that his hunch had been correct.

"How soon do you expect us to arrive at Fort Laramie?" Tess asked, her hand unconsciously kneading the small of her back.

"Just a few more days now," Hunter answered. "Are you anxious?"

"Very."

Hunter nodded. "I'm sure you'll enjoy being there. You'll be able to get some real rest."

"Rest," Tess sighed. "That's all I've been doing for the past two weeks. You know, there's really no reason why I can't continue to cook your meals for you. I think it would be good for me to . . . have something to do."

Hunter studied Tess's pale cheeks and fatigue smudged eyes for a moment, then shook his head. "There's no reason to push yourself. Mrs. Krenzke has been great about cooking and washing for me."

"But, it's my job," Tess protested. "Just because my brother—"

"Don't worry about it!" Hunter interrupted, his voice louder than he'd meant it to be. "I mean, it's okay. Just don't trouble yourself about things until we get to the fort. We'll talk then."

Before Tess had a chance to argue further, he tossed his hammer into his tool box and hurried off toward his horse, leaving her to stare after him in bewilderment.

"So, did you talk to her?" Dash asked, catching up with Hunter as he stowed his tools in his rucksack.

"No."

"Jared—"

"Shut up, Dash. I'll talk to her when the time is right."

"It's been two weeks since her brother died. What are you waiting for? You have to tell her that you know she's going to have a baby and that you're not taking her past Fort Laramie."

"I know what I have to do, but I've decided to wait to talk to her till we get to the fort."

"I don't understand. What's the point in waiting? You need to talk to her now!"

Hunter let out a long, frustrated breath. He almost wished that Dash hadn't been the one to discover Tess's condition. Ever since their talk the day of Joe Chambers's funeral, his friend had pestered him almost constantly to confront her with his knowledge. Dash's unrelenting prodding was beginning to wear very thin on Hunter's already strained temper.

Several times he had set out to talk to Tess, but something always stopped him. Maybe it was the sadness in her eyes or the wistful, lonely smile she turned on him when he approached her. Whatever it was, he just couldn't seem to bring himself to confront her with more news that he knew she would take badly.

His concern for her feelings angered him. Why should he be so reluctant to upset the girl? After all, she didn't mean anything to him—except trouble, of course. She had lied in order to get hired for a job she knew she didn't have the skills to do, and when he'd discovered that perfidy and had asked her, point blank, if there was anything else she was lying to him about, she'd simply lied to him again.

Even after their kiss—*God, why couldn't he forget that kiss*—she still hadn't confided in him.

So, why did he care if he upset her or hurt her or caused her more sorrow and worry? Although he had asked himself that question many times, he refused to admit what he knew to be the only plausible answer.

Glaring at Dash, he spat, "I said, I'll talk to her when we get to the fort. I get so damned sick and tired of you telling me what I have to do and when I have to do it. Try to get it through your head that I don't want your stupid advice. I just want you to leave me the hell alone!"

Dash's suddenly narrowed eyes reflected his offense at Hunter's rude words. "You can really be a son of a bitch when you want to."

"Go to hell, Dash."

Dash took an aggressive step forward, his fists clenched. For a moment the two friends faced each other like combatants.

Finally, Hunter held out his hands, palms up, and said, "Look, Dash, we've been friends way too long to let some deceitful, lying woman come between us."

The anger suffusing Dash's handsome face cleared and he relaxed his hands at his sides. "You're right. It's none of my business why you're not telling Mrs. Caldwell what you know, but I wish to hell you'd tell me, just to appease my curiosity."

Dash's guileless words brought a rare smile from Hunter. "You always have been the nosiest bastard I've ever known," he chuckled. "All right, I'll tell you. I've decided not to talk to the girl till we get to the fort because I figure, once she sees how much nicer it is to be there than on the trail, she won't be nearly as prone to argue when I tell her I'm leaving her behind."

The words sounded good—had sounded good every time he'd repeated them to himself—but even as he said them aloud, Hunter knew he was only kidding himself.

"Well, why didn't you tell me that before?" Dash questioned, laughing. "It makes perfect sense now. In fact, it's a hell of a good idea."

"Yeah, I thought so," Hunter muttered.

"I'm sorry about what I said before," Dash said contritely, holding his hand out in a gesture of friendship. "I should have known you had a plan. You always do."

"Forget it," Hunter smiled, shaking Dash's hand and giving him a good natured slap on the back. "We're all road weary, that's all."

"Hey, guess what I found in my kit?"

"What?"

"Just the thing to perk this group up."

Hunter looked at Dash warily. "Oh, God, not your . . ."

"Yup," Dash grinned. "My harmonica. I figure a

few choruses of 'Skip to My Lou' should brighten up everybody's spirits."

Hunter stared disbelievingly into Dash's sea blue eyes. "You're nuts, you know that? Do you honestly think these wild lumberjacks are gonna gather round a campfire and *sing*?"

"Sure," Dash answered. "Why not?"

"I suppose you think they're gonna dance too."

The mere thought of the burly, rough men dancing together made Dash laugh until tears ran down his face. "Lord I hope so," he wheezed when he could finally talk again. "I can't think of anything I'd enjoy more than seeing Blackie Wilson being waltzed around in Goldtooth Jones's arms!"

It was nearly sundown when Hunter and Dash finally parted. They had spent the late afternoon going over maps and charts, checking to make sure they were still on course and discussing whether they could make it to Scott's Bluff by the following afternoon.

As Hunter returned to Tess's wagon carrying two plates of food that Mary Krenzke had prepared, he spotted a long coil of steam rising toward the sky. With a muttered curse, he quickly set the plates down and raced around the back of the wagon.

"What the hell are you doing?" he demanded as he spied Tess bent over a washtub, energetically scrubbing.

Tess straightened, squeezing her eyes shut briefly as a persistent, nagging pain knifed through her lower back. "Since we stopped early today, I decided to do some laundry."

"Are you crazy?" Hunter demanded. "You're going to hurt yourself. Now, go lie down or something. I'll finish this."

Tess looked at him in bewilderment. "What are

you talking about? How would I hurt myself just by washing a few clothes?"

"I don't know," Hunter snapped. "Any number of ways, probably."

Tess's confusion deepened. "What?"

Hunter watched her press her hands against her back, her unconscious gesture only serving to confirm his fears. "For God's sake, Tess," he thundered, "don't you have any sense at all? Women in your condition shouldn't be scrubbing clothes. Any fool knows that!"

Tess's hands dropped away from her back as she stared at Hunter in startled surprise. "What do you mean, my condition?"

"Oh, for God's sake, drop the act," Hunter growled, walking over to the washtub and whipping the wet pair of dungarees she held out of her hands. "I know you're going to have a baby and I know it's gonna be soon." Furiously, he wrung the soggy pants out and threw them over the makeshift clothesline Tess had strung. Turning back to the stunned woman, he slammed his hands on his hips. "All I want is to make it to Fort Laramie before your time comes and I don't want you doing anything that might cause it to happen sooner. Is that understood?"

Tess didn't immediately answer his question. Instead, she said quietly, "How long have you known?"

"Since the day Joe was buried. Dash McLaughlin had his arm around your waist, remember? He said it was pretty hard to miss."

Tess dropped her eyes to the ground and nodded. "I see. If you've known that long, why haven't you said anything about it before?"

"What was the point? It's not like confronting you with yet another one of your lies would change anything. Besides, I figured you'd probably just deny it."

Tess looked down at her enormous stomach buried beneath the many layers of clothes. "No, I can't deny it."

Hunter let out a dispirited breath. Ever since Dash had told him of his suspicions, he had clung to the thought that maybe his friend was wrong. Now, even that faint hope was gone. "So," he said, walking over to where she stood, "when are you due?"

"Anytime now," she whispered.

Hunter rolled his eyes heavenward. "Great. Just what I need." Looking back at her, he added, "Have you had any signs of anything yet?"

Tess was mortified by Hunter's frank question and for a moment, she considered telling him it was none of his business. One glance at his cold, angry eyes quickly changed her mind, however. "No, not yet," she mumbled.

"What?"

"I said, nothing yet," she repeated, raising her chin and looking at him squarely. "I feel fine."

"Good. Let's try to keep it that way. You are to do no more washing, no more cooking and no more walking."

"Now, just a minute, Mr. Hunter. I feel better when I walk. Being jostled around in the back of the wagon is more uncomfortable than—"

"I don't care," Hunter interrupted rudely. "You will stay in your wagon on your cot. I know from experience that when you want to encourage a mare to give birth, you take her out and give her a little exercise. I'm not going to take that chance with you."

"I beg your pardon," Tess snapped, glaring at him, "but I am *not* a mare."

Hunter shrugged. "Female animals are female animals, Mrs. Caldwell. I doubt there is much difference between a horse, a dog, or a woman in regards to childbirth."

By now, Tess was truly offended with Hunter's high handed and insulting remarks and despite her vow not to antagonize him, she couldn't seem to help herself. "You, sir, are an odious and obnoxious boor."

Hunter's obsidian eyes suddenly blazed with fury. "And you, madam, are a liar and a fool."

"How dare you?" Tess gasped.

"How dare I?" Hunter bellowed. "How dare you? You lied to me to get on to my train, then when I caught you in that one and asked you if there was anything else you were keeping from me, you lied again. Why shouldn't I think you would tell me another?"

The angry fire in Tess's eyes faded, replaced by a look of hopelessness. "You don't understand," she choked, raising a shaking hand to push back an errant lock of hair. "I had reasons . . . so many reasons . . ."

"I don't care about your reasons!"

"I know you don't," she mumbled. "Now that Joe's gone, no one does." She raised her head, the light of battle again entering her eyes. "But that still doesn't give you the right to call me a fool!"

Hunter arched a brow. "Oh? And what would you call a pampered, spoiled city girl who joins a wagon train, minus a husband, when she knows she's due to give birth before reaching her destination?"

Tess hesitated a long moment before answering, and when she finally did, her voice was nearly inaudible. "I'd call her desperate."

Desperate? Why would she be desperate? There was only one reason Hunter could think of and he felt an immediate flash of anger at the possibility that Tess had duped him yet again. Could it be that she wasn't actually a widow after all? That she was, perhaps, an unmarried girl who'd gotten herself into a disgraceful situation?

Hunter knew a sudden, overwhelming desire to

have that question answered, and although he quickly told himself that Tess's marital status was no concern of his, his next words seemed to tumble out of their own volition. "Why, Tess? Why are you desperate? Tell me."

Tess shook her head. "No. It's none of your concern." Turning, she took a halting step toward the wagon.

Hunter moved quickly to the left, stepping into her path and effectively cutting off her escape. "Is it because you're lying to me about being a widow?"

Tess's look of stunned surprise answered that question even before she spoke. "Of course, I'm not lying! But, the reasons I joined your train are my business and no one else's."

"You're wrong about that. I told you once before, everything that happens on this train is my business."

Tess slowly raised tear filled eyes. "This isn't." Then, with a dignity that impressed Hunter despite his anger, she sidestepped his massive body and returned to the wagon, hauling herself clumsily up to the seat and disappearing into its canvas enshrouded shelter.

Hunter stared after her for a long moment, frustrated beyond all reason. "This isn't over between us, lady," he muttered angrily. "You *will* tell me what's going on in that head of yours. Maybe not tonight, maybe not tomorrow, but before we part company, I will know what's driving you." With a last, furious look at the silent wagon, he stomped over to the steaming pot and pulled another pair of dungarees out of the water, heaving them over the clothesline without even bothering to wring them first.

Much to Hunter's surprise, Tess obeyed his edict and stayed in her wagon for the next three days.

Although he found excuses to ride by frequently, he never once found her outside of its crowded confines. Twice he thought about stopping long enough to inquire about her health but, both times, he decided against it, realizing that if there were any problems, Matthew Bennington would inform him. Although the boy was, to his knowledge, unaware of Tess's condition, he would certainly recognize a woman in labor if he saw one.

Finally, the morning of the third day, Hunter could stand it no more. Pulling up to the wagon, he called, "Is everything okay, Bennington?"

Matthew smiled pleasantly and nodded. "Fine, Mr. Hunter."

"Mrs. Caldwell feeling all right?"

"Guess so. Haven't heard any complaints, anyway. I think she's sleeping. She seems to be awful tired today."

Hunter's brows knit with concern and after throwing Matthew an acknowledging wave, he rode around the back of the wagon, standing up in his stirrups to peer into the dusky interior.

Tess was indeed asleep, laying on her back on her hard cot, onc arm thrown over her head and the other laying across her stomach. In this position and with most of her heavy petticoats stripped off, Hunter had his first real glimpse of how enormously pregnant she really was. It was a curiously beautiful sight and he was shaken at how much her Madonna like condition affected him.

"Hold on, sweetheart," he murmured softly, not even aware of the endearment he voiced. "Just hold on till we get to the fort." He cast a last look at her, then wheeled his big gelding around and cantered thoughtfully back to the front of the train.

Scotts Bluff came and went—the majestic, castle shaped rock formations awing the travellers as they had all those who had gazed upon them before. Hunter wondered if Tess had awakened long enough to view the magnificent natural wonder of the bluffs, but he didn't allow himself to check on her again.

As the bluffs faded into the distance, the wagon train began the gradual climb up the North Platte Valley to Fort Laramie. The night before their expected arrival at the fort, they camped early, the settlers' spirits high with anticipation at the thought of once again being in the midst of some semblance of civilization.

"Are we really going to get there tomorrow?" Florette Kubes asked Hunter excitedly as he wandered among the camped wagons.

"We should, barring bad weather," he informed her.

"Wonderful!" she enthused, clapping her hands together. "At long last, we find ourselves at the gates of Paradise."

Hunter smiled, amused, as always, by Mrs. Kubes's flowery manner of speaking. "Just remember, Mrs. Kubes, Fort Laramie is a military post, not heaven. I wouldn't want you to be disappointed."

"Oh, I know that," Florette gushed, fluttering her hands expressively. "But, after all, it *is* to be our new home and it only makes sense to envision it in the most favorable of lights, don't you agree?"

"Absolutely," Hunter nodded, "as long as you understand that the reality might not be quite as romantic as the vision."

Florette smiled sublimely and cast her eyes up at him flirtatiously. "Oh, Mr. Hunter, you do have a most eloquent way of expressing yourself. Why, one would think you were a statesman or a man of the cloth to hear you talk."

"I assure you, ma'am, I'm neither," Hunter

responded quickly. Tipping his hat, he clucked to his horse and moved on, adroitly guessing that Mrs. Kubes was steering them toward a discussion that was bound to be far more personal than he was comfortable with.

As soon as Hunter rode off, Caroline Brooks joined Florette. "I saw you talking to Mr. Hunter."

"Yes," Florette answered dreamily. "You know, Caroline, I do believe he's the most handsome man I've ever met. That dark hair, those eyes, and that mouth! Have you ever in your life seen a mouth as perfect as Mr. Hunter's? I'll wager his kisses would make a woman swoon!"

Caroline's expression clearly betrayed her shock at her friend's provocative words. "Why, Florette Kubes, I'm ashamed of you! What a thing for a good, Christian woman to say. I can hardly believe you would be harboring such scandalous thoughts. Mr. Hunter's mouth, indeed!"

"Oh, come on, Caroline," Florette giggled, "don't tell me you've never noticed how . . . appealing . . . Mr. Hunter's looks are."

"Well, of course I have. But, to stand here and discuss how he might kiss is downright scandalous."

"Well, I can't help it if I find him devilishly handsome. He is! It's too bad he's so sad, though. He almost never smiles."

"Sad!" Caroline huffed. "He's not sad. He's just standoffish."

Florette looked at her in surprise. "Do you really think so?"

"I certainly do. I have tried every way I know how to be friendly to him, but he barely acknowledges my presence."

"Has he been rude to you?"

"Oh, no, he's polite enough. But, every time I ask

him to have supper with us, he declines, and if you ask him anything the least bit personal, he always changes the subject."

"He does that with me too," Florette admitted, "but I think it's because something terrible and tragic happened to him in the past and he doesn't want to talk about it."

"Oh, pooh!" Caroline scoffed. "You *always* think something 'terrible and tragic' has happened to people—especially if those people are handsome young men. I say the man is a snob. That's why he's so aloof. He just thinks he's better than the rest of us."

"Oh, Caroline, that's a terrible thing to say! He thinks no such thing! Just look at how nice he's been to Tess Caldwell. Why, ever since her brother was killed, Mr. Hunter has gone out of his way to be kind to her. Mary Krenzke told me he's so concerned about her well being that he has insisted she not walk anymore, that she just lay on her cot all day and rest."

Caroline looked at Florette incredulously. "He did?"

"Yes, he did."

"Well, this is certainly an intriguing little tidbit. Why didn't you tell me this before?"

"I didn't know you'd be interested."

"Well, of course I'm interested! Don't you find it a bit odd that Mr. Hunter is showing Tess so much attention?"

"Caroline Brooks, what are you insinuating?"

"Who said I was insinuating anything? I'm just saying that I find it fascinating that a man who seems so disinterested in all the other members of his party would show that much concern for the only eligible woman on the train."

"Her brother was killed and she's all alone! Of course, Mr. Hunter feels responsible for her, especially since she works for him."

"She doesn't work for him anymore," Caroline argued. "Mary Krenzke is doing all his chores for him now and Mr. Hunter is paying her handsomely for it. You said yourself that Tess spends her days lounging in the back of her wagon."

Florette's lips pursed so tightly that she looked like she'd been sucking lemons. "Caroline Brooks, I'm surprised at you. You're being most unkind, and here I thought you liked Tess."

Caroline raised her graying eyebrows in complete surprise. "Why, I do, Florette! What in the world would make you think I didn't?"

"Well, the way you're talking about her, a body would think that you suspect her of being Mr. Hunter's fancy woman."

"Nonsense. I think no such thing. Tess seems to be a very nice, God fearing woman. But, you have to admit, her relationship with Mr. Hunter is a bit—unusual. Just look at the way he kissed her the day her brother died. And, don't tell me you didn't notice either, because I know you did."

"Yes, I noticed," Florette admitted. "But, Mr. Hunter didn't mean anything by that. After all, Tess's brother had just been killed. He was simply comforting her."

Caroline's expression was dubious. "Maybe, but George never gave me a kiss like that until long after we were married. And when he did, it wasn't a gesture of comfort."

"You see?" Florette snapped, her excitable nature making her voice high and strident. "There you go again. In one breath, you say you like Tess and in the next, you make it sound like there's something . . . well, *unseemly* in her relationship with Mr. Hunter."

"I didn't say their relationship was unseemly. I just said that the kiss Mr. Hunter gave Tess that day was a bit, well, *personal*."

At that moment Mary Krenzke, having heard snatches of her friends' conversation, walked up and joined them. "What are you two talking about?" she demanded. "I can hear you screeching at each other all the way back at my wagon."

"Caroline is saying all sorts of unkind things about Tess Caldwell," Florette announced.

Mary, who had developed a strong maternal affection for Tess rounded on Caroline angrily. "Caroline Brooks, how could you? Why, after all that sweet girl has gone through, I can't believe you'd speak badly of her."

"I'm *not* speaking badly of her," Caroline defended hotly. "I just said that I find it intriguing that Mr. Hunter has taken such an interest in her. You noticed it yourself, Mary. Don't you remember when he bought that red sunbonnet for her? Even you thought there might be a romance sparking between them—and that's before we knew how young and pretty Tess really is!"

"I know I thought that," Mary admitted, "but I was wrong. Now that I know Mr. Hunter better, I believe there was a woman sometime in his past who broke his heart. "Just from little things he's said, I don't think he'll ever get involved in a romance again."

"See, Caroline?" Florette said smugly. "I told you the exact same thing."

"Besides," Mary interjected, "if any man on this train is interested in Tess Caldwell, it's Joshua Bennington. Why, every time he looks at her, you can see his heart in his eyes."

"Do you really think so?" Florette gasped. "Joshua Bennington?"

"Absolutely," Mary nodded. "Dash McLaughlin, too. He can't seem to take his eyes off her either."

Florette nearly swooned at this news. "You know,

I think that Mr. McLaughlin is the most handsome man I've ever seen! That blond hair and those blue eyes . . ."

"I thought you just told me that Mr. Hunter was the most handsome man you'd ever seen," Caroline laughed. "Now you're saying that Mr. McLaughlin is. I swear, Florette, you're the most frivolous woman I've ever known! What would Lloyd say if he could hear you?"

"Oh, Lloyd knows he's the only man for me, Caroline. But, I can't help myself. When I see men as handsome as Mr. Hunter and Mr. McLaughlin, it just makes me wish I was ten years younger!"

Caroline threw Florette a jaundiced look. "Try twenty years, Florette. That would be more like it."

"Oh, all right, twenty then," Florette huffed. "But, remember, Caroline, no matter how old I am, you're older. Leave us not forget that!"

"I beg your pardon!" Caroline bristled.

"All right, all right," Mary interrupted, "that's enough. It doesn't make any difference who's older, all three of us are far too old to turn the young men's heads anymore."

Florette, who had always been vain about her looks, threw her friend a devastated look.

"Oh, don't look so stricken, Florette," Mary laughed. "After all, we all had our day. Now it's Tess's turn."

"I guess you're right," Florette sighed. "I'm just disappointed that we won't be around to find out what happens with Tess and all her suitors. It almost makes me sorry that we're staying at Fort Laramie."

Caroline and Mary's looks of stunned disbelief were so comical that Florette burst into a peal of giggles. "Oh, come on girls, I said, '*almost*'!"

Chapter 14

Fort Laramie—or as Florette Kubes called it, "Paradise in the Prairie"—was little more than a hodgepodge of dwellings built against three foot thick, white-washed adobe walls. The fort was much smaller than the emigrants expected. Rectangular in shape, the entire structure was only 120 feet by 160 feet.

Built in 1834 by an enterprising businessman named William Sublette, the fort had, for many years, been an active trading post for fur trappers. By the mid 1840s, however, the fur trade had dwindled to the point that the fort was in jeopardy of closing.

Finally, in 1849, only a few months before Hunter's wagon train began its western trek, the United States Army had acquired the fort, turning it into a provisional outpost for the western pioneers, as well as a protective refuge against the Indians.

Despite the fort's disappointingly modest appearance, Florette Kubes, Mary Krenzke and Caroline Brooks were overjoyed by their first sight of their new home. After halting their wagons outside the main gate, they entered the fort's large center square, rhapsodizing expansively about the "endless possibilities" the fort and its surrounding area offered.

With characteristic forethought, Gerald Krenzke had, before leaving Missouri, engaged an enterprising carpenter by the name of Enzi Hobbs to construct a large pine building on the outskirts of the fort in which to house his store. Since all monies with which to construct the building had been forwarded to the unknown Mr. Hobbs in advance, Gerald was tremendously relieved when the man in question appeared at his side as soon as he climbed down from his wagon and announced that the building was complete. After speaking to the carpenter for several minutes, Gerald walked back to where Mary stood, smiling broadly.

"Wonderful news, Mary! Just as I predicted, everything is fine. That was Mr. Hobbs I was talking to and he assures me that the building is finished and ready to be provisioned. So, you see, he didn't fleece us like you were so sure he would."

Mary nodded, her expression mirroring her husband's relief. "That is wonderful news, husband, but I still say it was sheer madness for you to send nearly every penny we have in the world to a total stranger."

Gerald grinned and gave Mary's plump arm an affectionate pat. "It's like I've been telling you for the past seven hundred miles, you worry too much."

Mary shot Gerald a reproachful glance, but her good humor was soon restored as Hunter appeared, accompanied by Lloyd Kubes, George Brooks, and a tall, dignified military officer.

Nodding to the small party standing in the square, Hunter said, "Mr. and Mrs. Krenzke, Mrs. Kubes, Mrs. Brooks, I'd like to introduce Major Winslow Sanderson, commanding officer of the fort."

The merchants and their wives immediately began chatting animatedly with the major, telling him about their plans for their store. Major Sanderson listened with interest, then suggested that they all take a quick tour of the fort's facilities, including the Post Traders Store which was already in business within the compound. Eager to check out their competition, the couples promptly accepted the major's invitation and trooped happily away.

Hunter, who had been left standing alone in the square, spotted Dash McLaughlin chatting with a group of soldiers and sauntered over to join them. After the appropriate introductions were made, he turned to Dash and said quietly, "Have you seen Mrs. Caldwell?"

"Yeah, she's right over there."

Hunter looked in the direction that Dash pointed. An immediate frown tightened his lips as he spied Joshua Bennington, Matthew's older brother, solicitously helping Tess out of her wagon. "What the hell is Bennington doing?"

Dash swung his gaze back to Hunter, surprised by the obvious irritation in his friend's tone. Seeing Hunter's equally irritated expression, he grinned. "Well, it's just a guess, of course, but it looks to me like he's helping her out of her wagon."

"I can see that," Hunter snorted. "Where the hell is Matthew?"

"I don't know," Dash drawled. "Maybe Josh figured little Matt wasn't strong enough to lift Mrs. Caldwell down, so he's doing it himself. Or," he continued, trying hard to control the laughter that threatened, "maybe Josh has designs on the lady and this is his way of courting her. Who knows?"

Hunter threw Dash a withering look. "You tryin' to make me mad?"

"Heavens no!" Dash protested, clapping a hand to his chest and making a great pretense of reeling backwards in feigned shock. "You know I'd never do that, boss. I'm just answering your question."

"You're a real horse's ass, McLaughlin."

Dash could no longer contain his mirth and erupted in a roar of laughter. "Maybe you better hie on over there, Hunter. Looks to me like old Joshua may be gettin' ready to propose."

"I wish he would," Hunter growled. "It would solve a lot of problems."

"Oh, sure you do," Dash chuckled. "I can tell by that furious look on your face that you're just prayin' for a wedding between those two."

"Why wouldn't I be?"

"Because you want that little girl for yourself."

"You're nuts, you know that?"

"And you're in love," Dash shot back, "so why don't you just admit it and go get her?"

Hunter glared at Dash as if he'd just ordered him to go get himself a case of cholera. "You're nuts," he repeated. Absolutely nuts. You always have been and you always will be."

Pivoting on his heel, he stomped off. But Dash noticed that before he disappeared through the fort's main gate, he threw a last, angry glare at Tess and Joshua Bennington.

"Let's put the cans of beans up here with the peas and tomatoes right next to them. That way people will have their choice of vegetables."

Florette looked over at Mary and nodded. "Good idea. We can put the peaches and pears on the same shelf too."

"Oh, girls," Caroline trilled, turning from where she was removing jars of preserves from packing boxes. "Do you have any idea how much money we're all going to make here? Why, we'll be rich!"

"I think you might be right," Florette agreed. "After seeing the prices in the Post Traders Store, we can easily undercut them and still make a fortune."

"The prices those robbers charge are a crime," Mary snorted. "Did you see what they get for tobacco? Why, they're charging a dollar for five cents worth! As close as I can figure, they're making about an eighteen hundred percent profit on most items. That's just not fair."

Caroline nodded so vehemently that all three of her chins shook. "You're absolutely right. It's outrageous. Why, we can sell the same amount for eighty-five or ninety cents, and we'll get all their business."

"Oh, yes, Caroline," Florette giggled. "A sixteen hundred percent profit isn't nearly as outrageous as eighteen hundred percent."

Caroline frowned at Florette's wry comment, but before she could think of a retort, Tess walked through the front door.

"May I help?"

"Tess!" All three voices greeted her in unison.

"Come in, dear, come in!" Mary enthused. "We haven't seen you all day. Where have you been?"

"Major Sanderson gave me a tour of the fort," Tess explained. "Have you seen the inside of 'Old Bedlam', the officers' quarters? It's really quite charming."

"Is that the big white building with the veranda?" Mary questioned.

"Yes, and the veranda is wonderful—so cool, and a fresh breeze seems to waft through all the time. The major had tea served and we sat out there for quite a while, chatting. He is a very pleasant man."

"And, apparently, quite taken with you," Caroline noted. "He gave us only the most cursory of tours when we arrived yesterday."

"I'm not nearly as busy as you ladies are," Tess said quickly. "I'm sure the major noticed that."

"I'm sure what the major noticed," Caroline continued archly, "is that you are a young and beautiful woman, far more interesting than the three of us."

"Oh, I don't think that was it at all, Mrs. Brooks," Tess protested. "The major probably just thought that since I really don't have anything to do, I'd enjoy the diversion of a chat and a cup of tea."

"You don't have anything to do?" said Caroline. "Well, we can fix that soon enough."

"That's why I'm here," Tess said. "I thought I might be able to help you with your unpacking."

Mary glowered at the sharp tongued Caroline, then turned her attention to Tess. "How sweet of you to offer, dear. Perhaps you could put those jars of preserves up on the top shelf over there."

Tess nodded and picked up several of the jars Caroline had unpacked. "You know," she said, looking around the spacious room, "this really is going to be a wonderful store. The building is beautiful and the spot Mr. Hobbs chose for it is ideal. Why, with all those trees and that lovely patch of grass right outside, you're bound to attract everyone who passes by." With a smile, she reached up and placed a jar of blueberry preserves on a high shelf.

Florette glanced over at Tess to respond to her compliment, but what she saw made her swallow her words and gasp in shock instead.

"What is it, Florette?" Caroline asked. "Did you see a mouse or something?"

"No!" Florette answered quickly. "It's . . . it's nothing."

"Then, why did you gasp like that?"

"I . . . I cut my finger on this box."

"Oh, my dear," Mary cried, hurrying over. "Is it badly hurt?"

"No!" Florette said, hurriedly sticking her right index finger into her mouth. "It's nothing, really. It just stung for a moment."

Mary looked at her curiously. "Well, if you need a bandage, I have a box of medical supplies right over here. I'll be happy to find one for you."

"Thanks, but that won't be necessary." Pulling her finger out of her mouth, Florette held it up. "See? It's stopped bleeding already."

The other women glanced over at her for a moment, then, convinced that there was, indeed, no emergency, they returned to their tasks.

For the rest of the afternoon, Florette covertly watched Tess. By the time they decided to quit for the day and return to their wagons to start supper, she was positive that her suspicions about her were right.

As the four women left the store, Florette waylaid Mary and Caroline, using the slim pretext of wanting to discuss the next day's unpacking schedule. When she was sure that Tess was out of earshot, she turned to her friends, her eyes wide. "Are either one of you aware that Tess is going to have a baby?"

"What?" Mary gasped. "What in the world are you talking about?"

"She is! And very soon, too."

"Oh, Florette, you and your overactive imagination . . ."

"It's not my imagination, Mary! I saw it when she was putting those preserves on the top shelf. Every time she reached up, her dress flattened against her stomach. She's definitely in the family way. Very, very much so."

Mary looked at her frivolous friend for a long moment, but there was an uncharacteristic seriousness in Florette's expression that she couldn't ignore. "I can't believe this," she blustered. "Why wouldn't Tess have told us? Oh, Florette, you must be wrong! Being in the family way isn't something a woman can hide indefinitely."

"You can if you wear enough petticoats," Caroline interjected tartly.

"Well, I suppose it *might* be possible," Mary conceded, "and Tess does always seem to wear a lot of layers of clothing, regardless of how hot it is."

"Exactly," Florette nodded. "And now we know why."

Mary shook her head, still doubtful that what Florette claimed could actually be true. "I just don't understand why she would try to hide her condition from us. I mean, she might not want the men on the train to know but, surely, she could have told us."

Caroline looked at Mary speculatively. "What if . . . and I'm not saying this is true . . . but, what if Tess isn't really a widow?"

"Not a widow! Are you saying that you think she may have a husband back in Missouri? That she's running away, perhaps?"

"Why, I hadn't even thought of that," Caroline admitted. "I was thinking more along the lines of Tess not being married at all."

Mary's eyes filled with horror. "Oh, no, I don't believe that! Not dear little Tess! Why, she's far too nice a girl to get herself into . . . that kind of trouble."

"Oh, I don't know," Caroline said snidely. "You have to admit, if Tess is a widow like she says she is, then it's very peculiar that she'd not tell any of us that she's going to have a baby. After all, there certainly is no shame in it."

"It *is* a bit peculiar," Mary agreed, "but I'm sure she has a good reason."

"Oh, I'm sure she does too," Caroline said, her voice dripping with sarcasm.

Mary frowned at the catty woman, wondering briefly how she was ever going to spend the next twenty years of her life in her company. "Well, one thing is for sure, Caroline. If Tess is as far along as

Florette thinks she is, she can't continue on with the train. She'll have to stay here with us, at least until next spring."

"Oh, Mary!" Florette cried, clapping her hands together. "What a wonderful thought! Imagine, having a precious little baby around for the whole winter. Why, I can't think of anything I'd enjoy more. In fact, I'm going to talk to Lloyd tonight about the possibility of Tess living with us for the winter."

"Living with you!" Mary huffed. "Don't be ridiculous, Florette. She'll live with Gerald and me. We already have a house under construction and, after all, Tess is *my* friend."

"*Your* friend! What makes you think she's only your friend?" Florette argued. "She's my friend, too."

"And mine," Caroline chimed in.

This comment was met by jaundiced looks from both Florette and Mary, causing Caroline's mouth to purse with offense. "Well, she is!"

"Look," Mary said, "there's no sense in our standing here arguing about this. Why don't I, as Tess's *closest* friend, go talk to her? I'm sure this can all be settled with one simple conversation."

Florette and Caroline glanced at each other, but neither of them could think of any reason to argue with Mary's suggestion.

"All right," Florette agreed. "You go talk to Tess. But, remember, she's not to make any decisions about who she wants to live with until I've had a chance to talk to her too."

"All right," Mary nodded. "Fair enough. Agreed, Caroline?"

"Yes," Caroline answered reluctantly. "I guess so. But, remember, my offer for her to live with George and me still stands too—depending, of course, on what Tess tells you."

"What do you mean, 'depending on what Tess tells me'?"

"Well, Caroline bristled, "George and I couldn't possibly take her in if it turns out she's not married. That just wouldn't be proper and I couldn't risk my good reputation just to . . ."

She paused, startled by the black looks of rage being cast at her by her friends. "Oh, never mind," she said quickly. "Just go talk to her, Mary."

Chapter 15

"Why didn't you tell us, dear?"

Tess and Mary sat together on the cot in Tess's wagon, taking advantage of the little bit of privacy the enclosed vehicle offered.

"I guess I just felt it was my business and no one else's."

"But, surely, you could have trusted me."

"I know, Mrs. Krenzke, and I probably should have told you, but . . ."

Mary looked at Tess kindly, her heart going out to the troubled girl. "But, what, dear?"

"But, I figured if I told you, you'd want me to stay here at Fort Laramie, and I can't do that."

Mary's eyebrows rose in surprise at Tess's astuteness. "Tess, dear, I'm your friend. You should know that I would never try to force you to do something you didn't want to."

"I know that," Tess nodded, summoning a wan smile, "but I also knew that you'd think I was every kind of fool if I told you I was travelling on to Oregon, despite the fact that I won't make it before the baby's born."

Mary sighed and reached over to pat Tess's hand. "It *would* be very foolish of you, Tess. There's not a woman in her right mind who would choose to have a baby in the back of a covered wagon. Believe me, I've had four, and that's not where you want to do it."

"I'm sure hundreds of women have done it before me," Tess argued.

"Yes, but not by choice, I'm sure . . . and not without another woman around to help with the midwifery."

Tess threw Mary a sideward glance. "So, you *are* here to try to talk me into staying at the fort, aren't you?"

"Yes," Mary admitted. "Mostly, I'm here to tell you that Gerald and I would be delighted to have you spend the winter with us. Our house will be finished in just a few weeks and we are building on an extra bedroom in case one of our sons decides to join us next year. You and the baby can stay there. Or, if you prefer, you could stay with the Brookses or the Kubeses. But, I think you'd be happier with us."

"Mrs. Krenzke . . ."

"Call me Mary, dear."

Tess smiled gratefully. "I really appreciate your offer, Mary. It's very kind of you. But, I have to get to Oregon this year."

"Why?" Mary asked, genuinely puzzled. "What real difference does it make if you get there this year or next?"

"My sister is expecting me this year. If I don't arrive, she'll think something has happened to me. She might even think I'm dead. I couldn't let her worry like that—not for a whole year."

"Oh, stuff and nonsense, Tess!" Mary scoffed. "All you have to do it write your sister a letter and explain your situation. Does she have children of her own?"

"Yes, three little boys."

"Well, then, she'll certainly understand your delay."

Tess shook her head stubbornly. "No, I have to go this year."

Mary pressed her lips together in frustration. "Tess, you're being very difficult about this. Now, there's not a reason in the world that you have to get to Oregon this year, and . . ."

"You don't understand," Tess murmured. "I want to be with my sister. I *need* to be."

"Why do you *need* to be?"

Tess hung her head, loathe to tell the kindly woman her troubles. "It's . . . it's hard to explain," she stammered. "I've had a very difficult year. My husband died, I . . . lost my home, now I've lost my brother. My sister is quite a bit older than I am. After our mother died, she was almost like a mother to Joe and me. I just feel that I need to be with her now." *There. It wasn't the whole truth, but it was close enough.*

"And you *shall* be with her," Mary soothed. "But now is not the time. You need to be someplace safe, someplace secure when your baby is born, and that place is here."

Tess tried very hard to maintain her smile, but it wasn't easy. She didn't need the pressure that Mary Krenzke was applying. That's all she'd had for the past year—pressure, pressure, pressure—from everyone. Her husband, William; Margaret, Joe, Hunter, and now, Mary. Why couldn't anyone understand that she had to do what *she* thought was right? She'd be so much better off if everyone would just leave her alone!

Despite her smile, tears welled in Tess's eyes. "I have to get to Oregon, Mary. Please try to understand. *Please!*"

Mary looked at Tess with stricken eyes, overwhelmed with remorse that she'd made the poor, overwrought girl cry. "Oh, honey," she crooned, hugging her to her ample bosom. "I didn't mean to upset you. Please, dear, don't cry."

"I'm sor..sorry," Tess sniffed. "I just have ss..so much on my mind right now."

"I know," Mary said, rising, "and I certainly didn't mean to add to your burdens. I'll tell you what. Why don't you get some sleep? We can talk about this again tomorrow." Seeing Tess's anguished look, she quickly amended, "Or some other time." With an apologetic little nod, Mary backed out of the wagon and climbed down to the ground, her face a mask of pity as she heard Tess give vent to her tears.

Florette and Caroline were already at the store when Mary arrived the next morning.

"Did you speak to Tess?" Florette asked excitedly. "Was I right? Is she in the family way?"

"Yes," Mary nodded, pulling off her shawl and draping it over an empty packing box. "I did talk to her and, yes, she is going to have a baby."

"So, what did she say?" Caroline demanded. "Who does she want to live with?"

"None of us," Mary answered. "She wouldn't listen to reason. I talked until my face was blue, but she just kept saying that she wanted to be with her sister—that she '*needed*' to be with her sister, and that she was going on to Oregon, regardless of her condition."

"Well," Caroline shrugged, "then, that's that. After all, it's Tess's life. She's not a child and if she's bound to go, then I guess she'll have to face the consequences of that decision."

"Oh, Caroline, how can you say that?" Florette gasped. "We have to stop her! She doesn't know what she's getting herself into."

"She's a grown woman," Caroline repeated stubbornly. "She knows perfectly well what she's getting herself into." Turning to Mary, she narrowed her eyes speculatively. "So, is she really a widow?"

"I'm sure she is," Mary answered. "She certainly didn't say anything that would make me think she wasn't."

"But, did you ask her?"

"Not in so many words. But she spoke about losing her husband."

"Of course she's a widow!" Florette snapped, firing a withering look at Caroline. "She's said all along she is, so she is!"

"Maybe yes, maybe no." Caroline huffed.

"You know, Caroline," Mary said quietly, "you almost act as if you hope Tess is lying."

"I don't either. I'd just like to know the truth."

"Well, then," Mary continued, "why don't you just accept Tess's word as the truth? She says she's a widow and that's good enough for me."

"Me too!" Florette enjoined, glaring at Caroline. "But, what are we going to do to shake some sense into the girl and convince her she's better off staying with us for the winter?"

"There's only one thing to do," Mary said sagely. "And I'm going to do it."

"What?"

"I'm going to tell Mr. Hunter."

This statement was met by simultaneous gasps of shock from the other two women.

"Oh, Mary, do you really think you should?" Florette asked. "It seems like it would be betraying a confidence."

"Not to mention having to discuss such a delicate subject with an unmarried man," Caroline added.

"What has to be done, has to be done," Mary said stoutly. "And, yes, Florette, you're right. I *do* feel like

I'm betraying a confidence, but sometimes I believe a body has to do that if it is for the good of someone else."

Florette nodded slowly, but her eyes were still full of doubt.

"So," Mary continued, standing up and wrapping her recently discarded shawl back around her shoulders, "I might as well do it before I lose my nerve."

"Now?" Florette gasped. "You're going to talk to him now?"

"No time like the present," Caroline encouraged. "The sooner you talk to him, the sooner Tess can get out of that awful, cramped wagon and start getting settled. I understand that Major Sanderson is temporarily renting rooms in Old Bedlam to any member of the train who decides to settle here. Maybe Tess can take up residence there until one of us can offer her something permanent. At least she'd have a roof over her head."

Mary nodded and started for the door. "Caroline, that's the first decent thing I've heard you say in two days. Maybe there's hope for you yet."

She didn't pause to see what Caroline's reaction was to her sarcastic jibe, but based on Florette's immediate giggle, she knew it must have been choice.

"Mr. Hunter, I need to talk to you, please."

Hunter looked up from the mule he was shoeing. "Sure, Mrs. Krenzke. I'm a little busy right now, though. How about after dinner?"

Mary shook her head. "I'm sorry, but this can't wait."

Hunter dropped the mule's hoof. "Riley!" he barked. "Come finish up with this mule. I have something I have to take care of."

Jack Riley, who was sprawled in a nearby haystack with a bottle of cheap whiskey, glared over at his boss.

"Damn it, anyway," he muttered. "Why in tarnation does he always have somethin' he's gotta take care of just when I get settled in for a little relaxation?"

"I heard that, Riley," Hunter laughed.

Turning his attention back to Mary, he said, "Now, what can I do for you, ma'am? Are you having problems at your new store?"

"Oh, no, it's nothing like that," Mary assured him. Leaning closer, she whispered, "It's something rather personal. Could we go somewhere where we won't be overheard?"

Hunter's eyebrows shot up questioningly, but he merely nodded and led the portly woman over to a tree situated well out of earshot. After they'd settled themselves comfortably in the grass, Hunter looked over at Mary expectantly.

"It's about Mrs. Caldwell," Mary began without preamble.

Of course it is, Hunter thought tiredly. What clandestinc conversation *isn't* about Mrs. Caldwell?

"What about her?"

"Well, I'm afraid we have a bit of a problem."

Of course we do. When isn't she a problem?

"A problem?"

"Yes." Mary paused, looking away in embarrassment as she tried to think of the appropriate words with which to broach the delicate subject of Tess's pregnancy. "You see, it has recently come to my attention that Mrs. Caldwell is . . ."

Pregnant, Hunter finished silently.

"Expecting a baby." Mary's already florid face turned even redder than usual and her plump hands fluttered nervously in her lap.

"I already know that, Mrs. Krenzke."

Mary's embarrassed expression immediately disappeared, replaced by one of outright astonishment. "You do? You mean, she told you?"

"Not exactly."

Mary stared at him expectantly.

"Someone else did."

"How long have you known?"

"For a couple of weeks."

"Does Tess know that you know?"

"Yes."

Mary frowned, wishing that Hunter would elaborate more on his answers. "Mr. Hunter, I am very concerned about Tess's well being and I'd appreciate you being candid with me."

Hunter looked at her in surprise. "I thought I was, Mrs. Krenzke."

Mary sighed, thinking that it was just like a man to believe that one word answers were all that was necessary to explain a situation. "I guess what I'm saying is that I'd like to know what you and Tess talked about when you discussed her condition."

Hunter shrugged. "Not much, really. I just told her that I knew she was in the family way and that I wanted her to start resting more and riding in the wagon instead of walking."

Mary thought about this for a moment, then shook her head. "Surely, Mr. Hunter, you can't be thinking of letting her continue on to Oregon with the train."

Hunter reached out and plucked a blade of coarse grass, rolling it thoughtfully between his fingers. "No, I'm not."

"Well, I'm certainly glad to hear that. Have you said anything to her yet?"

"No." *I've been avoiding it like the plague.* "I was planning to speak to her this evening."

"Or sooner," Mary advised. "I told her yesterday that I thought she should stay here at the fort until next spring, but she refused to listen to reason. Perhaps if you talk to her, you can change her mind."

My talking to her would probably be the last thing in the

world that would change her mind. Hunter shrugged and threw the piece of grass down. "There's really nothing to talk about. I'm just going to tell her that she can't travel any further. As wagon master of this train, it is within my authority to make that decision for any member of the party. Mrs. Caldwell has no choice but to submit to my decision."

"Oh, I don't know about that," Mary said dubiously. "I think you're going to get quite an argument."

Of course I am! She argues about everything. "She can't argue. My decisions regarding this train are final."

Mary smiled at him pityingly. "I'm afraid, Mr. Hunter, that you don't know Tess very well. You're going to get an argument whether you expect one or not. She's very determined."

Hunter stood up and brushed off the seat of his pants. "So am I, Mrs. Krenzke. And, regardless of how determined Mrs. Caldwell might be, she can't go on. There's no one on the train to assist her when her time comes since the entire company will now be only men. She has also lost the protection of her brother and there's no one else with the time or inclination to watch over her."

"I'm not sure that's true," Mary interjected. "I think Joshua Bennington might happily take on that responsibility if she asked him."

Over my dead body, Hunter thought, his lips tightening ominously. "No, he won't."

"Have you already spoken to him about this?"

"No, but Mr. Bennington is in no position to take on the responsibility of a woman and baby. I'll not allow it, even if he offers. That's that."

Mary looked at Hunter thoughtfully. The telltale strain in his voice at the mention of Joshua Bennington's possible relationship with Tess spoke volumes. Maybe she hadn't been wrong, after all, when she'd told Gerald that she thought there might be a romance blooming between Tess and Hunter. Too bad it would never have the chance to blossom . . .

"It's getting late," she said suddenly, holding her hand up so Hunter would help her to her feet, "and I have to get back to the store. I do think the best thing is for you to speak to Tess as soon as possible. I wouldn't advise waiting until this evening."

Hunter nodded. "Okay, I'll do it right now."

Mary smiled at the handsome man and laid her hand on his arm. "Be gentle," she advised. "Tess is very vulnerable right now. Try not to upset her."

"I'll be as diplomatic as I can," he promised. *Please, God, make me remember that when she starts being impossible.* Turning, he walked away, heading for Tess's wagon.

"You're going to need a whole lot more than diplomacy to change that girl's mind," Mary whispered as he disappeared from sight. "What you're going to need is a miracle."

Chapter 16

"You can't go, and that's the end of it!" Hunter yelled angrily.

"You are truly the most odious man I've ever met!" Tess railed back at him. "Get out of my wagon. I don't ever want to see you again."

"Gladly!" Whipping open the wagon's canvas cover, Hunter leaped down. Furiously, he marched over to a nearby grove of trees, pounding his fist against the trunk of a poplar and cursing roundly. Never, *ever* had he met a woman who could infuriate him as fast as Tess Caldwell could. She was impossible. Impossible! Thank God that after tomorrow morning, he'd be rid of her.

Slumping against the tree, Hunter raked his fingers through his hair and glared at Tess's wagon. What had gone wrong? Their conversation had started amicably enough . . .

"Hi. Are you trying to take a nap or could I talk to you for a minute?"

Tess, who was resting in the back of her wagon, sat up and quickly straightened her wrinkled skirt. "No, I'm not napping. Come in."

Hunter climbed into the wagon and sat down next to her on her narrow cot. Folding his hands between his knees, he stared down at them for a second, carefully choosing his next words. "I have something to tell you that I'm afraid you're not going to want to hear, but it's for your own good and it's got to be said."

Tess's eyes narrowed warily. "What is it?"

Hunter blew out a long, bracing breath. The moment he'd dreaded for so long was finally upon him. Even though he'd spent a great deal of time during the past couple of weeks thinking about how he was going to break this news, right up until this minute, he had still not decided whether just to tell Tess point blank that she couldn't travel on or try to finesse his way through with a lengthy explanation. But now, looking over at her shuttered, defensive expression, he realized there was no point in being anything but straightforward. It was obvious she was expecting the worst. He might as well give it to her and be done with it.

"When the wagon train leaves tomorrow, you can't go." There. It was out. Covertly, he sneaked a peek at her from the corner of his eye. She was staring straight ahead, her face stony.

"I am going," she said flatly.

"Mrs. Caldwell, listen to reason—"

"No," she gritted, her voice rising, "you listen to me. I am sick and tired of everyone telling me what I should and should not do, what I can and cannot do. I have paid my fare—or at least Joe paid a fare which I figure should transfer over to me—and I'm going."

Hunter chewed on the inside of his bottom lip for

a moment, trying desperately to keep his temper in check. Mentally, he began reciting Mary Krenzke's parting words. *"She's very vulnerable right now. Be gentle."*

"I understand your logic," he began again, "really I do. But, please, just hear me out. We're only a third of the way to Oregon—the *easy* third—and you're in no shape to make the climb over the Rockies. It's grueling, even for men. But for a woman in your condition, it's an impossibility."

"Nothing's impossible if you want it badly enough."

Hunter ignored this interruption and continued on as if she hadn't spoken. "You don't seem to understand. You couldn't ride in the wagon. You'd have to walk. It's uphill, sometimes nearly straight uphill. And it's over rocks, not soft, level grassy plains. You're not going to be able to do it, Mrs. Caldwell, believe me. I've been over this trail before. A pregnant woman can't do it."

"Maybe by the time we get to the really difficult climb, I won't still be . . ."—she swallowed, barely able to make herself say the scandalous word, but unwilling to let Hunter think she wasn't sophisticated enough to match his language—"pregnant."

"Oh, that's great!" he barked. "All that means is that instead of having to worry about a woman about to give birth, I'd have to worry about a newborn baby and a woman recovering from her confinement."

"I'll be fine."

Hunter closed his eyes, praying for patience. When he finally opened them again, he pierced Tess with a glacial look. "And just who do you think is going to assist you with this birth? Your three adopted mothers aren't going to be there. No one is. Do you think you can deliver this baby yourself?"

"If I have to."

"For God's sake," Hunter hissed, gritting his teeth in frustration.

"Look, Mr. Hunter, I'm not trying to be difficult, really I'm not—"

"Oh, no! Not in the least!"

It was Tess's turn to ignore the interruption. "I *have* to get to Oregon this year. That's all there is to it. Now, I understand that conditions aren't ideal and I'm sorry if I'm causing you a problem, but I *am* going. And that's the end of this conversation."

Hunter shot her a look of outraged disbelief as she threw his customary comment back in his face. Jumping to his feet, he glared at her furiously. "No, that's *not* the end of this conversation, Mrs. Caldwell, because you're not going and that's that!"

Pulling his thoughts back to the present, Hunter rubbed his forehead tiredly. After that point, their discussion had quickly deteriorated into a screaming match, ending with Tess ordering him out of her wagon.

So, now what? They were obviously at an impasse and short of gagging her and tying her to a chair in one of the empty rooms in Old Bedlam, there was very little he could do to prevent her from hitching up her team and joining the train.

Hunter couldn't help but smile to himself as he thought about how much he would enjoy gagging the feisty girl and giving her a real piece of his mind, knowing that she couldn't verbally retaliate.

But, his smile soon faded. Unfortunately, binding and gagging were not options. Moreover, he only had until daybreak tomorrow to come up with a truly feasible plan of how to keep Tess at the fort.

"You'll think of something," he told himself. "You always do." Rising, he headed back to the blacksmith's shack. "Just go back and shoe a couple more mules. Something will come to you."

* * *

By nine o'clock that night, nothing had. Desperate for advice, Hunter sought out Dash. Quickly, he explained his problem, then sat back, waiting for his friend to come up with a bit of brilliance.

Dash didn't fail him.

"I think the answer to this is pretty simple," he shrugged, pulling a new bottle of whiskey out of his saddle bag and pouring them both a generous portion.

Hunter looked at him hopefully.

"You've been trying to reason with the wrong person in this little drama, Jared. If you can't get the girl to agree to stay behind, then you're just going to have to chop her off at the wheels, so to speak."

"What the hell are you talking about?"

"The Bennington brothers. They're your answer. Even Mrs. Caldwell can't be foolish enough to think she can drive herself. She has to be counting on Matthew or Joshua to do it for her."

"And I'm sure either one of them would be happy to agree," Hunter interjected sarcastically.

"Not if you tell them you forbid it."

Hunter leaned back on one elbow, taking a long swallow of his drink as he ruminated about this possibility. "You know, Dash, you just might have something there. Why the hell didn't I think of that?"

Dash grinned, his blue eyes dancing with deviltry. "I don't know, Whitaker," he sighed. "I guess some of us have it and some of us—"

"Oh, go to hell," Hunter said absently, turning the plan over in his mind.

"If I go to the Benningtons and tell them that I won't allow them to drive for Tess, then she has no choice but to stay here . . ."

Dash gestured to Hunter with his glass. "Unless, of

course, the Benningtons kick up a fuss. Not Matthew, necessarily, since he's just a kid. But if Josh has it as bad for Mrs. Caldwell as he appears to, you might have a hell of an argument on your hands."

"I can handle him," Hunter said confidently. "Joshua Bennington is a rule follower. You can tell that by the way he lives his life. And, in this case, I'm the rule maker. He knows that. I don't think he'll buck too hard."

"What is Josh decides to stay here with the widow?"

"He won't. He can't. He and his brother aren't just transient 'jacks, you know. They've bought a parcel of timber in Oregon and they plan to start their own operation. I can't believe Josh would throw that away just because he's got a case on a girl."

"But, what if he does?"

"If he does, he does," Hunter shrugged, trying desperately to sound nonchalant. "It's his business, not mine. My only concern is that Tess Caldwell isn't on the train when we leave tomorrow morning."

Dash smiled knowingly. "Oh, yeah? Do you really expect me to believe that's your only concern?"

Hunter leaped to his feet, slamming his glass down so hard on a nearby tree stump that it broke. "Damn right, I expect you to believe it! And, what's more, I want you to quit trying to make something out of nothing. After today, I'll never see Tess Caldwell again and that's exactly the way I want it. I don't give a damn if she marries Joshua Bennington, Matthew Bennington, Jeremy Bennington, or all three of them at the same time. Do you understand me?"

Dash's expression remained infuriatingly bland. "You know what I think, Whitaker?"

Hunter's eyes flared. "No, I don't know what you think, McLaughlin, and I don't care. But, so help me God, if you start quoting Shakespeare to me again, I'm gonna knock your block off!"

* * *

"So, you see, Mrs. Caldwell, although my brothers and I would be more than happy to drive your wagon the rest of the way to Oregon, Mr. Hunter won't allow it. I'm real sorry, ma'am. I hope you'll understand this was his decision, not mine."

Tess looked up into Joshua Bennington's earnest, sympathetic face and summoned a small smile. "It's all right, Mr. Bennington. I do understand."

"Do you have any idea why Mr. Hunter doesn't want you to continue with the train?"

Tess lowered her head and nodded. "Yes," she sighed. "We've discussed it already."

Josh's face registered his surprise. "Oh! So, then, you already knew you weren't going to be travelling on."

"No," Tess corrected him. "I was planning to continue on with the train despite Mr. Hunter's objections."

Joshua looked clearly appalled at Tess's mutinous words. "But, Mr. Hunter is the wagon master. His word is law! Didn't you and your brother sign an agreement stating that you understood that and would abide by it?"

"Yes, I suppose we did," Tess nodded tiredly.

"Well, then, I don't see how you were going to . . ."

"It's all right, Mr. Bennington," Tess repeated. Looking up into the man's plain, square face, she smiled, touched by his concern for her. Joshua Bennington was as good a man as she'd ever met—forthright, law abiding and honest to a fault. Tess knew by his actions of the past few weeks that Joshua was developing an affection for her, and although she was flattered, she had never had any intention of fostering it. What Joshua Bennington needed was a wife as forthright, law abiding and honest as he was. What he didn't need was Tess Caldwell.

Getting up from where she sat in the tall grass near the evening's campfire, she reached out and placed her small hand in his meaty paw. "I truly appreciate all you and Matthew have done for me since my brother died," she said softly. "Please don't feel guilty that I can't continue on with this train. I'll just wait here at the fort until next spring."

Joshua was elated that Tess didn't blame him for the awkward situation, and his relief was obvious on his face. "Thank you for saying that," he smiled. "I feel much better now." He continued to stare at her for a moment, kneading his battered old hat in his hands self consciously. Finally, summoning up his courage, he said, "Mrs. Caldwell, I wonder if I can ask you a question?"

Tess sighed inwardly, knowing that whatever it was Joshua wanted to know, it was probably something she didn't want to share. Still, she supposed that she owed the man some sort of explanation since her problems with Hunter had put him in such an embarrassing position. "Of course, Mr. Bennington. What is it?"

"Well, you just said that you knew why Hunter didn't want you to continue on with the train."

"Yes?"

Joshua shrugged, his heavy shoulders silhouetted against the dancing firelight. "Why?"

"Actually," Tess murmured, looking away in embarrassment, "it's a personal problem between us."

"I see," he nodded. "So what they've all been saying is true."

Instantly, Tess's eyes flew back to his face. "What? Has someone been talking about me?"

"Oh, it's nothin'," Josh said quickly, cursing himself for having opened his mouth. "Just idle talk among the men on the train. I've really got to go now, ma'am. My brothers and I have a lot of packing up to do before we pull out tomorrow." Clapping the battered hat on his head, he turned to leave.

"What idle chatter, Mr. Bennington?" Tess demanded, stopping his hasty flight.

Without turning around, Josh muttered, "Well, some of the boys have it figured that there's something going on between you and Mr. Hunter, and that the reason he doesn't want you to travel on is that the two of you had a lover's quarrel."

Tess sucked in a horrified breath. "Well, they're wrong! There's *nothing* going on between Mr. Hunter and myself! I hardly know the man and what I do know about him, I don't like."

Her agitated statement made Joshua spin around and look at her with renewed interest. "Really? There's nothing between you two?"

"Absolutely not," Tess assured him.

"But, then, why won't Hunter let you stay on the train? You said that it's something personal, but if there's nothing between you, then it doesn't make sense . . ."

"I'm going to have a baby, Mr. Bennington," Tess blurted.

Joshua's wide, square jaw dropped open. "A baby?" he gasped. "But everyone just thought you were . . ."

"Fat?" Tess finished. "Yes, I know they did. But, the truth is, I'm going to have a baby, and very soon, too. Mr. Hunter found out about . . . my condition . . . and didn't want me to be alone and without female assistance when my time came, so he insisted I stay here at the fort with the other ladies."

Joshua considered Hunter's edict for a moment, then nodded his head. "He's right. You should stay here. A lady in your delicate state shouldn't be jostled around in the back of a wagon."

"I know, I know," Tess said, holding up her hand. "I've heard all this before. There's no need to lecture me, Mr. Bennington, I know when I'm licked."

"Oh, Mrs. Caldwell," Josh cajoled, trying hard to keep his eyes from straying to Tess's thick middle, "it won't be so bad. You can catch the first train in the spring. That's only about ten months from now."

"Yes," Tess sighed, "ten months from now. But I wanted to get to the Willamette Valley this year."

"The valley will still be there next spring," Josh smiled, "Honest, it will. Where exactly are you headed?"

"I'm going to live with my sister. She has a farm outside of Oregon City."

"Really!" Josh crowed, his face lighting with undisguised pleasure. "Why, that's the same area where the boys and I have bought our timber stand. Maybe we'll be neighbors."

"Maybe," Tess responded doubtfully, "but it's a very big area from what I hear."

"Yeah, I've heard that too, but still, we're bound to run into each other sometime."

"Who's going to run into whom?" came a deep voice from out of the darkness. Tess and Joshua both whirled around in startled surprise as Hunter stepped out of the heavy night shadows.

"Mrs. Caldwell and I were just discussing that since we're headed to the same place, we'll probably be seeing each other again," Josh explained, grinning.

"Have you also discussed the fact that you won't be driving her there?" Hunter asked rudely.

"Yes," Josh answered. "We were talking about seeing each other next spring."

"Good." Pulling a heavy gold watch out of his

pocket, Hunter made a great show of snapping it open and looking at the time. "Getting pretty late, Josh. Don't you think it's time to turn in? We're leaving at daybreak, remember."

"You're right," Josh nodded. "It *is* getting late." Turning back to Tess, he once again whipped his old hat off his head and executed a clumsy bow. "Mrs. Caldwell, it's been a pleasure. Until next spring, then."

Tess smiled graciously. "Yes, Mr. Bennington, until next spring."

With a last nod at Hunter, Joshua turned and walked off into the darkness.

As soon as he was out of earshot, Tess rounded on Hunter. "Well, you finally won, didn't you?"

"Won?" he asked, feigning innocence.

"Yes, won! You managed to block every opportunity I had to complete my trip, so now I have no choice but to stay here until next year."

Hunter dropped his cocky stance and took a step toward the furious woman. "Tess, please don't be angry. It's the best thing for you, you know it is." *And the best thing for me, too,* he added silently.

Tess studied his handsome face for a long moment, then exhaled a defeated breath. "Maybe you're right. Maybe it *is* the best thing."

Hunter smiled, the first genuine smile Tess had seen him display in a long time. "I'm glad you've finally seen reason." Reaching into his pocket, he lifted out a thick envelope. "Here," he said, extending it, "this is for you."

"What is it?"

"It's the balance of Joe's passage money. I figured I only got you a third of the way to where you were going, so I'm giving you back one hundred and fifty dollars."

"That's not necessary," Tess said, thrusting the envelope back at him.

"Don't be foolish," he argued, waving the envelope away. "You're letting your pride rule your head. You're going to have a baby to support and more passage money to pay in the spring. Keep it."

Tess looked at the envelope for a moment, loathe to take anything from the hateful man. But he was right. "All right," she nodded curtly. "Thank you."

A moment of silence ensued, then Hunter took a step toward her. "Tess . . ."

"I probably won't see you in the morning," she said quickly, taking a step back, "so I want to wish you God's speed. I hope the rest of your journey is successful and without incident." Inclining her head in a brief farewell, she turned away.

"Tess . . ." Without even realizing he was going to make a move, Hunter's arm shot out and caught the retreating woman around her non-existent waist. "For God's sake, wait!"

Whirling back toward him, Tess opened her mouth to admonish his scandalous behavior, but before she could say a word, she found herself wrapped in a crushing embrace. "Hunter . . ." she breathed as his mouth descended on hers.

Hunter's kiss this time was far different from their first embrace. Full of longing and unfulfilled passion, his lips feasted on hers, dragging a response from so deep within her that it was like drawing water from the bottom of a well.

His fingers wound into her freshly washed hair, releasing the silken mass from its confining pins until it tumbled down her back and over his arms. He groaned, burying his face in the fragrant softness and breathing deeply of her sweet scent. "Tess," he moaned, his lips tasting the soft skin of her temple and eyelids, "God, how I wish . . ."

"What?" Tess gasped, pulling away and staring up into his dark eyes. "What do you wish?"

"So much," Hunter muttered, "so many things." His lips again dropped to hers, coaxing and caressing until her silky tongue answered his silent call.

Their kiss went on endlessly, their mouths communing with a harmony that their personalities had never allowed them to share. Finally, Hunter stepped back, his fingertips brushing against her cheeks as he looked deep into her eyes. "Someday," he whispered, kissing her one last time, "someday, we'll meet again."

Then, suddenly, with the stealth and swiftness of a great hunting cat, he was gone, leaving Tess standing alone and bereft in the darkness.

Chapter 17

The brightness of the nearly full moon was a Godsend. As Tess threw her small satchel of clothing into the back of her wagon, the silvery sheen of moon glow on the prairie grass made it almost as easy to see as full daylight.

Thank God she'd gone out of her way to make friends with the mules, she thought as she led two of them over to the wagon. At least they hadn't kicked or bitten her. Although they were balky and stubborn in their reluctance to be taken away from their comfortable pasture, neither of them had laid back their ears or bared their teeth.

"Come on, Sue, come on, Patty," she clucked as she backed them into the traces. "Be good girls and stand still now." Slowly, she slipped the heavy leather collars over their necks, sucking in her breath nervously when Sue's eyes began to roll. "It's okay, girl," she soothed. "I'm not going to hurt you." To her relief the testy mule quieted, staring at her balefully as she began buckling the harnesses.

It took her almost a half hour to get the four mules

harnessed but, finally, she was ready. Standing back, she brushed her dirty hands together in satisfaction. "Not a bad job if I do say so myself," she murmured.

Gathering up her skirt, Tess hauled herself onto the wagon seat and picked up the heavy leather reins. She paused for a moment, turning around and taking a last look back at the fort. A needle of guilt pricked her as she thought about how upset Mary, Florette and Caroline were going to be when they found her gone. The women had been so kind, so good, so generous with their affection that she hated to hurt them. But, she had to get to Oregon. She simply *had* to.

With renewed resolve, she faced forward again, clucking softly to the mules. "Giddap," she coaxed. "Come on, Sally, come on, Bob, let's go."

To her astonished delight, the mules leaned into the traces and the wagon started to roll slowly down the lane leading away from the fort.

By God, I did it! Tess thought excitedly. "Harnessed them up and moved them out." Throwing back her head in sheer elation, she slapped the reins happily over the mules' backs, then nearly toppled backward off the seat when they suddenly surged forward.

"Whoa, babies, whoa," she called anxiously, pulling back on the reins. "Take it easy there."

Swallowing hard, she drew a deep, steadying breath, realizing that her exuberance could get her into very big trouble if she wasn't careful. "Settle down," she warned herself. "You've got a lot of catching up to do. You've come this far. Don't ruin it now by being too anxious."

For the next fifteen minutes, she drove slowly and cautiously, concentrating on the moonlit road. Finally, though, she could contain herself no longer. "I'm coming, Deborah," she cried happily, calling to her sister in Oregon as if she could hear her. "Despite them all, I'm coming!"

"Gerald! Gerald, come quickly!"

Mary Krenzke stood in the doorway of the store, a piece of paper clutched in her hand and a frantic look on her face.

"Mary, what is it?" Florette called, running across the grassy yard. "Has something happened? Have we been robbed?"

"No, we haven't been robbed," Mary sobbed, tears running down her weathered cheeks. "It's much worse than that! GERALD!"

At the sound of his wife's frenzied calls, Gerald Krenzke came tearing out of Major Sanderson's office. Racing across the compound, he skidded to a halt in front of his distraught wife. "What is it,?" he gasped, holding his hand over his chest to still his racing heart.

"It's Tess," Mary shrieked, waving the paper in his face, "she's gone!"

"Gone!" Gerald cried.

"Gone!" Florette echoed.

"Who's gone?" Caroline demanded, hurrying up to where the small knot of people were gathered.

"Tess. She's gone!"

"But, where did she go?" Florette cried, throwing her arms wide.

"To Oregon," Mary wailed, thrusting the note at Gerald and burying her face in her apron. "She's gone off to Oregon—by herself!"

"That's crazy," Gerald snorted, unfolding the crumpled piece of paper and reaching into his pocket for his spectacles.

"What does it say?" Caroline demanded.

"Well, just hold on a minute and I'll read it!" Looping his spectacles over his ears, Gerald shook out the paper.

Dear Mary,

I hope you'll understand what I have to tell you. After much thought, I have decided that I must join my sister this year and, so, I am continuing on to Oregon alone.

Please do not worry about me. I am well provisioned with food and water. Although I am sure Mr. Hunter will not allow me to rejoin the wagon train, I plan to follow closely behind so I won't get lost.

My thanks to you and your husband for your many kindnesses to me. I wish you much success with your store.

Kindest regards to the Brooks's and the Kubes's.

Sincerely,
Tess

"The girl is crazy," Gerald said, taking his spectacles off and shaking his head. "How does she think she can manage on her own?"

"Well, she can't!" Mary snapped. "That's all there is to it. We have to go after her."

"You're right. I'll see if Major Sanderson can spare a couple of men and we'll get started right away. She can't have gotten far."

"Now, wait a minute," Caroline interjected. "What good will it do to go after her? If she left once against everyone's advice, she'll probably just do it again, even if you do bring her back."

Gerald considered Caroline's words. "You know, Mary, Caroline may be right. If Mrs. Caldwell is so determined to get to Oregon that she'd take off in the middle of the night, we're probably not going to be able to stop her from setting out again."

Mary turned stricken eyes on her husband. "Oh, Gerald, surely you can't be considering not going after her. Why, she could die out there! She's alone, unprotected, and about to have a baby. How can you even think of not fetching her back?"

Gerald looked from Caroline back to his wife, his face a mask of indecision. "I just don't know . . ."

"I really don't think anything is going to happen to her," Florette offered. "Of course, I would prefer to see her back here where's we *know* she's safe, but Hunter isn't going to let anything happen to her."

Mary swung around to Florette, glaring at her angrily. "Hunter doesn't even know she's out there!"

"He will soon enough," Gerald said. "Dash McLaughlin will find her. He scouts behind the train, as well as in front."

Mary looked at Gerald in surprise. "He does?"

"Certainly, he does. He has to, in order to be sure there are no Indians or other brigands tracking the train. He'll find Mrs. Caldwell. In fact, he's probably already spotted her even as we speak."

"But, then what?" Mary railed. "Even if Mr. McLaughlin finds her, Hunter won't let her rejoin the train."

"Yes, he will," Caroline said positively. "He'll have no choice. Even Hunter isn't unfeeling enough to leave a solitary woman alone and defenseless. He'll either let Tess rejoin the train, or he'll bring her back here himself."

Mary looked around, unable to believe the conversation that was swirling around her. Could these people truly be contemplating not going after Tess? It was unthinkable! "Oh, I don't care what you all say," she barked. "Gerald, I want you to go after her,and if you don't then, by God, I will!"

Gerald's eyes widened at Mary's unprecedented ultimatum. Never, in all their many years of marriage, had he seen her so adamant about anything. "All right, my dear," he said resignedly, "if you really feel so strongly about it, I'll go. But, the more I think about it, the more I agree that it's a mistake. First of all, even if I can coerce Mrs. Caldwell into returning to the fort with me, she'll probably leave again at the first opportunity. And, secondly . . ." He paused, leaning close enough to Mary's ear that Florette and Caroline couldn't hear. "You have said all along that you think there's a spark between Tess and Hunter. Have you thought about the fact that maybe, just maybe, that attraction had something to do with her decision to follow him?"

Mary's eyes flared wide at this titillating thought. "Do you really think so?" she whispered back.

Gerald shrugged. "It's possible. And even if that thought wasn't uppermost in her mind, why don't we just let nature take its course? You were hoping a romance might blossom between them. Maybe this is fate's way of making that happen." He stepped back, wiggling his eyebrows meaningfully.

For a long moment, Mary stood and chewed on her lower lip, darting tortured glances between the three faces staring back at her. "But, what about the baby? Tess isn't going to have anyone with her when that baby is born."

"Yes, she will," Gerald responded confidently. "She'll have Hunter."

"Oh, what does he know about delivering a baby!"

Gerald cocked his head and threw Mary a penetrating look. "Probably nothing, but he's an intelligent man. He'll figure it out. You've said yourself, many times, that it's pretty much just common sense. Besides, if there's a problem, what could you do that he couldn't? Every birth is ultimately in God's hands."

Mary sighed heavily and turned to Florette and Caroline. "What do you think? Do you agree that we should just let well enough alone?"

Without hesitation, they both nodded.

"Oh, I don't know!" Mary wailed, shaking her head. "I just don't want anything to happen to Tess."

"Nothing will," Florette assured her. "I'll bet Hunter has her tucked under his wing already and we're all worrying for nothing. And like Gerald says, when Tess's time comes, there's nothing we could do for her that Hunter can't."

"Do you really think so?"

Florette nodded. "Absolutely. He'll take care of her. In fact, I wouldn't be at all surprised if we got a letter from Tess next spring telling us that she and Hunter are married. I've always thought there was a little something between those two."

Caroline snorted. "I don't know if I'd go so far as to say they'll get married, Florette, but I agree that there's something between them. In fact, I wouldn't be surprised if we find out someday that Hunter is actually that baby's father. And, if he is, then who better to deliver it?"

"Caroline!" Mary gasped. "How can you say such a thing? Why, you know perfectly well . . ."

"I don't know anything 'perfectly well'. All I know is what Tess wanted me to know and that doesn't necessarily . . ."

"Oh, Caroline, you're horrible! I can't believe that you'd even think something like that about dear, little . . ."

The heated conversation between the women faded away as they entered the store, slamming the door behind them.

With a sigh, Gerald walked down the store's front steps and headed back toward Major Sanderson's office, wondering how in the world he was ever going to put up with the three of them for the rest of his life.

Chapter 18

"Hey, Hunter, wait up!"

Hunter slowed his horse and swiveled around in the saddle, waiting for Dash to catch up. "What's going on?" he asked as his friend cantered up beside him.

"We've got company."

"What kind of company? Indians?"

"No, not Indians," Dash said, shaking his head. "But, I'm afraid when you hear who it is, you'll wish it was."

Hunter's eyes narrowed warily. "What in hell are you talking about?"

"It's your little widow," Dash explained. "She's following us."

Hunter's jaw dropped. "No! You mean Tess Caldwell?"

Dash chuckled. "She's the only little widow I know."

"She's following us?"

"That's what I said."

"Where?"

"About half a mile back."

"Is she alone?"

"Far as I can tell."

Hunter blew out a long breath. "Well, I'll be damned. You mean to tell me that she's out here in the middle of nowhere by herself?"

"Yup."

"Is she riding?"

Dash shook his head. "Nope. She's drivin' her wagon."

"*She's* driving? All by herself?"

Dash rolled his eyes impatiently. "Aren't you listening to me, Whitaker? I just said, Tess Caldwell is following the train about half a mile back. She's all alone and she's driving her wagon. You got it now?"

"Yeah, I've got it," Hunter nodded, "I just don't believe it."

"What part don't you believe?"

"That she'd be fool enough to think she can cross some of the driest, dustiest, most treacherous land in the country by herself in a wagon she doesn't know how to drive with a team of mules she doesn't know how to control when she's gonna have a baby any minute. That's what I don't believe!"

"Well, she is," Dash laughed. "Now, the question is, what are you gonna do about it?"

Hunter shook his head, wondering which god he had offended to give him such problems. "I don't know what I'm gonna do about it. Damn fool girl. She's gonna put me in my grave."

"If she doesn't put herself in hers, first," Dash added wryly.

"There's truth to that. Well, I guess the first thing I'm gonna do is go back and have a look myself."

"What's the matter? You still don't believe me?"

"Oh, I believe you all right. I'm at the point where

I guess I'd believe just about anything concerning Mrs. Tess Caldwell. I just want to see her for myself before I decide what to do about her."

Dash nodded and nudged his horse into a trot. "Straight back," he called over his shoulder. "You can't miss her."

"I'm sure I can't. Subtlety has never been her strong point."

Fifteen minutes later, Hunter sat on a rise overlooking the well beaten trail and stared down at the lone wagon. Sure enough, there she was, creaking and rattling her way along the south bank of the Platte. Even from this distant vantage point, he could see the sweat glistening on her face and the gnats buzzing around her face. She had to be miserable, travelling in the train's wake. It was close to ninety degrees and dusty as hell, yet here she was, forging along on her insane journey.

Hunter removed his hat, wiping the back of his sleeve across his own brow to remove some of the dust and sweat. God, it was hot!

Looking back at Tess, he saw her pull back on the reins, bringing the mules to a halt and climbing slowly down from the wagon. Once on the ground, she pressed her hands into the small of her back, then walked along the trail's edge for a few minutes, stretching her legs and arms. After looking around to make sure she was alone, she lifted her skirts high above her knees, standing with her feet apart as she tried to take advantage of the slight, cooling breeze.

Hunter shook his head, not sure whether he should admire her for her tenacity or curse her for being the stupidest woman God had ever created.

Squinting his eyes, he stared closely at the wagon.

Her water barrel was full. The mules were sound and appeared to be properly hitched. He wondered, briefly, if she had actually accomplished the complicated process herself or if someone back at the fort had done it for her. No, she must have hitched them herself, he decided. Certainly, no one at Fort Laramie would have been crazy enough to aid her in her ridiculous flight. His eyes dropped to the wagon's wheels. Although he'd heard them creaking more noisily than he would have liked when he'd ridden up, they all appeared to be in round and, at least from this distance, he couldn't see any signs of the metal tires coming loose.

He sat back in the saddle, satisfied with his long distance inspection. At least for now, she seemed to be all right and in little danger of a breakdown.

Several minutes passed before Tess crawled laboriously back up into the wagon and picked up the reins. Hunter watched her cluck to the mules, then set off down the road again. With a last snort of disgust, he reined his horse around and headed back to the wagon train.

"Well, did you find her?"

Hunter looked over at Dash who seemed to appear out of nowhere. "Yeah," he grunted, "I found her."

"What did she have to say for herself?"

"I didn't talk to her."

"You didn't? Why not?"

"Didn't see any reason to."

Dash gazed at Hunter in complete bewilderment. "Just what do you think is gonna happen here, Jared? Do you think she's just going to magically go away?"

"Yup."

Bewilderment turned to astonishment. "Are you crazy?"

Sighing in resignation, Hunter jerked his head in the direction of a small stand of trees. "Come over here where we don't have to yell. These wagons are creaking so damn loud that I can't hear a word you're saying."

With a nod, Dash joined him under the shady trees. "Nice under here," he commented.

"Yeah, it's a bitch out in that sun today."

"Only gonna get worse, buddy. You know that."

"Yeah, I do know that, and that's what I'm banking on to solve our problem."

Dash stared at him vacantly.

"Mrs. Caldwell, Dash. We're talking about Mrs. Caldwell."

"We are?"

"Yeah. Did you take a good look at her?"

"Not really. I just got close enough to identify who it was, then I hightailed it back here to report."

Hunter unscrewed his canteen and took a long swig of water, then dumped some over the top of his head. "Well, I *did* take a good look and she's hot. Real, real hot. So hot, in fact, that I think she's probably about ready to give it up and turn back."

Dash watched Hunter douse himself, then picked up his canteen and did the same. "You really think so?"

"Yup. In fact, I'd wager that the thought of that nice cool fort with those thick adobe walls is looking better and better to her every minute."

"So, you're not gonna do anything about her? You're just gonna wait and see if she goes back on her own?"

Hunter nodded. "That's the plan—for the time being, at least."

Dash frowned. "Jared, she's all alone back there!"

"We'll keep an eye on her. She's only half a mile behind us. In fact, she's close enough that I could tell she's eating our dirt. She took her sunbonnet off while I was watching her and her hair is white as snow from the alkali dust. Anyway, it doesn't take more than ten or fifteen minutes to get back to where she is. Once every couple of hours, one of us can ride back and check on her."

"What about at night?"

"That's not a problem, either. After I get the train settled down, I'll go back and camp out near her. She'll be okay."

Dash was still not convinced. "And what if she does turn around and head back? How are you going to know if she gets there?"

Hunter shrugged. "Guess I'll have to follow her."

"All the way back to the fort?"

"If I have to, I have to."

"Sounds like a whole lot of needless horsing around to me," Dash groused. "Why don't you just confront her and make her go back now? Save yourself some time."

"*Make* her go back?" Hunter scoffed. "Have you ever tried to make that woman do anything?"

"Well, no."

"If I rode up and demanded that she go back, she'd travel on all the way to Oregon for sure, just to spite me. Better that we try it this way first. I think, after a day or two of swallowing our dust, she'll realize she's made a mistake and go back all by herself. Besides, the only way we're gonna be sure that she stays there once she gets there is if she goes back on her own."

Dash nodded reluctantly, still not sure he agreed with Hunter, but unable to think of a better plan. Pulling out his pocket watch, he snapped it open.

"Okay, it's one thirty now. I'll go back around three, then you at five. By that time we should be camped for the night."

Hunter checked his timepiece too, then nodded in agreement. "Thanks, Dash. I appreciate the help."

"Oh, sure," Dash sighed. "You know me, Jared. Never could resist a lady in distress."

As usual, Hunter had underestimated Tess's iron will. Three days went by and still she followed the train—always staying a half mile or so behind, but doggedly keeping up her pace.

Late on the afternoon of the third day, Hunter and Dash stood together behind a small cluster of scraggly trees and watched her lumber by.

"I just don't believe her," Hunter fumed. "I would have sworn she would have given up by now."

Dash smiled. "You know, I can't help but admire her courage. It can't be easy for her, especially in her condition, and yet, she just keeps comin' on."

"Yeah, when I wake up, she's already up and hitching those mules. They're mean bastards, too. One of them tried to bite her this morning, but she didn't bat an eye. She just hauled off, gave him a smack and kept on buckling the harnesses, like she's been doing it all her life."

"Guess she's made of heartier stuff than you thought."

Hunter pressed his lips together hard to squelch the smile that unexplicably threatened. "Guess so."

"So, what now? It's obvious she's not going back to Laramie. When are you gonna admit that and let her rejoin the train?"

"Who said I was going to let her rejoin?"

"What else can you do?" Dash demanded. "You can't let her continue alone indefinitely."

"Well, I could," Hunter snapped, his voice testy, "but I guess I won't."

Dash frowned at him impatiently. "When, Jared?"

"Tomorrow. I'll come back tonight and camp here, then tomorrow morning I'll bring her in."

"Are you gonna stay here now? Looks to me like she's gettin' ready to make camp for the night."

"No, I've got some things to do and I want to get some supper. I'll come back later. She'll be okay here for a couple of hours. She's secluded by these trees, she has a good spot to build her fire, and there's plenty of grass for the mules. She'll be fine until I get back."

Dash nodded, then looked back at Tess who was just climbing down from the wagon. "Looks like she's got a backache," he noted, watching her press the heels of her hands against her spine.

"Yeah, she's been doing that for a couple of days now. It's got to be killing her back to sit up on that hard bench all day."

"Poor thing," Dash clucked sympathetically. "No woman in her condition should be doin' what she is."

"You're right," Hunter agreed. "I guess I'm gonna have to ask Matthew Bennington to start driving her again so she can spend the days resting on her cot."

"How soon do you think she's gonna have that baby?"

Hunter shrugged. "I don't know. She told me over a week ago that it could be anytime, but I sure as hell hope she waits until we get to Fort Cooper."

"Why? It's not much of a place. They just finished building it this spring and I heard there aren't even a hundred soldiers garrisoned there yet."

"Yeah, but maybe one of those hundred is a doctor. Anyway, anything's better than being on the road. At least at the fort, she could be inside a building. No matter how primitive the place is, it's a damn sight better than having a baby in the back of a wagon."

"I suppose you're right," Dash nodded. "Okay, then let's make it our goal to get to Fort Cooper as quick as we can."

Hunter nodded. "And pray a lot that it's quick enough."

Chapter 19

It was very late by the time Hunter was able to return to Tess's campsite. When he'd gotten back to the wagon train that afternoon, he'd discovered there had been an accident. One of the wagons had lost a wheel, causing it to hurtle down an embankment and tip over. Although no one had been seriously injured, it had taken several hours to right the wagon, pull it back up the embankment, and put a new wheel on.

Now, as he neared the spot where he'd left Tess, he looked up at the sky, judging by the position of the nearly full moon that it was close to midnight.

He rounded the bend where he had last seen her wagon, then drew in a sharp, angry breath when he saw it parked by the side of the road, the mules still harnessed and shifting restlessly in the confining traces.

Kicking his horse, he galloped over to the campsite. As he drew near, he noticed there was no campfire, nor was there a lantern lit. "What the hell," he gritted. "She went to bed without even unhitching the team? Damn her!"

Dismounting, he strode over to the back of the wagon, intending to give Tess a tongue lashing she'd never forget, but his steps were suddenly halted by an eerie, keening wail coming from within.

Reflexively, he pulled his gun, crouching down and slinking along the wagon's far side. As he moved stealthily down the vehicle's length, the moans from inside the wagon suddenly turned into high, piercing shrieks.

Lurching to his feet, Hunter swung around the back of the wagon, training his gun directly into the dark interior.

The sight within brought a gasp of shock. Quickly, he uncocked his piece and shoved it back into the holster, aghast at what he was seeing. There was Tess, lying on the cot, her arms circling her swollen stomach as she rolled back and forth in agony.

"Tess," he cried, leaping into the back of the wagon, "my God, what's wrong? Is it the baby?"

Tess opened pain-filled eyes and gazed up at him as if he were an apparition. "Hunter?" she croaked.

"Yes, it's me." Crouching down next to the bed, his eyes swept her sweat soaked form, settling on her distended stomach.

"Oh, Hunter, I hurt so much!" she groaned, reaching for his hand and clutching it in a death grip.

Instinctively, Hunter ran the back of his knuckles across her forehead, brushing back her wet hair in a soothing gesture. "How long has this been going on?"

"I don't know. Hours."

Again his eyes slid warily down to her stomach. "Are you having a pain now?"

"No."

"How close are they, Tess?"

She opened her mouth to answer, but her words were suddenly cut off as another contraction seized her. Squeezing Hunter's hand so hard that he was sure his knuckles were being crushed, she let out another scream.

With his free hand, Hunter pulled his watch out of his pocket, checking the time, then setting the timepiece down next to him.

Finally, the pain subsided. Tess loosened her grip on his hand and looked up at him. "I'm so hot," she panted.

"I know, it's like an oven in here." Leaning forward, Hunter unbuttoned the top two buttons of her bodice, then looked around for something with which to wipe her perspiring face. Spotting a pile of clothes stacked in a corner of the wagon, he leaned over and rummaged through it till he found a clean petticoat. Gently, he ran the soft cloth over her face.

Suddenly, the wagon rocked precariously, nearly pitching him over on top of Tess. With a muffled curse, he straightened. "Will you be okay if I leave for a minute?"

"Leave?" she asked weakly. "Are you going to leave me?"

"Just for a minute," he repeated. "I want to unhitch the mules."

"Do you have to?" Despite the weakness in her voice, Hunter could tell that she was afraid he might abandon her.

"It'll just take me a second, Tess. I'll be right back."

Turning, he jumped out of the wagon, racing up to the front and unhitching the team so quickly that he spooked them with his abrupt movements. Ignoring their rolling eyes and laid back ears, he led the double brace over to a grassy area and tethered them. That done, he raced back to the wagon, just in time to hear Tess let out another anguished moan.

He reached for his watch, then swore softly as he realized he'd left it inside. Raking his fingers through his hair, he threw back his head and stared at the starry sky. "Don't panic," he told himself fiercely. "You've got to stay calm. Now think. *Think*! What needs to be done?" He tried to remember everything he'd ever heard about the process of childbirth, but his knowledge of the subject was so limited that there wasn't much to recall. Suddenly, he snapped his fingers and muttered, "Water. Boil some water."

He had no idea whatsoever why he needed to boil water, but he'd always heard it had to be done. In a frenzy of haste, he began gathering up twigs and bits of other debris with which to build a fire. Once he had one going, he grabbed a large cooking pot off the side of the wagon and filled it from the water barrel, setting it carefully over the flame. All the while, he could hear Tess moaning, but feeling that it was important he make all the preparations he could think of for the birth, he responded to her calls only by rushing to the back of the wagon and shouting words of encouragement.

He knew he needed something to wrap the baby in once it came, but, what? For a moment, he looked around frantically, as if he might find his answer lying somewhere on the ground. Finally realizing how ludicrous his search was, he closed his eyes, focusing on what he could use for a blanket. The petticoat, of course! Hefting himself up on the horseshoe step he'd fashioned, he reached into the back of the wagon and grabbed it off the end of the cot. Next he pulled his knife out of his pocket and began slicing through the soft material till he was satisfied he had enough swaddling.

When the petticoat lay in shreds, he stood back and surveyed his handiwork. Everything appeared to be in order except that he needed something sterile to cut the cord with once the baby was born. Looking down at the knife he still held, he tossed it into the steaming kettle. "So, *that's* what the boiling water's for," he murmured with satisfaction.

He hurried back to the water barrel and poured a small amount into a bowl, thinking that maybe Tess would feel better if he bathed her off with some cool water.

Again, he entered the stifling confines of the wagon's interior and sat down next to the laboring woman. "How are you doing?" he asked quietly.

For a long moment, she lay perfectly still and didn't answer.

A shimmer of fear rippled through him. "Tess?" he said more loudly, reaching over and gently shaking her shoulder. "Are you okay?"

Slowly, her eyes opened. "Hunter? I thought you'd left me."

"No," he smiled, "I wouldn't leave you." Picking up one of the strips he'd ripped from her petticoat, he dipped it into the bowl of water. Squeezing it out, he ran it across her forehead and down her cheeks, dabbing some of the moisture against her parched lips.

"That tastes good," she croaked, running out her dry tongue to catch the drops. "I'm so thirsty."

"Do you want a drink of water?"

She shook her head. "It'll make me sick." Her last word ended on a shriek as another pain knifed through her. Hunter quickly picked up her hand, instinctively knowing that it helped the pain if she ground his knuckles together. This time, the pain seemed to last much longer and when Tess finally let out an exhausted sigh and lay back, he was afraid she had lost consciousness.

"It's so damn hot in here!" he cursed. Carefully, so as not to disturb her, he stepped outside, dragging in deep draughts of the fresh night air. "She'd be better off out here," he mumbled absently. He stared off in the distance for a moment, pondering this thought, then quickly climbed back into the wagon. Pulling a small feather tick down from the canvas wall, he hurried outside, spreading it on the grass. Then he dived back inside and retrieved a sheet, folding it around the makeshift pallet. Returning one last time to the airless, stuffy wagon, he knelt down beside Tess.

"Sweetheart, are you awake?"

She didn't move.

"Tess, I'm going to move you outside. It's much cooler out there and you'll be a lot more comfortable."

Tess opened glazed eyes and stared up at him dully. "I can't walk," she mumbled. "Please, don't make me walk."

"No," Hunter smiled, "this is one time I won't make you walk." Slipping his arms beneath her shoulders and knees, he lifted her off the cot and carried her outside, carefully setting her on the soft little bed. "There, now isn't that better?"

Tess opened her eyes again, looking around in confusion.

"You're outside," he supplied helpfully.

She wagged her head in what Hunter assumed was a nod, then again closed her eyes. Her respite was brief, however, as another pain grabbed her, sending her nearly upright as she jackknifed her legs and grabbed her stomach.

Hunter bit his lower lip, wishing fervently that there was something he could do to help her, but knowing there was nothing. Although he'd never witnessed the birth of a baby, he'd sat with mares during their labor and he knew that human or animal, the pain of childbirth was something that just had to be gotten through. The only remedy was time.

When Tess finally lay back down, panting and

exhausted, he grabbed his cloth and again dabbed at her lips. "You know," he said conversationally, "I think you've shown a lot of courage coming after us the way you did. Most women wouldn't have the guts to set out on their own like that. You really are determined to get to Oregon, aren't you?"

Tess nodded without opening her eyes.

"Does your sister have a big farm there?"

Another nod.

"And she and her husband work it?"

"You don't have to talk to me, Hunter," Tess muttered, her voice so soft that he had to lean forward to hear her. "Just please don't leave me."

"I'm not going to leave you," he assured her. "Don't worry about that anymore. I promise you, I won't leave." He felt her hand begin to tighten around his and knew that another pain was coming. This time as the contraction seared through her, he put his arm around her back and braced her until it subsided. "Did that help?" he asked hopefully.

"Yes." Slowly, she opened her eyes and tried to smile. "Thank you, Hunter."

"You're welcome." Hardly realizing what he was doing, he picked up her limp hand and kissed her knuckles. "If there's anything else I can do to make this easier for you, just let me know."

"Tell me your first name."

"What?"

"Your first name."

"It'll make you feel better to know my first name?"

Weakly, she nodded.

Hunter hesitated. Could he really tell her what she wanted to know? In all the many months since the war had ended, he'd never divulged his name to a living soul. Could he now trust his secret to a woman who had deceived him so many times in the past? For a long moment, he stared down into Tess's pain enshrouded face. "Jared," he said quietly. "My first name is Jared."

Somewhere, deep in Tess's mind, a bell went off. "Daulton Whitaker," she mumbled.

Hunter's jaw unhinged. "What did you say?"

"Daulton Whitaker. Jared Daulton Whitaker."

Hunter's heart leapt to his throat. *His name. She had said his full name. It had been so long since he had heard those three words spoken together that the sound of them made a chill run down his spine.* "You . . . you know who I am?"

"Jared Daulton Whitaker," Tess repeated for a third time.

"How do you know that, Tess?"

Before she could answer, another contraction built, crescendoed and finally subsided.

After resettling her in the pillows, Hunter checked his watch. The pains were coming every minute now. Surely the baby was about to be born, he thought desperately. After all, how much more could she take? "Come on, damn you," he silently railed, staring at Tess's stomach. "Get yourself out of there."

As if there had been no pause in the conversation, Tess suddenly said, "Joe told me."

Hunter's attention snapped back to her face. "Joe told you what?"

"That you're Jared Daulton Whitaker. He knew you—in the war."

Hunter picked up the damp cloth and absently unbuttoned two more buttons on Tess's bodice, drawing the cool material across her neck and the upper curves of her heavy breasts. There was no sense denying it any longer. "Yeah," he said quietly. "I know he did. He was in my company."

"You were his hero," Tess whispered.

Hunter squeezed his eyes shut, trying hard to block out those words. The last thing he wanted to hear was that anyone had ever thought of him as their hero. "He was a fine soldier, Tess." Glancing upward, he quickly begged forgiveness for his lie. He didn't remember Joe Chambers at all, but maybe telling Tess that he did and assuring her that her brother had been a brave soldier might bring her some little measure of comfort.

"I wish he'd known you thought so. He would have been so happy."

Hunter lowered his head, ashamed of himself that he'd never admitted to the kid who he really was. Why was it that you always wished you had done things after it was too late?

Several minutes passed by without another pain. Hunter sat quietly next to Tess, hardly moving for fear of disturbing her rest. The silence was so deep and pervading that when she suddenly spoke again, he jumped with surprise.

"May I call you Jared?"

He hesitated a moment, then said, "Sure, as long as we're alone. In fact, I'd like you to." He was surprised to realize that he meant his words. It had been so long since anyone except Dash had called him by his given name that it hardly seemed familiar anymore. But, somehow, the thought of Tess Caldwell calling him Jared pleased him.

His thoughtful reverie was suddenly interrupted by another sharp cry. Thinking that Tess was having another contraction, Hunter automatically reached behind her. His assistance was quickly rebuffed, however. She pushed his arm away and stared down at herself in horror. "I'm wet!" she gasped.

Looking down at her skirt, Hunter noticed that she was, indeed, soaked. "What is it?" he cried in alarm.

"It's the waters," Tess panted.

"Waters? What waters? Is this supposed to happen?"

"Yes. It's all right." Her voice trailed off, then rose again in a loud groan."

"What's wrong now?"

"I have to push!" Bracing herself up on her elbows, she bent her knees, then screwed up her face in an agonized grimace and pushed with all her might.

"Oh, my God, it's coming, isn't it?" Hunter cried. Quickly, he left his position at her side and knelt between her bent knees. Unconsciously, he pushed her heavy, wet skirt up until it was bunched around her waist and placed his palm flat against her enormous stomach, massaging gently.

He could feel the tightness of her contracting muscles beneath his palm, then felt them relax at the same moment as he heard her sigh of relief.

He continued to rub his hand against her abdomen and almost immediately, he felt the muscles tighten again. This time, when the pain ebbed away, he looked at Tess's face over the huge mound of her belly, accurately reading her look of embarrassment.

"It's okay," he said softly. "Trust me."

She said nothing but simply nodded, then closed her eyes, trying to rest a bit before the next pain seized her.

Their vigil continued for another hour. Tess became more and more exhausted, the strain of her labor causing deep violet circles to appear beneath her eyes. They said little, though once, between pains, she asked if he had everything he needed for when the baby actually came. Hunter briefly explained what he had prepared and she reminded him that they would also need string with which to tie off the cord. For a moment, he was at a loss, trying to think of what he could use for this. Then, suddenly, he had an inspiration. A corset string would be perfect.

He asked Tess where she stored her corsets, then, despite their circumstances, nearly laughed out loud when he saw the look of embarrassment that crossed her face as she explained which trunk they were in. He was still smiling as he hurried back to the wagon. Considering that they were in the midst of sharing one of life's most intimate experiences, the fact that he knew of the existence of corset strings hardly seemed worthy of Tess's scandalized blush.

When he returned, she was having yet another pain, only this time as he knelt between her legs and looked downward, the baby's head was clearly visible.

"Tess, the baby's coming! I can see its head. Come on, sweetheart, just a few more minutes and you'll be all done. Push now. *Push*!

Tess did as he bade, letting out a impressive bellow as she bore down again. Hunter cupped his hands at the opening to her body and suddenly found the baby's head cradled within them.

"Almost, Tess!" he shouted. "Come on, just one more push and it'll be here!"

Tess lay back a moment, then drew a deep breath, raised herself up and dug her elbows into the ground. With the last bit of strength she possessed, she pushed one more time.

Suddenly, Hunter's arms were full of a slippery, squalling, brand new bit of humanity. "It's a girl!" he crowed, tears coursing unashamedly down his cheeks. "It's a beautiful little girl!"

He grabbed a piece of linen, wrapping the baby in it and laying her on Tess's stomach. Reaching for his knife, he swallowed hard, saying a quick prayer that he was doing everything right, then cut through the cord and tied off the end closest to the baby's stomach with a bit of corset string.

"Look at her," he breathed, his voice choked with tears. Picking up the tiny bundle, he laid the baby gently in Tess's arms. "Isn't she wonderful? Oh, look, Tess. She's absolutely perfect."

Tess gazed up at Hunter, her eyes shining despite her exhaustion. "The sun's coming up," she remarked, her eyes drifting past his face to the eastern horizon.

"And it has a whole new life to shine down on today," he whispered. "Oh, God, Tess, she's so beautiful. You're both so beautiful . . ." Leaning down, he touched his lips gently to hers. "You did it, sweetheart," he murmured.

"No, Jared," Tess answered, her eyes closing wearily as she cradled her daughter close, "*I* didn't do it. *We* did it."

Chapter 20

Dash was worried. It was well past eight o'clock and Hunter and Tess still hadn't arrived. Hunter had told him the previous night that he would be back with Tess by sunrise, but that had been almost three hours ago and still there was no sign of them.

The wagon train had already moved out, plodding steadily along the barren, dusty track toward Fort Cooper. The night had passed without incident, except for Dash's discovery that one of the lumberjacks had picked up a prostitute at Fort Laramie and had kept her stowed in his wagon for the past four days. Dash had done little more than deliver a black eye to the devious traveller and promise him that Hunter would deal with him upon his return. If he ever returned . . .

For the tenth time that morning, Dash rode up to the top of the ridge in whose shadow they had camped and peered out at the endless horizon. Still no sign of a wagon, a horse, or even the telltale plume of dust that would herald a vehicle's approach.

"Damn it," he muttered, reining his horse around

and heading back toward the train. "Where the hell is he?"

Catching up with Jack Riley who was bringing up the train's rear, he yelled, "I'm gonna go look for Hunter. He should be back by now."

Jack nodded. "I'll keep 'em movin' here. D'ya think somethin's happened to the boss?"

"Naw," Dash said quickly, not wanting to alarm the other man, "but I want to check on him anyway—find out what the hold up is. You never know, the widow's wagon might have broken down and he may need another strong back to fix it."

Again Jack nodded, seemingly satisfied with Dash's hastily contrived excuse. "See ya' later," he shouted.

Dash touched the brim of his hat and turned away, his set smile quickly fading to a grim mask of concern as he galloped off back down the trail.

Half an hour later, he reached Tess's wagon. The eerily silent vehicle was standing exactly where he and Hunter had spotted it the day before, the mules tethered nearby, contentedly grazing. As Dash drew closer, he sucked in an alarmed breath. Hunter's big roan gelding was grazing with the mules, proof that he had returned here yesterday as planned. But, where was he now? There were no signs of life anywhere around the wagon and the only sounds to be heard were the whistling songs of mockingbirds and the droning buzz of cicadas.

Pulling his gun, Dash slipped off his horse and crept toward the wagon. "Hunter?" he called softly. "You here?"

He paused, waiting for an answer, but there was none.

Dash was becoming more apprehensive with each passing moment. Something was very wrong here. Fearful that he might be a target for some sort of ambush, he stood still and listened intently, his eyes darting in every direction, his gun at the ready.

Silence.

Again he took a wary step forward, moving along the wagon's near side. He paused when he reached the back of the vehicle, then with an arcing swing of his gun, he wheeled around the far side, crouching down in a marksman's stance.

His eyes widened in astonishment. He wasn't sure exactly what he had expected to see—a band of brigands, perhaps, with rifles trained at his head or, even worse, the dead bodies of his friend and the girl—but, certainly not this. Just a few feet in front of him lay Hunter and Tess, curled up together under a blanket—very much alive and very much asleep.

"What the hell," Dash cursed, his fear instantly turning to anger. "Hunter! Wake up!"

With a soldier's instincts, Hunter's eyes immediately snapped open and in one lithe movement, he gained his feet, his eyes scanning the area for some unseen foe. Instead, they settled on the face of a furious Dash McLaughlin.

"What in the hell is going on here?" Dash demanded, holstering his gun and crossing his arms in front of him.

"Shut up," Hunter hissed, looking down at the sleeping Tess. "You'll wake her and the baby."

"The baby!" Dash blurted, paying no heed to Hunter's command. "She had her baby?"

Hunter stepped over Tess and grabbed Dash by the arm, leading him over to the side of the road. "Yes, she had her baby. And it took all night too, so she needs some rest."

"Well, I'll be . . ." Dash breathed, his gaze swinging back to Tess. "Were you here when it was born?"

The deep lines of exhaustion beneath Hunter's

eyes disappeared as his face split in a reminiscent smile. "Yeah. I was here the whole time."

"What did she have?"

"A girl. A beautiful, perfect, little girl. Sarah Elizabeth."

Dash's eyebrows lifted with interest at Hunter's effusive response to his simple question. "Why Jared, you old scoundrel," he chuckled. "You sound as proud as if you were the papa. Are you thinkin' of takin' up that role?"

Hunter's smile immediately disappeared. "Don't be ridiculous," he snapped. "Of course not. I'm just happy it's over and everybody's okay." Wearily, he rubbed his eyes with the heels of his hands. "It was a long night."

"I'll bet," Dash commented wryly. "What time was the baby born?"

Despite his fatigue, another smile lit Hunter's face. "At the crack of dawn. I swear, Dash, the first rays of sun came over the horizon and that little girl appeared just in time to see it. It was really something."

Dash eyed his friend speculatively for a moment. It had been many a year since he had seen such a light in Hunter's eyes or heard such a happy, uplifted tone in his voice.

Who would have thought that the birth of a child who was no relation, born to a woman whom Hunter professed to dislike, would be the cause of such a transformation? Strange, how things sometimes worked out. "Can I see her?"

Hunter, who had been staring absently at the far off foothills, pulled his attention back with difficulty. "See who? Sarah?"

"Yes, Sarah," Dash chuckled. "I've seen Mrs. Caldwell before."

Hunter frowned doubtfully, too tired to appreciate Dash's quip. "I don't know, Dash. She's over there sleeping with her mama. I don't want to disturb them."

"I won't disturb them," Dash promised, heading back toward where Tess lay. "I just want to take a peek. I like babies."

"Be very quiet," Hunter warned, hurrying to catch up. "Tess needs her sleep."

Dash threw Hunter a jaundiced look. "I wasn't plannin' to beat a drum in her ear," he muttered.

Squatting down next to the prone woman, Hunter gently lifted a corner of the blanket, exposing the peacefully sleeping baby to Dash's view. Looking up at his friend, he grinned proudly, then carefully lowered the blanket again. "Isn't she beautiful?" he asked as they again walked away.

"Oh, I don't know," Dash teased. "She's kind of red and wrinkly, if you ask me."

"Of course she's red and wrinkly," Hunter bristled. "She's three hours old, for God's sake. Babies are all red and wrinkly the first few days. You just wait a couple of weeks, then you'll see what a little doll she is."

Dash could barely conceal his delighted grin. Tiny Sarah Elizabeth Caldwell might be only three hours old, but as far as Dash was concerned, she had already performed a miracle. She had done what neither time nor space nor forgetfulness had been able to. She had brought Jared Daulton Whitaker back to life.

"So, when are you gonna bring Tess and the baby back to the train?"

Dash and Hunter were sprawled out in the grass, sharing their fifth celebratory drink. At first, Hunter had declined Dash's usual offer of a glass of whiskey, but when Dash reminded him that every baby's birth deserved to be toasted, he had changed his mind. Now, lulled by whiskey and a languid sense of well being, the push to move on as quickly as possible didn't seem as important as it had the day before.

"I'm not sure yet," Hunter drawled. "I don't want to move her today. I just want her to sleep and get her strength back."Propping himself up on one elbow, he lazily plucked at a blade of grass. "She had a hard time, Dash. It went on for hours and hours and she was so tired . . . so weak. I honestly don't know how she did it. It just seems like there should be an easier way to bring a baby into the world than what Tess went through."

Dash threw back his head and laughed heartily. "Well, Colonel, you're going to have to talk to the Man upstairs about that, but I don't think he's gonna change things anytime soon. This method, good or bad, has seemed to work for a couple thousand years now."

Hunter grinned at Dash's foolishness. "I guess you're right. But it sure does seem like a tough way to get the job done."

Their sympathetic reverie was suddenly broken by a high pitched, angry squall coming from the direction of Tess's makeshift bed.

"I think Miss Sarah Elizabeth is awake," Dash commented, getting to his feet and swallowing the last of his whiskey.

"I think you're right. I wonder what she wants?"

"Probably her breakfast," Dash said dryly, "and since, at this point in her life, that's a rather personal event, I guess I'll be on my way."

Together, the men headed back over to Dash's horse. "So, you think you'll be startin' off tomorrow?"

"Yeah, if Tess feels well enough to travel. We shouldn't have any trouble catching up if you keep the train moving steady, but don't rush."

"Gotcha," Dash nodded, mounting. "Oh, by the way, we've got a new member in our little group."

Hunter looked at him in puzzlement. "Who?"

"Sam Waters picked up a fancy woman at Fort Laramie."

Hunter's face darkened. "And he's got her with him? How the hell did that happen?"

Dash shrugged. "How should I know? I'm the scout, remember? It's *my* job to keep track of the Indians and *your* job to keep track of the emigrants."

"Damn!" Hunter cursed. "All I need is some Skirt flaunting her wares around all those horny lumberjacks. She could cause real trouble, Dash. We've got to get rid of her as quick as we can."

"I know, but there's not much we can do until we reach Fort Cooper. I figured you could drop her off there. Until then, I've told Waters that he's to keep her in his wagon and out of sight. Actually, he didn't seem to have any problem with that idea."

Hunter sighed tiredly. "No, I suppose he didn't. Well, I'll just have to take care of it when I get back."

"Where do you want me to say you are if somebody asks?"

"I don't care. Tell them the truth if you want to. They're going to find out anyway as soon as Tess and I get back."

Dash nodded and gathered up his reins. "Hey, Jared, can I ask you somethin'?"

"Sure."

"What are you gonna do with the little widow? Leave her at Fort Cooper along with Sam's whore?"

"No," Hunter negated quickly. "That's no place for a woman of quality, and neither is Fort Bridger.

She's just gonna have to continue on with us until we reach someplace suitable. Fort Hall, maybe."

"You're still not planning on letting her go all the way to Oregon with us?"

Hunter hesitated a moment, not sure that even he knew the answer to that question anymore. There were so many reasons to drop Tess off somewhere. So many good reasons to do it . . . and only one not to. And that one was too preposterous to even consider. "No," he said suddenly, "she can't go all the way to Oregon with us. I definitely plan to leave her somewhere."

"I think she's proved herself to be quite the little trooper, "Dash said." Why not let her continue on?"

"Because I still don't believe she can make it on her own and I don't want the responsibility of having to watch over her," Hunter said fiercely. "We're going to have to drop her. I just haven't decided where yet."

"Well, maybe things will work out that you won't have to worry about it."

"Why? Do you think now that she has the baby, she'll make the decision to get off herself?"

Dash shook his head. "No, I don't think that at all. Now that she has the baby, I think she's going to be even more determined to join her sister. In fact, I'll bet she'd do just about anything to get to Oregon, including marrying Joshua Bennington." Quickly, he shot a covert glance at Hunter to see what his reaction would be to that statement. And when Hunter's mouth tightened just as Dash had expected it would, he could hardly quell his smile of satisfaction.

"You're nuts! She's not going to marry Bennington."

"I wouldn't count on that," Dash said blandly, running his reins idly through his fingers. "Bennington's been sweet on her from the beginning, even when he thought she was fat and forty. Now that she's had that baby, everyone on the train is gonna see how young and pretty she really is. If Joshua was interested in her before, he sure as hell is gonna be now."

"That doesn't mean they'll get married, for God's sake!"

Dash held up his hands in mock surrender. "Hey, take it easy! I'm just speculatin' here. You say you don't want the responsibility of watchin' over the lady and I'm tellin' you that I don't think you're going to have to worry about her much longer. Old Josh will probably be more than happy to take over that job for you. Hell, Jared, I thought you'd be *glad* to hear that you probably won't have to be fussin' with Mrs. Caldwell much longer."

Hunter's expression was as stormy as a June afternoon in Kansas. "Fine," he growled, "*Mrs. Caldwell* can marry anybody she wants, as soon as she wants. And you're right. I *will* be happy to have her out of my hair. God knows, she's already given me enough trouble to last a lifetime. Let somebody else deal with her and her foolishness for a change. Why, the woman can't even wash a load of clothes!"

"Sure, Jared," Dash said pleasantly. "That's just what I was sayin'. You don't want her, Joshua Bennington does, so everybody's happy, right?"

"Right!" Hunter snarled. "Now, you better get back to the train. I've got things to attend to here."

"Okay, boss, see you in a couple of days." With a farewell nod, Dash began to move off, then suddenly pulled back on the reins and turned around in his saddle. "You said to go ahead and tell anybody who asks that you're bringin' Mrs. Caldwell back. Do you want me to tell them about the baby too?"

"No!" Hunter barked, his voice far too loud. "I

mean, that's Tess's news. She should be the one to make the announcement."

"Can I at least tell them that she's going to have a surprise for everybody?" Dash needled.

"Don't say anything to anybody! And, especially, don't say a damn word to Joshua Bennington! Do you understand me?"

"Oh, yeah," Dash laughed, unable to conceal his glee a moment longer, "I understand everything. In fact, the whole situation is crystal clear!"

Chapter 21

It was very late that evening. Hunter was sitting on the ground next to Tess's pallet, drinking a last cup of coffee before retiring.

"Do you think you'll feel strong enough by tomorrow to travel a little bit?" he asked. Seeing the look of skepticism that crossed Tess's face, he quickly added, "Of course, I realize you're not up to sitting up or walking, but maybe we could get a few miles behind us with you resting on the cot."

Tess sighed inwardly. She was so tired and so sore, the last thing she wanted to do was be jounced around in the back of the wagon all day, but she also knew that if they didn't get started, they might never catch up with the rest of the train. "That'll be fine," she said, forcing a thin smile.

"You're sure?"

"Yes, of course. I know we need to get back to the train. You've already been over the next few miles. Is it terribly bumpy?"

"Not terribly. About the same as the last ten or so. But since we're crossing the driest area in the whole trip, it's important we don't linger here. There's almost no fresh water that's fit to drink, so we want to get past this stretch as fast as we can."

"I understand, and Sarah and I will be fine." Tess looked around, wrinkling her nose with distaste. "This really is a terrible place. That white dust that the wheels kick up is so thick it chokes you."

Hunter nodded. "Alkali. It poisons the water. In fact, I might as well warn you right now, you're going to be seeing a lot of carcasses for the next few days. Back in the early forties, the emigrants didn't know that the water holes were tainted. It killed a lot of people as well as hundreds of animals. Their bones are still out there and it's a pretty grisly sight."

"Their compatriots didn't even bury them?"

"They didn't dare take the time. They were too afraid that if they stopped to bury the dead, they'd meet the same fate since they didn't know how far they'd have to go to find pure water. They felt, and wisely so, that they had to keep moving."

"Do we have enough water?" Tess asked fearfully.

"Oh, yeah, plenty. Besides, I know which pools are safe. But, it's still a good idea to get through this area as fast as possible because sometimes the animals get so thirsty that they stampede toward a bad pool. If they do that, it's pretty hard to get them away from the water before some of them poison themselves with it."

Tess shuddered. "Then, by all means, let's get out of here tomorrow."

"We won't have to travel all day," Hunter said sympathetically, "but if we can put a few less miles between us and the others, I'll feel better."

Tess studied him for a moment, alarmed by his tense expression. "Is there something else you're worried about, Jared?"

Hunter blinked in surprise, still not accustomed to

hearing himself called by his true name. God, but it sounded good.

"No," he answered hastily, not wanting to scare her by telling her that a solitary wagon this far into Indian country was easy prey. "I just don't want to get too far behind. Three days travel is a lot to make up."

Tess nodded and they again lapsed into silence. Hunter finished his coffee, then rose to his knees and took the pot off the fire. "Want any more before I pour this out?"

"No, thanks," Tess answered, glancing down lovingly at the baby who had awakened and was beginning to fuss. It was time for her to be fed again.

"Jared, I wonder if you'd do me a favor?"

Hunter had heard the baby's tiny cries and guessed that Tess needed to feed her. "Sure," he answered, getting to his feet. "I'll just go over to the other side of the wagon for awhile. Maybe check on the mules."

"No," Tess murmured, ducking her head in embarrassment. "That's not what I meant."

Hunter looked at her quizzically. "Oh?"

"I have to . . ." Her voice trailed off as she tried to think of a delicate way to state her need for some privacy.

"There's a good patch of brush over there," Hunter said quickly, understanding what she was trying to tell him.

Tess nodded, her cheeks flaming. "I wonder, while I'm gone, if you'd consider holding Sarah?"

Hunter drew in a sharp breath. "Hold her? Can't you just lay her down somewhere for a minute?"

Tess's expression hardened at his rebuff. "Certainly. Never mind." Getting painfully to her feet, she carried the fussy baby over to the pallet and laid her gently down on the blankets. Then, without a backward glance, she headed off toward the brush Hunter had pointed out.

Hunter frowned as he watched her slowly make her way to the bushes, then his gaze swung back to the baby. Now that Sarah had lost the security of being in someone's arms, she started squalling in earnest, her tiny fists flailing angrily.

He grimaced with indecision, then walked over to where she lay. "Got quite a temper, don't you?" he asked, raising his voice to be heard over the baby's furious wails. "A good set of lungs, too," he added. For a long moment, he stared down at her, noting with concern that her tiny face was turning crimson. "Oh, all right," he relented, bending down and picking her up. "If it will make you feel better, I'll hold you."

To his complete astonishment, Sarah immediately quieted and looked up at him with somber eyes.

"Well, what do you know?" Hunter murmured, instinctively cuddling the baby closer and gently rocking from side to side. "That *is* all you wanted, isn't it?"

Sarah continued to stare up at him, her expression so earnest that Hunter couldn't help but smile.

Looking up, he saw Tess returning from the bushes. "She's looking at me," he laughed.

"I don't think she can see you, though," she answered, surprised and secretly pleased that Hunter was holding the baby after all.

"What do you mean? Of course, she can see me. It's not that dark."

Tess reached out and gently lifted the baby out of his arms. "That's not what I meant. Mary Krenzke told me that newborn babies are almost blind. They look like they're staring at you, but they're really not seeing anything but shadows."

"I don't believe that," Hunter bristled. "She was looking right at me—and she quit crying too, so you know she was interested in what she was seeing. Shadows wouldn't make her react like that."

"Okay," Tess smiled. "Whatever you say."

"By the way, she's wet."

Tess rubbed her hand along the baby's damp bottom. "She certainly is. If you wouldn't mind getting me another square of linen from the wagon, I'll change her."

Hunter nodded agreeably and disappeared to do her bidding. When he returned again, he said, "We're going to need more of these. We've almost used up all the ones I made out of your petticoat last night."

Tess laid the baby down on the tailgate of the wagon and began to remove her wet diaper. "I have a lot more in the small trunk."

"You do? Good, I'll get them."

Again, he disappeared into the interior of the wagon. Tess finished changing Sarah, then carried her over to the pallet, sitting down gingerly and unbuttoning her bodice. She searched around for something with which to cover her exposed breasts and was just reaching for the corner of the blanket when Hunter jumped out of the wagon, carrying a large pile of white cloth.

"Found 'em," he said, walking toward her. "I didn't bring all . . ." His words suddenly died in his throat as his eyes lit on Tess in her semi-nude state. She made a frantic grab for the blanket and he quickly turned away, but both of them knew he had seen her alabaster breasts.

"I'm sorry," he mumbled, keeping his face averted as he set down the diapers. "I didn't know you were . . ."

"It's my fault," Tess interrupted, her cheeks flooding with color. "I should have told you I was going to feed her now."

"I'll just wait on the other side of the wagon." He backed away so quickly that he nearly fell over the fire. "Call me when you're . . . done."

Tess nodded, keeping her head down so he wouldn't see her flaming face.

Hunter tore around to the other side of the wagon and leaned against it heavily. He closed his eyes, seeing again the madonna-like beauty of Tess with the baby suckling greedily at her breast. He knew he had never seen a more beautiful sight in his life and, for a fleeting moment, he considered sneaking around the back of the wagon so he could take another look.

"Stop it!" he ordered himself. "What kind of man are you, anyway?" Pushing away from the side of the wagon, he hurried over to where the stock was tethered, checking their water buckets, even though he'd just filled them an hour before.

Pull yourself together! You're acting like some green kid who's never seen a woman's breast before. After all, you saw a whole lot more than that last night.

But, even as he tried to comfort himself with that thought, Hunter knew that that situation had been entirely different. Somehow, last night, Tess had been just a body—a female animal struggling through the trial of childbirth. But, tonight, she was a woman—and the sight of her nursing her baby had again stirred the embers of emotion deep within him that he had thought long dead.

It wasn't the first time this woman had had that effect on him—and it scared him to death to think it also might not be the last.

* * *

Three days later, they caught up with the wagon train at Independence Rock. Because the travellers had reached the famous landmark right on schedule on the fourth of July, Dash decided to give them a day of rest, allowing them to celebrate the nation's seventy-fourth birthday by writing their names on the great stone "Record of the Desert", as well as giving Hunter an extra day to catch up.

The days that Hunter and Tess spent travelling alone together had been uneventful. Tess spent most of her time lying on her cot, cuddling Sarah and trying to keep the all pervasive dust and grit out of the baby's mouth and nose. The air was so bad that she and Hunter couldn't even talk, except late at night when the wind died down.

Hunter was very careful to keep his distance from Tess, making sure that whenever Sarah cried, signalling that she wanted to be fed, he made himself scarce. Neither of them had said anything about the embarrassing incident when he had seen her breasts and he was relieved that Tess was obviously as anxious to forget it as he was.

His budding affection for the baby continued to increase, and by the end of their third day together, he was as comfortable holding her and walking her when she fussed as her mother was.

The night before they rejoined the train, they camped by a small pool of fresh water. While Hunter settled the animals for the night, Tess took advantage of the solitude and clean water to give Sarah and herself a sponge bath. They ate a light supper, then, as had become their custom, settled down in front of the fire to share a cup of coffee.

"You know," Tess said, smiling over at Hunter who was holding the sleeping baby, "I don't know what I'm going to do without your help. You've been just wonderful these past few days and I just want you to know how much I appreciate your kindness. You've made everything a lot easier for me."

Hunter's heart slammed against his ribs at her tender words. It had been a very long time since anyone had told him that anything he did made a difference in their lives. Looking down at the baby lying so peacefully in his lap, he was hard pressed to choke back his emotions.

"I was glad I could help," he said, desperately trying to keep his voice impersonal, "but I am concerned about what you're going to do now that I have to go back to running the train."

Tess cast a covert glance at him from the corner of her eye, trying to determine if there was some hidden meaning behind his simple words. Was he, perhaps, trying to tell her that nothing had really changed between them? That once they rejoined the expedition, he would go back to ignoring her? Or worse yet, was he trying to allude to the fact that he didn't think she could make it alone and that he was again planning to leave her behind at the next frontier outpost they reached?

"I'll be fine," she said with far more assurance than she felt. "I know that you're going to be busy from now on, but I'm feeling stronger every day and I'm sure I'll be able to take care of Sarah on my own. Besides, it's not as if I don't have friends on the train. I really think that if I need help with something, someone will assist me."

Hunter's imagination immediately conjured up a vision of Joshua Bennington, sitting as he was now, holding Tess's baby and chatting intimately in the quiet of the late evening. "You can't count on that, Tess. Everybody is going to have all they can handle taking care of themselves for the next couple of months. We're really going to start climbing now—all the way up to South Pass. It's one of the hardest parts of the whole trip and there's not going to be anybody who has the time or energy to take care of you and Sarah."

Tess's mouth tightened angrily. Reaching over, she plucked Sarah off Hunter's lap. "I understand," she snapped, getting to her feet and marching off toward the wagon, "and you don't need to worry. I don't plan to be a burden to anybody."

Hunter cursed under his breath, furious with himself for ruining their last evening together. "That's not what I meant," he called, jumping to his feet and following her. "I know you don't *plan* to be a burden, but you have to face the fact that you can't make the rest of this trek on your own. You have Sarah to think of now. How are you planning to drive your wagon and take care of her, too?"

Tess whirled around, glaring at him in fury. "You don't have to remind me of my duty to my daughter," she spat. "I understand that I have to care for her. But, I thought . . ." She paused, swallowing hard as she realized that what she had taken for granted might not be possible if the man standing before her decided to prevent it.

"What?" Hunter demanded.

Lifting her chin, Tess looked him directly in the eye. "I thought that Matthew Bennington could maybe drive for me again."

"Matthew Bennington is a boy!" Hunter barked. "He doesn't have the skill to drive a wagon over the Rockies by himself."

"Well, then maybe Jeremy or Joshua could do it," Tess said desperately.

"Oh, of course," Hunter growled, his nostrils flaring angrily as jealousy coursed through him. "Joshua will do it. I'm sure you think that Joshua will do anything you ask him to, don't you?"

Tess gaped at him incredulously. "What are you talking about?"

"Don't you think I know that Joshua Bennington is in love with you? Why, every time he looks at you, he reminds me of a lovesick cow."

"You're being ridiculous," Tess snapped, settling Sarah into the temporary cradle Hunter had fashioned out of a small clothes basket. "Joshua Bennington has never been anything but polite, and he's certainly never shown any sign that he harbors any deeper feelings for me than just simple friendship. In fact, he's never made an advance of any kind."

"His kind never do," Hunter snorted. "He probably still won't, even after you marry him."

"Marry him!" Tess gasped. "Who said anything about Joshua Bennington and me getting married! I assure you, he hasn't asked me and if he did . . ."

Before she could finish the sentence, Hunter took hold of her shoulders to prevent her from walking away from him.

"What would you say?" he demanded. "If Joshua Bennington asked you to marry him, what would you say?"

"That's none of your business!" Tess cried.

"I've told you before," Hunter snarled, holding her so close that she could feel his warm breath on her face, "as long as you're on my train, everything you do is my business."

Tess opened her mouth to deliver a stinging retort to this high handed declaration, but no words came out. Instead, their eyes locked, and before either of them could stop themselves, they came together in a searing kiss, their mouths melding in a frenzy of need and frustration.

Hunter's tongue plundered the sweet interior of Tess's mouth with the passion of a starving man at a banquet, tasting each sweet crevice of the warm, soft cavern.

His hands were everywhere, tangling in her luxurious hair, then dropping lower to run down the length of her back and bracket her newly discovered waist. Bringing his hands around, he pressed his palms against her ribs, then swept his fingers upward to cup the fullness of her breasts.

It was the explosion of desire deep within his loins that finally brought him to his senses. Wrenching away from her, he took a stumbling step backward. "I'm sorry," he panted, clapping his hand over his eyes as he sought to gain control over his raging emotions. "My God, you've just had a baby . . . I shouldn't have . . ." Wheeling around, he took several lurching steps away from Tess, gulping in the cool, calming air. It took nearly a minute before he finally felt he was again in control. "Please forgive me," he said softly. "I promise you, it won't happen again."

Tess walked slowly over to him, laying her hand lightly on his arm. "It was just a kiss," she murmured. "We've been through a lot together in the past few days. I don't think there's anything wrong with us sharing a kiss."

Hunter nodded gratefully but he took another step backward, effectively breaking her gentle hold on his arm. "I'm sorry for what I said about Joshua Bennington. You're right. What you choose to do with your life is none of my business."

Turning away, he walked over to where his bedroll lay, picking it up and moving it to the far side of the campfire.

With a sigh, Tess picked up Sarah's basket and walked over to her own pallet, setting the baby down and crawling beneath the light blanket. For a long while, she lay staring at the stars.

A silent chuckle suddenly shook her. So, Jared thought she was going to marry Joshua Bennington, did he? Turning her head, she gazed over at his stiff figure. "Not likely, Colonel Whitaker," she whispered, "unless he can kiss as well as you do."

Chapter 22

"Lord above, am I glad you're back!" Galloping up to Tess's wagon, Jack Riley flashed his nearly toothless grin at Hunter. "See you got here jus' in time for supper. You never been late for a meal in yur life, have ya, boss?"

Hunter shook his head. "Hey, Jack, how are things?"

"Well, I'll tell ya, Hunter, things've pretty much gone to hell since you been gone. Why, it's a wonder there's a man jack alive on the whole damn train the way they all been fightin' over that whore and. . . . what's that?"

Jack cocked his head, listening intently to the tiny mewling sound coming from the back of the wagon. "You pick up a kitten somewhere?"

"No," Hunter said mysteriously, "I didn't pick up a kitten." Winding the reins around the brake handle, he turned around and looked into the back of the wagon. "We're here. Why don't you come and show Jack your surprise?"

"Surprise?" Jack asked, edging his horse closer

to the wagon. "What surprise? Who's got a surprise?"

"Mrs. Caldwell has a surprise," Hunter answered, jumping down.

"Did *she* pick up a kitten?"

Hunter shook his head. "Much better than that."

Tess emerged from the back of the wagon and placed Sarah into Hunter's waiting arms.

Jack's squinty old eyes rounded into saucers. "Well, lookee here," he cried, climbing down from his horse as fast as his arthritic old legs would allow. "Looks to me like somebody done had herself a baby!"

"Jack Riley," Hunter said formally, "meet Miss Sarah Elizabeth Caldwell."

Jack stood on his tiptoes and grinned down at the baby. "It's a real pleasure to make your acquaintance, Miss Sarah Elizabeth," he chortled. Looking back up at Hunter, he added slyly, "So, that's where y'all have been all this time. No wonder it took ya so long to get back here. Had to stop along the way and take care of a little business, huh?"

"Yes," Hunter said, handing Sarah to Jack so that he could help Tess out of the wagon, "we did, indeed."

Jack beamed down at the tiny child, enthusiastically bouncing her up and down in his arms. "And, you, missy," he said, turning a questioning eye on Tess, "how did you manage to keep this little bundle a secret all this time?"

"It wasn't easy," Tess smiled, reaching out and taking the baby out of his arms, "especially toward the end."

Jack's eyes dropped to Tess's newly slender waist. "Woowee, you sure do look different all of a sudden. Lost a little weight this week, ain't ya?"

"A little weight and a lot of padding," Tess confessed, sending the old man into a fit of laughter.

"You sure did have us all hornswoggled. Why, even Hunter here, talked about how fat you was."

Hunter threw Jack a killing look, but Tess just laughed. "Mr. Hunter was right, Mr. Riley. I *was* fat. And what Sarah didn't do for me, five petticoats did."

"But, why did ya want to keep the baby a secret?" Jack asked. "There's no shame in a widow lady bein' in the family way."

Tess ducked her head, a bit nonplussed by the old man's frank question.

"She had her reasons," Hunter said evasively. "Now, Jack, suppose you tell me about what's been going on here."

Tess threw Hunter a grateful look which he answered with a conspiratorial wink. "I'll be back in an hour or so," he called as he and Jack ambled off.

"Fine. I'll get supper started."

"Don't overdo," Hunter warned. "I'm not particular. Anything will be fine."

Jack looked at Hunter incredulously. "Since when?" he demanded. "Last I heard, nothin' that little gal cooked was good enough, now anything will do? Boy, somethin' sure must've changed while you was gone."

Hunter smiled, but didn't respond. A lot of things had changed while he was gone, but that was between him and Tess. It certainly wasn't anything he was going to share with the nosy Jack Riley.

"So, what were you saying about a problem with this woman Sam Waters has been hiding?"

"Oh, yeah," Jack nodded, forgetting Tess. "You wouldn't believe the problems Dash has been havin'. I tell ya, Hunter, it has been one hell of a mess. Ya see, Sam Waters has this whore that he picked up in Laramie."

"I know about that. Dash told me."

"Well, this here fancy woman—Rona Rose is her name . . ."

"Rona Rose?" Hunter blurted, disbelief evident in his voice.

"Yeah, Rona Rose. What's so funny about that? Well, anyway, she was hidin' in Sam's wagon for the first few days and ev'rything was fine. But, Dash found her when she was out in the bushes doin' her private stuff and then ev'rybody found out 'bout her and it's been hell ever since."

"Why? Is she hawking her wares with the other men?"

"No, she ain't really done nothin' wrong a'tall. She just stayed in Sam's wagon where she belonged, but the men, well, they keep goin' up to the wagon and tryin' to make a deal with her for a little lovin'. Sam didn't take too kindly to that since he figures she's his woman now."

"No, I imagine he didn't."

"Anyway, night before last, a bunch of the boys went over there while Sam was playin' poker and tried to force the lady to come out and dance with 'em. She told 'em she couldn't, but they kept insistin'. Then, suddenly, Sam came back to get some more gamblin' money and that's when all hell broke loose. Quicker'n you could blink an eye, ev'rybody was swingin' and punchin' and fightin'. You know how it goes when boys are horny and then they get liquored up . . .

Hunter sighed. "Yeah, I know how it goes."

"Dash and me and those three Bennington boys tried to break it up, but we wasn't much of a match for all them drunk 'jacks."

"So, what happened? Was anybody hurt?"

"Naw, nothin' serious. One of 'em landed a hell of a gut punch on poor Dash, though, and he hit the dirt pretty hard, but while he was down there, he got his pistol out and fired a few rounds in the air. That seemed to calm ev'rybody down some."

As Jack paused to take a breath, Hunter shook his head, fighting back an urge to find Sam Waters and throttle the life out of him.

The thought of bandy-legged little Jack Riley and the three taciturn Bennington brothers taking on fifty or so drunken lumberjacks was nothing short of insane, yet Hunter couldn't help but be grateful that at least someone had tried to restore order.

"How do things stand now?"

"Well, Dash, he called the whole group together yesterday mornin' and told 'em that anybody that caused any more problems was gonna be thrown off the train—said he'd personally chain 'em to their wagon wheel and leave 'em behind to fry in the sun."

"And, did they believe him?"

"Guess so, 'cause there ain't been no more trouble."

"What about the girl?"

"What girl?"

Hunter clucked his tongue impatiently. "Rona Rose, or whatever Sam's tart's name is."

"Oh, she's still in his wagon. She ain't come out once since all the hullabaloo started."

"Well, she won't be a problem much longer," Hunter gritted. "We'll drop her at Fort Cooper."

"I don't know, boss, old Sam's taken a real shine to her. He's tellin' ev'rybody who'll listen that he's gonna marry her first chance he gets."

"Not if he wants to stay on my train, he isn't."

Jack looked over at Hunter skeptically. "You'd really throw him off?"

"Damn right. I'm not putting up with that kind of trouble. This is a man's train only. They all know that. Hell, they all signed a paper, agreeing to that, including Waters. Now, if he wants to stay at Fort Cooper with his fancy woman, that's his business, but she's not going all the way to Oregon with us, and that's the end of it."

"But, boss, if this is only a man's train, then how do you explain Miz Caldwell?"

Hunter turned to Jack, his gaze chilly. "That's different."

"How so?"

Hunter's glare became even blacker. "She works for me. Besides, she'll be getting off pretty soon too. Probably at Fort Hall."

"So, you're gonna dump her again, are ya? What makes ya think she won't just come taggin' along behind, like she did last time you tried to get rid of her?"

Hunter's stormy eyes narrowed ominously. "You know what, old man? You ask too many questions."

Jack shrugged, not intimidated in the least by Hunter's sudden surliness. "Maybe, but if ya don't ask questions, how'll ya ever find out anything? Besides, I think Joshua Bennington wants to marry Miz Caldwell, and if he does that, you gotta let her stay on or throw him and his brothers off too. Why, at the rate you're talkin' about dumpin' folks, by the time we get to Oregon, there won't be nobody left 'cept you, me, and Dash."

Hunter clenched his fists at his sides, admonishing himself to hold on to his quickly unraveling temper. "Where is Waters's wagon?" he snarled. "I'm going to go down and have a few words with him."

" 'Bout Miz Rose?"

"Yes, about Miss Rose."

"We already passed it," Jack announced, turning and pointing back down the line. "It's about ten rigs back." Suddenly, he squinted his eyes and cupped his hand to his forehead. "That's funny."

"What?"

"Looks like Miz Rose finally come out."

"What?" Hunter barked, pivoting on his heel and scanning the line of wagons. "You mean she's outside?"

"Yup. Sure is. But, she's not at Sam's wagon, she's at yours."

"Mine!"

"Well, Miz Caldwell's, I mean. And it looks to me like they're makin' friends. Who knows, maybe she likes babies, or maybe she just seen there was another woman on the train now and decided to . . ."

Before Jack finished his sentence, Hunter was gone.

"You can just call me Rona, honey. No need to stand on ceremony. What's your name?"

"Tess. Tess Caldwell."

Rona Rose looked at Tess intently. "Tess. That's a pretty name. You know, you look real familiar to me. Have we met somewhere before?"

"I don't know how we could have," Tess answered, a wave of unease washing over her. "I'm from the East. I've never been west before." Quickly, she turned away, pretending to be absorbed with adjusting the baby's blanket.

Shooting a covert look back at the other woman, Tess found her still staring at her curiously. Not wanting Rona to think that she was uncomfortable under her close scrutiny, Tess forced herself to smile.

Rona was a striking woman with black hair, emerald green eyes and a wide mouth that was painted brilliant red. She was tall and slender, with big breasts that Tess thought looked like they might spill out of her partially unbuttoned bodice at any moment.

As Tess took a closer look at her, a warning bell went off. Rona *did* look slightly familiar. Dear God,

Tess thought dismally, wouldn't it be just my luck to be out here a million miles from nowhere and have someone recognize me.

Leaning over, she scooped up the baby who had begun to cry, then turned back to Rona. The other woman was shaking her head as if she was trying to remember something that just wouldn't quite come to her.

"So," Tess said, careful to keep her voice light and impersonal, "did you join the train at Fort Laramie?"

"Yeah. I'm with Sam Waters."

"Sam Waters," Tess mused. "Is he a member of the expedition?"

Rona nodded. "He's one of the 'jacks."

"I see."

Rona looked at Tess quizzically. "I heard you been on the train ever since Missouri."

"That's right."

"And you still don't know Sam?"

Tess shook her head. "No. I'm afraid I don't know very many of the men."

Rona smiled a bit sadly. "And I'm afraid I've known far too many."

Tess blushed as she grasped what the woman was alluding to. One only had to look at Miss Rose to guess her profession—the gaping bodice, heavy lip rouge and smears of kohl around her eyes were dead giveaways. "Are you travelling all the way to Oregon?" Tess asked, wanting to change the subject.

"That's my plan, although you never know. If Sam gets tired of me, or if that devil man wagon master everybody keeps talkin' about decides he don't like me, I could find myself sittin' on my suitcase by the side of the trail somewhere."

"Devil man wagon master!" Tess blurted. "Do you mean Mr. Hunter?"

Rona shrugged. "I guess that's his name. Is he that

dark brute of a man I saw you ride in with a while ago?''

"Well, yes," Tess stammered. "But he's certainly not a brute . . ."

Rona waved a dismissing hand. "Sorry. I didn't mean to offend you. I heard you tell him you'd start supper. You and he ain't married, are ya?"

"No! I . . . I just work for him."

"Oh?" Rona's eyebrows rose with interest.

"Cooking and doing his laundry," Tess added quickly. "Things like that."

Rona nodded. "Tough bein' a workin' girl, ain't it? So, where's your husband, sweetie?"

"I'm a widow."

"That's a shame. He died makin' the trip, huh? What was it? Cholera?"

Tess shook her head, rocking Sarah who refused to be comforted and was now squalling lustily. "My husband passed away last winter. I was making the trip with my brother, but he . . . he met with a fatal accident before we reached Fort Laramie."

Rona clucked her tongue sympathetically. "You've had your share of bad luck, ain't you, honey? Where'd ya say you was from back east?"

"Boston."

"Boston," Rona mused, again studying Tess intently. "I used to live in Boston too—for awhile, anyway. You sure we never met?"

"Yes, I'm sure," Tess insisted. "I better get supper started now."

"Don't worry 'bout it," Rona smiled. "Looks to me like you've got your hands full there with your baby."

Tess looked down at the screaming infant and nodded helplessly.

"Tell you what. Why don't I gather up some chips and start a fire for you?"

"Oh, would you?" Tess asked gratefully. "Sarah's so fussy today, I can't imagine what's wrong with her. I've fed her and changed her, but she's still cranky."

"She's probably hot," Rona ventured. "Why don't you take that blanket off her? I bet she'd feel better. This heat is enough ta make anybody cry."

Tess looked at Rona incredulously. Did this strange woman actually know something about babies? If she did, it could be a Godsend. "Do you have children?" Tess called as Rona sashayed away to look for buffalo chips.

"Lord, no, that'd be all I'd need. I had nine younger brothers and sisters, though. When you're the oldest of a tribe like that and you've got a sick ma and a worthless drunk for a pa, you gotta help. I figure I raised kids for 'bout fifteen years. You're bound ta pick up some tricks along the way to keep 'em quiet, otherwise you'd go insane."

Tess's eyes widened with astonishment. This woman, who didn't look to be much older than she was, had raised nine children? Impulsively, she lay Sarah down and removed the heavy blanket, leaving her covered by only her diaper and a light linen sack. To her delight, the baby immediately quieted, kicking her arms and legs happily as the cooling evening air filtered through the soft cotton.

"Better now, ain't she?" Rona smiled, returning with a small bucket filled with chips.

"Yes, she is," Tess nodded. "Thanks so much for the advice."

"Sure. Anytime. Believe me, if there's two things I know about, it's men and babies. And, speakin' of men, what d'ya want to feed yours tonight? I'll get it started for you, then I'll go rustle up somethin' for me and Sam."

"He's not 'mine'," Tess protested quickly. "He's just my employer."

"Sure, honey, whatever you say. By the way, what did ya say your last name was again?"

"Caldwell," Tess answered, her heart in her throat.

"Caldwell . . . Caldwell. The name's kinda familiar and so are you, but I just can't put my finger on where I've met you before. Musta been in Boston, 'though I can't imagine that you and me was in the same social circles." Rona laughed heartily, her ebony hair streaming down her back as she threw her head back in good natured mirth.

"Miss Rose?"

Rona's raucous amusement came to an abrupt halt as Hunter's voice sliced through the evening air. Spinning around, she found herself nearly toe to toe with the imposing man. "Well, actually, the name is Rosenbaum, but that's too hard to remember, so Rose will do."

"I want to talk to you."

Tess shot a bewildered look at Hunter, unable to imagine what was causing his obvious ill humor. "Oh, Mr. Hunter," she bubbled, hurrying over to where he and Rona stood, taking each other's measure. "Miss Rose has been such a help. She gave me some advice about Sarah that stopped her crying. She knows all about babies since she helped raise her nine brothers and sisters. And besides that, she gathered . . ."

"Miss Rose, I want to talk to you . . . Now!" Hunter barked, rudely cutting into Tess's effusive babbling.

Rona cocked her hip and looked up into Hunter's face unflinchingly. "Why, you're just as friendly as everybody said," she purred sarcastically. "C'mon, then, let's go have us a talk." Turning back to Tess, she forced a smile, but Tess could tell that she was nervous. "See ya tomorrow, honey. Maybe by then, I'll remember where we met."

Tess nodded weakly, saying a silent prayer that

Rona's memory would continue to fail her. "Thanks again for all your help."

"You bet." Swinging her gaze back to Hunter, Rona crooked her finger enticingly. "Well, come on, Mr. Trail Boss, let's get this over with."

Tess noticed a muscle jumping in Hunter's cheek, further indicating the depth of his anger. Looking at his tense, set face, she didn't envy Rona the next few minutes in his company. "Supper will be ready in just a little bit," she called lamely.

"Good," he growled, taking Rona's arm and leading her off into the darkness. "This won't take long."

Rona turned around and threw Tess a naughty wink. "But, if we're gone more than ten minutes, don't come lookin' for us, 'cause we'll most likely be occupied. I promise I'll send him back in one piece, though, so keep his supper warm."

Chapter 23

"Okay, lady, just so you know, you're off this train as soon as we get to Fort Cooper. Until then, I don't want to see you out of Sam Waters's wagon. Is that clear?"

Rona Rose looked up into Hunter's dark eyes, wondering if there was any trick in her deep bag of feminine wiles that would make him change his mind. Unfortunately, she didn't think so.

She'd heard tales about the enigmatic Hunter—the man with no first name, no friends, no home, and no past—and the cold, emotionless giant she was facing now bore out every grim story she'd been told.

"Oh, come on," she wheedled, placing her hand on Hunter's broad chest. "What dif'rence does it make if I stay on the train all the way to Oregon, long as I hide out in Sam's wagon?"

"It's a Men Only train, for starters," Hunter growled.

"That ain't true! You have Mrs. Caldwell with you, and . . . She paused, her eyes suddenly widening with excitement. "*Mrs.* Caldwell . . . Tess Caldwell! Of course! Now, I remember!"

"What are you babbling about?" Hunter demanded, swiping her hand away from his chest with an irritated swat.

"Tess Caldwell. I knew I'd met her someplace. Now, I finally remember!" Rona started to laugh, her pretty but careworn face lighting in genuine amusement. "My, my, how the mighty have fallen."

"What in hell are you talking about?" Hunter repeated. "Are you saying that you know Mrs. Caldwell from somewhere?" *My God, where would Tess have ever met this soiled dove?*

"Indeed I do," Rona said slyly. "And . . . I might be willin' to tell you where from if you let me stay on the train."

Hunter snorted. "No deal, lady. It doesn't make any difference to me where Mrs. Caldwell is from." *Like hell, it doesn't.*

Rona considered Hunter for a moment. The years spent pursuing her unsavory vocation had made her an excellent judge of character and, despite Hunter's attempts to keep his face impassive, Rona knew he was actually extremely curious to find out what she knew. With a smug smile, she reached up and stroked his lean cheek. "You're lyin', Mr. Trail Boss. You'd just *love* to know what I know 'bout your servant girl, now wouldn't you?"

Hunter's brow lowered threateningly. "Not unless it has some effect on me or this expedition." It was a bald faced lie and he knew it, but he was damned if he'd let this conniving whore know how curious he really was.

"Well," Rona drawled, "would the fact that one of the richest families in Boston has an army of detectives lookin' for her int'rest you?"

"What?" Hunter gasped, losing his battle with feigning disinterest.

Rona giggled delightedly. "You really *don't* know

who she is, do you? You prob'ly think she's just some no account emigrant woman who didn't have the money to pay her passage west, so she took a job with you ta earn it. Ain't that 'bout right?"

Hunter swallowed his astonishment at Rona's astute guess. "Look, I don't care who you think Mrs. Caldwell is. As far as I'm concerned, she's exactly who she says she is—a widow from Boston who's travelling west to join her sister in the Willamette Valley."

"I'm sure that's true," Rona nodded, "as far as it goes. But, there's more to the story, Mr. No First Name Hunter. Much, much more. And the 'more' is the real interestin' part, believe me."

"Well, it's of no interest to me," Hunter lied, turning away to signal that the conversation was over.

"Maybe not, but I bet it would be to plenty of the men on this train who'd like to collect the reward."

Hunter spun back around. "What reward?"

"Ten thousand dollars for information leadin' to Mrs. Caldwell's whereabouts." Idly, Rona reached down and smoothed out the wrinkles in her garish skirt. "And I'll wager I could find a man or two hereabouts who'd be more than happy ta split it with me if I tell him what I know. Of course," she mused, "I *could* just tell Sam. He's wantin' ta marry me, and if he collected the reward on Mrs. Caldwell, that money would give us a real nice start in Oregon."

"Are you trying to blackmail me?" Hunter snarled.

"Blackmail?" Rona gasped dramatically. "Certainly not. I'm willin' to give you the information for nothin'. You don't even have ta split the reward with me, that's how generous I'm feelin'. Just let me stay on the train and quit givin' me a hard time."

Hunter hesitated a moment, loathe to give in to the wily woman's underhanded demands. But, if he didn't, he had no doubt that she would do exactly as she threatened and sell her information to someone else. No telling what jeopardy that might put Tess in. Hunter blew out a long, frustrated breath, knowing he'd been bested. "Okay, I'll agree to let you stay on with the train on one condition."

"I'm listenin'," Rona smiled sweetly.

"You tell me and no one else what you know. Not Sam, not anybody. I find out you've talked and I'll drop you off by the side of the trail and let you starve or freeze or get eaten by wolves. And, don't think I won't do it, because what happens to you is of no consequence to me. You double cross me and you're off the train, no matter where we are. Understand?"

"My, my, ain't we protective of our hired help, though," Rona singsonged. "Sounds to me like you might be just a little bit sweet on the lady."

Hunter glared at her menacingly, furious that he was obviously being so transparent. "My feelings toward the 'lady' are none of your business."

"You're right," she retorted flippantly, "they ain't. Okay, Mr. Trail Boss, you got yourself a deal. But, I don't want no guff from you for the rest of the trip. You leave me alone, I'll leave you alone. Understand?"

Hunter nodded reluctantly. "Just stay out of sight," he warned. "I won't tolerate the men fighting over you."

"Oh, Mr. Hunter," Rona sighed, "men have been fightin' over me since I was fifteen years old. I ain't never found a way yet to stop it."

"Staying in your wagon and minding your own business is a start."

Rona shrugged elaborately. "Okay. That's what I was plannin' to do, anyway."

"Good. Now that we understand each other, tell me about Mrs. Caldwell. How do you know her?"

"Well, I don't exactly *know* her," Rona hedged. Hunter's brow lowered and she quickly amended, "I mean, I *met* her in Boston. We worked together for awhile."

"Worked together?" Hunter blurted. "Do you expect me to believe that Mrs. Caldwell was a . . ."

"Whore?" Rona finished, a tinge of bitterness creeping into her voice. "No, no, no, Mr. Hunter. What she was, was a star."

"A star? What kind of star?"

Rona sauntered over to a tree and slid down the trunk into a sitting position. Now that she'd won her battle to stay on the train, she was feeling much more secure and her natural good humor bubbled to the surface. "This is quite a story, so why don't we get comfortable?"

Hunter was far too agitated at this point to "get comfortable". Pacing irritably up to Rona, he glared down at her. "Just tell me what you know."

"You ever been to Boston?"

"Yes," Hunter admitted. "I've been to Boston."

"You been to the theater there?"

"Look, lady," Hunter gritted, "I'm not here to play Questions and Answers with you."

"All right, all right. I'll just tell ya straight out, then. Mrs. Caldwell was the biggest theater star in Boston."

"You mean she was an actress?"

"Exactly. She didn't use the name 'Tess Caldwell', though. She was known as 'Miss Theresa Chambers'." Rona trilled Tess's stage name off her tongue theatrically, making a wide, sweeping gesture with her arms.

Hunter's heart leapt into his throat. Of course. Theresa Chambers. It all suddenly made sense. Tess was short for Theresa and her brother Joe's last name was Chambers. Theresa Chambers was actually Tess's maiden name.

Unbidden, a nearly forgotten memory floated through Hunter's mind. That last night in Boston with his fianceé, Sophie Westhover. He'd taken her to see Shakespeare's comedy, "Much Ado About Nothing" starring the beautiful and highly renowned Miss Theresa Chambers. Hunter closed his eyes for a moment, picturing again the lovely young actress on the stage that night. Yes, now that he thought about it, that girl could have been Tess with her blond hair and melodic voice.

If only he'd paid closer attention. But, he'd been far more intrigued with Sophie than with the play, and since he'd returned to his military duties in Mexico the following day, he'd never seen Theresa Chambers on stage again.

"So?" he asked, forcing himself back to the present, "Mrs. Caldwell was an actress in Boston. What does that have to do with anything?"

"You can't have spent much time in Boston if ya don't know the rest of the story," Rona smirked.

"I didn't," Hunter said shortly, "so, tell me."

"Well, I got a week's work as one of them people who stand around in the background in a play she was in. You know, one of 'em Shakespeare things? 'Much Ado About Somethin'', or is it 'Much Ado About Nothin'? I can never remember. Anyway, it don't matter what play it was. The point is, I got this job in the play and Miss Chambers was the star. That was right around the time that William Caldwell started courtin' her."

Hunter nodded.

"You know who the Caldwells are, don't ya?"

"No."

"Lord, you *ain't* spent much time in Boston! The Caldwells happen to be one of the wealthiest families in town. They own a ship buildin' company that's practically the biggest on the whole East Coast—'cept for the one that Wellesley family owns, of course, that's the very biggest—but, still, the Caldwells are rich, rich, rich and very Beacon Hill, if ya know what I mean."

Hunter nodded impatiently. "Yes, I know. Go on."

"Well, William Caldwell was the only son in the family, so he was heir to the company and all the money. His mama had set her sights on him marryin' some rich, snobby girl and, let me tell you, she wasn't one bit happy when he set his sights on Theresa Chambers, the actress!"

"But they got married, anyway."

"Yeah," Rona nodded. "Ran away to Maryland and got married. Theresa quit actin' right away, of course, so I sorta lost track of what happened after that. I heard they was livin' with Will's mama and daddy in their big house. About a year went by, then, all of the sudden, Will got sick and just up and died. Nobody even knew there was anything serious wrong with him and, just like that, he was dead. Strangest thing, a young man like that—and with all that money too. A real shame."

Hunter nodded, gesturing impatiently with his hands for her to move on.

"After that, Theresa just disappeared. Nobody at the theater knew where she went. Even her friends that she still saw after she got married didn't know. There was lots of rumors, though."

"What kind of rumors?"

"Mostly that old Mrs. Caldwell had sent her packin'. Some even said that the old lady threw her out of the house the day after Will's funeral. The whole thing was real sad. In fact, people are still talkin' about it." With a final nod, Rona sat back and smiled with satisfaction.

"Is that it?" Hunter asked.

"Well, almost, 'cept for the detectives, of course."

Hunter rolled his eyes in complete frustration. Why in the world didn't the woman just tell him the rest of the story and get it over with? It was just his luck to get strapped with a would be actress who obviously wanted to milk the drama of the tale for everything it was worth. "What about the detectives?"

Rona wiggled her bottom around on the hard ground, trying to get more comfortable, then smiled beatifically up at Hunter. "I'm gettin' to it. Keep your britches on."

Clapping her hand over her mouth, she giggled girlishly. "Now that's somethin' ya don't often hear a girl in my line of work say."

"Just tell me the rest of the story, for God's sake!" Hunter exploded.

Rona immediately sobered, looking up at him with a pouting expression. "You're no fun a'tall."

"The story, Miss Rose?"

"Okay, okay. I guess it was about, oh, maybe three months after Will died. I wasn't in Boston anymore. I'd moved on to Chicago, but it was in all the papers there and since my mama learned me how to read and write when I was just a little girl, I read all about it."

Hunter nodded, acknowledging Rona's obvious pride in her literacy.

"Well, there was a whole bunch of articles in the papers 'bout how the Caldwells was tryin' to find their 'dear daughter' who'd disappeared a few months before. It said too that they was offerin' a big reward for information about where she was. I never heard anymore about it after that, and that was way last spring. Guess she was with you, huh?"

Hunter ignored Rona's last question and, instead, shot one of his own back at her. "Why do you think Mr. Caldwell's family suddenly wanted to find her?"

"Who knows," Rona shrugged, "unless the stories about Mrs. Caldwell throwin' her out were lies and the old lady really did care about her."

Hunter's eyes narrowed as he pondered this possibility. "I doubt that. If Mrs. Caldwell and her late husband's mother were close, why did she disappear in the first place?"

"It's a mystery, that's for sure," Rona sighed, getting to her feet and brushing off the back of her skirt. "Why don't ya ask her?"

Hunter looked at her in surprise. "Because it's none of my business."

"Well, then, guess you'll never know, will ya? Say, I gotta go now. Sam's gonna be 'spectin' his supper and he can get real cranky if his food is late."

Hunter nodded absently. "Can you think of anything else that you haven't told me yet? Something you might have forgotten?"

"No, that's it." Rona looked at him warily. "Now that I've told ya, though, you ain't gonna go back on your word 'bout lettin' me stay with the train, are ya?"

"No," Hunter answered. "As long as you don't cause any trouble and you keep away from the men, you can stay."

"Can I still visit with Miz. Caldwell? I mean, after all, we do know each other—sorta."

"You can visit during the day while we're moving—if she invites you to. At night, though, I expect you to stay in your wagon."

Rona nodded agreeably, then shambled over to Hunter and ran a yearning hand down his arm. "Ya know, I still think you're kinda sweet on her. It's a shame, too, 'cause you and I could've had a lot of fun between here and Oregon."

Hunter scowled and shook her hand off. "I'm not in the market, Miss Rose."

"I know, I know. It just goes to show, some women have all the luck and some of us don't have none."

"What do you mean?"

"I mean, Will Caldwell was a real good lookin' man and so are you. Some women just seem to get all the pretty ones without hardly even tryin', and the rest of us get what's left. Don't seem fair, somehow."

Hunter looked down at Rona, noticing for the first time, a few carefully concealed strands of gray hair blending in with the black. To his utter astonishment, he felt a moment of pity for her. When her looks were gone, what would she have left? How would she support herself in the rough environment of the Oregon lumber camps when her big breasts started to sag and her voluptuous hips turned to fat?

"Life isn't always fair, Miss Rose," he said quietly, "but I have a feeling that you'll be just fine."

"Oh, sure I will," Rona nodded, pasting on a smile that didn't quite reach her eyes. "After all, I got Sam now. He'll take care of me—probably even marry me if I want him to. What more could a girl ask for than that?"

With a jaunty little toss of her head, Rona turned on her heel and swaggered off toward her wagon, leaving Hunter standing under the tree, staring after her thoughtfully.

Chapter 24

"Hi," Hunter said quietly, walking up to where Tess sat on the tailgate of the wagon, rocking Sarah. "How's everything with you?"

"Fine," she answered. "There's some stew in the pot that I kept warm for you. I'm afraid all I had was some dried beef to put in it. I hope that's okay."

"It's fine," Hunter assured her, scooping up a hearty portion. "There's just not much meat to be had in this area. Once we get a little higher up into the hills, there'll be more game."

Carrying his full plate and a cup of coffee back to the wagon, he leaned his hip against the tailgate. "So, how's Miss Sarah this evening?"

Tess smiled down at the dozing baby. "It was so hot that she had kind of a bad day, but she's much better now. In fact, she's just about ready to go to bed."

Hunter nodded, then frowned over at the clothes basket that served as Sarah's cradle. "How attached are you to that little table you brought with you?" With a jerk of his thumb, he gestured to a carved cherry wood curio table inside the wagon.

"It was Joe's," Tess answered. "He figured maybe Deborah might like to have it for her front room. Why?"

"Because I thought I might break it down and build Sarah a cradle out of it. She deserves better than a clothes basket and I think there's enough wood there to make a cradle big enough to hold her for a year or so."

Tess smiled at Hunter gratefully, thinking how handsome he looked with the chiseled planes of his face reflected in the dancing firelight. "That's very thoughtful of you, Jared. Thank you."

They sat together for several minutes in companionable silence, Hunter eating his stew and Tess rocking the baby. Finally, she drew a deep breath and asked the question that had been plaguing her all evening. "What happened with Miss Rose? You were gone a long time."

Hunter set his plate aside. "We had an . . . interesting conversation."

"Are you going to let her stay on the train?"

He nodded, absently reaching over and stroking the bottom of one of Sarah's tiny feet. "Yeah. She and I came to an agreement about that."

Tess was glad to hear this news. She had enjoyed the short time that she and Rona had spent together that afternoon, despite her worries that the other woman might recognize her. "You came to an agreement?"

"Yeah. She promised not to cause any trouble with the men and to stay in her wagon after we camp every night. If she can stick with that, she can stay."

Tess smiled, pleased to see this new, more understanding side of Hunter. "I'm glad," she murmured. "I enjoyed having another woman to talk to again."

"I could tell you did," Hunter nodded, picking up his coffee cup and taking a swallow. "She asked if she could visit with you during the day and I told her that as long as it was okay with you, I didn't mind."

"It's okay with me," Tess confirmed.

Hunter threw her a penetrating look. "Even though she knows who you really are?"

Tess's breath caught in her throat. "What do you mean?"

"She knows, Tess, and she told me."

Tess's hand reflexively clutched her throat. "I don't know what you're talking about."

Hunter frowned at her, surprisingly disappointed that she would feel it necessary to prevaricate with him. "What I mean is that Miss Rose told me that she was a background player in a production of "Much Ado About Nothing" in Boston some time ago. It seems this production starred one Miss Theresa Chambers who eventually left the company because she married a very influential and wealthy man by the name of William Caldwell. Does any of this sound familiar?"

"Yes," Tess whispered.

"And," Hunter continued, "she also said that the same William Caldwell died suddenly last year and that after his death, his widow disappeared."

Tess nodded without meeting Hunter's eyes.

"Now, it seems that Mr. Caldwell's family has decided they would like to find their son's widow and they have hired a group of detectives to locate her."

"Oh, my God," Tess moaned. "They're *still* looking for me?"

Hunter reached out and hooked a finger beneath her chin, raising her head till their eyes met. "Yes, they are. Would you like to tell me why?"

Tess stared at him for a long moment, searching his dark eyes as if to convince herself that she could trust him. Hunter met her intense gaze steadily. "Tell me, Tess. Why are you running?"

"Because they want Sarah," she blurted, tears springing to her eyes, "and I'll never let them take her. Never!"

Hunter's brow furrowed with bewilderment. "Are you saying that William's family wants to take Sarah away from you?"

"Exactly," Tess nodded miserably. The tears swimming in her eyes suddenly overflowed, streaming down her cheeks and causing her shoulders to shake uncontrollably.

"Come here," Hunter murmured, curling his arm around her shoulders and pulling her into his solid embrace. "Now, I want you to tell me everything."

"It's such a long story," Tess choked, "I hardly know where to start."

Without thinking, Hunter buried his face in her hair. "I've got time, sweetheart. Just start at the beginning."

Tess dashed a tear away. "William's family objected to our marriage from the very beginning. In fact, they forbade him to marry me, so we eloped to Maryland. We made sure that by the time we returned to Boston, the marriage was . . ." She hesitated, embarrassed by what she was about to confess. ". . . was already consummated, so there was nothing his parents could do to annul it."

Hunter nodded slowly, his cheek rubbing comfortingly against her hair. "Go on."

"When we got back to Boston, we moved in with Will's family until we could build a house of our own. At first, it was terrible. His mother, Margaret, hated me and made no attempt to hide it. She did everything she could think of to tear Will and me apart, but it didn't work. Finally, I think she realized that, and things got a little better. I knew she still didn't like me, didn't approve of me as Will's wife, but at least she was no longer openly hostile toward me.

Then, just a month before we were supposed to move into our new house, Will got sick. At first, it just seemed like a nasty bout of influenza and, for awhile, he seemed to get better. But, then, he suddenly got worse again. The doctors told us it was pneumonia and that there was nothing they could do. He lingered for a few more days, but on the twenty-seventh of January, he . . . he died."

Her last word ended on a sob. Hunter winced, hating the fact that he was forcing her to resurrect all these sad memories, but feeling like he had to know the truth of what had happened to her in order to be able to help her . . . to protect her.

"Then what happened?" he coaxed gently, threading his fingers through her hair in a soothing gesture.

Tess drew a shuddering breath. "The day after Will's funeral, Margaret called me into the parlor. I thought she wanted to talk about his will or, perhaps, discuss what my plans were regarding the new house. But, that's not what she wanted at all."

"What did she want?"

"What she wanted was to order me out of the house. She told me to pack my bags, leave by the servant's entrance, and never show my face in the neighborhood again. Those were her exact words. 'Leave by the servant's entrance!' Can you imagine anyone being that cruel? Then she called me all sorts of terrible names. She accused me of being a cheap floozy and a selfish, unprincipled fortune hunter. Oh, God, it was horrible!" With a groan of misery, Tess buried her head in her hands. "She acted like it was my fault that Will had died. As if something I had done had been responsible for him getting sick."

"Shh, sweetheart," Hunter crooned, guiding Tess's head down to his chest. "Don't cry. It's all in the past now."

Tess raised her head, looking up at him with beseeching eyes. "I wasn't a fortune hunter, Jared. I loved Will with all my heart. It didn't matter one whit to me whether he had money or not. I would have married him even if he'd been a pauper. I swear to you, there was nothing selfish about my feelings for him. And he loved me too. Why, the last thing he said to me before he died was how much he loved me . . . how happy I'd made him."

Hunter felt a twinge of envy at Tess's impassioned words. Never had anyone felt that kind of love for him. For the briefest instant, he let his mind drift, trying to imagine spending his life within the warm embrace of a woman's unconditional love. With a quick shake of his head, he shrugged off his wistful thoughts, forcing back his feelings of regret and envy. Fate had decreed that he would never know that tender emotion, so there was no sense brooding about it. Turning back to Tess, he said, "So, where did you go after Mrs. Caldwell banished you?"

"That's when I went to St. Louis," Tess sniffed. "I took some of the jewelry that Will had given me during our marriage and sold it to pay my passage. Then, I got on a train and went to Joe. I didn't know he was planning on joining Deborah and Clay in Oregon. I only found that out after I arrived. But, once Joe told me his plans, I decided to go along. Besides, by that time I knew I needed to get as far away from Margaret as possible. Oregon seemed perfect."

"Had you heard that she was looking for you?"

Tess nodded. "Yes. A detective came to Joe's house asking about me. Joe suspected why he was investigating and didn't let on that I was there, thank God."

Hunter shook his head in bewilderment. "What I don't understand is, if Mrs. Caldwell threw you out, why did she then hire detectives to try to find you?"

Tess's expression hardened. "I'm sure she found out about the baby."

"She didn't know before you left?"

"No. I had just found out myself a week before Will died and I didn't tell anyone but him."

"Then how did she find out?"

Tess shrugged. "One of the servants, probably. They were always lingering outside of Will's sickroom. One of them might have overheard me when I told him about the baby. Or maybe it was Dr. Wright. I suppose he might have told her, although he had been my doctor before I was married and he knew how I felt about Margaret. I don't believe he would have betrayed me."

"You never know what people can be induced to betray if enough money crosses enough palms," Hunter said cynically.

Tess sighed. "I know. Anyway, the real reason I've been so determined to get to Oregon is to get away from Margaret. I have no doubt that if she finds me, she'll try to take Sarah away from me."

"She can't do that," Hunter snorted. "You're the baby's mother. You were legally married to Sarah's father. She doesn't have a leg to stand on."

Tess laughed bitterly. "You don't know Henry and Margaret Caldwell. They're very powerful people. If they want something, they won't rest until they get it—and I'm sure Margaret wants her only heir. She'll probably try to have me declared unfit because I was an actress. I know that shouldn't make any difference, but I'm not taking any chances. That's why I have to get away where no one will ever find me."

"And Will's father goes along with all this? He'd condone his wife taking your baby away from you?"

"I don't know," Tess said thoughtfully. "Actually, Henry was always very kind to me in a detached sort of way. But, Margaret is a beast and he generally goes along with her. I think he's found over the years that it's just easier to give in than fight her."

"What makes you think they won't have their detectives follow you all the way to Oregon?"

"Well, for one thing, I don't think they know Deborah is in Oregon. I don't remember ever mentioning that she and Clay had left Missouri. And I don't believe it would occur to them that I'd be travelling on a wagon train. The detectives never came back to Joe's after he sent them away that one time, so I don't know how they would have found out that I headed west. Even if they followed up and found out that Joe had gone west, they wouldn't know that I'd gone with him. But still, I worry about it all the time. You don't think Miss Rose will tell anybody, do you? I heard the Caldwells are offering a substantial reward and if she knows that, what's to keep her from reporting me and collecting it?"

"She won't," Hunter said positively. "She and I discussed that very thing this evening. She won't."

Tess straightened and looked at Hunter curiously. "What did you do, threaten her?"

"No," he laughed. "Like I told you before, she and I just came to an agreement about some things—and her silence regarding who you are was one of them."

"Still," Tess sighed, "people have been known to break their word when money is involved."

Hunter smiled and pulled her back into his arms. "Let me worry about Miss Rose," he whispered. "You just worry about taking care of yourself and Sarah."

Tess looked up at him incredulously. "You'd do that for me?"

"What?"

"Worry about Miss Rose?"

"Yeah," Hunter murmured, gazing down into her sea blue eyes, "I'd do that for you."

Slowly, he lowered his mouth to hers, a little thrill of excitement shooting through him as he watched her lips part in anticipation of his kiss. When it came, the intensity of passion between them startled them both. Hunter turned her in his arms until she was cradled across his lap, gently stroking the side of her breast as he kissed her mouth, her jaw and the delicate skin beneath her ear.

His breathing became hoarse and ragged as Tess responded to his caresses, although deep in the back of his mind, he knew he had to stop. After all, the woman had just had a baby less than a week before. He tried to pull back, but Tess prevented him from breaking their embrace, going with him as he began to raise his head. Hunter felt a stab of guilt as he realized his normally ironclad will was quickly slipping away, but Tess's breathy "Don't stop, please don't stop," made him throw caution to the winds. She just felt so good, so right in his arms, that he couldn't seem to stop kissing her, touching her.

"You're so beautiful," he breathed, nibbling at the soft hollow where her neck met her shoulder.

"So are you," she whispered back.

With a moan, he kissed her again, his tongue playing with hers provocatively as it emulated the consummation he was starving for.

You can't do this! his mind screamed. *You have to stop before you disgrace yourself in front of her.*

Wrenching his mouth away from hers, Hunter sat back, squeezing his eyes shut as he dragged in breath after breath of fresh, cool air. Gently, he set Tess away from him, his hands shaking as he reached up to give her cheek a last caress.

To his surprise, Tess raised her hand, covering

his own with her slender fingers. "You know," she whispered, "Joe was right about you."

"How so?" he rasped, his voice still hoarse with unfulfilled desire.

"You *are* a hero. For years, you were his. Now, you're mine."

Chapter 25

You're my hero.

Over and over the three words pounded through Hunter's brain like a litany. He didn't want to be Tess's hero. He didn't want to be anybody's hero. Why couldn't anyone understand that being a hero was what he was fleeing from? What he was trying so desperately to escape?

What had he ever done to deserve the hated moniker? He'd killed a lot of people. That was all. And for that, they called him a hero? To his mind, 'murderer' would have been a more fitting title.

Now, even Tess was calling him a hero. What had he done to make her lay that burden on him? Yes, he'd saved that Indian's life, but only because she'd shamed him into it. If left to his own devices, he would have abandoned the wounded warrior to his fate.

And, yes, he'd delivered her baby for her, but what choice had he had? If she'd only known how badly he'd wanted to turn and flee that night, to ignore her cries and just ride away into the dark solitude that had become his life, she certainly wouldn't think so highly of him.

And now, just because he'd told her that he would make sure Rona Rose kept her mouth shut, she was again attributing all sorts of ludicrous virtues to him. There had been nothing virtuous about that decision. It was simply that he knew if word got out that there was a bounty of ten thousand dollars on Tess's head, some one of the ruffians on the train would undoubtedly kidnap or even kill her to gain it. That was the only reason he'd negotiated with the prostitute for her silence. There had been nothing heroic in his actions.

There had never been anything heroic in his actions. Why couldn't they all realize that and release him from this prison of expectation that had been built around him?

With a deep sigh, Hunter forced himself to close his eyes. He was exhausted. It had been a long, torturous day and one just like it lay ahead. He had to get some rest. Silently, he played the old game he'd used so many times when trying to block out the horrors of battle.

Empty your mind. Think of nothing except the smell of flowers and a quiet, blue pond. Now, float. Float on the pond. Smell the flowers . . . Float . . .

As always, the soothing mind game worked. His eyes closed, his muscles relaxed, his mind began to drift . . .

Then he heard the gun shot.

He was on his feet in a trice, grabbing his pistol out of its holster and taking off at a dead run in the direction of the sound.

He didn't have to go far. Eight wagons in front of Tess's, chaos had broken out. Men were running, shouting, and brandishing pistols wildly in the air.

As he ran toward the melee, Hunter spied Jack

Riley trying to pull apart two burly lumberjacks who were slugging at each other with murderous intent. Pushing the diminutive Jack out of the way, Hunter launched himself between the men, knocking one of them down with a well placed blow to the jaw and grabbing the other by the front of his bloody shirt. "What the hell is going on here?" he thundered.

"They're fightin' over that whore again," Jack shouted back, successfully bringing down another man with a well placed knee to the groin. "I think somebody shot Sam Waters."

"Son of a bitch!" Hunter bellowed. "Where's Dash?"

"Over there." Jack pointed to a large group of men who were lustily brawling on the other side of Sam's wagon. Hunter sprinted around the back of the wagon and dove into the pile of thrashing arms and legs.

"Glad to see ya," Dash yelled, ducking a flying fist and knocking his assailant cold. "I could use some help here."

Hunter looked around wildly, trying to ascertain who was fighting whom. His eyes lit on the loyal Bennington boys doing their best to break up a group of drunken roughnecks who seemed intent on pummeling each other into pulp. However, like the previous fracas that Jack had described to him, the Benningtons seemed to be the only members of the expedition who were trying to bring an end to the violence. Everyone else appeared to be reveling in it.

For a split second, Hunter contemplated stepping back and letting the lumberjacks beat each other senseless, thinking that it might be the most effective way of ending the trouble. Maybe, if he let them have their way with each other, they'd beat each other to the point that all of them would be too sore and bruised to want a rematch any time soon.

His innate sense of responsibility quickly put his mutinous thoughts to rest, however. He was the leader of this expedition and as the leader, it was his job to maintain order. And, whether he liked to admit it or not, Jared Daulton Whitaker was a man who always did his job, regardless of how odious the assignment might be.

Stepping out of harm's way, he raised his gun into the air and fired off five shots. Almost instantly, fifty pairs of eyes turned toward him and a heavy silence fell over the winded, bloody group.

"That was five," he shouted. "There's still one bullet left in this gun and the next man who makes a move toward anybody else is going to get it between his eyes."

Hurriedly, Jack and Dash also drew their guns and joined Hunter where he stood facing the sullen lumberjacks.

"And when that one is gone, I've got six more here," Dash added, training his pistol threateningly on the group at large.

"And six more here," Jack echoed, holding his piece up too.

"Hey, Hunter," a man at the edge of the crowd called, "you got a dead man over here."

Hunter looked over to where Jeremy Bennington, the oldest of the three brothers, stood over Sam Waters's still body.

Hunter walked over to where Sam lay, looking down at the sightless, staring eyes. "Who did this?" he asked, his voice as cold as the steel in the gun he held.

"Arnie Butcher did it," came a frightened female voice from the back of Sam's wagon.

Hunter swiveled around and threw a killing look at Rona Rose. She was standing inside the wagon, holding together the gaping shreds of her mangled nightdress. "Get back inside," Hunter ordered. "I'll deal with you later."

A man with a badly bruised eye and a cut lip stepped forward. "She didn't do nothin', Hunter, and she's right about what she's sayin'. She and Sam was in the wagon together, mindin' their own business when Arnie and a bunch of his cronies decided they wanted some of Miss Rose. Sam got out of the wagon to stop 'em, and they started fightin'. Then Arnie pulled out his gun and told Sam to get out of the way, that he was gonna have his woman whether Sam liked it or not. When Sam said 'no', Arnie shot him dead. Sam wasn't even armed."

During the course of the lumberjack's explanation, Dash slipped through the crowd and collared Arnie Butcher, hauling the resisting man over to Hunter.

"This story true, Butcher?" Hunter asked.

"The woman's a whore, Hunter," Arnie cried, trying to wrench himself free of Dash's grasp. "A whore just ain't for one man—a whore belongs to everybody. Sam was bein' selfish and he deserved what he got."

Hunter looked at Arnie solemnly, then said, "You'll hang, first light, Butcher."

"What?" Arnie screeched. "Now wait a damn minute, here. You can't hang a man without a trial."

"You just had it," Hunter snarled. Turning to Dash, he said, "Get him out of here. Chain him to his wagon wheel and don't leave him."

Dash nodded and led the kicking, screaming murderer away.

Turning to the rest of Arnie's cohorts who were standing together, staring at him warily, Hunter said, "I understand that when a fight like this broke out a couple of nights ago, Dash told you that the instigators would be tied to their wagon wheels and left to fry in the sun. Guess you boys weren't listening."

With a slight nod of his head, he signalled Jack

and the Bennington brothers to surround the five men. Pulling a long length of rope off the side of Sam Waters' wagon, he threw it to Joshua Bennington. "Tie 'em up."

The men put up a token resistance, but most of them were so battered they could hardly hold their heads up, so their protests had little effect. Once Jack and the three brothers had them lashed together, Hunter strode over to them, his pistol still cocked.

Turning back to the rest of the crowd, he said, "These men may very well die for what happened here tonight and that's also gonna be the fate for any of the rest of you who decide to repeat it. Keep that in mind next time you feel like Miss Rose is someone to be shared. And, by the way, until we get to Fort Hall, she'll be travelling with Mrs. Caldwell. As you know, that's my wagon too, so the next time you decide to tangle with somebody to get to her, remember that I'm not Sam Waters. I don't sleep without my gun." His icy gaze swept the crowd of men, daring any one of them to argue. No one said a word. "Good," he nodded, "I'm glad we understand each other. Now, go to bed, all of you."

Reaching up into the back of Sam's wagon, he lifted Rona unceremoniously to the ground and hauled her back down the line toward Tess's wagon.

"You're not gonna do nothin' to me, are you?" she asked fearfully. "It was just like that man said. Sam and me, we wasn't doin' nothin'. We was in our wagon just like you said we should be."

"That may be," Hunter growled, "but, you're trouble, lady, and I don't like trouble on my train."

"You're gonna go back on your word, ain't ya?" Rona accused hotly. "You're gonna throw me off, leave me sittin' by the side of the road somewhere, even after you promised you wouldn't, ain't ya?"

"I haven't decided what I'm going to do yet,"

Hunter responded. hustling her over to Tess's small campfire and pushing her down on to his bedroll. "For now, you're going to lie down here, shut up and go to sleep. Understand?"

Rona nodded and quickly stretched out on the bedroll.

Hunter walked over to the back of the wagon and peeked in through the oval opening in the canvas. "You okay, Tess?" he whispered.

"Yes," she whispered back, "just a little scared. "Are *you* okay?"

"Yes. Everything's fine now. There won't be any more trouble tonight, so try to get some sleep—and don't come out of the wagon tomorrow morning until I tell you to."

"All right."

Turning away, Hunter trudged over to the campfire and sat down tiredly next to it.

"Mr. Hunter?"

He angrily jerked his head in Rona's direction. "I thought I told you to shut up and go to sleep."

"I know and I will, but I just wanted to thank you."

"Thank me? For what?"

"For savin' me from those men. By the time they'd've finished with me, I'd be as dead as Sam."

Hunter thought about this for a moment, realizing that Rona was probably right. "You're welcome, Miss Rose," he said finally. "Now shut up and go to sleep."

"Okay, but thanks again. Not a lot of men woulda done what you done tonight—just to save a whore. You're a real hero, you know that?"

Hunter didn't answer, but as Rona stared across the campfire at him, she could have sworn she heard him moan—almost like he was in pain.

* * *

It was nearly eight o'clock the next morning before Hunter finally got the wagon train rolling. To Tess's surprise, he tied his big roan gelding to the back of her wagon and climbed up on the seat, picking up the reins.

"Are you driving?" she asked.

"For awhile. Just stay back in there and don't come out."

"Hunter," she protested, "I don't understand why I have to stay in the wagon."

"Just do as you're told and don't ask questions."

Tess's mouth tightened mutinously at his autocratic directive. Why couldn't she sit up front for a little while? The back of the wagon was hot, stuffy and airless, but the morning breeze felt glorious wafting through the canvas hole. Impulsively, she made up her mind to disobey Hunter's high handed command. Grabbing hold of the wagon bows, she pulled herself forward and crawled over the seat.

"Just for a minute," she said by way of explanation, settling herself on the bench. "It's so much cooler up here, and I don't see . . ." Her words died in her throat as her eyes lit on the grotesquely swinging body of Arnie Butcher. "Oh, my God!" she cried, clapping her hand over her mouth in an effort not to lose her breakfast. "You hanged someone!"

"Get in the back!" Hunter roared, giving her shoulder a hard push.

Swinging her legs over the bench, Tess hurtled herself back into the wagon bed, still fighting the urge to vomit. "You hanged someone!" she repeated, her voice accusatory.

Hunter craned his neck around, glowering at her angrily. "Yeah, you're right, we did. That's what happens to men who murder other men."

"But, Hunter," Tess railed, "you're not a judge. How can you make that decision?"

"Out here I *am* the judge," Hunter retorted, "and all decisions ultimately fall to me."

"Who are those other men I saw? The ones chained to their wagons?"

"They're being punished too. They were warned once that if they caused any more problems, they'd be left behind."

"What? You're going to just leave them there? My Lord, they'll die in the sun!"

Hunter shrugged. "If they do, they do."

Tess stared at the back of Hunter's head in open mouthed horror. "I can't believe this," she said, shaking her head. "I thought I knew you, but I guess I was wrong. I don't know you at all."

"This is the frontier, Tess, and it demands frontier justice. It has to be swift and irrevocable. If I don't make an example of these men, I'll have mutiny on the train."

"You call this justice? I call it murder."

"Call it what you want," Hunter gritted, "but it's the way things are out here and if you're planning to live here, you better get used to it. You're not in Boston anymore and you would be well advised to remember that."

"Now I understand why you didn't want me to get out of the wagon this morning," Tess accused. "You didn't want me to see your 'frontier justice', did you?"

"That's right," Hunter nodded without turning around, "because I knew this is how you'd react. I was trying to spare your sensibilities."

"Sensibilities have nothing to do with this!" she shot back. "Any decent person with the tiniest shred of human compassion would feel exactly as I do."

Hunter's lips flattened and with a hard jerk on the reins, he brought the mules to a halt. "Now you listen to me," he growled, turning around and pinning Tess with a frigid look, "for your information, that man swinging from that tree back there is doing so because first, he decided he wanted to have sex with Miss Rose and second, because he killed Sam Waters when Sam tried to stop him. Think about it, Tess. If I allowed that sort of incident to go unpunished, what's to say that after he got tired of Rona over there, he wouldn't demand the same of you?"

Tess swallowed hard and averted her eyes. "And what about the other men?"

"They were Arnie Butcher's cronies," Hunter spat. "They were planning on having their turn with Miss Rose once Arnie was done with her. When my men tried to dissuade them of that notion, they resorted to brawling."

"But I still don't think they should be left to die for that . . ."

"They're not going to die," Hunter said quietly. "I just decided to let everybody think they are. I'm leaving them to sit there for a day or two. With water," he added, holding up a finger to halt the argument he knew was coming, "and then Jack Riley will cut them loose. I just want to make sure that the rest of the train is far enough ahead of them by the time they're freed that they can't catch up. They're being banished, not killed. So, you see, Mrs. Caldwell, I'm not quite the heartless murderer that you're accusing me of being."

Without waiting for a reply or an apology, Hunter swiveled back around, picked up the reins and slapped them over the mules' backs.

For a long time, Tess sat contemplating all that he had just told her, trying to come to terms with the "swift and irrevocable" justice he deemed necessary. Finally, after many long minutes of thought, she crawled back up to the front of the wagon and sat down beside him. "Hunter?" she said quietly, reaching over and touching his arm to get his attention.

"Yeah?"

"I understand."

"But you still don't agree with my methods, right?"

"No," she admitted, "I can't say that I agree, but I do understand."

Hunter gazed over at her for a moment, then nodded. It wasn't what he'd hoped to hear but, for the time being, it was enough.

Chapter 26

Hunter pounded the last nail into the side of Tess's wagon and stood back to admire his handiwork. "There," he said, smiling. "It's done."

"It's a brilliant idea," Tess complimented. "In fact, you could probably sell those and make a fortune."

Hunter laughed and scooped Sarah out of her mother's arms. "Now you can get fresh air and sunshine every day, little girl. No more riding in that hot old wagon for you." He turned back to Tess with a pleased grin.

It had taken Tess several weeks to get over being upset regarding his treatment of Arnie Butcher and his cohorts but, finally, as Sarah passed her one month birthday, their relationship again seemed to be back on an even keel.

Hunter had been surprised, and more than a little disturbed, at how much he had missed Tess's company during the long tense days following the incident and, even now, he was loathe to admit that the fact that she was finally over her anger was the reason for his renewed good spirits.

Despite his persistent denial that Tess's attitude toward him was the cause of his sudden twists of mood, there was not a person on the train who wasn't relieved that the two of them had obviously patched up their differences and the volatile wagon master was once again smiling and talking.

"Well, I see you finally got it done." As was her wont, Rona seemed to appear from out of nowhere, smiling at Hunter and adding, "I gotta admit, Hunter, nailing a cradle on to the outside of the wagon is a great idea. Think of how many times it'll save me and Tess from havin' to crawl into the back of that dang wagon to see what little Sweetie here is hollerin' about."

Tess smoothed the soft bedding she'd laid in the little wooden box and plucked Sarah out of Hunter's arms. "Okay, darling, let's see how you like this." Laying the baby gently down in the little nest, she stood back and beamed with pleasure. "Look at her. She loves it!"

Indeed, Sarah waved her arms and legs exuberantly, seemingly delighted to be out in the fresh air.

Hunter grinned. "She likes it so much, she's smiling at me."

"I keep tellin' ya," Rona snorted, "she's not smilin'. She's got gas on her stomach, that's all. She just looks like she's smilin' when, actually, she's probably sufferin' a terrible bellyache. Babies don't smile for real till they're a coupla months old, at least."

"And I keep telling you that you're crazy," Hunter argued hotly. "Sarah is smiling at me. You're just jealous because she never smiles at you."

"He's got a point there, Rona," Tess laughed. "Hunter does seem to be the only one Sarah smiles at."

The irrepressible Rona clapped her hand over her

mouth to cover her guffaws. "Then that must mean Hunter's the only one who gives her gas!"

Dash McLaughlin and Jack Riley stood nearby, watching Hunter, Tess and Rona with amused expressions on their faces. "Have you ever seen a happier threesome?" Jack chuckled.

"Or a stranger one?" Dash added.

Jack cocked his head to one side. "Strange, maybe, but I ain't never seen Hunter so happy as he is with them two women and that baby. D'ya s'pose he might be fallin' for one of 'em?"

Dash picked up his saddle and threw it over his horse's back. "You just realizin' that, old man? Why, I've known for weeks that he's head over heels for Mrs. Caldwell and I think she feels the same about him. Trouble is, she's too shy and he's too stupid to admit it."

"You just may be right about that, boyo," Jack laughed. "But where does that leave Miss Rona? Looks to me like she might be carryin' a torch for Hunter too."

"Well, if she is, she's out of luck," Dash said, tightening the saddle cinch. "She hasn't got a chance with him. He's taken, and everyone knows it. It's just too bad he doesn't, because he's gonna leave Mrs. Caldwell with a broken heart and he's never even gonna realize it."

"Well, they all seem to be happy as pigs in shit now," Jack noted. "And the last few weeks since we got rid o' the rowdies and Hunter settled in with his little harem have been the best this train's seen. I don't remember ever makin' the climb up to South Pass with less fuss and fightin' than this outfit has. It's like that bastard Arnie Butcher took all our problems with him when he went."

"Well, I don't know if I'd go that far," Dash countered, "after all, we've lost six men to Mountain Fever."

"Yeah," Jack sighed, "and it's too bad too, 'specially considerin' we got through the desert without a single case o' cholera. Just don't seem fair to finally make it up to the good air, then get hit with Mountain Fever."

"I still think it's those ticks," Dash insisted.

"Aw, you're crazy, you and your ticks. It's somethin' in the air, just like cholera is somethin' in the water."

Dash shook his head stubbornly. "If it was somethin' in the air, then everybody would get it. Besides, you know yourself, that every man that came down with the fever had those bug bites on their bodies. It's that tick we keep seein', I know it is. They bite you and leave somethin' behind that gives you the fever. I'm just sure of it."

"Okay, Dr. McLaughlin, think whatever you like," Jack said, becoming bored with the scientific twist the conversation was taking. "When d'ya think we're gonna make the pass?"

"A few days. We should reach the Ice Slough by this afternoon."

"Woowee!" Jack whooped, pulling off his dusty old hat and pounding it excitedly against his leg. "My favorite part of the whole trip."

"Yeah. What I wouldn't give for some fresh lemons."

"Lemons, hell," Jack scoffed. "What I wouldn't give for a pint o' fresh whiskey!"

"It's ice! I tell you, there's a whole field of ice straight ahead."

Joshua Bennington looked at his brother, Matthew, in patent disbelief. "You're loco, boy. Why, it's got to be close to eighty degrees. Now, how would ice form in this heat?"

"I tell you, Josh, there's ice up ahead. Tons and tons of it. I saw it myself."

"He's right," Dash said, joining the two brothers. "There is an ice field ahead." Dash had been riding by the Benningtons wagon when Matthew had made his grand announcement and now he pulled back on his horse's reins long enough to corroborate Matt's story.

"Get out of here!" Josh laughed. "Ice?"

"Yup," Dash nodded. "I read an article about it in a newspaper once. Some scientist type travelled here to check it out since he'd heard emigrants' stories about it. He says it's somethin' to do with the earth being thin right here. That, and the fact that we're up so high makes ice form underneath."

"Sounds plum crazy to me."

"I know it does, but whatever causes it, it's there. When we reach it, you might want to add some of it to your casks. It sweetens the water. Besides that, if you put some in a cup and let it melt, it'll give you a chance to have a nice, cold drink."

"A cold drink," Joshua sighed. "What a wonderful thought. Hey, Dash, do you suppose Hunter will let us stop there for awhile?"

Dash shrugged. "Probably. It's late enough in the day that we might even camp near there. Why? You want to spend all night drinkin' cold water, Josh?"

Joshua grinned. "No, but I've got a couple of lemons I've been savin' and I thought maybe Mrs. Caldwell might like to share a glass of lemonade with me."

Dash's brow furrowed. "She might at that, but you better ask Hunter first."

Josh's grin disappeared. "Why? Does she have to get his permission to have a glass of lemonade?"

Dash could almost smell the trouble that he knew was about to arise, and he was determined not to get into the middle of it. "Just ask Hunter," he advised. Then, with a nudge of his heels, he cantered off toward the front of the train.

"Ask Hunter, hell," Josh grumbled as Dash rode away. "I'll just ask Mrs. Caldwell. If she says 'yes', then Hunter doesn't have anything to say about it. After all, he's not her husband or even her sweetheart. What the hell business is it of his what she does with her evenings?"

"So, you wouldn't mind looking after Sarah for an hour or so?"

Rona tossed Hunter an arch look. "Okay, let me get this straight. You wanna take Tess up to the ice slough after supper and you want me to stay here and take care of the baby?"

"Yeah. Will you do it?"

"Well, that depends now. How bad d'ya wanna go up there, Hunter?"

Hunter sighed wearily. "Come on, Rona, don't make a deal out of this."

Rona let loose with one of her raucous laughs. "Honey, to my way of thinkin', *everything* is a deal."

Hunter shook his head. In the past few weeks spent in Miss Rona Rosenbaum's nearly constant company, he had found her to be one of the most exasperating women he'd ever met—and, also, one of the shrewdest. "Okay, Rona, what are your terms this time?"

Rona looked around surreptitiously, making sure that no one could overhear them. "I'm gonna tell ya somethin' about yourself, Hunter. Somethin' you probably don't even know."

Hunter's guard immediately went up, causing Rona

to break into another peal of laughter. "Scarin' ya, ain't I?"

"Come on, Rona, I don't have all day."

"Okay, here it is. You're in love with Tess. Crazy, mad, wild in love with her—*and* that baby of hers."

"Rona . . ."

"Don't interrupt me. I know what I'm talkin' about. Lord, lord, do I ever know what I'm talkin' about. Now, here's the deal. The only way you two are ever gonna find out if bein' together is the right thing is if you have some time alone together, and I figure I'm the one that can make that happen."

"Oh? And how do you figure that?"

"Well, you two ain't got no chance for any romancin' at all with that baby between you. That's where I come in."

"Here it comes," Hunter muttered.

"Right," Rona grinned, "here it comes. You let me stay on the train all the way to Oregon City—no droppin' me off at Fort Hall—and I'll watch the baby whenever you feel the need to . . . ah . . . get away alone with Tess for a spell. What'd'ya think?"

"You want to know what I think, Rona? I think you're crazy as a loon. Mrs. Caldwell and I are friends, nothing more. There's absolutely nothing romantic going on between us."

Rona shrugged, unperturbed by Hunter's name calling. "And you know what I think, Mr. No First Name Hunter? I think you're lyin' through your teeth, and what's more, I think you know it."

Hunter's gaze narrowed. "Be careful, Rona."

"Aw, quit glarin' at me like that. I know ya way too well to be scared of ya anymore. Besides, you're too handsome to be frownin' all the time. You should try smilin' once in a while."

Hunter rolled his eyes, feeling like he was aboard

an out of control merry-go-round, a feeling he often had when trying to reason with Rona.

"So, back to business," she said briskly. "You wanna take me up on my offer or not?"

Hunter stared down at her for a moment. Rona was everything he didn't like in a woman—loud, immodest and totally indiscreet—but despite her many faults, he had developed a genuine affection for her. Perhaps it was because Tess seemed to like her so well, or perhaps it was because he saw in her a person who had been as misunderstood by society as he had. He had already decided to let Rona continue on with the train to their destination. She had caused no trouble since Sam Waters's death and she was an enormous help to Tess with the baby. Still, something stopped him from taking her up on her offer—and he knew that that something was the knowledge that by doing so, he would also be admitting his feelings for Tess. The mere thought of it scared him to death.

"I'll get back to you, Rona," he said suddenly, turning away to escape the woman's penetrating stare.

"Okay," she shrugged, "but don't wait too long. If you don't ask Tess to go to the Ice Slough with you pretty soon, somebody else is gonna."

Hunter immediately turned back. "You think so?"

"Think so, honey? I know so. In fact, you might already be too late. Joshua Bennington was sniffin' 'round here not a half hour ago lookin' for Tess. He's prob'ly found her by now. On the other hand," she added slyly, looking at Hunter out of the corner of her eye, "Tess was all the way down at the creek, washin' out diapers, so maybe he hasn't. Still, if I was you, I'd hurry with that decision you gotta make."

Hunter considered Rona for a long moment, then shook his head in defeat. "Okay, lady, you win. You can stay on the train."

Rona laughed delightedly. "Why, thank you, Mr. Hunter, sir. I just knew you'd some to your senses and see things my way—eventually."

Tess stood holding two cups filled with a mixture of lemon juice, sugar and water while Hunter knelt on the ground, chipping away at a huge block of ice. "I can't believe we're doing this," she laughed. "I feel so wicked, leaving the baby and coming up here to drink lemonade."

"You deserve it," Hunter said, smiling at her over his shoulder. "Even new mothers deserve an few hours away once in awhile." Picking up some chips of ice, he motioned for Tess to bring the cups, then dropped the ice into the golden liquid. "There, now, just wait a minute and let a little of that melt."

Tess handed Hunter one of the cups, then followed him over to a large, flat rock where she sat down. "Do you think it's been long enough yet?" she asked eagerly.

"Probably," Hunter nodded, reluctant to spoil her excitement by making her wait any longer. Holding his cup up to hers, he said, "Let's make a toast."

"All right. What should we toast?"

Hunter thought a moment. "To Sarah Elizabeth Caldwell. May all the dreams she ever dreams come true." Gazing at Tess over the rim of his cup, he saw her eyes soften. The tin cups clinked together and they each took a sip. Hunter laughed as Tess's eyes closed and her nose wrinkled in reaction to the tart drink.

"Not enough sugar?" he asked.

"No, it's wonderful!"

"Good. Now you make a toast."

Tess cocked her head, thinking for a moment, then lifted her cup again. "To Colonel Jared Daulton Whitaker, whoever he may be."

Hunter's hand froze with his cup in midair. "I don't think I can toast to that," he said quietly.

"Yes, you can," Tess answered, her voice equally soft.

Their eyes met; his haunted, hers beseeching. Then, with a nearly imperceptible nod, he reached out and tapped his cup against hers.

Tess smiled at him as they took another swallow, then patted the rock next to her, inviting him to sit down. "May I ask you something?" she said when he was settled comfortably next to her.

"Sure. I'm not guaranteeing I'll answer, but go ahead."

"Where did the name, 'Hunter', come from?"

To her surprise, he chuckled. "I've had that name for a long, long time. Since way back when Dash and I were at West Point."

"West Point Military Academy? You went to school there?"

"Yes. Dash and I both did. And that's where I got the name."

"But, where did it come from?"

Hunter shifted on the rock, not sure he wanted to confess the origin of his nickname. "I don't think . . ."

"Oh, come on," Tess coaxed. "Tell me!"

"Well, there were a lot of girls in the town . . ."

"And you would go *hunting* for them!" Tess finished. Her teasing smile quickly turned to a look of amazement as she saw Hunter redden with embarrassment. "I'm right, aren't I?" she gasped.

"Yeah," he muttered. "But, that was a long time ago."

"Oh, but you know what they say," Tess giggled. "Once a rogue, always a rogue."

"Do they say that?"

"Indeed they do." She took another sip of her lemonade. "You know, now that I know about your reputation, I'm not sure that I should be out here alone with you."

Hunter gazed into her laughing eyes, the very nearness of her in this wild and primitive place making his heart pound against his ribs. Never had he wanted to touch a woman as badly as he suddenly wanted to touch Tess. Reaching out with shaking hands, he took her cup out of her hand and set it aside. "You have nothing to fear," he said softly. "I would never do anything you didn't want me to do."

Tess sobered as she saw the flame of desire ignite in his eyes. "I know you wouldn't," she whispered.

"How would you feel if I told you I wanted to kiss you?"

"Lucky."

"Lucky?"

Tess nodded slowly. "Remember, I've been kissed by you before."

Hunter drew a deep breath, his senses filling with the sight and smell of her. "Tess," he moaned, gathering her into his arms.

"Kiss me, Jared."

Hunter was more than happy to comply with her softly murmured request. His mouth descended on hers, feasting hungrily on her honeyed sweetness. Slowly, he lay her back on the rock, covering her body with his own as she tangled her fingers in the ebony silk of his hair.

The sensation of her fingernails running lightly over his scalp caused a sensuous chill to run all the way down to his toes, making him shiver.

Tess was so enthralled with their passionate kiss that she was only vaguely aware of Hunter's hands fumbling with the front of her bodice. It wasn't until she felt his rough, calloused fingers feathering over her bare breasts that she realized he had unbuttoned her all the way down to her waist.

"So soft," he murmured as his thumb swept over a pebbled nipple. Pulling his lips away from hers, he kissed his way down the long column of her throat. When his mouth reached the swelling curve of her breast, he paused, lifting his head and gazing down at her reverently. "Your skin is like alabaster," he whispered.

"And yours is like sculpted bronze," she returned.

For the first time, Hunter noticed that she had unfastened the snaps on his shirt front. He looked down into her languid eyes as she splayed her fingers over the hard wall of his chest. Her index finger traced the chiseled contours of his pectoral muscles, then drifted over to caress the sensitive skin surrounding his flat nipple.

Hunter emitted a low moan as he felt himself begin to harden. "Tess," he gasped. "You don't know . . ."

"Kiss me," she breathed, arching her back as she offered herself to him.

Hunter's hands were shaking as he lifted her breasts, pressing the lush globes together and burying his face in the exquisite softness. Parting his lips, he ran his mouth seductively over her tingling flesh, his tongue tracing a warm, wet trail as it moved inexorably closer to the rosy, peaked buds.

He glanced up into Tess's face, his excitement increasing tenfold as he saw the breathless anticipation in her expression. Lowering his head, he swirled his tongue around and around her nipple, then closed his mouth over it, making love to the taut bud until Tess squirmed and moaned beneath him.

Hunter's breath quickened as he felt his erection strengthen, pressing insistently against the front of his tight denims. With every fiber of his being, he longed to reach down and release the turgid length from its torturous confines, but the nagging voice of reason which plagued him so often when touching Tess stopped him.

With a groan, he sat up, throwing his head back in agonized frustration as he willed his overheated body to cool down. He opened his eyes, staring over at the huge blocks of ice and wishing that he could throw himself on one.

"Jared?" Tess whispered, sitting up also and looking over at him in bewilderment. "Is . . . is something wrong?"

"Yeah," he laughed mirthlessly, "everything is wrong."

Tess shook her head, not understanding what he was trying to say. "Did I do something . . ."

"No!" he blurted. "You didn't do anything." Getting to his feet, he moved painfully away from her, turning his back while he pulled vainly at the front of his denims. "We should get back, that's all."

"But . . ."

Whirling around, he threw her an angry look. "We shouldn't be doing this, Tess."

"You're right," she nodded, a deep flush of embarrassment staining her cheeks. "It's still too soon . . ."

"That's not what I meant! I meant, we can never do this." Walking back to where she sat, he glared down at her, his eyes afire with a combination of unquenched desire and self loathing. "Don't you see? A month from now, we'll be in Oregon. You'll go your way and I'll go mine. There's no future for us, Tess, and if I make love to you now, there could be the possibility of . . ."

"I understand!" Tess broke in, throwing up her hands to stop him from saying more. "You don't need to spell it out for me. Believe me, I know what can happen." Dropping her eyes, she suddenly noticed that her bodice was still gaping open. With a gasp of dismay, she jerked it together, then turned away to quickly button it again. Jumping up from the rock, she smoothed her tangled skirts. "I'd like to go back to the wagon now. If you'll just point the way . . ."

"I'll walk you back."

"No! I mean, I'd rather go alone."

Hunter gazed at her, his expression a mask of pain and regret. "It's straight down this path," he muttered, pointing. "You can't miss it. Your wagon is about twenty back tonight."

Tess nodded, careful to avoid making eye contact. Without a word, she turned away, hurrying down the path.

Hunter watched her until she disappeared into the darkness. With a groan of agonized self-recrimination, he walked over to a granite ledge, leaning his head against it tiredly and unfastening his denims. With a shuddering sigh, he released his still throbbing manhood, staring down at it with a murderous expression.

"You fool," he muttered furiously. "What made you think you could be friends with her? What made you think you could have a casual relationship with her? When will you ever learn that relationships bring you nothing but pain?"

Squeezing his eyes shut, he ground the heels of his hands against them. "When, Whitaker? *When* will you ever learn?"

Chapter 27

Rona winked broadly at Tess as she crawled into the back of the wagon. "How was the . . . lemonade?"

"Fine."

Rona's eyebrows plunged into her bangs. "Fine? That's all? Just fine?"

"Yes, it was fine. How's Sarah?"

"Fine," Rona parroted. "She slept the whole time you was gone."

"Good. I'm glad she didn't bother you."

"That little sweetie? She couldn't be no bother, no matter what."

"I'm going to bed now," Tess announced, reaching under her pillow to get her nightdress.

Rona studied her friend closely for a moment, sensing that something portentous had happened at the Ice Slough, but not sure if she dare ask about it. After a moment's consideration, however, her curiosity got the best of her and she blurted, "My God, Tess, what the hell happened up there? You look like you just lost your last friend. Did the man throw you down and have his way with ya or somethin'?"

To Rona's astonishment, Tess burst into tears. "No, he didn't."

"Then why the hell are you bawlin'?"

"*Because* he didn't!"

"What? Are you crazy, girl? You wanted him ta take advantage of ya?"

"Of course not," Tess sniffed. "But, don't you see, Rona? He wouldn't have been taking advantage."

Rona sat back, shaking her head sympathetically. "Oh, so that's how it is. You're in love with him, ain't ya?"

Tess nodded, reaching for a handkerchief and blowing her nose loudly.

"And ya figured if he tried to give ya a toss, it would show that he's in love with you too, right?"

"Sss . . . something like that."

"Well," Rona mused, "have ya considered the fact that maybe, it's 'cause he loves ya that he *didn't* try to have his way with you?"

"No," Tess wailed, "that's not it at all. The reason he didn't do anything is because he doesn't find me attractive. He's not interested in me . . . that way."

"Bull horns!" Rona snorted. "The man can't take his eyes off you. Anybody can see he's crazy 'bout you."

Tess's eyes widened at Rona's colorful epithet, but she didn't comment. "You're wrong, Rona. He isn't interested at all."

Rona shrugged philosophically. "Okay then, so, make him interested."

"How do I do that?"

"First of all, tell me what he said."

"He said that we couldn't do . . . what we started to do because pretty soon we're going to get to Oregon and we'll never see each other again."

"So, you did *start* to do somethin'."

"Well, yes."

"How far did ya get?"

Tess blushed to the roots of her hair. "Rona!"

"Oh, for God's sake, honey, now ain't the time to be modest. You need help—and, believe me, I'm just the one to give it to you. There ain't nothin' 'bout this subject that I don't know."

"Well," Tess gulped, hardly able to believe what she was about to confess, "we went pretty far."

"Did he toss your skirts over your head?"

"No!"

Rona shrugged. "Then, ya didn't go *that* far."

"We did too! He . . . he unbuttoned my bodice and . . . kissed me."

Rona's eyes sparked with renewed interest. "Kissed you . . . there?" she asked, pointing at Tess's chest.

"Yes."

"Well," Rona smiled with a envious little shiver, "lucky you!"

If possible, Tess's face became even redder.

"Then what? What did you do to him?"

"I . . . kissed him back."

"Where?"

"Where!"

"Yeah, where? I mean, his lips, his shoulders, his chest? Where?"

"Yes."

"What'd'ya mean, 'yes'?"

"All of those places."

Rona smiled with satisfaction. "Did he still have his clothes on?"

"Of course!"

"Oh. So, you really wasn't kissin' *him*, you was just kissin' his shirt?"

"Well, no. His shirt was unbuttoned."

"That's more like it! So, you was kissin' his bare chest and his shoulders and his lips?"

"Yes."

"But, that was all?"

Tess threw Rona a perplexed look, causing her to frown impatiently. "I mean, nowhere . . . lower?"

"No!"

"So, nothin' else happened."

"No."

It was Rona's turn to look perplexed. "Honey, that just ain't natural. What'd'ya do? Push him away?"

"He pushed me away!"

"No! He did?"

"Yes. Then he got up and walked away. That's when he told me that we couldn't do what we started to do."

"Damn," Rona cursed. "Wouldn't you just know he'd be one of them honorable types?"

"Oh, Rona," Tess moaned, wiping away a fresh wash of tears, "I was so embarrassed."

"Yeah," Rona nodded thoughtfully, "that would be kinda embarrassin'. Bein' all ready for it and not gettin' it."

Tess gulped. "I can't talk about this anymore. I have to go to sleep now."

"Now, wait a minute, honey. Just tell me one more thing."

"I can't, Rona! It's . . . too hard to talk about, even to you."

"Oh, pshaw. If you can't talk to the likes of me, who can ya talk to? That's the trouble with you society ladies. You never talk 'bout the important stuff. All you talk about is recipes and church sermons and better ways to clean the stove. Prob'ly not a single nice woman of your aquaintance has ever gotten the big prize in bed."

With a knowing jerk of her head, she added, "And prob'ly you ain't, either, Tess. Maybe if you'd all talk a little more 'bout important things, you'd figure out what you're missin' and how to get it. 'Course I s'pose

I shouldn't be sayin' this, 'cause if you ladies figure out all the secrets of really pleasin' a man, your husbands and sweethearts wouldn't be needin' the likes o' me anymore and I'd be out of business."

Tess clapped her hands over her cheeks and stared at Rona in fascinated horror. "You know, Rona, I've never met anyone like you. The things you say are positively wicked!"

To Tess's astonishment, Rona smiled as if she'd been given a compliment. "Yeah, well, they may be wicked, but they're also true. Now, here's what I wanna know and I don't want ya to screw up your face and act all embarrassed. Just answer my question, okay?"

Tess cringed visibly as she tried to imagine what incredibly indelicate thing Rona was going to ask next. "Well . . ."

"Say yes, Tess."

Tess swallowed hard. "Okay, yes."

"Good. Now, then, you been married. You know how a man gets when he's . . . well, when his blood's boilin' for ya?"

Tess shook her head. "How he *gets*?"

Rona sighed dramatically and threw her hands up in frustration. "Yeah, how he *gets*! You know, excited and shakin' and out of breath."

Never in her life had Tess ever participated in a conversation like this one, but as shocked as she was by Rona's frankness, she was also dying to find out what words of wisdom the experienced woman might have to share. Taking a deep breath, she murmured, "Yes, I know what you mean."

Rona nodded approvingly. "Good. Now, my question is this. Did Hunter get like that with you? When he was kissin' you . . . there." Again, she stabbed a finger in the direction of Tess's breasts. "Was he moanin' and pantin' like he wanted to do more?"

Tess closed her eyes, too embarrassed to meet Rona's questioning gaze. "Yes."

"Well, okay then," Rona chuckled, "things ain't near as bad as you think they are!"

Tess opened her eyes, staring at her beaming friend in complete bewilderment. "What in the world are you talking about?"

"It's simple, honey. If the man was actin' like that when he was kissin' ya, he's interested. Take my word for it, *he is interested.* But, it's just like I suspected. Hunter's bein' a gentleman 'cause he knows you're a lady. He prob'ly figures he don't want to take advantage since he don't see no future for you two since he's not the marryin' kind."

"I know that!" Tess said impatiently. "What I don't know is how to change his mind."

"That's easy," Rona laughed, waving her hand carelessly in Tess's face. "You don't have to do nothin' 'cept be available. He'll come 'round."

"What makes you think so?"

"Take my word for it, sweetie. Once his blood's up, it's only a matter of time till he's gonna find a way to make love to you, and once he does, he'll marry you. Men know they can't have your kinda woman without marriage. You got him as good as at the altar, unless, of course, marriage ain't what you're lookin' for. In that case, ya better stay away from him, 'cause you're not the kind who's gonna be able to dally around with a man and then walk away without feelin' guilty."

"I wish I knew me as well as you seem to," Tess sighed. "I honestly don't know what I want. After Will died, I never expected to find anybody else that I'd care about, and then Hunter came along. At first, I didn't even like him, but these last few weeks, especially since Sarah was born, everything has changed, and all of a sudden, I realize I'm falling in love with him."

"I know," Rona smiled. "I could tell that the first time I saw the two of you together. And, whether you believe it or not, he feels the same way 'bout you too.

"I don't think so. There are a lot of things in Hunter's past that none of us know about. I don't think he'll ever settle down."

Rona shrugged. "Maybe not, but I still say, the man's in love with you and he's also lustin' for you. In my book, that combination spells marriage, no matter what's happened in his past."

Tess sighed thoughtfully and began unbuttoning her dress. "I guess only time will tell."

"Yup, it always does." Rona yawned, extinguishing the small lamp and stretching out on the wagon floor. "But, I'm tellin' ya, Tess, you don't have a thing to worry about. If you want him, the man is yours."

"So, how was the lemonade?"

Dash propped himself up on an elbow and grinned lecherously at Hunter.

"What are you doin' still awake?" Hunter muttered.

"Stayed awake on purpose so I could hear all the details."

"There aren't any details. How the hell do you even know where I've been?"

"Everybody in camp knows where you've been," Dash chortled. "Seems Joshua Bennington had the same idea about drinkin' lemonade with Tess that you did, and when you got to her first, he wasn't too pleased. He groused about it all evening to anybody who'd listen."

Hunter snorted with ill disguised disgust. "The man's makin' an idiot of himself over that woman."

"He may be, Colonel, but he's an idiot with honorable intentions and I'll bet my last dollar that's more than you have."

"You're right. I don't have any intentions at all."

"Is that why there aren't any 'details'?"

"For God's sake, Dash, what did you think I was gonna do? Take the girl up to the Ice Slough and ravish her?"

For a long moment, Dash watched Hunter pace back and forth in front of the fire. "Based on how testy you are, I'd say the thought must have at least crossed your mind. And I'd also say it didn't happen."

"Nothing happened."

Dash smiled slyly. "Nothing?"

Hunter whirled around and glared at his old friend. "No, nothing! Why the hell do you keep yammering about this? *Nothing happened.*"

"Then, how come your shirt's buttoned wrong?"

Hunter glanced down at the front of his shirt, then grasped it near the neckline and ripped the snaps open clear to the waist. "I probably put it on wrong this morning."

"No, you didn't," Dash drawled, lying back down and grinning. "I saw you right before you left for the slough and it was buttoned just fine then."

"Okay," Hunter gritted, stalking back over to where Dash lay. "So we kissed a little. Are you satisfied now?"

"Considering your shirt, it's my guess that you kissed more than a little. Tell me, Jared, does Tess's blouse look the same as yours does?"

"Knock it off, McLaughlin!" Hunter exploded. "It's none of your damned business what we did and I'm not gonna stand here and answer your stupid questions. This conversation is over!"

Dash's smile never wavered. "Okay, okay, just calm down."

Hunter stormed over to the other side of the campfire, throwing his blanket on the ground and flopping down on it. "Jesus Christ," he muttered, "you'd think we were kids back at school, comparin' notes on who made the most conquests in the last month."

"Well, I'm real sorry to say that I haven't made any," Dash sighed, "but if Rona Rose doesn't quit smilin' and eatin' me alive with those big green eyes of hers, that may change very soon."

"You're lustin' after *her*?"

"Pretty hard not to when every time I look at her, her eyes are runnin' all over me."

"Have you totally lost your mind? My God, Dash, she's a professional. She'd probably *charge* you!"

Dash smiled confidently. "Oh, I think I could talk her out of that."

Hunter shook his head, his shoulders shaking with amused disbelief. "Well, be careful, buddy. That woman knows every trick in the book."

"I know," Dash laughed. "Why do you think I'm so interested?"

The men settled down to go to sleep. Several silent moments passed and then Dash spoke again. "Hey, Jared, you know how you've been talkin' about maybe givin' up this life and buyin' a little spread somewhere?"

"Yeah?"

"Well, I think you should do it, and fast."

Hunter squinted into the fire's dying flames, looking over at his friend curiously. "Why?"

"Because the way you're twitchin' around over there, it's only a matter of time before you and the little widow—how should I say this—succumb. And once you do, you're gonna have to marry her."

"You're nuts," Hunter muttered. "I'm not gonna 'succumb' to anybody."

"Oh, yes you are," Dash chuckled. "It's as plain as the nose on your face that you're in love with the girl and, besides that, now you've got the old horns of lust ridin' you. In my book, that's a combination that spells m-a-r-r-i-a-g-e."

"Hey, Dash?"

"Yeah?"

"Shut up."

Dash smiled with satisfaction. "Hey, Jared?"

"Yeah?"

"I give you two weeks."

Hunter frowned and turned over on his side. "Nuts," he muttered. "Always has been, always will be."

Chapter 28

A week later they reached South Pass. Throughout the trip, the travellers had heard about the famous pass which crossed the Continental Divide and brought them their first glimpse of the long awaited Oregon Country. They were surprised, however, to find that it was not the narrow, rocky channel they had anticipated but, rather, a wide, gently sloping valley that rolled along for miles.

Except for the fact that many of the emigrants suffered from dizziness and shortness of breath, and the animals became exhausted after only a few hours of travel, it was hard to realize that they were actually over seven thousand feet above sea level. The terrain was green and rolling, more closely resembling a huge meadow than a mountain top.

The travel weary group crested the Wind River Mountains summit and began the great descent down the western slope without incident, thanks to Dash's excellent guidance and Hunter's careful overseeing of the climb.

"You know," Rona said one morning as she and

Tess ambled along, gazing at the spectacular snow capped peaks surrounding them, "it seems funny not to see the Sweetwater River no more. We followed it along for so many weeks that I kinda miss it."

"Oh, but it's so beautiful here," Tess marveled. "I don't think I've ever seen anything as beautiful as these mountains. Besides, Dash told me we'll be coming to the Snake River soon, so you'll get to see water again."

"I feel better when there's a river in sight," Rona confessed. "Guess I spent too much time in that dry, dusty hellhole."

"You didn't like Fort Laramie?" Tess asked.

"No. I hated it. That's why I decided to go with Sam when he asked me. I kept hearin' how beautiful it was once you crossed the Divide and I wanted to see it for myself."

"What are you going to do once we get to Oregon?"

Rona shrugged. "Don't know. Settle down in a town somewhere, I guess. A town means a saloon and a saloon means men, so as long as I find a town, I'll find work."

"Rona," Tess asked quietly, "have you ever thought about, well, settling down somewhere—with just one man?"

"Sure, but I gotta find one first, and when you've lived the life I have, that ain't easy."

Tess looked at her friend sympathetically. "No, I suppose it isn't."

"Hey," Rona chided, reaching over and nudging Tess playfully, "we all got our problems, right? Nobody ever said it was gonna be all fun. I mean, look at you. You've found the man you want, but you don't hardly even speak to him no more. Ever since that night you two went up to the Ice Slough, you ain't said ten words to each other. Now, that's just plum crazy, if ya ask me."

Tess shook her head, her face mirroring her unhappiness. "It's better this way."

"How can it be better?"

"If he really feels there's no future for us, it's better that we end it now. If we had let things . . . develop . . . it would have just been harder to say goodbye later."

"You're prob'ly right," Rona sighed. "A man as big and bold as he is, ya prob'ly would've ended up with another little Sarah on your hands and the last thing ya need is *another* baby to raise with no daddy." Squinting her eyes against the bright morning sun, she scanned the wagons ahead of them. "And speakin' of big and bold, there he is now, and he's comin' this way."

Hunter was, indeed, riding toward them. Waving to Matthew Bennington who was driving Tess's wagon, he angled his horse over to the women and pulled the roan to a halt. Without so much as a greeting, he said, "Where's Sarah?"

"In her cradle," Tess replied, pointing at the little box hanging off the side of the wagon. "Why?"

"Get her out of there, and then all of you get in the wagon for awhile."

"What's the matter, Hunter?" Rona asked, her senses suddenly alert.

"Nothing, except that Dash spotted a party of Indians a couple of miles ahead. I'm sure they probably just want to do some trading and that there's nothing to worry about, but I don't want to take any chances."

"Oh, my Lord," Tess gasped, clapping her hand over her chest. "Indians!"

Hunter frowned at her impatiently. "Now, don't you go having a fit of the vapors. I told you, I don't think there's anything to worry about. Just stay in the wagon and out of sight. Everything will be fine."

Tess nodded, but her expression remained doubtful.

With a final nod, Hunter reined his horse around and rode up to the front of the wagon, speaking briefly to Matthew Bennington, then continuing on down the line.

Tess turned to Rona, looking at her with wide, frightened eyes. Rona was just as scared as Tess, but with her customary bluster, she said, "Well, don't just stand there lookin' like a scared rabbit, get the baby and let's get in the wagon!"

Shouting at Matthew to stop the wagon, Tess ran up to Sarah's cradle, scooping the baby out from under the protective netting and hurriedly climbing into the back of the wagon. "What should we do now?" she whispered, sitting down next to Rona on the narrow cot.

"Wait," Rona answered, "and pray."

They didn't have to wait long. Twenty minutes later, they heard shouting, followed almost immediately by the wagon jolting to a halt as Matthew pulled back hard on the mules' reins. Turning his head slightly, he hissed, "Stay quiet, ladies. There's a bunch of 'em and they're rovin' all over the place."

Tess and Rona exchanged frightened glances, then Tess unbuttoned her bodice, putting Sarah to her breast to ensure the baby's silence.

The minutes dragged by endlessly as the two women sat in paralyzed silence, gripping each other's hands for support. Matthew had gotten down from the wagon seat and disappeared, so they didn't even have the small comfort of his whispered reports.

Finally, Rona could stand it no longer. Getting up from the cot, she crept to the front of the wagon and peeked out.

"What's going on?" Tess whispered.

"Matt was right," Rona responded quietly. "There

must be a hundred Indians out there. They're all on horses and they're all armed."

"What are they doing?"

"Talkin' to Hunter and Dash."

"Do they seem mad?"

"I can't tell. They're throwin' their arms 'round, though, and Hunter looks mighty peeved."

"Oh, God," Tess moaned. "We're all going to get killed, I just know it."

"Wait a minute," Rona said. "Jack Riley is walkin' this way." She was silent for a moment, then Tess heard her calling softly to someone outside the wagon. The muted conversation went on for several seconds, then Rona turned back to Tess, her eyes huge. "They want you, Tess."

Tess's heart stopped. "What?"

"Jack says the Indians been watchin' the train for a coupla days and the chief says he wants the yellow haired woman. Says if he gets her, they'll leave peaceable."

"And if he doesn't?" Tess squeaked.

Rona shrugged. "I don't know, but Hunter's already told him he can't have ya. Accordin' to Jack, Hunter told the chief that you're his woman and he's not givin' you up."

From outside, Rona heard Jack saying something more and immediately peeked out again. When she drew her head back in, she said, "Jack says the reason they want you is 'cause you're blonde. He says Indians love blonde women 'cause all their women are dark." Silently, Rona thanked the fates that had graced her with raven hair.

Rona returned to her post, then suddenly gasped and dived back into the wagon's interior.

"What's wrong?" Tess demanded, her voice shaking with fear.

"It looks like the chief is gettin' mad. I think him and Hunter are gonna fight."

"No!" Tess gasped. "My Lord, Hunter could get killed! I've heard Indians don't fight fair, that they do whatever it takes to win, even if it means pulling a knife or having one of their friends throw a tomahawk."

"I heard that too," Rona nodded, "but it looks like Hunter's gonna fight him, anyway. Looks like they've come to some sorta agreement 'bout it."

Tess clapped a hand over her mouth, staring at Rona in horror. "Go see what's happening now."

Rona nodded and again rose to look out the slit. "Yup, they're gonna fight, all right."

"I have to stop this!" Tess cried, clutching the baby to her desperately. "Maybe they don't really want me at all. Maybe all they want is my hair."

Rona frowned at Tess impatiently. "So, what'd'ya gonna do? Let 'em scalp you?"

"No," Tess answered, her voice suddenly calm and decisive. "I'm going to cut my hair off and give it to them."

"What? Are you crazy?"

"If it will save Hunter, it's a small enough price to pay. Tell Jack to run and ask Hunter if the chief will settle for my hair."

Rona looked at Tess as if she'd lost her mind, but having no better plan in mind to save their skins, she did as her friend bade.

"What did he say?" Tess asked as Rona again sat down on the edge of the cot.

"He says he'll ask, but he don't think Hunter will agree."

"I don't give a damn what Hunter thinks!" Tess snapped. "If it will save our lives, then they can have my damn hair!"

"Tess!" Rona said, her eyes widening with admiration. "I never heard you cuss before."

"Never mind about that," Tess retorted. "Go take another peek."

For the third time, Rona got up and looked outside. "Jack's comin' back." She waited a minute, then turned back to Tess. "Hunter wouldn't even ask the chief. He told Jack to tell ya to quit bein' ridiculous and to just stay in the wagon till this is over."

"Oh Rona, tell Jack to ask the chief himself!" Tess implored. "Hunter's going to get killed and all over a hank of hair!"

Rona relayed Tess's message and again Jack took off. "He's talkin' to Hunter now," Rona announced. "Oh, Lordy, you should see Hunter's face. He's furious! Now, Jack is turnin' t'wards the chief like he's gonna ask himself. He's sayin' somethin'. The chief's noddin'. My God, Tess, Hunter just punched Jack!"

"This is enough!" Tess cried, laying the baby aside and jumping to her feet. "Where are the scissors?"

Rona whirled around, gaping at her in disbelief. "Are you really gonna cut your hair off?"

"No. You are. Now, where are the scissors?"

Rona stared at Tess for a moment, then reached over and opened a bureau drawer. "Right here," she said, holding up a large pair of sewing scissors.

"Good," Tess nodded. Reaching up, she pulled the pins out of her hair, letting the heavy mass of curls fall down her back. Taking a deep breath, she turned to Rona. "Okay, cut it off, right at my neck."

Rona looked at her beseechingly. "Oh, Tess, do you really think . . ."

"Cut it!"

With a resigned sigh, Rona crawled over to where Tess sat. Grabbing hold of the luxurious fall of hair, she clamped her tongue between her teeth and started cutting.

Tears sprang to Tess's eyes as she felt the drag of

the scissors, but she bit down hard on her bottom lip, refusing to give in to her anguish.

It took Rona almost a minute to finish her task, but finally, she laid the scissors down. "Okay, here it is."

Tess whirled around, looking at the long fall of curls Rona held. Her hand trembling, she reached out and took the hair from her friend. "Watch the baby while I'm gone."

Rona nodded, her own eyes swimming.

Tess jumped out of the back of the wagon and ran toward the crowd of men. As she neared the tense and wary group, she saw Hunter stripping off his shirt. "Wait!" she screamed. "Stop! There's no reason to fight!" Skidding to a halt in front of a fierce looking Indian in a feathered headdress, she held out the hank of hair. "Here. This is what you want. Take it and go!"

A collective gasp rose among the men and Tess suddenly found her arm being locked in an iron grip. "You little fool!" Hunter snarled. "What in the hell do you think you're doing?"

"Saving my baby's life!" Tess shot back, refusing to admit to the enraged man that she was trying to save his as well.

Again, she turned back to the astonished Indian. "Here! Take it!" Angrily, she shook the mane of hair in the chief's face.

The Indian shouted something at Hunter in a harsh, guttural tongue, his arms flailing wildly. Tess couldn't tell if he was angry or amused, but Hunter's snarled response left no doubt as to *his* frame of mind.

Looking back and forth between the two men, Tess waited for someone to explain what was going on. When no one did, she again shoved the hair at the Indian. "Do you want it or don't you?"

With a last, threatening glare at Hunter, the Indian

chief reached out and grabbed the hair out of her hand, then turned his pony around and took off at a gallop, whooping loudly and brandishing the hair above his head like a flag. The other members of the raiding party immediately kicked their horses into action, following their leader down the trail and disappearing into the heavy woods.

"I could kill you!" Hunter snarled, turning on Tess in a fury the likes of which she'd never seen.

"And he could have killed you!" she shouted back. "And Sarah and me and all the other members of this train."

Hunter looked around, suddenly aware that every man on the train was witnessing their heated confrontation. "Come here," he growled, hauling Tess off toward a copse of trees. When they reached the seclusion of the giant pines, he spun her around to face him. "For your information, I had gotten the chief to agree to settle this matter with a simple fist fight. If you'd just stayed out of it, it would all have been over in a few minutes."

"And what if you had lost?" Tess challenged. "You'd be lying dead and I'd be an Apache prisoner."

"They were Cheyenne."

"Who cares?" Tess yelled, her ire now coming close to matching his. "They were savages and I didn't care to spend the rest of my life with them, okay?"

"I wouldn't have lost!" Hunter thundered, his face clearly betraying his offense at her words. *My God, did the woman have so little faith in his fighting abilities that she thought he could be bested by one middle aged Indian?* "And you'd still have your hair!"

For the first time since she'd confronted the Indian chief, Tess remembered her shorn locks. A wave of self consciousness washed over her and she raised her hand, running her fingers across the back of her neck and feeling the ragged ends of her butchered hair. With a jolt of anguish, the enormity of her impulsive action gripped her and her voice dropped to a whisper. "What's done is done. It'll grow back in a couple of years."

In other circumstances, Hunter might have felt a twinge of compassion at the bereft tone in her voice, but right now, he was far too angry to be sympathetic. "If you ever, *ever* disobey one of my orders again, I'll throw you off this train so fast it will make your head swim! As it is, I've a mind to drop you at Fort Hall."

Tess's self righteous anger immediately reasserted itself. "Fine! Why don't you just do that? I'm tired of listening to your threats. Throw me off, throw me off, that's all you ever say. Why don't you quit talking about it and do it!"

"All right, goddamn it, I will! Plan on it!"

"Fine, I will!"

"And, this time, you better also plan to stay there, because I'm not coming back after you like I did when you pulled that stunt at Fort Laramie."

"Don't worry," Tess spat. "I'm not planning to follow you. I'll find some other way to get to Oregon City. The last thing I want is to be beholden to you anymore."

"Well, I'm glad to hear that. And until we reach Fort Hall, I want you in your wagon and out of my sight. Do I make myself clear?"

"Perfectly, but that doesn't mean I'm going to do it."

"You better or, by God, I'll chain you to your cot!"

Tess threw him a killing look. "That seems to be one of your specialties, Mr. Hunter. You're real good at chaining people up. I guess it's the simplest answer when you can't think of a civilized way to handle problems, right?"

Hunter drew in a sharp breath, hardly able to bear

the pain her icy words caused him. "Get out of here," he warned. "Go. NOW!"

"I'm going!" Tess cried, picking up her skirts as if to flee. "And I'll stay in my wagon, just like you ordered. Not because you ordered it, but because I don't want to see you any more than you want to see me." Throwing her head back to keep the tears from spilling, she covered her face with her hands. "Lord in heaven, how I regret the day I ever laid eyes on you!"

Hunter heard a sob tear loose from her throat, but before he could react, she was gone, sprinting across the emerald carpet of grass like a frightened doe running from a predator. Closing his eyes, he lowered his head, swinging it slowly back and forth. "I'm sure you do, sweetheart," he sighed miserably. "I'm very sure you do."

Chapter 29

Hunter stood enshrouded in the heavy, late evening shadows and watched Tess. She had been sitting under a pine tree for over an hour, not moving, not making a sound, just staring off into the distance at the mountains. It was a clear, moonlit night, and even though it was nearly midnight, he could see her features clearly. Although her expression was dispassionate and void of anger, there was no sign of contentment in her face. Rather, there was a sad, defeated look about her that troubled him, preventing him from approaching her and saying what he had come to say.

Since their argument that afternoon, he had been tongue lashed by nearly everyone he'd come in contact with. Dash had given him a piece of his mind, then Jack, and even Rona had braved his wrath to tell him that she thought he was "the stupidest, selfishest, stubbornest jackass" she'd ever met.

Planting her fists on her voluptuous hips, Rona had dressed him down like an irate mother chastising a recalcitrant child, berating him for his lack of gratitude toward Tess for sacrificing her hair to save him, and warning him that if he did anything more to wound Tess's delicate heart, he'd have to answer to her. When he'd coldly reminded her who was the head of the outfit, Rona had simply tossed her dark hair, pinned him with a stony look and announced that if she lived to be a hundred, she'd never understand why a "sweet little darlin'" like Tess would be in love with a jackass like him. She'd then ended her tirade by calling him by a few names he'd never dreamed a woman would even know and flouncing away, leaving him standing open mouthed, furious, and strangely chagrined.

He'd then gone in search of Tess, determined to set things to rights between them. It had taken him almost an hour to find her, seated on the heavily carpeted forest floor in a secluded cluster of trees, her head and back braced up against a tall, Jack Pine.

Drawing a deep, bracing breath, Hunter stepped forward, intentionally scuffing loudly through the pine needless so as not to frighten her with his approach. He saw her glance toward him out of the corner of her eye, then hurriedly look away again, trying to pretend that she hadn't seen him.

"You shouldn't be sitting with your head against that tree," he said quietly, standing above her. "You're going to get pitch in your hair."

Tess remained silent for a long moment, then slowly reached up and touched the back of her head, testing to see if it was sticky. "What hair?" she asked ruefully.

Hunter closed his eyes, the quiet resignation in her words so wrenching that he could hardly bear it. "Tess," he whispered, dropping to his knees beside her. "I'm . . . sorry about what happened today."

"It doesn't matter."

"Yes, it does matter." Moving around in front of

her, he picked up one of her icy hands, lifting it to his lips and gently kissing her palm. "It matters very much and I want to explain."

She pulled her hand away, keeping her eyes trained on some far off point in the distance.

Hunter frowned, wishing she'd look at him, but knowing it would be a grave mistake to demand she do so. In a voice so low that it was hardly audible, he said, "I was angry because I thought you didn't trust me."

"Trust had nothing to do with it."

"I understand that now, but I want you to know that I would have taken care of the situation. You needn't have sacrificed your hair to help me."

"I didn't do it to help you," she flared, lifting her chin and glaring at him mutinously. "I did it to save my baby."

"Okay," he nodded, "I can understand your reasoning, but you should know by now that I wouldn't have let anything happen to you or Sarah."

"I appreciate your concern for us," Tess said, trying desperately to keep her voice cool and unemotional, "but I am used to taking care of my own. I don't need any help from anybody, especially you."

A new surge of pain shot through Hunter's heart. "Especially me . . ." he repeated wearily. "All right. I won't bother you anymore." Slowly, he got to his feet, taking a halting step backward. "I just wanted to thank you for what you did and tell you I'm sorry."

He started to move away, but Tess's strangled little cry stopped him. "Jared . . . don't go."

Suddenly, he was beside her again, dropping to his knees and gathering her into a crushing embrace. "Oh, Tess, sweetheart," he moaned, pressing his face into her neck, "I almost died when I saw you running toward that warrior."

"I didn't want him to hurt you," Tess cried, burying

her fingers in the soft silkiness of his hair. "I was afraid he wouldn't fight fair and that you'd end up dead."

Hunter raised his head, gazing into her teary eyes incredulously. "That's why you didn't want me to fight him? Not because you thought I couldn't handle him?"

"Of course I didn't think that. Any fool could see that you were stronger than he was and in a fair fight, he wouldn't stand a chance against you. But I've heard terrible stories about these renegade war parties. I didn't want you to end up with a tomahawk in your back over something as ridiculous as my hair." She paused, then added, "That *is* all he wanted, isn't it? My hair? I mean, he's not going to come back to get the rest of me, is he?"

"No," Hunter soothed, "he's not. He originally wanted to take you, but I think he was so flattered that you cut off your hair for him that he was willing to accept that instead. He considered it a gift."

"A gift," Tess chuckled sadly. "A gift that left me looking like a scarecrow."

Hunter gazed deep into her blue eyes, his expression soft and yearning. "You're wrong about that," he breathed, leaning forward and feathering kisses over her eyes and cheeks. "You're the most beautiful woman I've ever seen, long hair or short."

"Oh, Hunter . . ."

"Call me Jared," he whispered, kissing her beneath her ear. "I love it when you call me Jared."

"And I love it when you're *being* Jared."

Hunter lifted his head, peering at her curiously. "*Being* Jared?"

"Yes," Tess smiled. "When you're like this, with your arms around me, kissing me, whispering to me, then you're Jared. That's when I love you the most."

Hunter drew in a startled breath, wondering if Tess

even realized that she'd just confessed she loved him. "Tess," he groaned, shaking his head, "I don't want you to love me. My life is in ashes. I have nothing to offer you—no money, no future, not even a name anymore."

"My life is in ashes too," Tess responded softly. "But maybe we can be each other's phoenix . . . at least for tonight."

Hunter looked at her searchingly for a long moment. He wanted her so badly. Wanted to hold her, kiss her, make love to her until they both lost themselves in passion's sweet surcease, until all the lonely realities of his empty life faded away—if only for just tonight. If he just had tonight, perhaps it would be enough. He could hold on to it forever, remembering this place and this woman and this moment. Gaining strength and comfort in the long, solitary days ahead that for one, magical summer evening, he had been allowed to forget his tortured, haunted past and just be Jared again. Not Hunter. Not Colonel Whitaker. Just Jared.

"Help me forget," he moaned, his lips brushing against hers provocatively as he laid her back in the pine needles.

"We'll both forget," she promised. "For tonight, let's forget everything except each other."

Their kisses deepened, becoming hot and sensuous as mouths melded, tongues touched, and breath mingled. Hunter's fingers deftly unbuttoned Tess's bodice, spreading the fabric wide and exposing her full breasts. "So beautiful," he breathed, kissing the soft white skin reverently. His lips traced a path across the round globes until his mouth settled over a nipple, his tongue toying with the hard little bud. Tess's head fell back and her lips parted with ecstasy.

Hunter felt her hands run down the front of his shirt and heard the sharp ping of snaps giving way.

Then she pulled him back to her, rubbing her breasts against the sensitive skin on his bronzed chest. He closed his eyes and smiled, the sensation of her skin touching his a sweet agony that he wished would never end. They kissed again, drinking deeply of each other's essence until, finally, Hunter sat back on his haunches, his eyes roving greedily over the beauty of her semi-nude body. "I want to see you," he whispered, raising her shoulders to push her bodice down. "All of you."

Tess smiled dreamily. "But you've seen all of me before."

"That was different," he rasped, raising her hips and pulling off her dress and petticoat. "So different."

Tess coyly crossed her legs, preventing him from stripping off her stockings. "No more," she teased, eyeing the masculine bulge in his denims, "until I get to see all of you."

Hunter didn't need any encouragement. With a throaty laugh of anticipation, he turned away, pulling off his boots and shinnying his tight pants down his thighs. The moonlight shone on his bare back, illuminating the heavy ridges of muscle in a silvery glow. He could feel Tess's gaze roaming over his lean hips and muscular buttocks, and the mere thought of her eyes feasting on his nakedness made him shiver with need. Glancing down at his impassioned manhood, he thanked the fates for the gift of this night. It seemed like a lifetime since he had felt the hot, pulsing excitement of sexual arousal throbbing through his blood and a feeling of renewal coursed through him as he looked down at his rigid, straining length.

Turning around, he stood proudly erect, unabashedly displaying his physical magnificence to the woman before him. He shivered with anticipation, then looked down at her, his breath catching in his throat when he saw that she had also divested herself of the rest of her clothing and was as unashamedly naked as he.

"Kiss me again," she whispered, holding her arms up to him.

Hunter pulled her to her feet, wrapping one arm around her shoulders while the other circled her hips, pressing her hard against his hot, aroused body. Dipping his head, he kissed her, their bodies fitting together like perfectly cut pieces of a puzzle. Soft curves melded into hard planes, lush breasts pressed against steely chest muscles, satiny hips pressed into muscular loins. With a little shudder of excitement, Tess moved one foot, spreading her thighs just enough to allow Hunter's rigid staff to slip between her legs.

A bolt of desire shot through him, seeming to settle in the hot pulsing shaft nestled so intimately between Tess's thighs. With a groan, he subtly undulated his hips, causing the moist tip of his manhood to probe with heated demand at the threshold of her femininity.

Tess moaned, clutching at his shoulders as her legs began to buckle. Hunter caught her to him, lowering them both to the pile of discarded clothing strewn around their feet. Laying her back, he looked down into her passion glazed eyes. "Are you comfortable?" he murmured, his voice shaking with desire.

"Yes."

The shy eagerness in her voice forced him to look away, drawing on every reserve of will he possessed as he reminded himself that she was fragile, vulnerable, and unused to lovemaking. He had to go slowly with her, regardless of how much his overheated body demanded release. This could very well be the only moment they would ever have together and he wanted it to be perfect. Anything less would be a travesty.

He began kissing her again, his lips sweeping down her neck, past her breasts and settling on the soft skin of her belly. He inhaled deeply, intoxicated by the sweet essence of her femininity. "You smell like flowers," he whispered.

Tess smiled, very glad that she'd taken Rona's suggestion and stolen a few moments for a bath that afternoon.

Hunter swept his hand up the inside of her thigh, settling it over the warm, moist nest between her legs. Sensuously, he toyed with her, caressing her dewy skin until she writhed beneath him.

He moved upward again, covering her entire body with his own as his lips descended upon hers. Lying on the cool fragrant ground, they kissed passionately, both of them reveling in the shared heat of their bodies, the taut excitement radiating between them.

With a sigh of surrender, Tess raised her knees, shifting her hips upward as she invited Hunter to greater intimacy. Instantly, he answered her beckoning call, rising to his knees and pressing the tip of his throbbing organ seductively against her.

A long, enraptured groan escaped him as he felt Tess's cool hand touch him. Her soft, stroking fingers made every fiber of his being cry out for release, but he was loathe to deny himself the pleasure of her intimate caresses and held himself back until he knew he could wait no longer.

With a groan of ecstasy, he gently entered her, careful to go slowly as he sheathed himself within her delicate body. He heard Tess sigh with pleasure as she took him into her, surrounding him with her warmth and calling up feelings of love and longing within him that he had thought forever dead. Slowly, exquisitely, Hunter made love to her, rocking gently as he subtly coaxed her to join him in passion's ancient dance.

Tess shyly responded to his seductive thrusts, gradually acquainting herself to the nuances of his rhythms until they moved together as perfectly as if they had been lovers for years. Slowly, their cadence increased, as did their ardor. Hunter's strokes became faster, deeper, more heated and demanding as they strove together in their lovers' quest. When their moment finally came, they hurtled off into passion's far flung universe, their moans of satisfaction giving way to sighs of ecstasy as they settled back to earth, replete and exhausted.

Never, in all his many romantic encounters, had Hunter ever experienced the joy he felt having Tess wrapped in his arms. He lay atop her for a long while, still intimately joined while their bodies cooled and their hearts slowed. Finally, he gently withdrew and rolled onto his back, pulling her up against his side and nestling her head cozily in the hollow of his shoulder.

"That was incredible," he murmured, kissing the top of her head.

"It was for me too," Tess smiled shyly, gazing up at him. "Rona told me that what we just shared is called the 'Big Prize', and this is the first time I've ever experienced it."

Hunter looked at her incredulously. "The *Big Prize*?" he gasped.

Tess nodded languidly. "That's what she called it."

"Well, I guess it suits," he chuckled. "And you've never before . . ."

Tess shook her head, smiling at him shyly. "Never." Laying back, she sighed wistfully. "It was so wonderful that it almost makes me wish it wasn't over . . ."

Hunter felt a sizzle of renewed desire race down his spine. "You know what?" he chuckled.

"What?"

"Underneath that demure Bostonian matron's facade, you're a little tiger."

Tess blushed becomingly. "Tonight anyway," she murmured, snuggling against him and lightly running her fingertip across his taut nipple.

"Oh, I see." With a smile full of promise, he lifted her chin till her eyes met his. "Then, I'm happy to tell you, Mrs. Caldwell, that tonight is far from over . . ."

Tess rolled over on top of him, kissing him lustily. "Oh, Mr. Whitaker, I was so hoping you'd say that."

Chapter 30

"Mornin', Hunter."

"Mornin', Dash. Great day, isn't it?"

Dash turned away from the horse he was saddling and looked at his friend curiously. Normally, Hunter's mood first thing in the morning ranged from silent to surly. The pleasantness that he was displaying this morning was so unprecedented that Dash could hardly believe his ears.

"Well, don't you look like the cat that got the cream this mornin'," Dash noted, turning back to his horse. "Or . . ." Suddenly a huge grin lit his face. ". . . maybe I should say, the man who got the girl?" Craning his head around, he shot his friend a questioning look.

Hunter smiled blandly and moved off toward his own mount.

"By the way," Dash continued, slipping the bridle over his horse's head, "where did you sleep last night? I made rounds before I turned in, but I didn't see you anywhere."

Hunter's smile widened into a grin. "That, my man, is none of your business."

Dash gaped at his friend in astonishment. "Well, I'll be damned! I *am* right!"

Hunter remained silent, but his grin remained.

"I *am*, aren't I?" Dash prodded.

"I don't know what you're talking about. Now, what's the plan for today? Think we'll make Soda Springs?"

Dash clucked to his horse, leading the big gelding over to where Hunter stood. "Maybe. Be nice for you if we did. Soda's kind of a romantic place, what with those hot springs and all."

Hunter blew out a resigned breath, realizing that Dash was not going to let him off the hook. "Okay, McLaughlin, let's get this out of the way. Where I was and what I was doing last night is my business and my business only, so you might as well quit with the innuendos because I'm not going to tell you anything."

"I know, I know," Dash laughed. "A gentleman never tells."

"Right," Hunter nodded. "Assuming, of course, that the gentleman has something *not* to tell."

Dash leaned in close, cocking his head and looking intently into Hunter's eyes. "Oh, Colonel," he teased, "all a body has to do is look at those heavy eyes of yours to know that you definitely have something not to tell!"

"Get the hell away from me!" Hunter ordered good naturedly, giving Dash a swat with his reins. "We've got work to do."

"Hell if we do. The train isn't gonna be ready to pull out for a half hour yet. We've got time for a cup of coffee . . . and a chat."

"Coffee, yes," Hunter agreed. "But, a chat? Not on your life."

Dash shrugged and moved off to get the coffee. "Can't blame a man for tryin' " he grumbled. "The way my love life is goin' these days, it looks like the only way I'm gonna get any thrills is by listenin' to somebody else."

Hunter squatted down next to Dash, accepting the cup of coffee he held out with a grateful nod. "What happened to your plans with Miss Rona?"

"Well, you know, that's a funny thing," Dash drawled. "I went over to her wagon last night to ask her if she might like to take the air with me, but she told me she couldn't. You know why?"

Hunter was careful to keep his expression impassive. "No. Why?"

"Seems she was takin' care of little Sarah Caldwell for her mama who was off God knows where. Anyway, Rona said that she had no idea when Mrs. Caldwell would be returning and, until she did, Rona couldn't leave."

"Did you go back later to see if Mrs. Caldwell had returned?"

"Once, about an hour later, but she still wasn't back."

"So, what did you do then?"

Dash shrugged. "I gave up. In fact, I came lookin' for you to see if you wanted to play a hand of cards, but strangely enough, I couldn't find you either."

"Guess you were just out of luck for company," Hunter chuckled.

"Guess I was. I finally just hunkered down alone in my blankets and slept until the time came for me to take the watch."

"Pretty boring evening, huh?"

"Yup, sure was." Throwing Hunter a teasing glance, he added, "So, how about yours? Was it as boring as mine?"

"Nope."

Dash waited, but when it became apparent that Hunter wasn't going to say anymore, he finally blurted, "Come on, Jared. I'm your best friend. If you're not gonna share any of the details, then just tell me one thing."

Hunter stared at him over the rim of his cup and waited.

"Was it special?" Dash asked, his voice suddenly quiet and full of concern. "Was it worth everything you've gone through with her?"

The look of Hunter's eyes as they closed in remembrance answered Dash's question even before he spoke. "Oh, yeah," he murmured. "It was worth everything."

"I'm glad, Jared," Dash said sincerely. "So, what happens now?"

Hunter's languid gaze refocused on his friend. "Nothing."

"Nothing! How can you sit here looking like a pie eyed kid and then say 'nothing'?"

"It was one night, Dash. She and I agreed about that. Just one night."

"You're crazy. You've gotten this far with this woman and now you're just gonna throw it all away? Why?"

Hunter's mouth tightened. "You know why."

"No, I *don't* know why, except that you've got some fool idea that because you were forced to do some ugly things during the war and then your fiancée jilted you, you're incapable of loving someone and being loved in return. I've told you for years that that's a pile of shit, but you just keep on believin' it. Now you've got another chance, another woman, and you're gonna throw it all away? I call that goddamn stupid!"

Hunter tossed out the dregs of his coffee and got to his feet. "Okay, I've heard enough. You see, Dash, this is why I don't talk to you about stuff like this. You never just listen. You always have to throw in your two cents worth. Well, I don't need it. Not from you, not from anybody. I know what my relationship is with Tess and so does she. We both understand that last night was a very special moment in both our lives, but that's all. It's over and now, everything goes back to the way it was. And that's the end of this conversation."

Turning on his heel, Hunter stalked over to his roan and mounted, spurring the animal hard and taking off at a dead gallop toward the front of the train.

Dash stood watching his friend's headlong flight, his hands on his hips. "You're a fool, Colonel Whitaker. A damn fool. Always have been, always will be."

Hunter couldn't ride hard enough, fast enough, far enough to wipe Dash's words out of his mind. *Another chance, another woman.* Was it possible that Dash was right? Was it possible that he might make a new start with Tess?

"Don't be a fool," he muttered angrily, sitting atop his winded horse at the summit of a large hill. "Love brings nothing but pain. Why should it be different this time? Just let it go and leave things the way they are."

He drew in a startled breath as he faced the reality of his own wayward thoughts. He was in love with Tess Caldwell.

"No, you're not!" he argued desperately. "It's just the sex. You've confused passion with love, that's all. It's perfectly natural . . . and as soon as you get her to where she's going, you'll forget all about her."

Dismounting, he sat down heavily on the ground, crossing his arms over his bent knees and laying his head wearily on them. Who was he kidding? He'd never forget her.

How had this happened? How had this woman who had started their relationship by deceiving him, had lied to him more times than he could count, and had driven him nearly crazy with her mad determination to reach her goal, ever wormed her way into his heart?

Since the day he'd met her, Tess had annoyed him, infuriated him, and taken up his time. He'd spent most of the months in her company trying to find ways to get rid of her. Yet, somehow, in the midst of all that, he had fallen in love with her. Totally, irrevocably in love.

His mind drifted back to the previous night, seeing again her languid eyes as she smiled up at him in the moonlight, remembering her self-consciousness over her shorn hair—hair that she had cut off in an effort to save him from being hurt—feeling again the sensation of her hands on his body as she'd caressed him with a lover's touch.

They had made love all night long, sleeping only briefly when sexual satiation exhausted them to the point that they could no longer hold their eyes open. Then waking later to begin again. As the night progressed, their lovemaking had become more intimate, more passionate, more uninhibited. They had shared moments together that most married couples never knew and, yet, this morning when he'd left her at her wagon, she had not demanded vows of love or commitment from him. She'd merely touched his cheek and smiled, whispering that he had given her the most beautiful night of her life.

As Hunter's thoughts meandered back over the night just passed, he realized that Tess was everything a man could hope for in a woman. She was beautiful, gentle, loving, and sensual. So, why couldn't he just let their relationship develop as it would?

"Because it's bound to go bad. It always does." He shook his head, knowing it was better to end it now and remember that one perfect night than to let things sour and end up with regrets tainting his memories.

With a disconsolate sigh, he got to his feet, trudging tiredly over to his horse and riding back down the hill. "It's better this way," he told himself again. "Much better."

So, why did he feel like crying?

"You gonna tell me 'bout it, or do I have ta ask straight out?"

Tess leaned Sarah against her shoulder and gently patted the baby's back. "What do you mean?"

"Oh, come on, Tess, you know exactly what I mean. What happened last night?"

"Last night?"

"Yeah," Rona blurted, "remember last night? When you was gone six hours? It's a good thing little Sweetie Pie there slept all night. If I'd had to come find ya to feed her, it could've been a mite embarrassin' for everybody."

Tess looked at Rona in dismay. "Oh, Rona, I'm so sorry. I didn't mean to inconvenience you."

"You didn't inconvenience me," Rona relented. "You're just awful quiet this mornin' and I wanna make sure you're okay. That . . . nothin' bad happened."

Tess's eyes took on a dreamy, faraway look. "Nothing bad happened."

"And?" Rona prodded.

"It's not something I can talk about," Tess said softly. "It's . . . private."

"I know, it's private! Sakes alive, honey, I'm not askin' for details. Believe me, I know how it's done. All I wanna know is how you're feelin' this mornin'."

A rosy blush stained Tess's cheeks. "I feel fine. Wonderful, in fact."

Rona grinned. "Somehow I just knew that man would be good. So, now what're the two of you gonna do?"

Tess looked quickly away, not wanting Rona to see the bereft expression she knew she couldn't hide. "Nothing," she said, trying hard to keep her voice light. "It was just one night. Now it's over."

Rona frowned. "Bull horns. If ya really felt that way, ya wouldn't be avoidin' my eyes. I told ya once I didn't think you could dally with a man and then just walk away, and I still don't."

Tess smiled as Sarah emitted a lusty burp. "What a good girl," she crooned approvingly.

"And I still don't," Rona repeated, reminding Tess that she did not consider their conversation over.

"Well, I'm just going to have to walk away," Tess sighed. "I knew last night that was the way it was going to be. Now I have to live with it."

Rona sat down on the edge of the cot next to Tess and picked up one of her hands. "Will ya tell me somethin'? Somethin' real personal?"

Tess glanced at her warily. "What?"

"How many times did ya do it?"

Tess closed her eyes, wondering if Rona would ever cease to shock her. "Oh, Rona," she groaned in embarrassment, "the questions you ask."

Rona shrugged unrepentantly. "Just tell me."

"Why do you want to know?"

" 'Cause I'm tryin' to figure out what's goin' on here."

"But what does that have to do with anything?"

"Just tell me, Tess!"

Tess lowered her head and mumbled, "Three."

"What?"

"Three!"

Rona's eyes widened. "My God, Tess, three times? Did ya sleep at all?"

"Not much," Tess admitted.

"Well, I can tell ya one thing for sure. It ain't over. Any man makes love to a woman three times in one night has feelings a lot deeper than just lust. And I s'pose he kissed ya and held ya and stuff like that in between, right?"

Tess nodded.

"I figured as much." Rona grinned and patted Tess's hand happily. "Don't you worry none, Tess, girl. It ain't over between ya. Not by a long shot."

"Good mornin', Mr. Hunter," Rona smiled as she jumped down from the back of the wagon.

"Good morning to you, Miss Rose. Are you ready to begin the day's trek?"

"As ready as I'm ever gonna be, I guess."

"We should be reaching Soda Springs sometime today," Hunter informed her. "That should offer a pleasant little diversion this evening."

"Glad to hear it," Rona responded. "I'm sure everybody needs a diversion once in a while, whatever that means."

Hunter chuckled, amused, as always, by Rona's frankness. "A diversion is something pleasant that takes your mind off your day to day problems."

Rona smiled slyly. "Oh, I see. Well, in that case, you'll find your diversion inside the wagon dressin' the baby."

Hunter's eyes flared with embarrassment. "Thanks," he mumbled, dismounting and stepping up on to the wagon's tailgate.

Just as Rona had said, Tess was bending over the

cot, wrapping Sarah in a soft blue bunting. "How are you?" he asked quietly.

The sound of his voice brought Tess's head up with a jerk. "I'm . . . I'm fine," she murmured, not knowing quite how to act around him in the bright light of day.

"Are you ready to go?"

"Just about." Picking up Sarah, Tess made a great pretense of adjusting the baby's blanket so she wouldn't have to meet Hunter's questioning gaze.

"I saw Matt a minute ago," Hunter said pleasantly. "He's on his way down."

Tess nodded and moved toward the back of the wagon. "Then, I better put Sarah in her cradle."

Hunter stepped aside to let her pass, greatly bothered by the sudden awkwardness between them. You shouldn't have made love to her, he silently berated himself. It's ruined everything and she'll never be the same around you again.

Clenching his jaw in frustration, he climbed down from the wagon and followed her over to the baby's cradle. "Tess . . ."

"What would you like for supper tonight?" she blurted, her hands fluttering nervously as she spread the netting over the top of the cradle.

"I don't care what I have for supper," he retorted impatiently. "Look, Tess . . ."

"Oh, Matthew! You're here!" Whirling away, Tess nearly ran to meet Matthew Bennington. "Look, Mr. Hunter," she called, "Matthew's here now, so we're ready to start whenever you are."

Hunter stared at her for a moment, furious that she was so obviously avoiding talking to him. "Okay," he gritted, heading back for his horse. Mounting, he jerked the reins and moved the horse down the line, yelling, "All right, everybody. Wagons ho! Let's move 'em out!"

His cry was echoed and re-echoed up and down the length of the train as the caravan got underway. Riding back up to Tess, he muttered, "I want to talk to you alone, later."

Tess pretended to ignore his curt request, flicking a glance in the direction of Matthew Bennington, then saying blithely, "I'm sorry I didn't have a hot breakfast for you this morning. I'll see that you get a good meal at noon."

Hunter's furious eyes bored into hers for a moment, then he rode off again.

"Lordy, he's worse than usual this mornin', ain't he?" Matthew Bennington laughed. "I sure am glad I don't suffer a sour temper every mornin'. I think if I did, I'd be tempted to stay in bed till after noon!"

Tess smiled up at Matthew, trying hard to conceal her consternation at Hunter's black mood.

"What was that all about?" Rona asked, walking up to join Tess.

"Nothing," Tess shrugged. "Hunter just seems to be in a bad mood this morning."

"Really?" Rona asked, chuckling. "Maybe he didn't get enough sleep last night."

Tess threw her a jaundiced look which Rona answered with a smug smile. "Or maybe, the night just ended too soon for his liking."

"Or maybe," Tess interjected, "he's just cross this morning, like he is every other morning."

"That's possible too," Rona said agreeably, "but it's my bet that what's really eatin' him is that he said some things last night that he's regrettin' this mornin' and he don't know what to do 'bout it."

Tess looked at her in surprise. "What do you mean?"

"Oh, nothin'," Rona shrugged, reaching down to pick some wild flowers growing by the side of the trail, " 'cept that it's been my experience that when a man sets up rules for a game and then gets mad at someone just for followin' them, it usually means that he's regrettin' those rules, but he don't know how to go about changin' 'em."

Tess's brow furrowed in confusion. "I don't have any idea what you're talking about, Rona."

Rona laughed and handed Tess half of the flowers she'd picked. "Never mind, sweetie. Why don't you put some o' these in your hair? They're real pretty and, if people are starin' at the flowers, maybe nobody will notice how tired you look. I swear, Tess, you better go to bed early tonight. You're lookin' so peaked this mornin' that a person would swear that last night, you didn't sleep at all."

Chapter 31

Tess needn't have worried about fixing Hunter a hot dinner that day because he never showed up to eat it. Nor did he appear that evening to eat the light supper she prepared. By the next morning when his breakfast remained untouched, she began to worry and sought out Dash McLaughlin.

"Naw, there's nothing wrong with him," Dash informed her. "He's just in one of his moods and when he's like that, it's best to ignore him till he gets over it. When he gets hungry enough, he'll come around."

Her fears allayed, Tess returned to her wagon, deciding that until Hunter got over his mad, she would no longer continue preparing meals for him. Food was too precious to waste and for all she knew, he might never come around again.

As the days continued to roll by with no sign of him, her initial depression over the loss of his company gradually turned to resentment, then anger. By the end of the week, she was livid. Plodding along next to the wagon one morning, she turned to Rona. "How dare he make love to me and then ignore me like I don't even exist?''

Rona looked over at Tess sadly, knowing that her anger was masking a badly wounded heart. "I don't know, honey. Who's to say why men do what they do? I guess the way Hunter's actin' just goes to show that men are all the same. They get what they want and then forget you. I gotta say, though, I thought Hunter would be different.''

"Well, he's not!'' Tess huffed, barely keeping the tears at bay. The day after the night that we—well, you know—he told me he wanted to speak to me privately, but he never even came around to do that. I guess he figured I wasn't even important enough to explain why he was throwing me over.''

Rona frowned, shaking her head sympathetically. "The best thing you can do is just forget him,'' she advised. "After all, who needs him? You got Joshua Bennington now. They way he's been courtin' you this past week, I'm sure he's gonna ask you to marry him.''

"He already has,'' Tess said softly.

Rona's head jerked around, her green eyes wide with astonishment. "He has? Why didn't you tell me?''

Tess shrugged.

"So, what did you tell him?''

"That I'd think about it.''

Rona's eyes widened even further. "Think about it! Why would ya have ta think about it? Just say yes!''

"I don't love him, Rona. It doesn't seem right to marry a man when you don't love him.''

Rona grimaced, her face betraying how unimportant she thought that aspect of the decision was. "Maybe you could learn ta love him after you're married.''

Tess shook her head. "I don't think so. I don't think I'll ever love any man ever again.''

"Oh, pooh," Rona scoffed. "You're a woman who's made to be married. You just gotta get over Hunter and then you'll be fine. You'll see."

Tess looked over at her worldly wise friend hopefully. "Do you really think so?"

"Sure. You just gotta put Hunter out of your mind. That shouldn't be so hard. He never comes 'round anymore and I don't think I seen him three times since we left Fort Hall. Outta sight, outta mind, I always say."

Tess nodded bleakly. "You're right. I just need to remember that. 'Out of sight, out of mind'."

"That's the spirit, honey," Rona smiled. They walked on for a few minutes in silence, then Rona murmured, "Tess Bennington. You know, that has a real classy sound to it."

Tess forced a thin smile, but Rona noticed that her eyes continued to scan the horizon as if hoping to catch sight of the man she obviously couldn't put out of her mind.

Little did Tess know that Hunter was suffering from much the same anguish as she was. After their awkward altercation the morning after their romantic interlude, he'd decided that it would be to everyone's benefit if he just backed away from the situation.

What was the point in prolonging the inevitable? he asked himself over and over. There was no future for them, so wasn't it better for both of them if he just quietly ended it?

His reasoning was sound. He knew it was. So, why did his heart constrict in his chest every time he caught sight of Tess walking in the bright August sunshine or, worse yet, sitting by the campfire in the dusky mountain twilight, rocking Sarah and talking with Joshua Bennington.

Joshua Bennington. Hunter's jaw clenched whenever he thought about the two of them together. The man was all wrong for Tess—too placid, too taciturn, too dull. What Tess needed was a man with a fire in his blood to match her own. A man with determination. With brains! A man more like *him.* Not him, of course, he assured himself, but someone at least *like* him.

The past week had been hell. Hunter had eaten little, slept less and his temper was so foul that he had alienated nearly everyone he had come into contact with. Even the most rugged of the lumberjacks avoided him, and Jack Riley had come right out and told him that until he quit "actin' like a goddamn Grizzly with a burr up his butt", he didn't intend to have anything more to do with him.

The only person who still seemed willing to tolerate him was Dash. But then, he and Dash had always stuck by each other through every crisis of their lives. And, despite the fact that Dash had spent the better part of the past week telling him that he was the biggest ass on the face of the earth, Hunter knew his friend's insults stemmed from concern and that he could count on Dash to be there if he ever felt he could talk about what was eating him.

But, so far, Hunter hadn't been able to bring himself to do that. Even at Fort Hall, the British owned trading post where he and Dash had spent a long night getting drunk on good English brandy, he still hadn't been able to admit that he was miserable and lonely for Tess.

Now, as they slowly made their way toward the Snake River and Fort Boise, so much time had passed since he'd spoken to her that he could no longer think of any reason to approach her, even if he decided that they should talk.

It was Joshua Bennington who unwittingly supplied him with the excuse he needed.

It was early on a beautiful September morning. Hunter had ridden ahead of the train to scope out the trail leading to the Grand Round, a circular valley rimmed by a massive pine forest and spectacular mountains. As he sat atop his horse, looking down on the magnificence of the famous landmark, he heard someone galloping up behind him. Turning in his saddle, he was surprised to see Dash racing up the hill to meet him.

"What's wrong?" he called, his senses immediately alert to potential danger.

"Nothin'," Dash answered, pulling his winded horse to a halt. "I just wondered if you heard the news."

"What news?"

"Seems we're gonna have a weddin' on the train."

Hunter's heart slammed against his ribs. "Who?"

"Josh Bennington told me this mornin' that Mrs. Caldwell has finally agreed to marry him."

Hunter blanched under his dark tan. "Finally?"

"Yeah," Dash nodded. "Seems old Josh asked her some time ago and last night, she finally made her decision and accepted him."

Hunter stared off into the distance for a long moment, the pain that jolted through him so intense that he didn't know if he could speak. "Well, I guess I should go offer my congratulations, shouldn't I?"

"What?" Dash gasped. "Are you out of your damned mind?" Offer congratulations, for God's sake? Stop it is more like it."

"Why should I stop it?" Hunter asked, his voice frosty.

"Because you love her, that's why! I know it, Rona knows it, and if you would use your head for somethin' other than a rack to hang your hat on, you'd know it too. The only one who doesn't know it is Tess. She doesn't love Joshua Bennington. She's just agreed to marry him because she's still stinging from your rebuff."

"I haven't rebuffed her."

"No? Well, what the hell do you call it when a man takes a woman to his bed, then never speaks to her again. She's not some two bit whore who can shrug her shoulders and go on as if nothing happened, Jared, and you damn well know it!"

Hunter's fists clenched in fury. "I never thought she was a whore!"

"Then quit treatin' her like one!" Dash yelled. "Get on your horse, go find her, and tell her you love her before she marries that dolt Bennington and you end up out in the cold singin' 'Woe Is Me" for the rest of your life! And, believe me, if you do that, it's gonna be a solo because I'm not hangin' around to listen to you."

"Whether you 'hang around' or not is up to you," Hunter said stubbornly, "but, I can't ask Tess to call off her plans. I have nothing to offer her and she's better off with Bennington."

"How can you say that?" Dash raged. "You've said yourself that he's the dullest man you've ever met. And what the hell can he offer her that you can't?"

"A relationship that will last. A love that won't fade with time. Men like Bennington marry a woman and love them until they die."

"And you wouldn't?"

"How the hell do I know? I don't know anything about love. All I know is how to fight and destroy and kill. Regardless of what you think, I know that's what made Sophie give up on me. In the end, she realized that I was far better suited to being a killer than a lover."

"Oh, what a bunch of crap!" Dash spat. "I can't stand another minute of sittin' here listening to you extoll the virtues of Sophie Westhover. My God, Jared, when are you ever gonna wake up and face the truth about her? Everybody in Boston knew she was the flightiest, most fickle deb in town. Everybody except you, that is. You were just so infatuated with her that you couldn't see through her. Didn't you ever stop to think it was a little strange that she dropped that Lieutenant Hedden for Major Tompkins and then Tompkins for you? Whoever was the highest ranking hero of the day was who Sophie went after. And, when she finally found herself an honest to God, English blue blood, she figured that title was more impressive than all the military ranks put together and that's who she married! Sophie didn't throw *you* over because she thought you had murderous instincts, Colonel. She never thought that deeply about anybody in her life. Little Miss Westhover just found a better title. I swear, you're the only one dumb enough not to realize that. And, if you think Tess is anything like that, then, by God, you deserve to lose her!"

Hunter sat atop his horse and gaped at his friend in speechless disbelief. Dash McLaughlin was the most good-natured, amiable man he'd ever known and this morning's explosion of anger was so unprecedented that Hunter couldn't help but heed him.

Although he still thought Dash was wrong in his belief that he and Tess could have a future together, he knew he needed to explain things to her. To make her understand why it wouldn't work out between them. He cared far too much about her to be the cause of her diving into a loveless marriage. He had to stop her.

"Okay, I'll go talk to her."

"Do what you want," Dash muttered. "I don't give a damn." Jerking on his horse's reins, he pivoted the animal around. "You know, maybe I'll just marry Tess myself. I may not be as fascinating as the illustrious Jared Daulton Whitaker, but I'm a hell of a lot more interesting than Joshua Bennington!'' With an angry jerk of his head, Dash took off down the hill, leaving Hunter to stare after him in open mouthed astonishment.

Hunter found Tess exactly where he expected to, trudging along next to her wagon with Rona at her side.

"Come with me," he said, halting his horse near her and extending an arm to lift her up. "I need to talk to you."

Tess looked at him haughtily. "I'm sorry, but we're almost ready to make camp for the night and I have things to do. Perhaps some other time."

"I need to talk to you. Now."

"I just told you . . ."

"Miss Rose, will you watch the baby for a few minutes?"

"Sure!" Rona beamed, ecstatic that the stalemate between Hunter and Tess was obviously about to end. Ignoring Tess's furious look, she added, "I'll start supper too."

"Thanks," Hunter smiled. Without giving Tess a chance to argue further, he reached down, grasping her around the waist and pulling her up in front of him. The feeling of her slender body pressed against his chest sent immediate waves of desire rippling through him, but he ignored them, knowing that now was not the time to pander to his physical appetites.

"Let me down right now," Tess gritted, her body as stiff as a board. "How dare you think you can just ride up and tote me off like this?"

"Who's gonna stop me?" Hunter rasped, leaning close to her ear. "Joshua Bennington?"

Tess grimaced, realizing now what this little abduction was all about. "I'm sure he would if he saw you."

"He might try," Hunter retorted.

Incensed by his arrogance, Tess struggled against him, trying desperately to extricate herself from his grip.

"Stop that !" Hunter demanded, hoping she couldn't feel the arousing effect her squirming was having on him. "You're going to fall off."

"I hope I do!" she spat. "I'd rather break my neck than allow you to get away with this." To her fury, Hunter just gripped her more tightly, his heavily muscled arm pressing intimately against her breasts. She closed her eyes, praying that he couldn't feel her nipples pucker as his arm moved rhythmically against them.

They rode along in silence for several minutes until they entered a secluded grove of trees, moving deep into the shade. Finally Hunter pulled his horse to a halt. "You're too far away from the train to walk back, so if you're thinking of making a run for it when I let you down, don't bother."

Tess glared at him, infuriated that he had seen through her plans so easily. Slowly, Hunter lowered her to the ground, biting his lip as her body slid provocatively down his leg. He dismounted on the far side of his horse, giving himself the opportunity to take a quick glance downward. To his chagrin, the telltale bulge of his arousal was every bit as evident as he'd feared it would be. He clenched his jaw, admonishing himself to get control. The last thing he wanted Tess to think was that he'd brought her up here to seduce her.

As he came around the back of his horse, she crossed her arms over her chest and glared at him. "Okay, say whatever it is you brought me up here to say and then take me back."

Hunter gazed at her for a long moment, his eyes drinking in her beauty. He hadn't been this close to her in nearly two weeks and the sight and smell of her made him feel almost lightheaded with desire.

"Do you love him?"

Tess stared at him blankly for a moment. She had figured he wanted to talk to her about her engagement to Joshua Bennington, but she hadn't expected such an intensely personal question to be the first thing out of his mouth. "Of course I do."

Hunter breathed a huge sigh of relief. She was lying. Had she said that she had strong feelings for Joshua or that she was fond of him and felt that fondness might grow into love, he would have believed her. But, her response was too quick, too enthusiastic. She was lying and Hunter was a bit stunned at how happy that knowledge made him.

"No, you don't."

"Oh!" she huffed. "You think you're so smart. Well, I don't have to answer to you. My feelings for Joshua are none of your business." Spinning around, she stalked off in the direction they had come.

Hunter raced after her, grabbing her hand and turning her back to face him. "I told you, it's too far to walk back to the train."

"I don't care if it's a million miles!" Tess railed. "I'll be happy to walk it if it gets me away from you." To her complete mortification, tears sprang to her eyes.

"Let me go!" she cried, her voice suddenly pleading as she looked down at their clasped hands. "Please, Jared, just let me go!"

It was her use of his real name that was his undoing. With a hoarse, strangled cry, he grabbed her to him, embracing her with a desperate passion. "Why, Tess? *Why* are you marrying him?"

For a long moment, Tess didn't answer. Hunter waited, holding her close. He could feel the muscles of his chest pressing against her breasts, the scratchy stubble on his unshaved face rasping against her soft cheek, the hot, insistent bulge of his desire straining against the front of her thin skirt. He wanted her so badly that he could hardly stand the tactile sensations of their bodies touching so intimately, but still, he waited. Her answer was far more important than his desire.

When Tess finally spoke, her words came out in a fevered rush. "Don't do this to me!" she begged, wrenching out of his embrace. "Don't make me want you again. I know you don't want me so, please, just let me go."

"But, I *do* want you," he whispered, his voice rough with need.

"No!" she gasped, taking a lurching step away from him. "Not that again. Never that again."

Reaching out, he pulled her back to him. "That's not what I mean."

"What, then?" she sobbed. "What do you mean? I never know what you mean!"

"I mean . . . I mean that I love you."

At that moment, everything stopped. All awareness of their surroundings—the towering mountain peaks, the rustling trees, the singing birds—faded away into an all encompassing silence as they stared into each other's eyes.

"I love you too," Tess mouthed, her emotions so profound that she couldn't put voice to her words.

Hunter's breath came out in a shuddering rush as he buried his face in her hair. "Oh God, Tess, I've missed you so much . . . so much."

Tess threw her head back, her joy knowing no bounds as she smiled up into his dark eyes. "I'm here now," she whispered, her hands running frantically down the front of his shirt. Knowing how meager his wardrobe was, she felt a moment of guilt as buttons sprayed in every direction, but the deep rumble of laughter with which Hunter responded to her provocative impulse quickly assuaged it.

Clothes flew, as did guilt and recrimination. Shoes and boots were discarded, along with modesty and inhibition. They sank to the lush forest floor together; lips seeking, hands touching, bodies straining as they gorged themselves at passion's bountiful table.

Their movements, as they strove together toward completion, were so perfectly attuned that it was as if they had planned this moment; orchestrating every kiss, every caress, rehearsing every word of love until their dulcet murmurs were a symphony to each other's ears.

Hunter's hands and lips were everywhere, feasting on Tess's beauty as he touched, kissed and licked every inch of her. His erection pulsed and throbbed, demanding release, but he ignored his body's lusty call, taking the time to enjoy the sweetness of the skin at the back of her knee, the delicate silkiness of the underside of her breast, and the musky essence of her most secret flesh as he boldly made love to her with his lips and tongue.

Tess's sensual cries as she experienced for the first time this new and scandalous delight brought him close to the brink of his control, but still he denied himself the ultimate intimacy, waiting until he felt her near love's precipice before entering her with one, deep, soul shattering thrust.

Tess's gasps turned into shrieks of pleasure as she found her heaven, and the pulsing, rhythmic contractions of her climax quickly sent Hunter hurtling into paradise also. Groaning with erotic pleasure, he poured his essence into her, their satisfaction so complete that long after the waves of passion had faded, they continued to lie together in silence, savoring the unique joy of their union.

Finally, Hunter raised his head, smoothing Tess's

damp hair away from her forehead with a gentle, caressing hand. "You have to tell Bennington that you're not going to marry him."

"I know," Tess nodded. "I was foolish to accept him in the first place. I only did it because I was so hurt . . ."

"I'm sorry," Hunter murmured, kissing her one last time and sitting up. "I never meant to hurt you. I only want you to be happy, and I know you wouldn't be married to him. He's not the man for you."

"No," Tess smiled, running her hand idly down his muscular back, "you are."

Her innocent, heartfelt words made a knot of pain clench in Hunter's gut. "Tess," he moaned, rubbing his fingers across his forehead tiredly. "I'm not the one either."

"What?" she gasped, jerking upright and grabbing for her discarded dress to cover her nakedness.

"I'm not the man for you, either" he repeated.

"But, you just said you loved me!"

"I do. And that's why I have to let you go."

Tess shook her head, her mind spinning. "But, if you love me . . ."

"It would never work out between us, Tess. I have nothing to offer you. No home, no money . . ."

"I don't care about those things!" she interrupted hotly.

"There's more."

"Then, tell me."

Hunter studied her closely, wondering if he actually could bring himself to tell her the truth. Once she knew about him, it would surely be the end of their relationship. But, wasn't that what he wanted, to end this relationship before they got more involved than they already were? Drawing a deep breath, he said slowly, "You don't really know anything about me,

Tess. There are a lot of things in my past that are pretty ugly."

Silently, she waited, her face impassive.

"I did some things in Mexico that no man should do. I carried out orders that I should have disobeyed."

"What kind of orders?" she asked softly.

"Orders to attack villages. Villages full of old men and women and children. I led a charge at a place called Chapultepec that ended up being nothing more than sanctioned slaughter. I was responsible for children dying, Tess. Children who were only trying to protect their school. I was ordered to take the town by whatever means necessary and I carried out the order, even though it meant killing little boys. Then, when it was over and all I wanted to do was try to forget it, I heard that the government was going to give me a medal for bravery. For bravery, Tess! My God, how brave does a man have to be to kill children?"

Hunter buried his face in his hands, unable to meet her eyes. A long, silent moment passed and when he finally spoke again, his voice was muffled and hoarse. "So, I left. I just walked away, leaving everything behind—my friends, my home, my name, everything. I started a new life. This life. And even though I'll always have regrets about what I lost, I know I made the right decision."

His voice again trailed off and this time Tess reached out and took his hand. "We can work everything out together, Jared. I don't care about your past. All I care about is the future . . . our future."

"Tess," Hunter implored, "please try to understand. There is no future. I've chosen my path and it's a solitary one. There's no place in my life for you. In order for things to work out between you and me, I'd have to go back, and it's far too late to do that now."

Tess dropped his hand, her eyes blazing with a combination of disbelief, fury and pain. "Solitary?" she cried. "You've chosen a 'solitary path'? My God, Jared, how can you do this to me? You are the most despicable man I've ever met! You bring me up here, make love to me, and demand that I not marry Joshua Bennington. Then, you cavalierly tell me that you're not the man for me and that you 'have to let me go' because you love me! You're horrible, hateful, cruel . . . Oh, I can't think of anything bad enough to call you!"

Hunter looked away, unable to meet her anguished gaze. He knew that whatever names she was calling him were more than deserved. He'd called himself by all of them, and worse.

He hated himself for the pain he was causing her, but, it was done now and, in the deepest recesses of his heart, he knew it was for the best. "I'll take you back," he said quietly, getting to his feet and gathering up his clothes.

"No!" The last thing Tess could bear right now would be the close intimacy of the two of them atop Hunter's big horse. "I'll walk."

"You can't walk."

"I will!" she sobbed, scrambling to her feet and frantically trying to pick up her cast off clothing while still holding her dress in front of her. "Don't you dare tell me what I can and cannot do!"

"Tess, be reasonable. You'll never make it back before dark and Sarah may need you."

"I'm not riding back with you!"

"All right," he sighed. "Then you take the horse and I'll walk." He paused, peering at her closely. "You do know how to ride, don't you?"

"Of course I know how to ride!" she snapped. "Just get out of here so I can get dressed."

Hunter nodded desolately and moved off into the trees.

Tess waited until he was out of sight before giving vent to her tears. Yanking on her clothes, she mounted the well trained roan and turned him back toward the wagon train, riding away without ever looking back. She arrived back at the camp just as the sun was making its spectacular descent behind the mountains.

Rona was waiting for her when she reached her wagon. Handing her the fussing Sarah, she said simply, "You look like hell. What happened up there?"

"I don't want to talk about it," Tess said dully. "Please, just leave me alone." Stoicly holding back another wash of tears, she climbed into the back of the wagon.

She didn't come out again all evening, but far into the night, Rona heard her quiet sobs as she cried into the pillow on her hard, little cot.

Chapter 32

Joshua Bennington strode up to Hunter's campsite, the expression on his face grim and determined. "I want to talk to you," he announced.

Hunter, who had been sitting on his bedroll drinking a cup of muddy black coffee, nodded. "I've been expecting you."

"Well, if you've been expectin' me, then you must know what this is about."

Hunter nodded again and rose to his feet.

"I'll get right to the point, Hunter. Mrs. Caldwell told me that she ain't gonna marry me, after all, and I wanna know what you said to her that made her change her mind."

"I told her I don't think you're the right man for her," Hunter replied honestly. "And, she agreed."

Joshua's mouth tightened. "Then, why the hell was I the right man for her three days ago when she first said 'yes'?"

Hunter shrugged. "Look, Bennington, it's not my place to stand here and tell you what's on Tess's mind. You need to talk to her."

"Oh, I see. Now, it's 'Tess'."

"It's been 'Tess' for a long time," Hunter said quietly.

"Are you sayin' that she's not marryin' me 'cause she's marryin' you instead?"

"No."

"Then, don't you think you're bein' a mite familiar callin' her by her first name?"

"That's between her and me," Hunter retorted, "just like this situation is between her and you."

"Yeah, well, she won't give me any answers except to say that she's thought it over and she don't think it would work between us. It's my feelin' that the only reason she thinks that is 'cause of somethin' you said to her."

"You should know her better than that. If she really wanted to marry you, she'd do it, regardless of what I said. And, if she's having second thoughts, then better now than after you're married. That really would be a tragedy."

Joshua flexed his fists at his sides, frustrated by Hunter's unarguable logic. "That's your opinion. My opinion is that things woulda worked out just fine between us once she got away from you."

"I'm not the problem, Bennington."

"Hell you ain't!" Joshua exploded. "She's in love with you. Everybody on the whole damn train knows it. Why, there's even been talk that you and she been playin' husband and wife late at night after the rest of us are bedded down."

Hunter's eyes flared with fury. "Who the hell has said that?" he thundered.

"More men than you can whip," Joshua returned.

"Do you believe it?"

Joshua hesitated a moment. "I don't know what I believe anymore. All I know is that I found a woman I wanted to marry, she said she'd marry me, and now she's changed her mind. And, everybody's tellin' me you're the reason. That's mighty upsettin', Hunter."

Hunter looked at Joshua speculatively for a moment. "So, what do you want to do about it? Fight me? If that's what you want, then let's get to it. But, I warn you, even though smashing my face in may make you feel better, it won't bring Tess back to you."

Joshua emitted a long, defeated sigh. "I know it won't, so I guess there ain't much sense in us bloodyin' each other up, is there?"

Hunter shook his head.

"Besides," Josh added, "Tess prob'ly wouldn't have been happy livin' in the middle of the forest somewhere and takin' care of me and my brothers, anyway."

"Josh," Hunter said, his voice placating, "if it was meant to be, then nothing I could have said would have changed Tess's mind. But, you're right about one thing. She deserves better than a life spent cooking and cleaning and washing for three lumberjacks and a houseful of kids."

Josh's recently subdued temper flared again. "Oh? And I s'pose you think you can give her better."

Hunter shook his head. "No. I already told you, she's not marrying me either. If she deserves a better life than what you can give her, then she certainly deserves a better one than I could offer."

Josh cocked his head speculatively. "I'm not sure I believe that, either. I heard a lot of the 'jacks sayin' that you're actually that famous colonel that all the newspapers were writin' about last year. That Jared Whitaker."

"Well, I'm not," Hunter said quickly.

"Don't matter to me, one way or the other," Joshua shrugged. "Unless, of course, you are this Whitaker fella and you used all that glory they heaped on you to take Tess away from me."

"I didn't. Believe me, not only do I not have anyone

heaping glory on me, but I'm not taking Tess away either. Tess took herself away. Accept it and find yourself another girl."

Joshua looked at him dejectedly.

"Maybe you should talk to Rona Rose," Hunter suggested. "She's a hard worker and a pretty good cook, too. I bet she'd make you a hell of a wife."

Joshua held up his hands, quashing that idea. "No thanks. I know that wildcat would be more than I could handle. Besides, she's gonna end up with Dash."

Hunter's eyebrows skyrocketed into his shaggy hair. "What?"

"Yup. You mark my words. Them two will be hitched before we get out of Oregon City. Everybody says so."

"It sounds to me like 'everybody' is saying a whole lot about a whole lot of things," Hunter noted wryly.

"Yeah, well, the evenings get pretty long and there ain't much else to talk about 'cept you two and the women."

Hunter held out his hand. "Look, Bennington, regardless of what's been said about you or me or Mrs. Caldwell or anybody else, I'd like us to part friends. You're a good man and I've been proud to have you on my train."

Joshua stared down at Hunter's extended hand for a long moment, then clasped it in his huge, meaty grip. "Okay, Hunter."

After shaking hands, Joshua turned to leave. He took only a step or two, though, before he turned back. "Don't let me hear that you've broken that little gal's heart," he warned, "or I'll be back. And next time, we won't shake hands."

Hunter nodded solemnly, knowing that it was no longer possible to break Tess's heart. All the damage he could possibly do, he'd already done.

* * *

"Mount Hood," Rona sighed, smiling up at the magnificent mountain looming in the distance. "Oh, Tess, I can't hardly believe it. We're almost there!"

Tess pulled her heavy brown shawl closer around her face, fending off the persistent drizzle dampening the gloomy day. "What I can't believe is that we're expected to pay five dollars just for the privilege of driving our wagons down this horrible, muddy, rutted road."

"I thought you said you didn't have to pay the toll 'cause you're a widow and Mr. Barlow don't charge widows."

"I didn't," Tess admitted. "And it's a good thing, too, since my funds are running so low. I swear, Rona, I had no idea we would have to pay so many tolls to cross the rivers. When we started out, I thought I had plenty of money, but now it's almost all gone. It's just lucky for me that Mr. Barlow is generous with widows."

"Sam Barlow can afford to be generous," Rona laughed. "Think of the fortune he must be makin' by chargin' that high a toll for every wagon on every train. I wonder if he's married . . ."

Tess threw her friend a jaundiced look. "Is marriage the only thing you ever think about?"

"What else?" Rona shrugged. "I don't want to live the rest of my life alone, and you don't either if truth be told."

"You're wrong," Tess protested. "I'm perfectly content to be a widow. The only thing I need to make me happy is a real roof over my head, some dry clothes, and a decent meal."

"Oh, bull horns," Rona scoffed, using her favorite epithet. "Nobody but an old, dried up crone is happy bein' a widow. And, why are you complainin' about food now? We been eatin' great this past week since the men started fishin' in the Columbia. That fresh fish sure does beat hardtack and moldy bacon."

"That's true," Tess conceded, "but even salmon and Marion Berries gets boring after eight days straight!"

"Well, I think them berrics are wonderful!"

Tess chuckled wryly. "I'm amazed you'd say that, after you ate so many of them yesterday that you were up half the night with a bellyache. Your lips are still black!"

"They are?" With a look of horrified embarrassment, Rona began rubbing frantically at her lips with her fingers.

"You're wasting your time," Tess laughed. "That stain is going to have to just wear off. You'll never get rid of it by rubbing."

Rona dropped her hand. "Well, even if they did stain my face and make me sick, them Marion berries were just about the best thing I ever ate. You thought so too, yesterday. You're just cranky this morning, and I know why."

"I'm not cranky," Tess argued, "I'm just cold and wet and sick to death of walking, walking, walking. I just want to get where I'm going and have this trip over with!"

"It will be soon enough. Complainin' ain't gonna make it go no faster. Besides, no matter what you say, walkin' ain't what's botherin' you."

"Okay," Tess sighed. "I know you're dying to tell me what you think *is* bothering me, so go ahead and say it."

"What's botherin' you is Hunter, and you know it. I keep tellin' you to forget him and find somebody else."

"And I keep telling you that I don't want anybody else. And Hunter's not bothering me because I don't want him either."

"You can say all you want . . ." Rona paused, picking up her soggy skirts and stepping around a large, mud filled pot hole. "Damn this mud! Anyway, as I was sayin', you can say all you want about not wantin' another man, but I know that all you need is to find the right one and you'd change your mind fast enough."

"I already found the right man," Tess murmured sadly, "but he's laying in a cemetery in Boston."

"You'll find another one," Rona said confidently. "We both will."

Tess looked over at her in surprise. "I thought you already had. With the amount of time you and Dash have been spending together, I thought for sure he would have made his intentions clear by now."

To her astonishment, Rona blushed. "Oh, he has, honey, he has. And I can't say that I haven't been enjoyin' it. But, Dash ain't the marryin' kind. He's like Hunter. He's got a wanderin' foot. I don't think that man's gonna settle down in one place for a long, long time yet."

"I'm sorry to hear that," Tess said sincerely. "I really thought maybe you and he might . . ."

"Naw," Rona interrupted. "Dash just sees me as a way to pass some time, nothin' more. But, I'm used to that with men, so it's okay."

Tess flicked a glance over at her friend, noticing the tightness around her mouth. Her heart went out to Rona as she saw the unmistakable proof that she was far more enamored with Dash McLaughlin than she was willing to admit.

"Well, you never know," Tess said encouragingly. "It's still several more days before we get to Oregon City. Anything can happen between now and then."

Rona nodded, but Tess could tell that she didn't expect anything to change.

"Speakin' of Oregon City, Tess, what're you gonna do when we get there?"

"I'm going on to my sister's place," Tess explained. "I thought you knew that."

"I did. I just wondered who's gonna drive you?"

Tess shook her head worriedly. "I don't know yet. Deborah lives thirty miles northeast of Oregon City, and I don't think I can handle the wagon and the baby by myself for that distance. I guess I'm going to have to hire somebody to drive me."

"Somebody from the train?"

"Maybe, if any of the men are going that way. If not, I guess I'll just have to hire someone from the town. I just hope they won't charge me too much."

"How about Matthew Bennington?" Rona suggested. "Can't he do it?"

"No. I already asked him, but he says he has to go on with Joshua and Jeremy and they're headed farther north than I am. I thought I might speak to Dash. Do you think he'd consider it?"

"Maybe," Rona mused, "or maybe Hunter would."

"No!" Tess said abruptly. "I won't ask him, and I want you to promise that you won't either."

"Okay," Rona shrugged. "It don't make no never mind to me who drives ya. I was just makin' a suggestion."

"I know, and I appreciate you trying to help. But, I'd rather walk to Deborah's than ask Hunter for help."

A silence fell over the two women as they plodded along the muddy track.

Finally, Rona spoke again. "Ya know, Tess, I think you'd feel a whole lot better if you'd talk to somebody 'bout what happened between you and Hunter."

"There's nothing to talk about."

Rona stopped walking and looked over at Tess with a frown. "Well, somethin' sure happened that day Hunter took you away on his horse. You ain't been the same since."

"Rona, I really don't want to talk about it. Please don't ask."

"Okay," Rona sighed, disappointed that Tess wouldn't confide in her, "but I still think you'd feel a whole lot better if you did."

Tess shook her head stubbornly. "I just don't want to dredge it all up again. I've put it out of my mind and that's the way I want to keep it."

"Sure ya have, honey," Rona said kindly. "You've put Hunter out of your mind just like I've put Dash out of mine." She chuckled ruefully. "You know what, Tess girl?"

"What?"

"We're some pair of sorry women, and that's for sure."

"If you're not gonna take her to her sister's, then who the hell is?"

Hunter looked up from the gun he was cleaning and scowled at Dash. "I don't know. I just know it's not gonna be me. If you're so all fired worried about her, Dash, why don't you take her? After all, you're a scout. Who better to help her find her sister's place?"

"I can't. I've got my own stuff to do in Oregon City."

"Oh?" Hunter questioned, his eyebrows elevating. "And what 'stuff' is that?"

"Lots of stuff," Dash retorted defensively. "Get settled for the winter, for one thing."

"Oh, yeah. I forgot how long it takes to carry those saddle bags of yours into a boarding house."

"Who says I'm gonna stay in a boarding house?"

Hunter peered curiously over the flames of his campfire. "Where else would you stay?"

"Oh, I don't know," Dash hedged, "I may just think about settling down there. Build myself a little place and raise some sheep or somethin'."

"What?" Hunter gasped, laying his gun aside and looking at his friend in astonishment. "Are you telling me you're not going back with me in the spring? That you're going to settle in Oregon?"

"Maybe."

Hunter looked away for a second, trying to digest this disturbing bit of news. "I see," he said slowly. "Well, this is mighty surprising."

Dash shrugged noncommittally and picked up a piece of kindling. "Comes a time, Jared, when a man's gotta start thinkin' about puttin' down some roots." He rubbed his index finger absently across the piece of wood, then reached into his back pocket and pulled out a small knife, snapping the blade open and beginning to whittle.

"What ya makin?" Hunter asked, definitely not wanting to discuss "putting down roots".

"I don't know. Nothin', probably, although I have been thinkin' about whittling a little doll or a horse or something and givin' it to Mrs. Caldwell for Sarah. I've gotten mighty attached to that baby and I'd kind of like to leave her with a little gift."

Hunter nodded approvingly. "That's a nice thought, Dash."

"Maybe you should do the same. After all, that baby must mean something to you too."

"Yeah, she does, but I don't think her mama would accept a gift from me."

Dash studied Hunter's set expression for a moment. "You know, I wish to hell you'd tell me what happened between you two that day. Maybe I could help."

"Nope," Hunter said, getting to his feet and returning his gun to its holster. "There is no help for it, buddy. All that happened that day was that I told Tess how things had to be between us, and that was the end of it."

"You might have told her," Dash muttered, "but, knowin' Tess, I find it hard to believe that was the end of it."

"Well, it was," Hunter said with finality. "And that's the end of this conversation, too."

Dash said no more, but he covertly watched Hunter as he stretched out on his bedroll. A chilly mountain breeze stirred in the dense pine trees surrounding them. Dash shivered in the cold autumn air, then threw several more pieces of wood into the fire, including the one he'd been whittling.

"Didn't like the way that was coming, huh?" Hunter asked from his pallet.

Dash turned to look at him, surprised that he was still awake. "No, I didn't. I can do a better job if I work on it during the day when the light's good. That little Sarah is so special to me that I want whatever I give her to be the best job I can do."

"Yeah," Hunter murmured, "she's special, all right."

"And so is her mama," Dash added, pulling his blanket tightly around him and lying down.

Hunter was silent for a long moment. Then, in a voice so soft that his response was nearly swept away by the rustling wind, he muttered, "Right. And so is her mama."

Less than a minute later, Dash fell asleep, still wearing the smile that Hunter's response had prompted.

Chapter 33

Tess nearly jumped out of her skin, so startled was she by the sharp knock on her hotel room door.

"Who is it?" she called, her voice betraying her trepidation.

"Hunter."

Tess squeezed her eyes shut, her emotions chaotic. She had hardly seen Hunter since they'd arrived in Oregon City three days before. Although she'd spent a great deal of time thinking about him—missing him—now that he was standing on the other side of her door, she wasn't sure whether she wanted to open it or not.

Telling herself that she was being ridiculous, she took a deep breath, patted her short curls into place, and pulled open the portal.

"Hi," Hunter said matter-of-factly, glancing over her shoulder into the room as if to check out who might be inside.

"What do you want, Mr. Hunter?"

Hunter's dark gaze flicked back to her face, one eyebrow cocking questioningly at her formality. "I want to talk to you a minute. May I come in, or are you going to make me stand in the hall?"

Tess hesitated a split second, then nodded and waved him into the room.

Hunter took off his hat and ducked under the door frame, entering the chamber. Just seeing him in her room made it suddenly seem smaller and more confined, and Tess wasn't at all sure that she wanted to close the door and cloister herself with his overwhelming presence. But, knowing he would think it very strange if she left the door open, she reluctantly closed it and turned toward him.

"What can I do for you?"

Hunter looked at her hungrily, his traitorous mind thinking of at least a hundred ways to answer that question. Instead he said simply, "Where's Sarah?"

Tess pointed over to a spot near the stove where Sarah lay sleeping in the old clothes basket.

Hunter walked over to the makeshift cradle, covering the awkwardness between them by reaching down and running his finger lightly down the baby's cheek. "I've missed seeing her," he muttered.

Straightening, he turned back to Tess, trying to come up with a bit of light conversation to ease the crackling tension between them. "So, how does it feel to sleep indoors again?"

"Heavenly," Tess answered, forcing a thin smile. "I never thought I'd enjoy a simple country town so much but, right now, I think Oregon City has as much appeal as Paris ever did."

"Have you been to Paris?"

"Yes, several years ago when I was still on the stage."

For a moment they stood and stared at each other, both of them realizing how little they actually knew about each other.

"Did you consider the crossing a successful one?"

Tess asked, as desperate as he was to think of something inconsequential to talk about.

"Very. We only lost fourteen members of the expedition and that's excellent."

"Fourteen?" Tess gasped. "I didn't realize we had lost that many."

Hunter nodded. "Six to Mountain Fever, five drowned in river crossings, then there was the Sam Waters, Arnie Butcher problem and . . . your brother."

Tess closed her eyes, feeling again the searing pain that always ripped through her when she thought of Joe. "So many lives," she whispered.

"It's not a bad number, Tess. Some trains that get hit with cholera can lose two-thirds of their entire population in a week or less. We were very lucky. Of course, I realize that tragedy hit you very personally, and that makes a big difference in how you feel."

Tess nodded sadly, then gestured to a small table by the window. "Do you want to sit down?"

"No," Hunter answered, his eyes following the graceful sweep of her skirts as she moved toward the table. "I can't stay. I just came to ask you if you'd had any luck yet finding somebody to drive you to your sister's."

"No, I haven't. Everyone I've talked to wants so much money to escort me that I just can't afford it."

Hunter opened his mouth to respond, but Tess quickly cut him off, not wanting him to think that she was hinting for him to offer. "I'm sure I'll find someone soon," she said confidently. "I heard at the general store that there's another train expected in a few days. Maybe there will be somebody on that one who's going my way."

Hunter shook his head doubtfully. "It's another train full of lumberjacks, Tess. It's going to be just like ours with all of them headed west, not north where you want to go."

Her voice, when she answered, was so dejected that Hunter almost wished he hadn't told her that. "I see. Well, then, I guess I'll just have to keep looking. Someone suggested that I post notices around town stating what I'm willing to pay, then just wait and see if anyone responds."

"Don't do that," Hunter warned.

"Why not? I have to do something! Everyday I stay here just depletes my funds more and more. I'm not going to have anything left at all if I don't leave soon."

"Notices aren't the answer," Hunter maintained stubbornly. "You don't know what kind of riffraff you'd get advertising like that. There are a lot of tough men here who'd probably be willing to take your money now, then tell you later that they considered it a *partial* payment, if you know what I mean."

Tess looked at him blankly for a moment, then the true meaning of what he was telling her dawned and her face turned beet red. "I hadn't thought of that," she said quietly, sinking down in one of the little chairs flanking the table. "Well, then, I don't know what to do. I'm just so tired of everything being so difficult . . ."

Hunter clenched his fingers around his hat's brim to keep himself from rushing over and pulling her into his arms. Being in this small, cozy bedroom with her was sheer torture and it took every bit of will power he could summon not to grab her and kiss away the worry that etched her tired eyes. Instead, he blew out a long breath and said what he'd come to say in the first place.

"I'll drive you."

"No!"

Tess's response was so quick, so final, so totally negative that Hunter's face immediately reflected his offense. "What's the matter?" he gritted, taking a step toward her. "Don't you trust me to get you there safely?"

Tess almost blurted that it was herself she couldn't trust, but good sense prevailed and she merely shook her head. "I don't want to trouble you, that's all. I know you're busy."

"If I was too busy, I wouldn't have offered," he countered.

"I'll find somebody else."

"Why?"

Tess looked up at him with a tortured expression. "Because I don't think it would be a good idea for us to spend two days alone together."

"I wouldn't take advantage of you, if that's what you're worried about."

"No, I'm not worried about that."

You probably should be, Hunter's mind screamed, because it's taking everything I've got in me not to do just that right now.

Out loud he said, "Look, Tess, you were my employee for a lot of months. Anything that happened between us during that time is over now, but as your employer, I still feel responsible for you."

"You don't need to," she whispered, crushed by his blunt reminder that she'd not meant anything to him except a moment's pleasure. "Just as you said, Hunter, I *was* your employee. I'm not anymore. You got me safely to Oregon City which is all you promised to do. You don't owe me anything more than that."

"I know I don't owe you," he argued, "but . . ." He paused, trying to think of a plausible reason for his offer. Glancing around, his eyes lit on Sarah. ". . . for Sarah's sake, I feel responsible for getting you where you're going."

"Sarah's my responsibility, not yours."

"I know that, too!" he thundered, his voice getting

louder as his frustration with her obstinacy grew. "But, Sarah means a lot to me and I want to see her safely to her new home. Now, quit trying to make something more out of this than it is and just accept my offer. You haven't got many other alternatives that I can see."

"You don't know that," Tess retorted hotly, her own anger surfacing at Hunter's typical high handedness. "I haven't talked to Jack Riley yet. Maybe he . . ."

"Jack Riley is passed out drunk at a whorehouse down the street and, unless you're willing to break down some floozy's door and wrest him from her bed, I don't think he's going to be available for at least another week."

Tess's eyes widened at his coarse statement. "Oh, you!" she spat. "When does this stop with you?"

"When does what stop? What the hell are you talking about?"

"I'm talking about control, Hunter. You've been trying to control me ever since I joined your train five months ago! When does it stop?"

"Control!" he bellowed. "Well, if you aren't the most ungrateful, selfish, irritating . . . *Control!* I came up here to help you, nothing more! I felt responsible for your well being, but you . . . you have to turn everything into something personal between us! *Well, there is nothing personal between us, lady.* Got it? *Nothing!* I was just trying to help you out. That's all!"

Tess jumped up from her chair as Sarah began squalling in her basket. "Now look what you've done!" she cried. "I swear, the thing you do best is shout and yell and wake up innocent babies."

"Fine! Then, I'll leave!" Hunter stormed over to the door, yanking it open. "But, let's get one thing straight. I'm taking you to your sister's, if for no other reason than I want to get rid of you once and for all.

I'll be here tomorrow morning at sunup and you better be ready. Do you understand me?"

He glared at her menacingly, as if daring her to argue further but, to his surprise, she simply nodded her head. "All right, I'll be ready. Now, get out."

"Gladly!" he bellowed. "Just don't be late."

"What are you going to do if I am?" she taunted. "Leave without me?"

Throwing her a look that had brought grown men to their knees, Hunter strode out the door, slamming it so hard behind him that Dash and Rona, who were cozily ensconced in a bed in the next room, glanced at each other in wonder.

"Don't worry about it," Dash chuckled, returning his attentions to Rona's soft, full breast, "he's just in love."

Tess wasn't late. In fact, when Hunter pulled up early the next morning, she was already standing on the boardwalk outside the hotel waiting for him. Rona and Dash stood in the gloomy dawn with her, Rona holding the baby and sobbing loudly.

"I don't know what I'm gonna do without you," she wailed, handing the baby to Dash and hugging Tess. "I'm gonna miss ya so much, honey."

"I know," Tess answered, returning Rona's embrace as tears pooled in her own eyes. "I'm going to miss you too, Rona. But, we'll see each other again, I know we will. If you're going to stay in Oregon City, we'll only be thirty miles apart. I'll come into town and you can come stay with me at my sister's, too."

"Sure," Rona nodded, the tone of her voice betraying her doubt that any of Tess's predictions would come true. "I'm just bein' silly. We'll see each other again."

Tess moved her mouth closer to Rona's ear. "How are things with Dash? Do you think he's the one?"

Rona shrugged pragmatically. "Who knows? I kinda hope so, but we'll just have to wait and see."

"Come on, Mrs. Caldwell, let's go."

Tess looked up at Hunter who had already loaded her meager luggage into the back of the wagon and re-assumed his position on the high seat. Nodding, she gave Rona one last fierce hug and climbed up to join him. Reaching down, she took Sarah out of Dash's arms, pausing a moment to allow Rona one last teary kiss on the baby's soft cheek.

"Good bye, Mrs. Caldwell," Dash smiled, winking broadly at her. "Have a good, safe trip and come back and see us soon."

Tess looked down into Dash's handsome, smiling face, wishing she could tell him how much his unfailing friendship had meant to her. Instead, she just smiled at him tearfully and said, "Thank you again for the darling little doll you made for Sarah. I love it and I know she will too."

Then, she turned back to Hunter, crying, "This is so hard! Please, let's go now."

Hunter nodded and looked down at Dash. "I'll be back in four or five days. Start thinking about the fastest way to get back to Missouri so we can pick up another train by April."

"So *you* can pick up another train," Dash corrected. "I've decided to stay here."

Rona let out a little gasp, causing Dash to smile and throw a possessive arm around her shoulder. "How do you feel about sheep, Miz Rosenbaum?" he drawled. "I've a hankerin' to maybe try my hand at raisin' some."

"I love 'em!" Rona rhapsodized. "Sheep, cows, pigs, whatever you wanna raise, I love 'em. And if I don't love 'em now, I'll learn to."

Tess smiled down at the grinning couple, her feelings vacillating between joy and envy. "You two take care," she said as the wagon lurched forward. "I'll see you both soon."

Her last vision of them before she turned around in the seat was of Dash kissing Rona lustily while Rona held one arm over her head, waving frantically at the departing wagon.

"How nice that they've found each other," Tess said as they headed out of town.

"I suppose it is nice," Hunter muttered, "except for me, of course. Now, I've got to try to find a scout as good as Dash and that isn't going to be easy. He was the best in the business."

Tess could think of no response to Hunter's complaint, so she merely shrugged and sat back to enjoy the scenery. "The Willamette Valley," she sighed contentedly as they jounced along across a huge, emerald green meadow. "I can hardly believe that I'm finally here."

"Do you know where exactly your sister lives?" Hunter questioned, ignoring her effusiveness about the spectacular countryside.

"Not exactly," she admitted. "I know it's thirty miles northeast, but that's about all. Deborah sent specific instructions to Joe, but I don't know what he did with them. I never found them in any of his things."

Hunter frowned in annoyance. "Do you at least know your sister's last name?"

Tess's face flushed with anger at his pointed insult, but she knew he was trying to bait her and she was determined not to let him succeed. "Of course," she said sweetly, "it's Douglas."

Hunter nodded, disappointed that she hadn't bitten his head off for that inexcusable bit of rudeness. It would make this trip so much easier if he could just stay mad at her the whole time. God help him if she turned on that wonderful, laughing charm of hers. He'd never be able to keep his hands off her.

"I know approximately what area they must live in," he admitted. "I guess once we get there, we'll just have to question people till we find somebody who knows them."

Tess nodded agreeably, shifting the fretting Sarah from one arm to the other. "I have to go feed her," she announced when her attempts to placate the baby didn't work. "Could you stop the wagon for a minute while I get in the back?"

Hunter obligingly pulled over to the side of the trail and held the baby while Tess crawled into the interior of the wagon bed. "Tell me when you're ready," he muttered, handing Sarah to her.

A silent moment passed during which he didn't allow himself to contemplate what Tess was doing in the back of the wagon. Then he heard her say, "Okay, I'm ready. Go ahead." Clucking to the mules, they started down the road again.

They travelled in silence for several minutes, then Hunter heard Sarah's loud, contented burp and the rustling of covers as Tess laid her on the bed.

He closed his eyes for a moment, his mind painting a picture of Tess sitting semi-nude only a foot or two behind him. It was this stimulating vision that overrode his usual good sense and prompted him to steer the mules directly toward a large pothole in the road ahead of them. Just as he'd planned, the front wheels dropped into the large hole, causing Tess to let out a surprised grunt.

Hunter used the excuse of her little cry to swing around and look at her, drawing in a lusty breath as his eyes feasted hungrily on the alluring sight of her naked breasts.

Tess gasped as she saw where his gaze was fixed. Turning her shoulder to him, she cried, "Do you mind?"

Her irate admonishment brought him immediately to his senses and he wrenched around to the front again, shouting, "Whoa, mules. Whoa there!" The mules obediently stopped, but not before the back wheels fell into the same hole the front ones had.

Again, Hunter heard Tess's grunt, followed by a softly uttered curse. "I'm sorry," he called, suddenly appalled by his outrageous behavior. "Guess I'm wool gathering out here." He cringed, realizing that even *he* didn't buy that lame excuse.

"Just keep your eyes on the road," Tess directed through gritted teeth. "And don't you dare turn around again!"

Hunter bit his lower lip, mentally chastising himself. *You horny fool! How could you act like such an ass? Things were going pretty well here, and then you have to ruin them by gaping at her like some school boy peeping in a girl's window.*

They drove on for over an hour, neither of them speaking. Finally, Hunter couldn't stand it any longer and he sneaked another quick look. Tess was still sitting on the cot, her bodice now buttoned tightly up to her neck and her expression stony.

"Look, Tess," he began, once again reining in the mules. "I'm sorry about what happened back there. I wasn't trying to peek at you." He paused, waiting for a bolt of lightning to strike him dead for that lie. "I just wanted to make sure you weren't hurt. It was instinctual, that's all."

"Oh, I know it was instinctual," Tess retorted, obviously not believing his lie *or* his apology.

"Oh, come, now," he cajoled. "You should know me better than to think I would resort to cheap tricks like sending the wagon into a pothole just so I could have an excuse to gawk at you." Again, he glanced warily up at the heavens.

"Besides," he continued blithely, "what difference does it make, really? It's not like I haven't seen you before. I don't understand why you're so mad." As soon as those words were out of his mouth, he knew he had made yet another colossal mistake.

"I'll tell you what difference it makes," Tess hissed. "That was an entirely different time . . . a different situation. What was all right then, isn't now. So, I will thank you to remember that and keep your lecherous eyes to yourself. I didn't agree to let you take me to Deborah's just so you could ogle me for a couple more days."

I didn't agree to let you take me . . . That did it! Hunter was perfectly aware that he had been wrong to look at her the way he had, but he had simply lost his head for a moment. It could happen to any man. Besides, he had apologized. But, now, Tess was making it sound like she was doing him a *favor* by letting him escort her to her sister's.

And, here he was, he thought self-righteously, taking his valuable time to drive her out to the middle of God knew where, just so she could be with her blessed family! Well, he had had enough of her insults and now was the time to set her straight about a few things.

"Now, you listen to me, lady," he began, his eyes firing with indignation. "You think real highly of yourself, don't you? You think every man who so much as glances at you is dying to get under your skirts. Well, I can tell you that's no longer the case with me. It might have been once, but it isn't anymore." *Good Lord, how many lies was he going to tell this afternoon?*

"What just happened here was a mistake and I regret it. I said I'm sorry and I am, although you aren't gracious enough to accept my apology. But, if you're so conceited about your looks that you think I don't have any other way to get a thrill than to ogle you, then you're sadly mistaken. If I want a thrill, I assure you, there are plenty of ladies back in Oregon City who'd be more than happy to provide me with one."

Tess swallowed hard, suddenly embarrassed by her outburst. Hunter was right. She had seen for herself during her short stay in Oregon City how many women were throwing themselves at him. And, maybe his driving the wagon through that pothole *had* been a mistake. Maybe he hadn't done it on purpose just so he could turn around and stare at her bare breasts.

Now, as she sat in the back of the cramped, little wagon, she looked at him closely. He was right. He wasn't a man that would ever have to resort to trickery just to get a look at a woman's body. Narrowing her eyes, Tess studied him, pretending she was seeing him for the first time.

He was magnificent. Physically speaking, Hunter was everything any woman could ever dream of: tall, muscular, and so darkly handsome that it made her shiver just to look at him, despite the heat of the afternoon sun filtering through the canvas wagon cover.

But, Tess knew she couldn't really view him dispassionately. They weren't strangers—far from it, in fact. And in her mind, what surpassed the physical perfection of Hunter was the aspect of his character that the women in Oregon City weren't privy too—the gentleness and sensitivity of Jared.

It occurred to her that he was very nearly two different beings. There was Hunter—the powerful, dark and silent enigma, and then there was Jared—the caring gentleman, the sensitive, giving lover. And as potent as Hunter's allure was, it was Jared whom Tess loved. It was Jared whom she feared she might never see again.

"I'm sorry," she said quietly. "I know that what happened was a mistake and I regret taking you to task. I guess I'm just a little nervous about . . . everything."

"You have nothing to fear from me, Tess," Hunter said honestly. "All I'm doing is fulfilling a responsibility that I feel I have toward you. Nothing more."

Even as he voiced these last words, he knew they were yet another lie, but this time, he felt it was justified—even necessary.

In a day or two, he and Tess would part company forever. What good could it possibly do to tell her now that the mere thought of that parting was tearing him asunder? That the realization that he would never again see her beautiful face or touch her silken body was causing him to suffer a sense of desolation he hadn't even known he was capable of feeling.

It was that knowledge that had prompted him to intentionally drive the wagon into the pothole. That need to take one more intimate look so that he could lock the memory of her beauty forever into his mind.

What would she think if she knew the truth about his feelings, his motives?

Hunter told himself it didn't matter, but Jared desperately wished he knew.

Chapter 34

They made camp that night in a grassy meadow near a small creek. The spot was near a grove of trees, giving them shelter from the chill late September night breeze and fuel with which to build a fire.

As Tess climbed down from the wagon, she looked around happily, breathing deeply of the fragrant, evergreen scented air before plunging her hands and arms into the clear, cold water of the creek. She washed off the day's grime from her face and neck, then sat back, her hands braced behind her as she allowed herself a quiet moment to relish the beauty of her surroundings.

"Pretty place, isn't it?" Hunter asked, coming up to stand behind her.

Tess nodded. "I can see why so many people want to live here. It's like heaven."

"Think so?"

"Yes. If I were to picture heaven, this would definitely be it."

Hunter smiled as he looked out at the mountains to the west, outlined in hues of purple and gray as the sun sank behind them. "You may be right, although I think of heaven in different terms."

"Really?" Tess remarked, tipping her head back to look at him. "How do you think of it?"

"It's hard to explain. I don't think of it so much as a physical place. To me, heaven is a condition where there's no pain, no deprivation, no death. A situation where everyone is happy and content with no worries or problems . . . or regrets."

Tess looked at him closely, surprised by his rather profound answer. "That's an interesting theory."

"Why?"

"Because except for a few elements, what you describe is obtainable on earth."

Hunter squatted down next to her, his expression perplexed. "Do you really think so?"

"Yes. I mean, we may not be able to control pain and death and, certainly, we all have to live with some regrets but, other than that, I think it is. I'm a firm believer that we all have the ability to be happy and content, and with the right amount of thought and planning, I think it's possible to solve most of our problems."

"Have you ever been happy and content, Tess? I mean, truly happy and content?"

Tess cocked her head, her expression becoming soft and wistful. "Yes, I have."

"It didn't last though, did it?."

"No," she admitted, "it didn't. But, at least I know it's possible because, for a short time, I had it."

"Unfortunately, I never have," Hunter said flatly, getting to his feet and starting back toward the wagon.

"You will someday."

He paused, looking over his shoulder at her. "Why do you say that?"

"Because you deserve it."

Hunter retraced his steps, walking back to where she sat and peering down at her curiously. "I can hardly believe what I'm hearing. After our little, um, misunderstanding this afternoon, you were ready to cast me into the bowels of hell for being a voyeur and a lecher. Now you're saying that I deserve to be happy?"

"Well," Tess murmured, "I guess I can forgive you for that. But, I still don't want you ever to do anything like it again," she added quickly.

Hunter held up his hands, his gesture assuring her that he wouldn't. "I'm glad you're not still mad," he said quietly. "It'll make the next twenty-four hours until we get to your sister's a whole lot more pleasant."

Tess nodded, then got to her feet. "Do you really think we'll make Deborah's by tomorrow?" she asked as they strolled back toward the wagon.

"If she and her husband live where I think they do, we should be there by mid-afternoon."

Tess closed her eyes and clasped her hands together in front of her. "I can't wait. I haven't seen Deborah in almost three years and now . . . finally, *finally*, I'm going to be with her again. You can't imagine how excited I am. I have a whole new life beginning tomorrow, and I can hardly wait to get started living it."

Hunter sighed inwardly, wishing he could share her excitement. To him, tomorrow meant the end, not the beginning. Tomorrow, he would deliver Tess to her sister like a much anticipated gift, then head back on his solitary journey to Oregon City, then to Independence, only to turn around and begin the trek all over again. Despite the fact that this was the life he had chosen for himself, it sometimes seemed so pointless.

Shaking himself from his reverie, he said, "I'm

going to go cut some wood for a fire. Could you gather up some kindling and maybe find some stones?''

She grinned mischievously. ''Sure. I've become an expert at fuel gathering. Kindling, chunks of wood, stones, buffalo chips. You name it. If it's out there, I'll find it.''

Hunter smiled, amazed at how much Tess had changed from the frightened, uncertain and wholly unskilled woman who had sat so nervously in his office five months before. Perhaps the greatest satisfaction he'd found on this emotionally tumultuous journey was witnessing her maturity into the self-assured, confident woman he saw before him now—her eyes dancing with merriment, her short curls blowing seductively around her beautiful face.

Quickly, he turned away before the yearning he knew he couldn't hide became apparent in his face. ''I'll be back in a half hour or so. I won't be far, so call if you need me for anything.''

Tess nodded and hurried off toward the grove of trees to begin her task. The underbrush was plentiful and it was only a matter of a few minutes before she had gathered enough kindling to start the fire. Strolling back to the wagon, she was just setting her little cache down when she heard a loud crash behind her. Thinking that Hunter was already back, she turned to greet him, but her words died in her throat, turning into a startled screech of terror.

From out of the woods she'd just left lumbered a giant Grizzly bear. The brute paused at the sound of her scream, standing up on its back legs and pointing its nose at the sky as it sniffed her unfamiliar scent.

Tess clapped a trembling hand over her mouth so as not to scream again and draw even more attention to herself. She was no more than ten feet away from the wagon, but she didn't know if she should try to climb inside and risk trapping herself and Sarah within its small confines, or stay where she was.

She thought she remembered once hearing that it was best to stand perfectly still when confronted with a predatory animal. Something about abrupt movements startling them and setting them on the defensive where they might feel compelled to attack.

With huge, terrified eyes, she stared at the great brown beast. It had to be nine feet tall, standing on its back legs as it was, and the claws extending off the ends of its front paws looked to be at least six inches long.

One swipe and I'm dead, Tess thought desperately. I've got to do something! Careful not to move her head, she shifted her eyes from one side to the other, trying to spot anything that might serve as shelter—or a weapon.

She looked downward, gazing at the small pile of kindling at her feet. Maybe, if she could bend down without riling the bear, she could grab one of the bigger chunks of wood and throw it. No, she thought dismally, she'd undoubtedly miss and that would just enrage the bear.

She could climb a tree—she'd been a good climber as a child -but the bear could probably climb too and would just follow her up. Could bears climb? She wasn't sure, but it really didn't matter anyway since the only trees nearby were the ones she'd just left and the bear was now standing between her and them.

I'm trapped, she thought, tremors of oncoming hysteria seizing her. I made it all this way and now I'm going to die. I'd have been better off if I'd let the Indians take me.

She cast her eyes upward, praying frantically that the bear wouldn't find Sarah—that she, herself, would be . . . enough to satisfy it. A convulsive shudder ran through her and despite her vow to remain still and silent, a tortured cry of fear erupted from her throat.

The bear, who seemed to have momentarily lost interest in her, suddenly let out an ear shattering bellow and dropped back on to all four feet, malevolently swinging its huge brown head in her direction. For a moment, predator and prey eyed each other, then the bear suddenly began running toward her, roaring evilly as it ate up the ground with its huge strides.

As the animal came closer, Tess turned and began running blindly toward the creek as fast as her shaking legs would carry her. Another shrill scream of terror escaped her as she turned and saw the bear rapidly closing the distance between them.

Suddenly, a strange calm overtook her and she stopped running. It was no use. She couldn't outdistance the huge animal, so what was the use of trying? Turning to face her tormenter, she put her hands up to her mouth to stifle another scream, staring squarely at her enemy as she waited for the inevitable.

From far in the distance, Hunter thought he heard a scream. "What was that?" he muttered. Listening intently, he waited, but the only sounds he heard were the small woodland animals scurrying about their business high in the trees above him. He was just about to resume his chopping when he heard another scream, louder this time and more terrified. Throwing down the ax, he grabbed his rifle and took off running back toward the wagon. When a third scream pierced the silence, he picked up his pace, racing through the trees and bursting into the clearing where they'd set up their small camp.

His already pounding heart slammed against his ribs as his eyes lit on the terrifying tableau unfolding before him. There was Tess, sprinting toward the creek and screaming as if all the demons in hell were chasing her. But there was only one demon after her—a huge, enraged Grizzly who was quickly closing the gap between himself and his prey.

"Jesus Christ! Why the hell is she running?" Hunter cried, instinctively dropping to one knee. Bracing his rifle on his bent knee, he drew a deep, shuddering breath and willed his trembling hands to still.

"One shot," he muttered, "one shot right through the heart."

It was his only chance and he knew it. Closing one eye, he sighted down the barrel, training the gun along the bear's massive brown side until he had drawn the bead he wanted on the animal's heart. "Please God, don't let me miss," he entreated. Then he pulled the trigger.

With a roar of shock and pain, the bear fell, tumbling over and over itself as the bullet found its mark. Hunter's gaze immediately shifted over to Tess who, to his astonishment, had stopped running and was now standing and calmly staring at the fallen beast.

Getting to his feet, he started to run toward her, pausing by the wagon long enough to check on the baby who was still asleep in her little basket, blissfully unaware of the danger so close to her.

He ran a few more feet, the stopped again near the thrashing, dying bear. Pulling out his six shooter, he placed two more well aimed shots into the animal's head.

Suddenly, all was silent. Hunter looked up at Tess who was still standing exactly as he'd seen her earlier, staring at him and the bear with a vacant expression on her face.

"Damn it, she's in shock." Holstering his gun, he started toward her again.

"Tess!" he cried, reaching out and pulling her stiff

form to him. "Tess, sweetheart, can you hear me? It's okay. It's over. The bear's dead. He can't hurt you now."

Tess looked up at him blankly, her eyes registering neither recognition nor relief.

"Tess!" Hunter shouted, shaking her until her head wobbled crazily on her slumping shoulders. "Tess, it's me, Jared! Say something, for God's sake!"

"Jared?" she croaked, lifting her eyes to look at him. "Jared?"

"Yes, sweetheart, it's me." Tightening his arms around her, he held her close against him, shocked by how cold and limp she suddenly felt.

"That bear was going to eat me," she said absently.

"It's dead now, Tess. It can't hurt you anymore."

"It was going to eat me."

Jared bit his lip, fighting back the sense of helpless panic that was beginning to grip him. "Tess! Look at me. Do you know who I am?"

Absently, she looked up at him, her gaze vague and disoriented.

"Tess, it's Jared. Listen to me, sweetheart. The bear's dead. He can't hurt you. He's not going to eat you! Do you understand me?"

"You don't have to yell at me, Jared," she said placidly. "I heard you the first time."

Desperately, he tilted her head back again, trying to see some sign of awareness returning to her empty eyes. When he didn't, he did the only thing that occurred to him.

He kissed her.

Passionately, frantically, he kissed her, his mouth moving over hers with a desperate urgency, sucking on her lower lip, his tongue coaxing her to open to him in the hope that the erotic sensations of his hot caress might bring her back to reality.

To his astonishment, his ploy worked.

Suddenly, with a shriek that made his ears ring, Tess pushed him away, throwing her head back and screaming so loudly that a covey of birds rose out of the tall grass in frenzied flight. Hunter made no attempt to stop her, knowing that she needed a release from the terrible trauma she'd just endured and that a long, lusty scream was probably the best way for her to vent her terror.

When Tess finally stilled, she looked up at him for a long moment. Then, without warning, she launched herself into his arms, kissing him feverishly. "Thank you, thank you," she babbled, her lips running all over his face. "You saved my life, you wonderful, beautiful man. I thought I was dead. I could see myself dying. I really could, and I was so scared, Jared, so terrified, I just didn't know what to do."

Hunter, who was shamelessly enjoying Tess's rambling about his heroism as well as her unbridled kisses, said nothing. He just nodded and kissed her back, vastly relieved that she had returned from the empty void into which she'd plummeted, and loving the feeling of her being in his arms again.

"Why did you run?" he asked finally when Tess stood back to catch her breath. "Don't you know you should never run from an animal who's about to attack?"

"I know that. But, I also knew the bear was going to kill me, no matter what I did, and I wanted to get him as far away from Sarah as I could."

Suddenly, her eyes flared with renewed terror. "Sarah!" she gasped. "My baby!" Wrenching herself out of Hunter's arms, she raced off toward the wagon. She ran past the dead bear without so much as a look and hurled herself into the back of the wagon without ever breaking stride.

Hunter waited outside for her as Tess checked the baby. "Sarah's fine," she sighed as he lifted her back to the ground. "She slept through the whole thing."

"I know," Hunter nodded, wrapping her in his strong arms again. "I checked on her a minute ago."

Tess looked up at him gratefully, then her eyes slid away and settled on the bear. A tremulous shudder ran through her. Burying her face against Hunter's flannel shirt, she started to cry again. "I was so scared. So scared that I'd never hold Sarah again, never see you again."

"Shh," Hunter soothed, lifting her chin and gazing into her eyes. He wanted to kiss her—to feel her lips beneath his and prove to himself that she was truly all right.

He knew he shouldn't. Even now, his better judgment told him to release her, to step back, to move away.

"To hell with better judgment," he growled. And, lowering his mouth, Hunter kissed Tess with all the pent up passion and longing he had kept hidden for so long.

Tess's response was immediate. "Make love to me," she whispered against his lips. "Please. Right here. Right now."

"Tess, I can't. It wouldn't be right for us to . . . "

"I know, I know," she interrupted, "you've already told me there's no future for us, and I understand. But, I don't care. Not tonight. Please, Jared, just one more time. *Please,* love me."

With a primitive groan of desire, Hunter led her a few feet away from the wagon and out of the line of sight of the bear, then pulled her down into the soft grass. "You're sure you want to do this?" he panted as he frantically fumbled with the long row of buttons down the front of her dress.

"Yes," she answered, her voice just as breathless

as his. "More than I've ever wanted to do anything in my whole life."

He smiled, turning away to kick off his boots, then lying down on his back with his feet in the air as he yanked off his denims.

"In a hurry, Colonel?" Tess teased, amused by the frantic pace at which he was stripping off his clothes.

"I don't want to give you a chance to change your mind," he muttered hoarsely, rising up, naked, on his knees to loom over her like some ancient, aroused god.

Tess let out an awed breath as her eyes slid up the length of his body. "You're so beautiful." Shyly, she reached out and feathered her fingers down his jutting manhood. "The most beautiful man in the world. And tonight, you're mine."

Hunter shivered and drew in a sharp breath as Tess's fingers intimately stroked him. For a long moment, he remained still, his head thrown back, his lips parted in ecstasy. But, it had been so long since they'd been together, so many weeks since he'd felt her touch him that after a brief moment, he knew he had to stop her.

Gently, he guided her hand upward until it reached his chest, then he bent to kiss her. "I'm yours forever, my love," he whispered, his mouth toying with hers. "There will never be anyone else but you."

Gently, seductively, he slid her dress down over her hips, flinging it aside, then turning back to pull down her stockings. As he worked the soft cloth over her foot, he leaned down and kissed her arch, running his tongue along her toes until she squirmed with delight.

"Do you like that?" he whispered.

Tess nodded, her bottom lip clamped between her teeth to keep them from chattering with excitement.

Hunter smiled with satisfaction. "How about this?"

Lowering his lips to her ankle, he gently worked his way upward, running his tongue over the tight muscle in her calf, the back of her knee and slowly, slowly up the inside of her thigh.

Tess writhed deliciously beneath his sensuous torment, tossing her head back and forth, and moaning.

Hunter smiled and straightened, pausing so long that she opened her eyes and looked at him questioningly. "What do you want?" he asked, brushing his thumb lightly across her femininity.

Her face reddened with embarrassment. "I can't say that," she gasped, unconsciously wiggling her hips to entice him to touch her again.

Deliberately, he lifted his hand, holding it up and stroking the air with his thumb as he emulated the caress he knew she craved. "Yes, you can. Tell me what you want."

Tess shivered and shook her head. "I can't."

"Then I'll just have to guess, won't I? Is it this, maybe?" Bending over her, he stroked her once with his tongue.

A little spasm shook her. "Yes!"

"Ah," he chuckled throatily, "I thought so. Now, tell me that you want me to do that again."

"I can't say it, Jared. *Please*!"

"You can say it," he assured her, bracing his hands on either side of her head and running his tongue around her ear. "All you have to say is, 'Kiss me there, Jared'."

Tess's eyes flew open and she looked up into his dark, laughing eyes. "That's all?"

"Yes."

"Please kiss me there, Jared. She paused a moment, then added, "And then, I'll kiss you there, too."

Hunter's mouth dropped open in astonishment at her provocative offer. "I'm going to hold you to that promise, my lady," he rasped, his breath coming hard and fast as he thought about the delights to come.

Slowly, he trailed his tongue down her neck, her breasts and her soft stomach, finally dipping deep into the sweet, moist core of her until she cried out with the ecstasy of climax. When the little convulsions finally ebbed, Hunter lifted his head, smiling at her sublimely.

Tess exhaled a long, satisfied sigh and crooked a finger at him. "Come here, Colonel. It's your turn."

"Oh, God," Hunter groaned, glancing down at his huge, throbbing erection. "I don't know if I can take this."

"Oh, I'm sure you can," Tess drawled, running her tongue over her lips in seductive invitation. "Come up here and I'll show you."

Shaking with eagerness, Hunter moved up the length of her body until he was positioned above her, his knees on either side of her shoulders, his magnificent arousal standing rigidly away from his body.

He watched Tess close her eyes and reach up to fondle him, then she took him into her mouth, her tongue twirling around the sensitive tip. Throwing his head back, Hunter emitted a long, strangled groan of pleasure, his fingers digging into his thighs as he lost himself in the exquisite sensation of Tess's warm, moist mouth.

Looking down again, he watched Tess make love to him, knowing that he would remember this night for the rest of his life. Finally, when he could no longer control his body's demand for release, he withdrew from her sensuous ministrations and lay down in the grass next to her.

"Are we done?" she asked softly.

"No," he smiled. "Why don't you come sit on me and I'll show you how far from done we are."

Tess's eyes widened at his scandalous suggestion, but knowing this might very well be the last night they would ever have together, she wanted to experience everything. Casting him a come hither look that made him feel like he was on fire, she rose above him, straddling his lean hips and impaling herself on his hot, hard shaft.

A little gasp escaped her as his entire length slipped deep inside, but she soon accustomed herself to his huge presence and began rotating her hips suggestively.

Hunter looked up at her, thinking that he'd never seen anything more erotic than the sight of Tess sitting atop him, her head thrown back and her knees gripping him as she sheathed him deep inside.

As their passion built to a heady climax, Hunter placed his hands on either side of her hips, thrusting her up and down until they both screamed out in a simultaneous explosion of pleasure.

Tess fell forward on to his chest, her head nestled under his chin, her hands splayed out against his heaving chest.

"You are an amazing woman," he whispered, gently stroking her silken hair.

"I am? Why?"

"Because I've never known anyone who's such a lady in public and such a hellcat in bed."

Wearily, Tess lifted her head, looking at him with concern. "Is that bad?"

"Oh, no," he chuckled, kissing her gently and guiding her head back down to his chest. "It's not bad at all. In fact, it's perfect."

Chapter 35

They spent the rest of the night nestled together on the small cot in Tess's wagon. The chill autumn wind made it too cold to sleep outside and although they were cramped on the narrow little bed, neither of them complained or, in truth, even noticed.

They awoke just before dawn and made love again. This time, their interlude was slow and sensuous, their kisses endless, their stroking and fondling of each other's nude bodies almost reverent. And after it was over, they fell asleep again, their bodies entwined intimately in a lovers' embrace.

Sarah awoke shortly after the sun came up, screaming lustily for her breakfast. It was Hunter who got up and retrieved the baby from her basket, bringing her back to the small bed and handing her to her mother. Then he lay down again, and with the baby snuggled between them, he fondly watched Tess nurse her, knowing that this moment with the three of them together was the most peaceful and contented of his life.

They were on their way again by eight o'clock. They

talked little, both of them lost in their own sweet thoughts of the night just past, and wondering what the day ahead would bring.

Why don't you just tell her you love her and that you want to spend the rest of your life with her? Hunter asked himself. You know you want her. Why don't you admit it and ask her to marry you?

But he didn't, the haunting specter of his past preventing him. And, as the hours and the miles rolled quietly by and the glow of the previous night's rapture faded, he gradually convinced himself it was for the best that he hold his tongue.

Tess would go on to her new life and he would return to his old one. That solitary life he had worked so hard to build—no ties, no entanglements, no pain . . . no purpose. The mere thought of returning to his aimless existence was so painful that he felt like he was strangling, but still he said nothing.

Several times, he caught Tess looking at him as if she were about to say something. Each time he would hold his breath, fearing that if she gave him so much as one word of encouragement, he would get down on his knees and beg her to marry him, and knowing that was the worst thing he could possibly do.

But Tess said nothing, and by the time they reached the small settlement where Hunter thought Clay and Deborah might live, the silent rift between them was so wide that he knew it was too late to close it.

After stopping at three homesteads, they finally found someone who knew Tess's sister and directed them on to the Douglas farm. It was nearly dusk when they arrived.

As the small, roughly hewn log cabin loomed up in front of them, Hunter pulled back on the reins and looked over at Tess. "We're here," he said quietly. "You did it, Mrs. Caldwell, you made it to your sister's."

Tess's thoughts were so chaotic that she didn't know if she could speak. All day she'd been suffering from the conflicting emotions of anticipation and loss. Now, listening to the quiet finality in Hunter's voice, she did what she'd wanted to do all day. She burst into tears.

"What's wrong?" he cried, aghast at the torrent of water springing from her eyes.

Tess gazed over at his handsome, beloved face. "Oh, Jared, I'm just so . . . " But as the words she so longed to say began to tumble out, she saw a look closely resembling fear fill his eyes. With a quick intake of breath, she realized that he didn't want to hear what she was about to say and quickly, she changed her mind. "I'm just so . . . grateful to you for everything."

Hunter tried desperately to cover his disappointment at her brief, impersonal statement. "You're welcome," he muttered, the tone of his voice as dead as the bear he'd shot the previous day. "Come on, I'll help you down."

Winding the reins around the brake, he jumped down from Tess's wagon for the last time, coming around the back and holding his arms up for the baby. Cradling Sarah in one arm, he assisted Tess down, and, together, they walked toward the little house.

"It's awfully quiet," Tess commented, gazing around the deserted yard. "I hope they're home."

Hunter looked over in the direction of the barn just as a young man stepped out of the building's large door. "There's somebody," he said, pointing. "Is that Clay?"

Tess squinted into the fading twilight, then shook her head. "No. Are you sure we have the right farm?"

Hunter shrugged, then handed Tess the baby he was still carrying and strode over to where the young man stood, eyeing them warily. "Is this the Douglas place?"

"Yeah. Who are you?"

Hunter jerked his thumb over his shoulder. "I'm bringing Mrs. Caldwell to join her sister, Mrs. Douglas. Who are you?"

"Zeke Dayton," the boy replied, rubbing his hands on his dungarees and extending his arm. "I live down the road apiece with my pa and ma. The Douglases ain't here. They went to Portland to lay in winter supplies."

Tess, who had followed Hunter over to the barn let out a groan of disappointment. "Oh, no. When are they expected back?"

Zeke looked at her closely, his eyebrows raising with interest as his eyes roamed over her. "Coupla days. I'm stayin' here while they're gone, tendin' their stock. You really Mrs. Douglas's sister?"

Tess nodded dismally, disappointment rampant on her beautiful face. "Two more days . . . "

"Y'all are welcome to stay in the house," Zeke offered. "I'm sleepin' in the barn. Funny thing, ever since I came across last year, I don't like sleepin' in houses no more. Guess it's all them months of bein' out under the stars."

Hunter nodded, knowing that this was a common phenomenon among the western emigrants. He'd even heard stories of babies who'd been born on the trail refusing to sleep inside, causing their poor mothers many a troubled night as they tried to acclimate their offspring to confined quarters.

"You this lady's brother?" Zeke asked. "We heared he was comin' too."

Hunter glanced quickly at Tess, noting the bleak look of anguish that immediately clouded her eyes. "No," he replied quickly. "Her brother didn't make it. I'm just an escort."

"Oh, sorry," Zeke stammered, digging his toe into the dirt in embarrassment. "Well, if yur just an escort, then you can sleep in the barn with me." Seeing Hunter's mouth tighten, he quickly added, "Or anywhere else you've a mind to."

Hunter nodded. "I'll only be here for one night. I'm leaving at first light."

"Yur a widah woman, ain't ya?" Zeke asked, turning his attention back to Tess.

She nodded.

"Yeah, thought so. We heared all about you. You was an actress back east, right?"

Again, Tess nodded.

"Well, yur sister will be real glad to see ya. She's been awaitin' and awaitin' for y'all ta get here. Clay finally decided, though, that they couldn't wait no longer to get their supplies, so they left for Portland on Monday. 'Spect they'll be back by Friday or so." He paused and chuckled knowingly. "I *know* they'll be back by Sunday for sure, 'cause Miz Douglas done promised all the menfolks 'round here that she'd bring you to church if you was here by then. There's a whole lotta unmarried men just snortin' and stampin', they're so excited yur comin'."

This last statement caused Hunter to shoot Zeke a sharp, almost threatening look. "Come on," he said, taking Tess firmly by the elbow. "Let's get you settled in the house."

Tess nodded and, together, they hurried across the yard. Hunter stepped in front of her, opening the crude front door to the small dwelling, then stepping aside to let Tess enter.

"Kind of small, isn't it?" he commented as he walked into the main room behind her.

"It'll do," Tess answered, her expression giving lie to her words as her eyes quickly scanned the twelve foot by twelve foot structure.

"There's two little bedrooms over here," Hunter said, poking his head into the side by side rooms. "That's good."

"They have three children, so they probably felt they needed the privacy of separate bedrooms. I imagine I'll just sleep in with the boys." Walking over to where Hunter stood, Tess peeked over his shoulder into the second bedroom, her heart dropping dejectedly when she saw it was no bigger than a large closet.

Hunter walked back into the main room, looking dubiously at the dirt floor and spartan furnishings. As accustomed as he was to living in rough quarters, even he had never been faced with long term residency in such a primitive dwelling. "Were you and Joe both planning to live here?"

"Only temporarily. Joe and Clay were going to build us our own cabin in the spring."

It was Hunter's opinion that that was a plan that should still be implemented. Regardless of how much Tess loved her sister's family, he could not feature seven people living comfortably—or compatibly—in this tiny house.

"I guess it doesn't make much difference that I had to eject all my furniture along the trail," Tess sighed. "Deborah wouldn't have had any room for it anyway."

Hunter nodded, sympathizing with how disappointed Tess must be. For five months she had dreamed of this day and now, not only was her sister not here to greet her, but she was faced with the realization that she was going to have to spend the winter in a house that was little more than a shack, and with four children and two other adults.

"I'll go out to the wagon and fetch a few things for you," he offered.

Tess nodded and untied the worn strings of her faded red sunbonnet. "If you'll bring some wood in first, I'll light the stove and start supper. I'm sure Deborah must have something here that we can eat."

As Hunter started out the door, his eyes lit on the old sunbonnet. Surreptitiously, he swept it off the table where Tess had thrown it and stuffed it into his pocket. A momentary pang of guilt stabbed him for stealing back the bonnet that he'd given her so many months before, but he figured it was that bonnet that had started their relationship, and for some reason that even he couldn't explain, he wanted it.

He collected enough wood for Tess to start the stove, then walked out of the house again to unhitch the team. He was barely through the door before Zeke Dayton hightailed it across the yard toward him. "Anything I can do to help?" he called.

Hunter looked over at the eager boy, not knowing why he'd taken such a dislike to him. "No thanks," he said pleasantly, "I can handle it. I'm just going to take a few things into the house that Mrs. Caldwell might need for the baby."

"She shore is a beauty, ain't she?" Zeke remarked, whistling softly between his teeth.

"Who?" Hunter gritted. "Mrs. Caldwell's baby?"

"Naw," Zeke guffawed. "Babies is babies. They all look the same. I'm talkin' about the widah. Mr. Douglas, he done told my pa that she was pretty, but that don't even touch her. Just wait till the boys down at church see her on Sunday. I'll wager she ain't gonna be a widah for long if'n they got anything to say 'bout it."

"Oh, so you think she'll be married soon?" Hunter asked, clenching his fists at his sides in an effort to hang on to his quickly fraying temper.

"Shore thing. Why, a woman looks like she does, she can have her pick of every man in the county! I jus' wish I was a little older. I'd go for her myself."

A small muscle in Hunter's jaw began to pulse. "How old are you, boy?"

"Sixteen," he answered proudly. "Seventeen, come January. I s'pose a lot of folks would say I'm old enough to go courtin' myself, but I say, what's the rush? I wanna find me just the right girl 'fore I make permanent plans. Too bad the widah ain't a few years younger, though. Woman looks like that would be worth pushin' my schedule up for."

Hunter jumped down from the back of the wagon with a bundle of clothes and Sarah's little basket tucked under one arm. "That's important, all right," he agreed. "A man should make sure he's found the right woman before he starts making permanent plans."

"My feelin's, 'zactly," Zeke nodded. "Want me to put your team up in the barn? There's plenty o' room with the Douglases gone and all."

"I'd appreciate that," Hunter nodded.

Zeke looked over toward the house, his nose twitching as he caught the scent of wood smoke coming from the chimney. "Is the widah cookin' some supper?" he asked hopefully.

"The *'widah's'* name is Mrs. Caldwell," Hunter barked, his temper beginning to win the battle over his resolve.

"Oh, yeah, sure," Zeke said agreeably. "Well, is *Miz Caldwell* cookin' some supper?"

"Yes."

"S'pose she'd mind if I had a bite with y'all? I ain't had much to eat for the last coupla days since I been here, 'cept for the apples and bread my ma sent with me."

"I'm sure she wouldn't mind. Why don't I bring a plate out to the barn when the food's ready?"

Zeke's face fell as he realized that he was obviously not going to be invited in to eat. "Okay," he shrugged. "That'll be fine."

Hunter turned and strode off toward the house. It

wasn't until he was halfway to the door, however, that he realized how irrational he was acting.

You're jealous! Jealous of a sixteen-year-old kid! What difference does it make if he gawks at her? Tomorrow, you're riding out of here and you won't know who's gawking at her . . . or doing anything else, for that matter.

Impulsively, he turned back toward the wagon. "Hey Zeke?" he called.

"Yeah?"

"Why don't you come in and eat supper with us in the house?"

"Really?" Zeke cried, grinning from ear to ear. "All right! And don't worry none. I'll wash at the pump afore I come in."

Hunter nodded and disappeared into the house.

Hunter had almost forgotten how nice it was to sit at a table and eat a meal. Tess had fixed bacon and biscuits, and although it was the same repast they had eaten dozens of times on the trail, just the fact that it was served on a china plate somehow made it taste better.

After supper, Tess excused herself to feed Sarah, and Hunter and Zeke went outside to sit on the step and have a smoke. During the course of the meal, Hunter noticed that Zeke could barely take his eyes off Tess, but he was no longer concerned. The kid was a baby. A true innocent. Before supper was finished, Hunter came to the conclusion that his initial wariness had been a mistake and that Tess would be perfectly safe alone on the farm with Zeke until her sister returned.

Unfortunately, Zeke's first comment as they sat down on the step put him immediately back on the defensive.

"You know," Zeke said, "I think I could fall in love

with that lady real fast, and I *know* my brother Daniel's gonna feel 'zactly the same way when he gets here tomorrow."

Hunter's head jerked toward Zeke. "Your brother's coming here tomorrow?"

"Yup. Ma's sendin' him over with more provisions for me. 'Course, I won't be needin' 'em now that Miz Caldwell's here to cook, but I'm still glad he'd comin'. Boy, oh, boy, I can't *wait* to see old Dan's eyes pop out of his head when he gets a gander at her."

Hunter's fingers tightened around his cigarette. "*Old* Daniel?"

"Well, he ain't really old. Just twenty-five, but he seems old to me 'cause he's ma's firstborn and I'm her baby. There's five more of us in between, so Daniel just seems old. He's a real looker, though. All the ladies back in North Carolina used to say so. I'll be real interested to see what Miz Caldwell thinks of him."

"I'll be real interested too," Hunter gritted.

Zeke looked over at him curiously. "I thought you was leavin' in the mornin'."

"Nope. I've decided to stay on a couple more days. I'm in no hurry to get back to Oregon City and it's . . . pretty here. Think I'll just relax for a day or two before I make that long ride back."

"Oregon City," Zeke sighed. "I only been there once, but I thought it was a mighty excitin' place. I can't imagine wantin' to hang 'round here for even an extra hour if'n I had a chance to go to Oregon City."

"Well," Hunter drawled, leaning back on the step and taking a long drag of his cigarette, "I guess different folks have different ideas about what makes life exciting."

"Yeah," Zeke responded, leaning back in emulation of Hunter's casual pose, "I s'pose yur right, although I can't imagine what anybody would find excitin' 'bout this place."

Hunter glanced through the house's open door, spying Tess coming out of the bedroom, buttoning up her bodice. "Oh, you'd be surprised, boy," he smiled. "You'd be surprised."

Chapter 36

Hunter couldn't sleep. He had long ago heard the small clock on the mantle strike the midnight hour, but still he lay wide awake, staring at the ceiling. He had decided to sleep in the house and, now, as he lay in Clay and Deborah's large comfortable bed, he could hear Tess tossing restlessly in the next room. Obviously, she was finding the blessed forgetfulness of sleep as elusive as he was.

Turning over on to his side, he punched his pillow irritably, then flung it aside and got out of bed. Not bothering to pull on his pants, he walked out of the stuffy bedroom and turned toward Tess's door. He paused, noticing the portal was slightly ajar. For a moment he warred with himself, knowing that what he was about to do was insane, yet powerless to prevent it.

Reaching out, he gave the door a push, then stood, his nude body silhouetted against the dim lamp he had left lit in the main room, and stared at the woman lying on the small bed.

"Jared?" she whispered.

Hunter heard Tess's soft, yearning call and, without a word, he strode forward, scooping her out of the little bed and carrying her into Clay and Deborah's bedroom. Pushing the door shut with his foot, he laid her on the bed and stretched out beside her, his naked body covering hers.

Not a word passed between them as they began feverishly kissing, their mouths devouring each other. Hands were everywhere—stroking, caressing, fondling each other with a desperate need. Tess's nightgown seemed to simply evaporate and she sighed with pleasure as she felt the hard muscles of Hunter's chest flatten her breasts.

The night was moonless and cloudy, the small room inky black. Hunter couldn't see Tess's face, but he could visualize what she looked like; her eyes half closed, her mouth parted. He could smell the sweet essence of her, her skin as fragrant as roses since her leisurely bath that evening.

Although he was sure she didn't realize it, it was that bath that had led him to this moment. He had stood shamelessly outside the door to the children's bedroom as she had bathed, listening to the sound of the water lapping around her, imagining the smooth, silken path of the soap as it glided over the hills and valleys of her gorgeous body. Leaning against the door, he had closed his eyes, gritting his teeth against his body's immediate reaction to his heady imaginings.

He'd returned to his bedroom, determined not to give in to his desire, knowing that he should stay away from the bewitching woman in the next room. Another night spent in ecstasy together would only confuse him more. As much as he wanted her, he knew that making love to Tess again would be a grave mistake.

He'd battled with himself for over an hour, but it

wasn't until he heard her tossing restlessly in her small bed and realized that she wanted him as badly as he wanted her that he gave into his own primitive urges and went to her.

Now, as they lay passionately kissing and caressing each other, he didn't regret his impulsive decision. He loved her, he wanted her, he needed her and, for this moment at least, she was his.

With a sweep of his arm, he skimmed along the soft curve of Tess's hip, settling his hand over her womanhood and lightly stroking her hot, moist flesh. His finger slipped easily inside and he smiled with masculine satisfaction as he felt her convulse with the first blush of ecstasy.

Wanting to return the pleasure, Tess reached down and encircled him with cool fingers, her soft hand stroking and massaging his turgid shaft until he felt he might explode.

Rising above her, Hunter pressed into her welcoming warmth, shivering when he heard her moan. He set an easy rhythm, their bodies perfectly attuned to each other. But their gentle, easy lovemaking lasted only a moment before Hunter increased the pace, his primal thrusts becoming faster and deeper. Tess stayed with him, matching his ebb and flow in perfect harmony.

Together, they reached the crescendo of their sexual symphony, crying out lustily as they celebrated the carnal joy they found in each other.

Their impassioned moans gradually faded to sighs of satisfied pleasure as they floated back to earth, holding each other close.

Finally, as the mantel clock struck two times, Tess murmured, "I should go back. It wouldn't do if anyone caught us here together."

"Don't go," Hunter whispered. "I'll take you back in plenty of time. Besides, who's going to catch us?"

Tess needed no further encouragement to stay with him. With a contented little sigh, she nestled more deeply under the covers, snuggling up against Hunter's big, warm body and falling into a dreamless sleep.

Hunter lay awake long after Tess's breathing became slow and regular, gazing into her serene face and stroking her hair with an adoring caress.

How could he leave? he wondered desolately. For the first time in his life, he knew what it was to cherish someone—to dance that exquisite, elusive waltz of love, passion and friendship. Could he really just walk away? He closed his eyes wearily, his tortured thoughts running in mad, whirling circles in his tired brain.

If he stayed, would it be possible for him to truly shed the ghosts of his past? Could he rid himself of the cold, unfeeling shell of Hunter, and reweave the tangled, broken threads of Jared?

Unfortunately, his time was running out and he still had no answer to that question.

They were eating their noon meal the next day when Hunter heard a horse cantering into the front yard.

"Somebody's coming," he said, rising from the table and looking out the cabin's front window.

"Is it Clay and Deborah?" Tess asked excitedly.

"No. I think it's Zeke's brother."

Tess looked at him in surprise. "Zeke's brother? What is he doing here?"

"Zeke said he was coming over to bring him more food, but now that I'm staying until Clay and Deborah get back, Zeke might as well go on home with him. I can take care of the animals."

A little wave of pleasure rippled through Tess at Hunter's words. She had fully expected him to leave that morning but when he hadn't, she'd said nothing, preferring just to enjoy every minute they had left together. Now, however, she could hardly control her exuberance. "You're staying on for a few more days?"

"Yeah," he nodded, picking up his hat and heading for the door. "I don't want to leave you here alone."

Tess smiled happily and turned back to the stove. Two more days, she thought, nearly giddy with excitement. Two more days to spend together. And two more days also meant two more nights . . . She bit the inside of her lower lip, embarrassed by her scandalous thoughts and guilty about the fact that as much as she wanted to see Clay and Deborah, she was secretly hoping that they'd take their time in Portland.

Glancing out the window, she saw Hunter talking to a tall, good looking man of about her age. She watched as Hunter gestured toward the barn, then headed back to the house with the other man in tow.

Patting her hair and straightening her apron, Tess met them at the front door.

"Mrs. Caldwell," Hunter said formally, "I'd like you to meet Daniel Dayton, Zeke's older brother."

Daniel's gray eyes widened to huge proportions as he gaped openly at the beautiful blond woman standing before him. "Pleased to meet you, ma'am," he croaked, pulling off a disreputable looking hat and smiling broadly. "We're all real pleased that you're gonna be livin' here."

"Thank you, Mr. Dayton," Tess responded graciously. "Won't you come in and sit a moment?"

Daniel grinned and opened his mouth to accept Tess's invitation, but before he could utter a word, Hunter abruptly intervened. "No time, I'm afraid. Mr. Dayton is in the middle of harvesting potatoes and he's just staying long enough for Zeke to get his things together."

Daniel opened his mouth again as if to protest, but seeing the frosty look in Hunter's dark eyes, he abruptly closed it. "Clay should be back by the end of the week," he said, turning his attention back to Tess, "I hope you'll be comin' with him and Deborah to services on Sunday."

"I'd like that," Tess smiled. "Perhaps I'll see you there."

"Oh, you will," Daniel said eagerly. "You can count on me bein' there for sure."

Hunter could barely contain his annoyance as Daniel continued to gawk at Tess. Glancing impatiently out the front window, he said, "Oh, good. Here comes Zeke. Guess you can get back to your potatoes now, Dayton." Throwing an arm around the other man's shoulder, Hunter propelled him hastily toward the front door. "Sorry you had to make the trip all the way over here for nothing."

"No problem," Daniel responded, craning his head around to take one last look at Tess. "See you Sunday mornin', Miz Caldwell," he called as Hunter nearly shoved him out the door.

Tess nodded. "Yes, Mr. Dayton. I'll see you then." She followed the men over to the door, spotting Zeke standing in the yard holding the two horses. "Goodbye, Zeke," she called, raising her arm and waving. "See you Sunday."

Zeke's face reddened with pleasure and he returned Tess's farewell with an enthusiastic wave of his own.

Hunter walked back into the house and sat down at the small table, returning to his meal. "Better watch out for that one," he warned, his mouth full of stew.

"Who?"

Hunter swallowed and gestured at her with his fork. "Daniel. He's making wedding plans already. You could see it in his eyes every time he looked at you."

"Oh, that's nonsense," Tess scoffed. "Besides, I don't have any plans to marry . . . anyone."

Hunter looked at her for a long moment, then thoughtfully returned to his meal.

The next two days were halcyon with warm, sunny days and cool nights.

The evening after Zeke left, Tess and Hunter sat outside in the grass, sipping a cup of coffee and staring dreamily at the surrounding mountains. The hour grew late and, finally, Hunter got to his feet and held out his hand to Tess. "Come on, sweetheart, let's go to bed."

Tess smiled and without hesitation, took his hand. There was no discussion about where she was going to sleep. As if it were the most natural thing in the world, they walked into the main bedroom, shed their clothes and climbed into bed together. Hunter's sexual appetite that night was nearly insatiable, but he refused to allow himself to admit that it was the inexorable ticking of the clock counting down the hours until Friday that drove him to feast on Tess's seductive charms so greedily.

For her part, Tess asked no questions and made no demands. She simply relished every moment they had together and refused to think about what tomorrow might bring. She had long since reconciled herself to the fact that she and Hunter were a temporary thing, but she was so in love with him that she steadfastly refused to ruin what little time they had left together by thinking about the future. Instead, she savored each and every minute, locking the memories of these lovely, lazy days deep in her heart to be pulled out during all the lonely years ahead and savored again.

It was late in the afternoon on Thursday that they heard the wagon rattle into the yard. After exchanging knowing looks, Hunter raced across the room, grabbing Tess to him and kissing her with a desperate passion. "They're home," he rasped, brushing his thumbs gently across her cheeks.

"I know," she nodded. Disentangling herself from his fevered embrace, she straightened her bodice and hurried out the front door, running across the yard and throwing herself into Deborah's waiting arms.

Hunter stood in the doorway, feeling as if the earth were crumbling beneath his feet.

Clay and Deborah were back.

His time was up.

"I wish you'd stay on another day or two, Mr. Hunter. I'd like to get your opinion on a piece of land I'm thinking of buying."

Hunter looked across the breakfast table at Clay Douglas, a spark of interest igniting in his eyes. "I suppose I don't really have to leave this morning. There's nothing going on in Oregon City that can't wait another day."

Tess, who was standing at the board in the kitchen that served as a counter, glanced covertly over at him. When she saw that he was staring back at her, she quickly turned back to the potatoes she was peeling, hoping that the blush she could feel creeping up her cheeks wasn't apparent.

"Will you two be back in time for dinner?" Deborah asked.

Clay nodded. "Should be."

As the men rose to leave, Clay paused to give Deborah a smacking kiss. "Be good while I'm gone," he teased, running his hand lovingly over her protruding belly.

"I will," Deborah chuckled, placing her hand over

her husband's so he could feel his child within. "I don't have any problem being good when you're gone. It's when you're here that I get into trouble."

Everyone laughed heartily. The men clumped out the door and the sisters turned back to the dinner they were preparing. A peaceful silence filled the house.

It was Tess who finally spoke. "I don't think I told you, Deborah, how thrilled I am that I'm going to be an aunt again."

Deborah smiled and looked down at her huge stomach. "I just hope that this time it's a little Sarah, and not another Samuel. Three boys is enough for any woman to contend with."

Tess nodded. "I'm so glad I had a daughter. Considering that I have to raise her alone, I think it will be easier with a girl."

Deborah set down her paring knife and looked at her sister speculatively. "You don't think that you and Hunter will get married?"

Tess's heart jumped into her throat. "Heavens, no!" she laughed, trying hard to sound casual. "Whatever made you think that?"

"Oh, nothing," Deborah chuckled, "except that the two of you can't take your eyes off each other and when you're in a room together, there's so much heat between you that it warms the entire house."

"Deborah!" Tess gasped, her face flushing with embarrassment.

"Oh, come on, Tess," Deborah chided, "this is me you're talking to. I've known you since your first suitor came to the door when you were sixteen. I can see that you're in love with the man and I can also tell just by the way you look at each other that your relationship is an intimate one. Now, why aren't you going to get married?"

Tess sighed and set down her knife also. "He . . . he's not the marrying kind."

"Why not?"

"It's a lot of things. Things that happened in his past."

"Another woman?"

Tess nodded. "Yes. And the war in Mexico did things to him too."

"Including making him change his name?"

Tess's mouth dropped open in astonishment. "You know?"

"My Lord, Tess, how could you help it? Jared Daulton Whitaker's likeness was splashed over every newspaper in the country for months. All anyone has to do is look at Hunter and you know that's who he is. What I'm wondering is, why the subterfuge?"

"He's trying to escape from his past," Tess explained. "He hated the notoriety that his heroics in the war brought him, so after he left the military, he changed his name and began escorting wagon trains across the country."

"In other words, he's trying to run away from himself."

Tess nodded dejectedly.

"And having a wife would force him to settle down and confront his real identity."

She nodded again.

Deborah shook her head. "Well, I'm sorry to hear that, dear, because I've never seen a man more in love with a woman than he is with you. It'll be a real tragedy if he lets his past prevent him from finding happiness in the future."

Tess brushed away a tear. "I know all that, Deborah, but there's nothing I can do."

"Do you love him?"

"Yes. More than I ever dreamed possible."

Deborah shrugged philosophically. "Well, you just never know, Tessie. He may come to his senses yet."

"But, he's leaving tomorrow!"

"There's still today."

"This is a fine piece of land, don't you think?"

Hunter and Clay sat atop their horses, looking down on a large parcel of rich farmland. "Yeah," Hunter nodded. "I think you could grow just about anything in that soil."

"Well, the government only gives us six hundred forty acres and I've already chosen my piece, so if I want this one, I'm gonna have to buy it. I'm just afraid I'm not going to be able to come up with the money before somebody else grabs it."

"How much do they want for it?"

"A dollar an acre."

"Whew! Six hundred and forty dollars is a tidy sum to raise."

"Yeah, I know," Clay sighed. "It's just a damn shame that Joe didn't make it."

"Was this the piece he was going to farm?"

"Probably. It's the one I'd picked out for him, anyway. Since it butts up to my parcel, I was hoping to keep this whole section of the valley in the family."

Hunter shook his head sadly. "Joe had the makings of a fine man."

"Except that he didn't listen when he should have."

"Yeah, that's true. And, ultimately, that's what got him."

The men sat in silence for a moment, then Clay said, "You ever thought about settlin' down, Hunter?"

Hunter shot him a quick glance. "Thought about it."

"And . . ."

"Never had any reason to do it."

Clay frowned, discouraged by his evasive answers. "A good woman should be reason enough."

"Like Tess?"

Clay looked at him squarely. "Yeah, like Tess. The fact that you're crazy in love with her should help too." He waited, expecting Hunter to deny his statement, but he was met only with silence.

When Hunter finally did speak, his voice was so low that Clay had to lean toward him to hear. "Being crazy in love with her doesn't count for much when I don't have anything else to offer."

Clay's clear gray eyes narrowed. "Seems to me you have plenty. And if you'd just admit who you really are and take what's due you, you'd have even more."

Hunter's head jerked up and he eyed Clay warily. "What are you talking about?"

"Oh, come on, Colonel Whitaker, who do you think you're kidding?" Again Clay waited for a denial and, again, it didn't come.

"Look," he sighed, "Hunter or Whitaker or whatever your name is, it's not my business who you are or what happened to you that caused you to make the decisions you did. All I'm concerned about is my sister-in-law's happiness and it's damned obvious to me that you make her happy."

"So, are you offering me this piece of land?" Hunter asked, staring out at the rolling hills before him.

"If you want it. But Tess comes with it."

Hunter smiled, wryly amused by this whole situation. Clay Douglas was offering to let him have a piece of land he didn't even own. Still, he did so without flinching, caring deeply enough for his wife's sister's happiness that he was willing to make a fool of himself to try to ensure it. Despite the ridiculousness of his offer, Hunter couldn't help but be impressed by his concern.

"Thanks, Douglas," he said quietly. "I appreciate the offer."

"Just don't take too long to make your decision," Clay warned. "It'll take us several weeks to get a house up and you'll want to be settled before the bad weather sets in."

Hunter nodded and, without another word, the men turned their horses around and silently headed back for the farm.

Hunter spent the rest of the day alone, riding aimlessly through the huge valley that was Tess's new home as he struggled with the most important decision of his life.

He spent countless hours thinking about Tess, remembering fond moments from the last five months, and trying to imagine what his life would be like without her.

Finally, around supper time, he arrived back at the house, stepping through the front door with his hat clenched between his hands. Clay and Deborah looked at him expectantly.

"I'll be leaving first thing in the morning," he said quietly, his attention riveted on Tess.

She nodded once in response, then quickly turned away, walking into her little bedroom and softly closing the door behind her.

"Do you want some supper, Mr. Hunter?" Deborah asked, her voice quivering with pent up tears.

"No," he answered, "I'm not hungry. But thank you both for your hospitality."

And, turning on his heel, he walked out the door.

Chapter 37

Three weeks passed. Much to Tess's relief, neither Clay nor Deborah so much as mentioned Hunter and although he was never far from her thoughts, the lack of discussion about him made her loss a little easier to bear.

October swept in, bringing rain and wind that turned the grass brown and sent dead leaves swirling through the nippy air. As the month waned, the nights became cold and damp, causing the family to cluster around the fireplace, soaking up its comforting warmth as they spent their evenings in quiet conversation.

It was on one of these rainy, windswept evenings just as they were getting ready to retire that a knock sounded on the front door.

"Now, who the hell could that be at this hour?" Clay muttered.

"And in this weather," Deborah added. "Tess, are you expecting company?"

Tess shook her head. "No. Daniel Dayton asked me to have supper with him tonight, but I turned him down. Anyway, it's far too late for him to come calling."

Clay opened the door, revealing the silhouette of a large man standing on the step, his hat dripping water.

"Hunter!" he exclaimed. "My God, man, what are you doing out on a night like this? Come in!"

Tess let out a shocked little gasp, clapping her hand to her chest and grabbing for the door frame to steady herself.

Hunter took a step into the room, carefully taking off his soaked hat and shaking it outside before closing the door behind him. "I'm afraid I'm getting your floor wet," he said, his words directed toward Deborah, but his eyes feasting on Tess.

"Oh, don't worry about that, Mr. Hunter," Deborah laughed. "Let me take your coat."

"Thanks," he answered, "but the name isn't Hunter."

Clay cocked his head to one side, smiling with satisfaction. "No?"

Hunter shrugged off his wet coat. "No." With great effort, he pulled his gaze away from Tess and turned to face Clay. "In fact, if you'll permit me, I'd like to introduce myself. I'm Colonel Jared Daulton Whitaker, U.S. Army, Retired." With a grin, he stuck his hand out, grasping Clay's and shaking it heartily.

Tess, who still hadn't moved a step, clapped her hands over her mouth, hardly able to believe what she was hearing.

"I've come to ask your permission, Mr. Douglas, as head of this household, to seek your sister-in-law's hand in marriage."

With a little squeal of delight, Deborah swiveled around to look at Tess who was standing transfixed, her eyes glued to the man in front of her.

Clay inclined his head formally. "Colonel Whitaker, you have my permission *and* my blessing."

With an answering nod, Jared moved forward, picking up Tess's hand and lightly touching his lips to her knuckles. "Mrs. Caldwell, may I speak to you privately?"

Tess nodded, her emotions running too high to allow for words.

"Here!" Deborah said quickly, opening the door to her bedroom. "You can talk in here."

"But that's all," Clay warned with a chuckle.

Jared led Tess into the bedroom and closed the door softly behind him. Turning toward her, he lifted her hand to his lips again, this time kissing it tenderly. "I love you," he said, looking into her eyes. "Will you marry me?"

But, instead of the eager acceptance that he'd expected, Tess glared at him angrily. "Where have you been?"

Jared blinked in surprise. "Oregon City."

"Why? Did you have to go there to think about this? Talk it over with Dash and Jack, maybe? Did you assume that you could just walk out of here with no explanation, not even a goodbye, leaving me to cry my eyes out over you while you went off to decide whether I was worth marrying?"

"Tess . . ."

"Don't you 'Tess' me, Jared Whitaker. What made you think I'd still be here when you got back?"

Jared frowned, his eyes darkening with frustration. This moment was not going at all as he'd planned. For ten straight hours he'd ridden like a madman through rain, sleet, and wind so cold that it cut right through you, just to get here. And now that he'd finally made it, she was *mad*?

"I didn't go to Oregon City to 'think it over'," he

gritted. "I went to get my name back. I had to wire Washington, tell them where I was, give them my status *and* an explanation of my whereabouts for the past year and a half, then wait till they replied and issued the appropriate releases. It took time, Tess, that's all. And I couldn't leave until all the papers were signed."

"Why didn't you tell me you were going to do this before you left?" Tess asked, her voice suddenly soft and beseeching. "Why did you just walk out?"

Jared dropped his eyes. "Because I wasn't sure I could really do it. And I knew if I couldn't, there was no future for us. I had to get away from you to be able to think straight, to figure out if we could be happy together considering everything that's in both our pasts. As soon as I left, though, I realized how much I missed you, how empty my life was when you weren't there, and I knew I had to slay my demons once and for all and accept who I really was."

"I see," Tess murmured. With a haunted look, she gazed up at him. "And, you were able to do that?"

"Yes."

She smiled wanly. "I'm happy for you, I really am. But, that doesn't solve my problems. I still have Margaret chasing me, trying to get Sarah."

"No you don't," Jared said quietly.

"What?"

"She's dead, Tess."

Tess drew in a startled breath. "How do you know?"

"I made some inquiries while I was in Oregon City. Margaret Caldwell died three months ago. I also found out that her husband has called off the detectives so, obviously, he's not planning to pursue you."

"Margaret, dead," Tess breathed. "Poor Henry. Now he has no one."

"I know. I'm sorry."

Tess shook her head, forcing herself back to the

present. "It's all right," she said softly. "Margaret was a very sad woman and, in a lot of ways, I feel sorry for her. But, the fact that she's gone means that I don't have to spend the rest of my life looking over my shoulder and, for that, I'm extremely grateful." She paused, her eyes lifting to gaze at him solemnly. "I'm free, Jared. I'm finally free."

Jared smiled tenderly. "I know, sweetheart. We're both free." Drawing a finger down her cheek, he gazed at her adoringly. "I want you to marry me, Tess. Me, Jared. Not Hunter."

"I wouldn't marry Hunter anyway," Tess responded promptly.

Jared's eyes widened with alarm. "Why not? My God, Tess, don't tell me you've accepted somebody else already because if you have, I swear I'll—"

"No," she interrupted, pushing his hand away and giving him an irritated swat on the arm. "Of course I haven't. And, as usual, you're not listening to me. I said that I wouldn't marry Hunter. And I wouldn't, because it wouldn't be fair."

"Fair! What the hell are you talking about?"

"Oh, don't get me wrong," she continued as if he hadn't spoken. "Hunter's a fascinating man—a bit high handed for my taste—but fascinating, nonetheless. Still . . ." Her voice dropped to a husky whisper and she moved so close that her lips were a mere hairsbreadth from his. "I couldn't marry Hunter because it's Jared I love."

"Oh, Tess," Jared groaned, wrapping her in his arms and brushing her lips with his own. "I love you so. Please, *please* say you'll marry me."

All traces of humor fled Tess's face. "Yes, I'll marry you, Jared. And I'll live with you wherever you—"

The rest of her sentence died in her throat as Jared's mouth covered hers in a kiss so full of love and passion that it made her head swim. It was many seconds later when he finally lifted his head. "Come on," he rasped, his eyes aflame with desire, "let's find someplace where we can be alone. I want to spend the whole night making love to you. Where can we go?"

"Nowhere, until after we're married," she responded primly, pushing him away. "After all, I'm not some floozy that Hunter picked up on a wagon train just for a night's pleasure. I am the fiancée of Colonel Jared Daulton Whitaker, U.S. Army, Retired, and I'll thank you to remember that, sir, and mind your manners accordingly."

Jared looked at her in horrified astonishment. "But, we can't get married for weeks! I have to build a house first."

Tess stared back at him, her face suddenly reflecting his consternation. "You're right. It *will* be weeks and weeks before a house is finished . . . and that is an awfully long time, isn't it?"

Sensing that she was about to capitulate, Jared nodded eagerly. "Yes it is. A long, *long* time.

Tess sighed. "Well then, Colonel, I guess for the time being, you're just going to have to resurrect Hunter."

Jared looked at her incredulously. "Why in the world would I do that?"

Tess smiled naughtily. "Because Hunter's Tess wouldn't bother waiting for a wedding ring. In fact, his Tess has a real affection for that little bed in the back of her wagon.

"And where exactly *is* her wagon?" Jared asked, his voice muffled as he feverishly began kissing her neck.

"Out in the barn," she replied throatily, throwing her head back to allow him greater access, "parked right next to a great big pile of fresh, warm, dry straw."

"Mmm," he moaned, his passion escalating so quickly that he wasn't sure he was going to *make* it to the barn. "Then, what are we waiting for? Let's go!"

"Okay," Tess giggled as he led her toward the door. "I swear, Hunter, it's always the same with you. All you ever want to do is make love!"

"You're absolutely right," he laughed, sweeping her up in his arms as he rushed past a startled Deborah and Clay and out the front door. Tearing across the rain drenched yard, he burst into the barn, tossing Tess playfully into the pile of straw and smiling down at her lustily. "And that, my darling, is the end of this conversation!"

HISTORICAL ROMANCE FROM PINNACLE BOOKS

LOVE'S RAGING TIDE (381, $4.50)
by Patricia Matthews

Melissa stood on the veranda and looked over the sweeping acres of Great Oaks that had been her family's home for two generations, and her eyes burned with anger and humiliation. Today her home would go beneath the auctioneer's hammer and be lost to her forever. Two men eagerly awaited the auction: Simon Crouse and Luke Devereaux. Both would try to have her, but they would have to contend with the anger and pride of girl turned woman . . .

CASTLE OF DREAMS (334, $4.50)
by Flora M. Speer

Meredith would never forget the moment she first saw the baron of Afoncaer, with his armor glistening and blue eyes shining honest and true. Though she knew she should hate this Norman intruder, she could only admire the lean strength of his body, the golden hue of his face. And the innocent Welsh maiden realized that she had lost her heart to one she could only call enemy.

LOVE'S DARING DREAM (372, $4.50)
by Patricia Matthews

Maggie's escape from the poverty of her family's bleak existence gives fire to her dream of happiness in the arms of a true, loving man. But the men she encounters on her tempestuous journey are men of wealth, greed, and lust. To survive in their world she must control her newly awakened desires, as her beautiful body threatens to betray her at every turn.

Available wherever paperbacks are sold, or order direct from the Publisher. Send cover price plus 50¢ per copy for mailing and handling to Penguin USA, P.O. Box 999, c/o Dept. 17109, Bergenfield, NJ 07621. Residents of New York and Tennessee must include sales tax. DO NOT SEND CASH.

PUT SOME FANTASY IN YOUR LIFE – FANTASTIC ROMANCES FROM PINNACLE

TIME STORM (728, $4.99)
by Rosalyn Alsobrook
Modern-day Pennsylvanian physician JoAnn Griffin only believed what she could feel with her five senses. But when, during a freak storm, a blinding flash of lightning sent her back in time to 1889, JoAnn realized she had somehow crossed the threshold into another century and was now gazing into the smoldering eyes of a startlingly handsome stranger. JoAnn had stumbled through a rip in time . . . and into a love affair so intense, it carried her to a point of no return!

SEA TREASURE (790, $4.50)
by Johanna Hailey
When Michael, a dashing sea captain, is rescued from drowning by a beautiful sea siren – he does not know yet that she's actually a mermaid. But her breathtaking beauty stirred irresistible yearnings in Michael. And soon fate would drive them across the treacherous Caribbean, tossing them on surging tides of passion that transcended two worlds!

ONCE UPON FOREVER (883, $4.99)
by Becky Lee Weyrich
A moonstone necklace and a mysterious diary written over a century ago were Clair Summerland's only clues to her true identity. Two men loved her – one, a dashing civil war hero . . . the other, a daring jet pilot. Now Clair must risk her past and future for a passion that spans two worlds – and a love that is stronger than time itself.

SHADOWS IN TIME (892, $4.50)
by Cherlyn Jac
Driving through the sultry New Orleans night, one moment Tori's car spins out of control; the next she is in a horse-drawn carriage with the handsomest man she has ever seen – who calls her wife – - but whose eyes blaze with fury. Sent back in time one hundred years, Tori is falling in love with the man she is apparently trying to kill. Now she must race against time to change the tragic past and claim her future with the man she will love through all eternity!

Available wherever paperbacks are sold, or order direct from the Publisher. Send cover price plus 50¢ per copy for mailing and handling to Penguin USA, P.O. Box 999, c/o Dept. 17109, Bergenfield, NJ 07621. Residents of New York and Tennessee must include sales tax. DO NOT SEND CASH.

FUN AND LOVE!

THE DUMBEST DUMB BLONDE JOKE BOOK (889, $4.50)
by Joey West
They say that blondes have more fun . . . but we can all have a hoot with THE DUMBEST DUMB BLONDE JOKE BOOK. Here's a hilarious collection of hundreds of dumb blonde jokes—including dumb blonde GUY jokes—that are certain to send you over the edge!

THE I HATE MADONNA JOKE BOOK (798, $4.50)
by Joey West
She's Hollywood's most controversial star. Her raunchy reputation's brought her fame and fortune. Now here is a sensational collection of hilarious material on America's most talked about MATERIAL GIRL!

LOVE'S LITTLE INSTRUCTION BOOK (774, $4.99)
by Annie Pigeon
Filled from cover to cover with romantic hints—one for every day of the year—this delightful book will liven up your life and make you and your lover smile. Discover these amusing tips for making your lover happy . . . tips like—ask her mother to dance—have his car washed—take turns being irrational . . . and many, many more!

MOM'S LITTLE INSTRUCTION BOOK (0009, $4.99)
by Annie Pigeon
Mom needs as much help as she can get, what with chaotic schedules, wedding fiascos, Barneymania and all. Now, here comes the best mother's helper yet. Filled with funny comforting advice for moms of all ages. What better way to show mother how very much you love her by giving her a gift guaranteed to make her smile everyday of the year.

Available wherever paperbacks are sold, or order direct from the Publisher. Send cover price plus 50¢ per copy for mailing and handling to Penguin USA, P.O. Box 999, c/o Dept. 17109, Bergenfield, NJ 07621. Residents of New York and Tennessee must include sales tax. DO NOT SEND CASH.